Praise for

No Ey

"*No Eye Can See* breathes with au ... tion of women of courage, and inspire ... xpe-rience in faith and hope."

—PATRICIA LUCAS WHITE
best-selling author of *Edwina Parkhurst, Spinster*

"Come enjoy Jane Kirkpatrick's *No Eye Can See,* a novel that captures the rich historical path of eleven women pioneers. It's the autumn of 1852, and their journey west is drawing near to its destination of Shasta City, California. A new life awaits, one that will require courage, love, and faith even greater than the journey west. They are building for themselves and their families a place to call home. *No Eye Can See* comes alive under Jane's pen, a tapestry of faith woven together in beautiful words. It is a book that should not be missed by those who want to feel and breathe the journey west to settle a new frontier."

—DEE HENDERSON
award-winning author

"*No Eye Can See* is a poignant story of compassion, courage, and tender relationships. Rich with hope, it spoke gently to my heart."

—ALICE GRAY
editor of the Stories for a Woman's Heart series

"Sweeping in scope, *No Eye Can See* deftly draws the reader into another time and place. Through the wonderful cast of characters who people this novel, I came to feel as if I was one of them, a courageous soul building a new life in a strange new land. Kudos, Ms. Kirkpatrick!"

—ROBIN LEE HATCHER
author of *Ribbon of Years*

"Jane Kirkpatrick brings California's Shasta City back to life in this exuberant gold-rush tale of remarkable women making a place for themselves on the frontier. Sensitively written, vividly imagined."

—JoAnn Levy
author of *For California's Gold* and *Daughter of Joy,*
winner of the Willa Award for Fiction

"As few contemporary novelists can, Jane Kirkpatrick serves admirably as omniscient narrator. Not surprising with her credentials: seasoned historical novelist, inspirational speaker, Oregon rancher, consultant to American Indian communities. The dramatic question she constructs is simple: Can eleven pioneer women, their male counterparts lost to cholera, accident, or perfidy, complete an 1852 wagon train journey and make new lives in raw Pacific Coast communities? They lack money-earning and decision-making skills; one's blind, one's lovesick, two seethe over spousal wrongdoings; others are paralyzed with grief and uprootedness. Of Kirkpatrick's many skills, most magical is her ability to see her characters as souls-in-progress. Their choices are always unpredictable, yet once made, inevitable."

—Harriet Rochlin
author of *Pioneer Jews*

"Graceful and poignant, Jane Kirkpatrick's second book in the Kinship and Courage series imparts hope for the journey. We struggle with the courageous women we met in *All Together in One Place,* as they confront disappointment, disillusion, and heartbreak, wondering if Shasta really is the promised land. As the women stretch their faith in the certainty of things hoped for, we get a glimpse of what *No Eye Can See.*"

—Bobbi Updegraff
author of *Un-Nimble Thimble,*
fourth book of the Choir Loft Mystery series

No Eye Can See

OTHER BOOKS BY JANE KIRKPATRICK

NOVELS

KINSHIP AND COURAGE SERIES

All Together in One Place

DREAMCATCHER SERIES

Mystic Sweet Communion

A Gathering of Finches

Love to Water My Soul

A Sweetness to the Soul

(Winner of the Wrangler Award
for Outstanding Western Novel of 1995)

NONFICTION

Homestead

A Burden Shared

No Eye Can See

JANE KIRKPATRICK
AWARD-WINNING AUTHOR *of ALL TOGETHER IN ONE PLACE*

WATERBROOK
PRESS

No Eye Can See
Published by WaterBrook Press
2375 Telstar Drive, Suite 160
Colorado Springs, Colorado 80920
A division of Random House, Inc.

ISBN 1-57856-233-3

Library of Congress Cataloging-in-Publication Date
Kirkpatrick, Jane, 1946–
No eye can see / Jane Kirkpatrick.— 1st ed.
p. cm. — (The kinship and courage historical series ; bk. 2)
ISBN 1-57856-233-3
1. Women pioneers—Fiction. 2. Blind women—Fiction. 3. California—Fiction. 4. Widows—Fiction. I. Title.

PS3561.I712 N6 2001
813'.54—dc21

00-043869

Printed in the United States of America
2002

10 9 8 7 6 5

This book is dedicated to
my husband, Jerry,
for always helping me to see.

CAST OF CHARACTERS

The widows, *All Together in One Place*
Suzanne Cullver, a former photographer
Clayton and Sason, her boys
Mazy Bacon, a farmer
Elizabeth Mueller, Mazy's mother
Ruth Martin, a horsewoman and auntie to Jason, Ned, Sarah, and Jessie
Lura Schmidtke, a business-woman
Mariah, her daughter
Matthew, her son
Adora Wilson, a shopkeeper's wife
Tipton, her daughter, age 15
Charles, her son
Sister Esther Maeves, a contractor for mail-order brides
Zilah, Mei-Ling, and Naomi, the surviving Celestials

Shasta City characters
Seth Forrester, a white-collared man
Zane Randolph/Wesley Marks, Ruth's husband
David Taylor, a stage driver
Greasy, a gold miner
Oltipa, a Wintu Indian woman
Ben, her son
*Nehemiah Kossuth, hotel owner and silversmith
*Ernest Dobrowsky, jeweler and gunsmith
*Sam Dosh, editor, *The Courier*
*Rev. Hill, a pastor
*Koon Chong, a Chinese merchant
Johnny, a Cantonese helper
Estelle Williams, a banker

*Actual people in Shasta City, 1852

No eye has seen, no ear has heard, no mind has conceived
what God has prepared for those who love him.

1 CORINTHIANS 2:9 (NIV)

I'm not afraid of lightning nor the wolf at my door
I'm not afraid of dying alone, anymore.
But when journeys are over and there's fruit on the vine
I'm afraid I'll be missing what we left behind.

TRADITIONAL TRAIL SONG

Home is not only the place you start from, but the place you
come back to...where dreams are sustained, hurts healed,
where our stories are told.

FROM *LANDSCAPES OF THE SOUL*
ROBERT M. HAMMA

prologue

His arms outstretched, he called to her, his voice deep and far away. "Look up here, then. At me." Suzanne Cullver found his gaze behind round lenses, the sun glinting off the wire frames. "I'll catch you if you fall," he said.

She heard, wanted to believe, but she hesitated, watching her husband brace himself against the current as he stood in the middle of the stream. He didn't belong here. Something was wrong, but she couldn't imagine what. He wore butternut-colored pants with a row of silver buttons just below his waist. Water splashed up high on the pant legs he'd rolled up to his knees. Suspenders, two lines of cedar-red tracks, marked his bare chest. He looked boyish, hair falling over one eye, a wide grin of encouragement given just for her. "Put your foot on that rock, there." He pointed with his chin to a gun-gray stone smeared with moss of green.

"It looks…slick," Suzanne said above the water's rushing. Bryce's bare toes shimmered jagged beneath the water swirling around his legs. She could see the sinew and muscle of his calves, how he held himself steady against the push of water. He looked so sturdy. Then in an instant, he whooped aloud, arms circling like a windmill. His face took on a flush of worry—but then he laughed, his hearty life-loving laugh, as he straightened, keeping himself balanced.

"It's not so bad out here in the middle," he said. "Just look up. Keep your focus and you'll be fine. Just like the good photographer you are."

Her mind drifted with the word. *Focus.* She remembered something about the word in Latin meaning *hearth.* The hub of home. Why that word?

She felt a pain in her side, a sharpness that irritated her. She set it aside. Instead, she gazed down at her feet, surprised to be able to see them. Then she lifted the hem of her ruffled skirt and stepped forward into the stream. Stay focused? On what? The water, the rocks, him?

She became aware of sounds around her. Mules grinding at grain. Oxen bawling. Women chattering and the scent of lavender and herbs. The sounds floated through the air as she slid down the grassy bank—no, drifted—toward her husband.

Now Suzanne could see herself as though from a distance, her tapered nails holding the embroidery of her lingerie dress, her reticule dangling at her narrow wrist. She shivered with the coldness of the stream covering her slippered feet. She longed for the warmth of Bryce's hands.

"I'm falling!" She heard the warning in her own voice. "Bryce? I'm falling. Help me."

"You're fine. Keep coming."

He smiled, oh, how he smiled at her, so warm, so brushed with feathery love. He pushed the shock of dark hair from his eyes, adjusted the tiny round glasses, bent, and reached for her outstretched fingers.

She could see her own face reflected in the water then, her full lips, the blush of geranium petals she'd rubbed that morning against her rounded cheeks. Wispy strands of hair the color of spun gold drifted over her eyes, eyes as warm as summer, as rich as sable. Inviting, everyone said. Water pooled in them. Could that be? How could she see herself? And in such a fast-moving stream?

Suzanne felt a pain again at her side, then the cold and something else—an ache of knowing and not wanting to, of waking and not wishing to leave. "Bryce," she said again, a cry this time arriving on a wave of anguish that tightened her chest. "Bryce!" His name caught in her throat. She knew he could not stay in this still place while water swirled about, knew her cry could not keep her from waking to what already was.

She felt the wetness press at her eyes as the dream-state drifted away—taking with it the sight of the man that she loved.

Awake, she blinked back the tears. This was her life now. The sounds of the women and oxen, those were real. And the darkness—her darkness. She lay in it, resigned. She was not a wife reaching out to her husband, but a widow, a blind widow, wistful and full of desire.

1

eye for an eye

Autumn 1852, west of Fort Laramie

The sucking in of his own breath broke the desert silence. He forced himself to relax, open his mouth slightly. Noisy, this habit of breathing. He would have to change that once he reached his destination, change the way he took in breath as he'd changed the way he dressed, the way he'd now survive. The shallow breathing had allowed him life, when he merely existed inside the smell of his own stench, inside the walls of that Missouri prison. Back then, he took in gasps of air. He forced his tongue against the roof of his mouth and kept from crying out when the beatings couldn't be stopped.

But now he straightened his shoulders, inhaled deeply of the dry air around him. The trail west looked long and empty, but it lured him. Enticed him.

She enticed him.

He forced his heartbeat to settle into a rhythm as steady as a guard's night stick tapping against iron bars. Back then, he had transformed his pain and humiliation into something driven, something of steel that pounded inside him like a hammer. And he'd thought of her. Every day. A woman more loathsome than what he had become. It was her flesh the canes struck against; her body he imagined would someday lie awake as he had—listening for the raspy breathing of a guard or an inmate gone mad. Someday she'd hear her own breath sucked in with worry and confusion, hear her racing heart seek freedom. It was her world he would torment. He'd make her wonder whether the sounds she heard were rats scurrying across a floor or the steps of someone coming in the night for her as she lay unguarded.

2

a satchel named desire

1852, beside the Humboldt River

The last week in the life of the Celestial known as Zilah began as it had those past few days on the desert: hot, yet scented with hope. Trying not to wake them, Zilah pulled her trembling body from the straw mattress she shared with the boy Clayton and his mother, Suzanne. Out of habit, she looked up and scanned the narrow wagon, seeking the white shawl that held the baby, Sason, suspended in his cloth cradle from the wagon's iron bow.

All fine. Baby all fine, sleep.

She swallowed, took in a deep breath. Her heart raced.

No reason, no reason heart race like startled dog.

Zilah fluttered over the unseeing mother who said two, three times a day now, maybe more: "I'm so glad you'll be with us in California, Zilah. We couldn't do it without you, we just couldn't."

Why she say that? Not do what without Zilah? What she plan, that woman?

Missy Sue made moaning sounds but did not wake.

Neither did the boy, neither one. This was good. Once awake, the child Clayton moved like dust chased by whirlwinds, racing, racing. "Boy like satchel named desire, always looking, wanting, try fill it much," she told his mother once after a morning crawling after the child beneath wagons, whisking him, too close behind the tails of oxen switching at flies, too fast.

"I suppose you're right, Zilah," Missy Sue told her. "We all are just satchels of desire, wanting things to fill us up." Suzanne had twisted her yellow hair then, into a roll at the top of her head as they'd sat outside in the shade of the wagon. "Still, it's desire that drives us. All of us. Why should it be different with a small boy?"

Finished, Suzanne had stood and reached for the leather halter worn by the dog that behaved as the woman's eyes. "My husband always said that desire was nothing to fear. It need only be focused."

"Yes, Missy Sue," Zilah told her, almond eyes dropped to the ground. Zilah wasn't certain of the meaning of the word *focused.* Keeping safe, that was Zilah's wish, what she filled up her satchel of desire with. Spiders of fear ran up her spine. Who knew what kind of husband waited for her in California? Who knew what danger lurked behind the eyes of people? So much was uncertain.

This morning beside the Humboldt, all in this wagon slept on.

This good.

Zilah dropped through the oval canvas opening, landing on the earth soft, like a bat dropping from a clinging place. The wide blue silk pants fluttered at her ankles.

No more long dress now. Not wear dress. Catch on sage and stickers. Wear legs now. Better, like Missy Ruth.

Zilah looked for the slender woman dressed as a man, whip on her hip. Did not find her.

Must be with horses, always with horses.

Zilah, turned, listened, then looked up. Two red-tailed hawks danced above her. Wind threaded through their wings. She watched the pair rise, catching currents over the white desert sand like children catch snowflakes on their tongues—one moment there, then gone. Zilah sucked in a deep breath, cowered.

Bird hurt me! Fly close! Too close!

She swatted at them, swirled herself around in the dirt, batting at birds high above.

She watched then as something black with small ears and a long tail sniffed beneath a wagon.

Bear too close! No bear. Dog. Belong Missy Suzanne. Stay away! Stay away!

Zilah shook her head, took in a deep breath. All the other women still slept, and she felt alone in this vast bowl of sagebrush and sand held by mountains with purple arms. She headed out. Hard white pebbles pressed through her thin slippers as she shuffled past the wagons. The day promised more sand and rock and uncertainty once they left the safety of the Humboldt.

Today, they headed west, Seth Forrester said, away from the sureness of the river trail, out across the desert. Her stomach filled with butterflies. Her arms ached and she shook.

Carrying boy Clayton, too much. Make weak, steal strength.

She scowled, her eyes squinted into a thin, dark line. She patted her face, felt the pockmarks left there from a long-ago disease. Her face felt moist.

Child Clayton cause much energy to flow. Bad child. Need too much.

He already wore three summers on his narrow frame and moved quickly, tiring her.

Boy steal strength. On purpose hurt me.

Zilah noticed a band of moisture above her lip. She wiped at it with her palm, felt dampness there, too. Noticed the scar on her hand where a dog had once bitten.

No get sick, not now, not now!

She found the water bucket. The round of the wooden dipper settled at the narrow base before she tipped it slightly to cover the bottom of her porcelain bowl. She lifted the bowl and drank. Others shared the wooden dipper, but Zilah liked the bowl. Her bowl. Over the lip, she could see the heat of the amber desert build and shimmer like agitated snakes above the surface of the sand.

The water carried a sour taste, and she wrinkled her flat nose. The liquid reminded her of the time of the graves, foul tasting, laced with death. She swallowed. Her throat hurt more today. She did not wish to speak of it to anyone, did not wish to see the fear in their eyes the way she'd seen it when the others had died. She'd developed a cough in the last week, a thickening that made her swallow often and yet not cough it clear. Why now, when everyone else walked well? Why now did she fear illness and what it might bring? She clucked her tongue, dismissing. So much came wrapped in the rice paper of the unknown.

Zilah filled her cupped hands with water as warm as blood. As she drew her palms toward her face, her fingers looked pink instead of their usual olive and the lines in her palms seemed to move like tiny worms swimming across her wide hands. She splashed the water at her feet, staining her blue pajamas wet. She shook her head. She tried again to bring the alkaline liquid against her pocked face.

She stared at the bowl with the yellow bat on it that sat before her. When so much had been thrown out and left behind on this journey west, this precious gift from her sister still survived, still blessed her with the assurance of home and the sacrifices she'd agreed to make. It meant good fortune, the yellow color, and the bat itself stood for wisdom. The character for the word was the same as *prosperity,* and Zilah smiled at that thought as she washed her face with water held by both wisdom and riches. So far, on this journey of wagons with women, both had been her gift. Until the return of this sickness. She dabbed at her eyes with the wide silk of her sleeve.

Still, no one knew the future, one's "lot," as the woman Mazy called it. Mazy spoke of a Lord said to know all their lots who was a kind father who wanted the best treasures for his children, "to meet the desires of their hearts."

But Zilah had been orphaned early in her life and was unfamiliar with kind fathers.

Suzanne Cullver blinked her eyes open. She shivered with cold as her hands patted for the single blanket pulled from her. Probably her son Clayton gripped it in his pudgy fingers. No, he'd slept close to Zilah last night. She patted around, didn't feel the blanket or her son. She must have kicked it off herself. She felt the dry desert air take the moisture from her eyes, heard water again but knew now it was not the stream in her dream.

The Humboldt, that's what they'd called the river she could hear. They'd followed it for days now, and she could imagine the muddy banks with the lowering water levels like steps marked in varying colors on the side, but she could not see it. She'd heard about the green meadow surprising them at this ford, green in late September, and she'd felt the cool of the cottonwood trees and not just the shade of the wagon shadow at dusk.

She heard rustling sounds, muffled voices of the women she traveled with. Eleven women heading west to who knew what, bound together by the deaths of their husbands and brothers and loved ones—and their agreement to care for each other.

Then the lone man's voice, Seth Forrester's voice, reminding her that today was a different day. Seth had joined them at the Humboldt, had already been in California. He knew an "easier way through the Sierras," he said, and he would lead them on that new trail, lead them to their new homes by another way.

She took a deep breath. The changes tired her, or perhaps it was the constant interpretations she had to make, still getting accustomed to her world without sight, without Bryce.

At least one thing was certain: She had a plan for her own future once they reached California. This was her focus. She smiled. She was not yet willing to accept that perhaps the Asian woman was an answer to a prayer—not her prayer. She didn't pray much herself these days. But it might be Mazy's prayer, or Elizabeth's, that God answered. Those two insisted God was in their every day; he wasn't just someone sitting far off in a flowing robe.

Fate. That was what it was for Suzanne. Fate had placed her here as a blind widow, and now fate was tending her and her children. And fate would allow her to buy out the contract of the Asian woman known as Zilah. Doing so would help Sister Esther, who now had one too many Celestials for the number of husbands promised. Best of all, Zilah was someone who could tend her children but not interfere with Suzanne's life, not try to tell her how to raise them. It was a good blend of stepping out into newness while hanging on to something old and solid—it would accommodate Suzanne's need for independence.

"Clayton? Are you there? Zilah?" Suzanne listened for the breathing of her son. Odd, she heard no answer.

Maybe Zilah had taken him out already. "That won't be good," she said out loud.

Pig, the slobbery dog, barked outside the wagon Suzanne slept in. "I know, you heard me and now you're pestering. I'm getting up," she told him. The chill chased away the warmth. She felt her way into kneeling on the mattress, sweeping the air before her like a woman washing a table. She rose, then touched the hanging blanket that held her youngest son, Sason, a name that meant *joy.*

"I must have been delirious when I named you that," she said softly, her touch swinging the shawl hammock. She listened for the baby's coos. Heard only the smacking of his lips in sleep. "I haven't given you much joy at all, have I?" she whispered. Her breasts ached, but she decided to dress first since Sason slept. She'd change, step out and call for Clayton, then get Zilah to help her place the baby at her breast.

She thought of the dream as she pulled the ribbons of her nightdress, then lifted it off over her head. Her heart ached. She missed her husband, missed the scent of him, his tender touch. Only in her dreams did she see those she loved as they appeared before she lost her sight. Only in sleep-swept images did her husband still smile and gaze at her through eyes of devotion and love. In her sleep, Suzanne saw him and herself—ageless—along with familiar landscape and color and light. Only then and not when she chose. It was just one more desire out of her reach.

Suzanne Cullver, former photographer and wife, desired now to just get dressed by herself in a wagon near the Humboldt River. She sighed, slipped her arms inside the wrapper, pulled it around her. Her fingers fumbled at the buttons. Then she found an apron to tie against her waist, gathering the yards of material around her slender frame.

What had Bryce said? Keeping focus. A photographer's sound advice even to a woman without sight. She scoffed to herself. Bryce had always stained the world with positive colors.

Still, she had direction now: Zilah could care for her children while she found a way to make a living before her resources ran out.

Elizabeth Mueller yawned wide, glad for the cool nights that flushed the hot sand of its blistering heat. This place, this Lassen Meadows it was called, at least offered temporary shade. Even if the cottonwood leaves clattered in the fluttering wind making her think for a moment it just might be a rattler there beside her tent. Elizabeth grunted as she rolled in her blankets. She was big as a house but still lacked enough padding on her hips to scare off the morning pain. Ah, well, it could be worse, much worse, and for many on this journey of women begun as wives and sisters and daughters it was.

Faster than a flash flood, what began as a journey west from Wisconsin and Missouri and places even farther east became first eleven wagons of widows turning back home, then ended with three wagons turning west again. They tried to grasp that life as they knew it had ended. They could never go back to what was.

What they had now was each other, all together in one place. And they'd come this far, stretching themselves to do new things, helping each other, getting through storms, desert crossings, arguments and misunderstandings and grieving. Lots and lots of grieving. Elizabeth wore two years of widowing on her own broad shoulders, but for her daughter, Madison "Mazy" Bacon, it was now just three months wearing a widow's threads.

Elizabeth pushed her arm against the warm earth and sat up. The eastern sky unveiled a pink as deep as ripe cherries streaked white with wispy clouds. Wasn't there something sailors on Lake Michigan always said about morning pink meaning warning? Well, that couldn't apply to this part of the country. This land was made up of all sand and shore and not a sea in sight. Elizabeth counted on smooth sailing.

Zilah watched, wary. People stirred.

What they want? Trouble me. They trouble me.

She moved closer to her water bowl, the bat's wings on its side open in flight. Clayton ran under a wagon.

That a small boy or white fox?

Her attention turned to the sounds of the woman Elizabeth walking with her slip-hip from her tent to the bumbling woman Lura's tent. "Get up, Lura. Time's awasting."

Why so noisy? No need make noise.

Zilah pushed her hair back with wet fingers, twisted the shiny black strands into a butterfly at the base of her neck, held it hostage with long wooden sticks. Someday, she wanted ivory hair sticks and pure rice powder pressed against her cheeks to fill the pockmarks. But for now, she settled for the warm water and feeling clean if only for the moment. She shivered again and held herself with her arms, squeezing her eyes shut, hoping to stop the shaking.

"You ladies best bury those morning toilets," Seth Forrester said, walking up from behind her.

Why so loud? No reason, no reason make so much noise!

Zilah turned to him, scowled. The tall, yellow-haired Seth man—as Zilah thought of him—had been present at the crossing of the Missouri when there were many wagons, many men, husbands and sons. The Seth man offered kindness, tipping his tall hat even to her, a simple Asian woman on her way to marry a foreigner. Traveling with them the first few days out, he'd helped Sister Esther and her brothers teach English classes to Zilah and the other three Celestials, and then he'd ridden on, not bound to any wagon train or person. "I'm a gambling man," he told them all. "Though all of life's a game of chance."

"He no teach us chance games," Zilah had complained to the other girls. "Just English."

Then months later, just a day past, he'd ridden back to them from the west, already having taken a shortcut known as Noble's Cutoff.

All together, the women voted to let him lead them to Shasta City, California, leave the safety of the familiar trail where the dust drifted thick with the wheels and feet of previous travelers. They would rise up across the desert, then rumble through the mountains, not over them, but through, the Seth man said. To a new home in mining territory. Then Zilah and Mei-Ling and Naomi would take a wagon or the stagecoach south to Sacramento City, to their husbands, instead of walking there in quick-quick steps, beside this river as they had been.

"There's gold in every stream, I'm saying," Seth told them at the campfire. Zilah felt chilled and feverish even last evening, but she heard the words through the canvas as she helped put the boys Clayton and Sason to bed. "The place is humming with new blood, new life, wealth from the water and the land, and wealth to all the folks bringing in wares to supply them. Even folks from your homeland, Mei-Ling. Chinese by the dozens there, I'm saying, and not many women, of any race."

"Indians?" Adora asked, her voice a too-high whistle. The sound had grated on Zilah's ears. Adora traveled with her daughter, Tipton, and had lost a husband to cholera and a son named Charles to disappointment.

"Yes ma'am. There are Indians. All the miners and such moving in is stretching their ways a bit, but I think we'll work things out with them. They're reasonable, and there's gold enough to go around, by my eyes. Don't have to be greedy. Truth is, the Indians aren't interested in the gold, just the streams. They prefer the salmon."

Elizabeth grunted. "Best you talk to the Mohawk tribe and the Virginia slaves about our nation's history of reason and greed," she told him. "And how we use cruelty as a tool to get our way, too. *There's* a history to ponder."

"History can hold a soul hostage," Seth said. "Make you think you can't change. California, that's a place that welcomes change with open arms, says 'step right up and see what you can do you never thought you could.' Look at me, leading a train of women. Is that a risky gamble or just good luck?"

Zilah's eyes furrowed with the stream of words. She knew neither Mohawks nor Virginia slaves. She did know stories of cruelty. And women with little say in their own destinies.

Uncertain of what waited for them in "the States," as the Seth man called California, Zilah had voted for the plan to head to Shasta City. In her history, she had never been asked such a question, where she wanted to go. Even coming west had not been her choice, but a way to save face, to send money to her brother-in-law who had taken a worthless girl into his home and fed her to keep her alive. Yet in this new land, next to a dusty wagon, someone asked her desire, and she had nodded her head and said, "I go Noble's."

Then everything changed. Another death—Betha—this one not the cholera that took most of the men. This one leaving four small children needing more tending and new paths to walk. Her heart raced again.

No, no.

That death and the others had happened before the Seth man arrived to lead them from the river, hadn't it? Yes, she was sure now. An aunt returned to care for the four motherless children. Ruth Martin. Yes, the woman with the whip who rode horses. She wore men's clothes, with men's pants covering her legs, just as Zilah now did.

But that was before, weeks before. She pressed her fingers against her temples. Zilah's head felt full of webs, mixed up her thinking. Was that when her throat began to hurt, her eyes start their watering? She shook her head. She'd forgotten her straw hat.

Everything different here, like rice paper once wrapped around treasure that now crinkles, never smooth again.

She squinted at the morning sun. Seth closed in on her, where she stood beside the wagon. Her heart raced. He walked close enough to touch her, leading a pair of oxen. He tipped his hat, then stopped the oxen in front of Suzanne's wagon, talking and working them back on either side of the wagon tongue. His white hat shaded one of the animal's heads as he leaned to the oxbow. The man ran his hands along the oxen's backs, disrupting flies as he drew the chains to the wagon tongue.

The noise of the oxen shaking their heads at flies and the chain being strung startled Zilah. Her ears hurt, and her eyes ran water like snow melting from high mountains in spring.

Why crying?

She did not feel like crying, and yet the water came. She fisted her eyes, wished she could make the noise stop. It was the fault of the sounds and the sand and the heat.

"Make too much noise," Zilah said. Seth stood at her words, lifted his fingers to the brim of his hat. "Why you look at me?" she asked. "Too loud, too loud!" She put her hands to her ears.

"You're shaking," Seth said, reaching out his hand to her elbow.

Zilah found his words cunning, like a fox. She jerked away.

"Zilah? Something wrong?"

"Who Zilah?" she said, her shrill voice hurting even her own ears. "Name Chou-Jou. Who tell you my name Zilah?"

"Why, you did. And Sister Esther," he said.

"Who Sister Esther?"

Seth shook his head. "You know who that is, she's your…the woman who manages the marriage contracts, why you're heading to California. Maybe it would be good if you stepped over to her tent. Here, let me help you." He reached out.

Maybe he steady me. Maybe he strike me.

She couldn't be sure so she struck first, her fingernails leaving a track of red welts on the back of his gloveless hand.

"Hey!" he said, jerking away.

She could see by the look in his blue eyes that she startled him, but she couldn't think why. He was being thick, making a game of her. She had to defend.

"Looks like you're running a fever Zi—I mean Chou-Jou, is it?"

"You make fun of name," she screamed. Her heart pounded, and she couldn't catch her breath. She breathed through her mouth, gasping in air.

"Best you sit down, Zilah," he said. "I'll get us some help."

"Name Chou-Jou," she screamed, then, in her flatfooted gait, she brushed past him, holding the sides of her head, staggering toward Sister Esther's tent. Her eye caught something moving. *A dog! No, boy. Small boy. Clayton.* The child smiled at her as he stood next to the tall wagon wheel. He waved, and she thought she saw him sneer. *He show teeth! No boy, a dog. He try to bite! Stop him!* She had to catch him, had to protect. She turned and headed toward this danger.

In the mirror on the back of the wagon, Tipton watched Zilah lumber across the sand then turn toward Clayton. Good, someone was looking after the boy, keeping him from trouble. Suzanne certainly didn't notice. Well, she couldn't, Tipton guessed, not really. Tipton gazed at the mirror as she dotted alum onto the blemish on her narrow chin. Those Asian women had strange habits, running with their hands to their heads. Her eyes looked at the lupine-blue sky surrounding her heart-shaped face framed by wispy blond curls. At least her hair was growing back, and less of it remained on her combs when she pulled them out. Elizabeth said it was her eating that affected her hair. How ridiculous. Some old woman's thinking. Whatever the cause, neither her face nor hair could take much more filth and grime. She wore a bonnet every day to keep the sun off the peach complexion that everyone back in the States said "just belongs with that creamy blond hair." Without soap and decent water, she didn't feel clean, didn't feel the least bit creamy or peachy at all. She just felt parched and dry and old, much older than her fifteen—almost sixteen—years that had already seen the death of her father and fiancé and the disappearance of her brother, though the latter she considered a blessing. Charles Wilson was not a man to be trusted.

With the tips of her fingers she pinched her cheeks until they blushed red. At least she had blood left. That was something. "Good morning, Mr. Forrester," Tipton said, being bold. She watched as the man turned slowly away from his staring at Zilah, a frown on his face washing into warmth as he saw her. "You look quite smart this morning."

Seth Forrester tipped his hat and smiled, showing even teeth, all still there and not yellowed by tobacco like so many old men she knew.

Tipton thought to carry on the conversation with him, but he seemed distracted, rubbing at his hand. He turned as though looking for Zilah, then bent to the wagon tongue. She picked up her combs and wash basin and headed toward her mother's tent. Seth was a nice man but old, probably twice her age. Tyrell, her true love, had been older too, but he was different. He'd been perfect. And he was gone. She'd never find someone to love her like that again, of that she was sure. Still, it was good to know that despite the devastation of this journey, the blast of wind and sand acting as pumice to her skin, even with thinning, matted hair, she could still engage in flirtation.

"Already working us into a routine, I see," Mazy Bacon told Seth as she caught up with him. Mazy carried a line-dried linen that stuck out stiffly over her arm, and she held a bar of glycerin at the waist of her bloomers once red, but now faded to orange. "A woman needs routine," she told him, pushing her auburn hair, kinky from a just-freed braid, back from her face. A wide blue scarf tied into a band caught her hair at the back of her neck.

"Does she?" Seth asked.

Mazy carried herself like a woman used to wearing the weight of disappointment. Seth liked her spirit of determination and honesty when he'd met her briefly back in Kanesville. He found her even more intriguing these three months later, now a widow. She was young, yet the word *wisdom* came to mind when he looked at her. From what the others told him, Mazy somehow wove the women together and brought them this far without taking away their independence. That was no easy task. He'd seen a few officers in the war succeed at it, but a whole lot more fail.

"Routine has a way of getting changed out on the trail," Seth said. "Figured that'd be a truth you of all people would know by now."

"Doesn't mean I don't long for consuming certainty—for something more than that the desert'll be hot and dry. And that Tipton and her mother will clash."

Seth laughed. "Suppose so," he said. "Even so, one routine we do need to follow is to break camp earlier, try to get on the trail while it's yet cool. It's a distance between the watering holes. There'll be a couple of days of just plain hot and sand that could bog us down. Once we edge around the desert toward Black Rock, there's a cut, at High Rock, and a spring before we start the next desert stretch. Maybe we could take a day there, just for those routine things you women seem to need. Have you talked with Zilah this morning?" Seth said then.

"I imagine she's helping Suzanne, although I haven't checked."

Seth removed his hat and ran his hands through the thickness of hair. He needed a haircut. It would have to wait until he reached Shasta City. "Seems to be acting strangely," he said. "Told me her name wasn't Zilah, that it was Chou-Jou or something. Acted like she didn't know who Sister Esther was."

Mazy's green eyes grew larger. "What happened to your hand?"

"Strangest thing," Seth said. He put his hat on, then turned his hand to look at the back of his palm. "Don't think it broke the skin. She scratched at me."

"Zilah did? You weren't wearing gloves?" Mazy reached for his hand, clasped it firm in both hands, her thumb tracing along the welts. Good hands, she had. Strong. He looked at her face but couldn't catch her gaze, she was so focused on his wound.

A tamed antelope dragging a leash bounded out from behind Mazy and her mother's tent. Elizabeth Mueller shouted and laughed after it.

Mazy dropped his hand. "We'd better get Mother to take a look at that," she said. "Wouldn't want it infected." She waved toward her mother who signaled "in a minute." Mazy turned back to Seth. "Maybe Zilah misunderstood something you said. I could ask Naomi or Mei-Ling to translate. Their English is better. Or maybe she's just tired, wants to get where we're going to be for a time, wake up with the same view more than two days in a row. I understand how all this newness wears at a soul."

Seth shook his head, fingered the red welts. "More than that," he said. "She looked… I've seen that look somewhere before. Can't place it exactly, but I remember it wasn't good."

"Not…cholera." Mazy whispered the word.

"No," he said. "Not that." Seth coughed. He had to remember what these women had been through, not dwell on the troubles, but not forget them either. "Got to finish hitching up." He pulled on his silk neckerchief. "See if you can hustle along your lady friends. You surely don't need to pretty yourself more."

"If you're going to tell tall tales about how well a woman looks when she knows the truth, your credibility's bound to be brought into question. Not good for a new leader. I'd best go check on Zilah," she said, dropping her eyes. She turned and walked in her broad stride, away.

Seth nodded. He liked this woman. He liked her a lot. But he hoped her strength didn't grow from a rigid streak.

Suzanne slipped out of the wagon, as the dog, Pig, brushed at her knee. She felt for the leather harness, put it on the dog's back, then held the handle that stuck up stiffly. She'd dressed herself just fine. Now for the boys. "Clayton?" she called out. "Clayton? Where are you?"

"It's me, Mazy," the woman said, "approaching on your left." Suzanne smelled fragrant soap.

"Have you seen Clayton or Zilah?"

"Neither one. But Seth has. Zilah, at least. She's acting strange, he says."

"Left without telling me this morning. That's certainly not like her," Suzanne said. "And she's never taken Clayton without saying. The baby'll be awake soon." She reached for the bodice of her wrapper, the mere mention of the baby's waking causing her breasts to ache at their fullness.

"Have Pig take you to the morning fire. Lura has one going beside her tent. Maybe Mariah has Clayton—oh, there he is!"

"Where?"

"That's odd."

"What?"

"Zilah has him. They're out in the sand. Maybe he has to do his necessary thing. Are you training him, Suzanne? He's sitting down it looks like."

"I didn't tell her to do that. It's not safe, is it? Aren't there snakes and stickers?"

Suzanne heard Mazy's intake of breath. "What is she doing?" She clutched at Mazy's arm. "Tell me! Mazy?"

"Mother! Seth! Come quick!"

Suzanne heard her son wail. "What? What's happening?"

"Oh, Lord, please," Mazy whispered. "Zilah's—wait here!" Mazy peeled Suzanne's gripped fingers from her arm before Suzanne heard Mazy turn and run.

Boy making too much noise, too much. Follow all time. Put him by flower in garden, plant him. Water him. Make him wait, grow up, leave Chou-Jou be.

"No cry! You bad boy. Scare Chou-Jou. No hit Chou-Jou when walk by wagon. No hide! You stay in garden now. You stay. Sit dow. Sit dow!" The desert sand tripped her, made her feet heavy. She yanked at the boy, forced him hard again to his bottom, his wail piercing her ears. "No cry!" she screamed. "No cry!" She struck at the boy but he moved, quick like a fox. No, like a snake. He slithered between her legs, crawling, crying. She spun around. She couldn't see him; her eyes were filled with tears, her mouth, too, so many tears. She choked, coughed. She rubbed her hands across her lips, looked at the back of her palm. All white and foamy now. She felt Clayton move. She grabbed the boy's feet, held him, pinched his ankles. She could not breathe, not swallow. She looked up.

Sun, all yellow, mean good luck.

She squinted toward a noise at the wagons. Hot. Snakes run toward her! One wears hat, walks upright, calls her Zilah.

Not Zilah! Who Zilah?

She could not breathe. Her heart pounded. *Strike back! Stop snake on ground, snake up tall. Stop, stop.* Her world turned black, then white.

3

jane randolph's choice

Near the Decision Point, along the Oregon Trail

The horse stomped impatiently. The man yanked at the reins, and the horse, resisting, danced sideways. The animal spun around, twisting the lead rope of the pack mule. Zane jerked the lead over his head, spurring, and yanking on the leather reins. "Headstrong, are you?" he said. "No challenge for me."

In time, the big gelding tired, shook his head, and snorted. He stood, tail twitching. Behind them, the mule brayed.

"Much better," the man said. "Thought you'd know by now."

The sorrel lifted his head up and down, jangling the bit and cheek pieces. The animal pawed at the hard dirt but didn't dance.

The man stared then at the sign. It was handwritten in her pen. It seemed odd to see the loop of her letters here at the point of decision where people either chose the Oregon Territory or headed south to the States, to California.

It was his own name written on a piece of broken bed slat, written with a pen she'd held, a sight he had not seen for five years. *Zane Randolph, your family has gone to Oregon,* it read.

Not likely, though she was honest to a fault. It was one reason her testimony against him had been believed, he imagined. But she wouldn't have told him the truth about Oregon Territory. No, he'd find her in

California. He didn't know where or when, but he knew he would. He swallowed in anticipation and smiled. She knew he was following her, had foolishly hoped to turn him north. That was good. He heard the sucking of his breath and cursed. He had to change the habit. He was free now, free of the brick walls, the damp smells, the cries in the night. He was free.

He uncorked his canteen and drank from the warm water. He replaced the stopper, matching the black mark he'd made on it with the tiny dent in the lip. A perfect alignment. He liked things to be precise.

He'd waited at Fort Laramie, not sure at first if he was ahead of her. Before he left the States, he'd asked their neighbors—the ones who would talk to him—where Ruth might be. They'd shook their heads, unknowing. Or covering for her. Then he'd ridden to the home of his brother-in-law, Jed, that fat lawyer who'd helped carry the charge against him. He didn't live there anymore.

"Headed west," a toothless woman told him when he inquired. "Left with his wife and four children and his maiden sister." The sister would be her. Ruth. No maiden but Zane's wife.

Zane had headed west, taken a steamship up the Missouri to St. Joe, every day expecting to catch up with them. He'd decided they must have taken a northern route. Everyone stopped at Laramie, though. North Platte travelers and those like him, on the south. Once at the fort, he'd read the register to see if Jed Barnard and his brood and his "maiden sister" had signed in. When he failed to find their names, he relaxed. He'd gotten ahead of them. He could now just wait.

For a week, he spoke with his Southern charm to women and men looking tired and beaten, watched their eyes light up at the interest of a well-dressed stranger. He slipped in quick but pointed questions about who their traveling companions were as he nodded at their wearisome stories.

But like a knife tossed for sport, his blade never drew blood, came out streaked only with dirt. He listened with false interest to tales of "trail justice," people murdered by jealous husbands, or of women, all modesty lost, fawning after men not their husbands. Zane clucked his tongue as the storytellers expected him to. "Just no sense of honor anymore, anywhere, is there, ma'am?" he said. "What's the world coming to?"

Then as they walked away, he found himself wanting to bathe, to wash off the grime from being with people, put cologne on strong enough to block out the smells of the righteous.

Still, his time at Laramie fed him. One delicious morsel was a momentary conversation with a beautiful woman, blind and with child. Intriguing. She wore a shawl of independence heading west without a husband, yet carried vulnerability on her shoulders. If he'd had time, he might have pursued her, tamed her in his way. But the woman came first, his wife. And the next day he'd found he was on her trail.

Going back once more over the registry at the fort, he looked not for her name or Jed's this time, but he read every entry. A wrangler named Matt Schmidtke wrote a sentence about having someone's cows in tow, telling Betha and all howdy and announcing to "Ruth Martin" that her horses were fine. He saw the date—two weeks before he'd gotten there. Somehow this Schmidtke had gone ahead, and Ruth could not have been much behind. Zane had made a choice then: to assume he'd somehow missed her, she'd somehow passed him by. He'd had no choice but to follow.

Today, he knew for sure. The sign with his own name on it.

No, she wouldn't go to Oregon, not and tell him so. She'd do the opposite. And he would find her. And when he did, he would play her like a harp, tease her into believing she was safe, then slowly orchestrate her cunning heart, drive her to increased frenzy until, like him, she'd have no place to run.

He inhaled, his mouth open wide, his breathing raspy again. He must practice stillness, hold the rage he felt and bury it deep, fuel the only future he could imagine.

He reined the horse south.

He pictured Ruth, then, as he had a thousand times before. Sometimes, he dressed her slender frame in white, all ruffled and laced. He'd expose her shoulders and place a pearl choker at her throat to bring out the hazel of her eyes, the wet sand color of her hair. Sometimes, he imagined her with a long black skirt, her knees pulled up to balance on the sidesaddle, her hand holding a short quirt instead of that blasted whip she'd taken to cracking.

She was always smiling in his images, Ruth was. And when he was finished dressing her to perfection, he always laid her softly against purple satin. Sometimes, he placed a lithograph in her strong hands folded now across her body. He could see the still smoothness of her face, the fine bones, the shine of her hair.

His breathing calmed, the making of a new habit. He wiped his wet hands against his thighs.

Then came the best part in these images, when his thoughts dwelled upon her eyes. Sometimes those hazel globes registered surprise. Often, pleading, sadness, emptiness, fear. One thing always stayed the same—she was held in a confining box, a box he'd laid her in himself, one that he controlled.

The horse stumbled, caught itself, bringing Zane back to the present. Not long and he'd approach the Humboldt. He'd follow that lazy river, pass the time with camps and ask discreetly after Ruth, maybe even the blind woman. How many blind, pregnant women could there be on this trail? There'd been a huge dog with her. Easily noted.

A man could lose himself in country like this, choose something different than he'd been. And he would do that, choose something different. But only so it took him closer to his goal, his all-consuming goal of terrifying Ruth until she broke.

Just as she had thought she'd broken him.

4

breaks

Mazy swallowed. She was looking at an animal, cornered.

Zilah lunged from a hunch, a foamy alkali thickened on her lips. She twisted Clayton's leg with one hand, struck at Mazy with the other. Mazy felt Seth come up behind her, step protectively in front.

"You're all right, Zilah."

"Chou-Jou! You crazy!" Zilah shouted. The effort frenzied her more, her eyes wild without recognition.

Pig barked closer. Clayton screamed. Suzanne kept shouting, "What's wrong? What is it? Clayton? Zilah?"

"Chou-Jou! You no listen!" The girl struck out. Her mouth foamed, eyes like slits, her tongue hanging as though too large for her mouth.

The others moved into a circle around them, Seth closest to Zilah, his hands at his side, crouching as he spoke quietly. "It's all right now. All right." But the crazed woman jerked forward, then back, threatening Clayton as she yanked at his little leg. The wails of the child pierced the dry air and broke up the fast beating of Mazy's heart.

"Clayton?" Suzanne called out.

Seth's hands motioned them to stay back. Zilah turned then, her mouth open as though to chomp at the boy's flesh, when her body began shivering, the convulsions knocking her to the desert floor. Her unseeing eyes rolled back into her head.

"Clayton's all right, Suzanne," Mazy shouted, holding the blind woman's arm as it strained against her.

"Get a rope," Seth said.

Mazy turned to run, but there was no need. The Asian girl's tiny feet made impressions in the sand where her body writhed and then stopped. Even Clayton silenced, his face a pinch of tears as he stared at his keeper.

The stillness held them hostage until Suzanne pressed forward, her arms sweeping the air before her.

"She's...dead," Mazy said.

Sister Esther's fingers pressed white against her own lips as though to keep from crying out, as though she could not believe that one more woman in her care was gone. Shattered and gone.

Mazy turned from Esther and reached for the child wailing now, arms outstretched for his mother. Another loss, another tending interrupted. Mazy felt as hot as a fired iron and just as heavy. Somehow she'd thought Seth's leading them would keep them safe, but nothing could do that, not in this thankless wilderness her husband had brought her into. She felt a surge of anger flush her face. She wished for the hundredth time she could have shoved those feelings into Jeremy's hands. But he had died before experiencing the full range of her fury. She was forced to hold on to it alone.

Suzanne pressed Clayton's face to her bodice. "It's all right," she said. "It's all right. Mama didn't know Zilah was sick. I'm so sorry. I never should have asked her to watch you." She rubbed her hand over the down of his hair, kissed his temples until he calmed. "It's all right," she said. "It surely is," though she knew in that instant it wasn't.

"Is what she got...contagious?" Lura Schmidtke asked. "I been letting Mariah spend a lot of time around that woman and your boy there, Suzanne."

"Got to wait and see," Elizabeth said. "Best we get her buried. All right with you, Sister Esther?"

Suzanne heard Sister Esther tell the other Celestials how to lift Zilah, and with Seth's help they carried her back toward the camp. They wrapped the still body in one of Suzanne's quilts, one she'd had the privilege of making when she could see, when her husband provided a housekeeper so she had the luxury to sit and sew. Such a long time ago that was. A much safer time.

Suzanne heard a scraping as a hole was being dug in the roadbed. Mazy said they laid Zilah in it, covered it with dirt and tiny purple rocks, then ran the wagons across the grave so no one taking this trail—and no scrounging animals—would scruff up Zilah's remains.

She was at rest, Suzanne thought, her turmoil ended.

Suzanne's heart thudded in her ears. Her troubles had just begun.

Already Ruth Martin regretted her decision—not that regret was anything new. But she thought she'd learned on this journey west about making a firm plan and then staying with it, without always dancing back and forth like a circus bear with his leg chained in place. Seth Forrester just rubbed her the wrong way, she guessed, had all week long.

It was not in her nature to trust people first. She preferred to believe in them "when" they performed as they said they would, not like Elizabeth, who trusted everyone "until" she had good reason not to. And Elizabeth always found a way to forgive them even then.

"You need to keep your horses off to the side instead of riding in the back," Seth told Ruth just moments before, and it galled her, his telling her what to do.

"Why?"

"Save you some dust in your face and so you can see what's happening easier too. Seems your kids're climbing in and out, and it might be better if they waited 'til we stopped. Save on the stock if they'd walk and not ride. Good way to get hurt, jumping off a moving wagon."

"Are you suggesting I can't keep a good eye on the children?"

"We've got one less adult around to watch them now," he said. "Just thought it might be a way of your accommodating."

"I accommodate plenty," she snapped back. "And I'll take care of my children just fine."

He'd turned his horse and rode back to the front of the three wagons, his horse's tail flicking at flies.

What really irked her was that she knew he was right, about the dust at least. There was no reason to ride behind all the wagons. The desert was flat and wide, and she wasn't required to be last as she had been those months before when she was the only woman with a wagon of her own. She hadn't thought about the children getting into trouble. They were entertaining themselves was how she saw it, no different than rolling stones with sticks or playing with the few cloth dolls they had. Seth suggested she was being irresponsible—that was what stuck in her craw. Maybe it was Zilah's quick dying that had her on edge. She was tired of the dying, of starting to care about someone and then having them leave.

From behind, the wagons leaned liked stiff old men not able to bend at the waist, the wheels rolling up on a rock then dropping, hard. Another gully approached. They rattled awkwardly down into it, across the white sand, and then Ruth pressed her knees against Koda. His muscles tensed, responding immediately as he always did. She guessed that responsiveness without argument was what made spending time with horses so gratifying. That and knowing they wouldn't betray her the way people could.

In the distance, she could see Mei-Ling kneeling, her tiny hands resting on the back boards of the seat. That little Celestial had made the entire trip on her knees. Her thoughts looked far away. But she waved her small hand when Ruth lifted her floppy hat and arced it through the still air. As she did, horse flies clustered at the big gelding's neck lifted. Mei-Ling twisted around then and disappeared into the darkness of the wagon. Ruth imagined that she tended her bees who by now must have been as tired inside those white boxes as the rest of them, seeking a place they could at last call their own.

Ruth had her own worries to consider. She knew she'd have to find a good home for the children, locate someone to care for them. Then make contact with a solicitor back east. Once she had time to go through her brother's leather bundle of papers, she'd discover what estate was left for the children. Surely he'd made provision for them in the event of his death—he was, after all, a lawyer. With those arrangements secured and the children settled with good keepers, she could move north to locate her brood mares. She wondered if she ought to take Jessie with her. Maybe it would be a time to tell the girl the truth.

Ruth brushed at the dust on her woolen pants. Better would be Mazy agreeing to take the children on. Mazy and her mother would likely end up together, and the older woman for certain handled children well. She even played like one, always talking about tree houses and such. She even tried to convince the rest of them that they should lift their skirts and laugh out loud more often.

Ruth had danced a little jig the night they encountered Seth and made the decision to go by way of the Noble's Cutoff. Seth had told them their brass tacks would bring them cash in California. That seemed too good to be true. "Something to celebrate, I'll ponder," Elizabeth said.

Yet Ruth found little to laugh about in life. Living was serious business with serious consequences if she failed to pay attention.

"We may have voted for our own death warrant when we agreed to trust Seth to lead us through this," Ruth said, riding up to where Elizabeth walked beside Suzanne.

Elizabeth turned to her, surprise on her face. "Why, Ruthie, I think he's being just dandy, considering all."

Ruth could see the wagon where the children were performing their circus acts, bare round hills in the distance. "Hey!" she shouted. "You kids need to be watching Clayton, not jumping up and down." She could see Clayton with Mariah walking off to the side. "Clayton's fine, by the way," she told Suzanne. "Now get off of there," she shouted at them.

"Aw, Auntie." Ned stuck his head out the back of the wagon that the Celestial named Mei-Ling rode in.

"You heard me," Ruth shouted back. "You'll be bothering Mei-Ling's dowry. Don't want to upset the bees." She watched Ned make a leap from the wagon box, careful to jump out far and avoid the heavy wheels. Then Jason jumped, then Sarah, holding the skirt of her jumper with one hand. Ruth was surprised at the girl's willingness to risk the way the boys did. Jessie would be last, Ruth could bet on that.

"Why are you so critical of Seth?" Suzanne asked.

"We really don't know much about him except that he's a white-collared gambling man. Where's Jessie?" she yelled at Ned, who pointed toward the wagon box. "And Zilah was perfectly fine before Seth joined us."

"You're not blaming Seth for Zilah's death," Elizabeth said. "That girl just plain died of hydrophobia. The look of a wild dog foaming on her face. Thank goodness Mazy grabbed her before she took a chunk out of Clayton's foot. She must have gotten bitten herself somehow, sometime. Maybe when they chased a skunk for oil. She had a scar on her hand. Or maybe some mad dog no one remembers."

"Sister Esther doesn't know when she was bitten? Or the Celestials?" Suzanne asked.

"Not that she recalls."

"Maybe it was a bat," Suzanne said. "Zilah used to talk about bats being good things." She shivered.

"So much of this country looks alike," Ruth said, back on her subject. "I hope Seth remembers where all the watering holes are."

"It's his thirst to quench too, Ruthie," Elizabeth said. "I expect Seth'll see us through. That Rabbit Hole springs was the best these parched lips have tasted since forever. And the bunch grass fed up

Mazy's cows until I feared they'd bloat—which they didn't, Suzanne. Just to let you know."

"It feels hot," Suzanne said. "Is anything growing around here?"

"Nothing," Ruth said. "Feel the sand? This place is Hades' parlor. I'm heading on up to see what's keeping Jessie."

"Maybe she's showing good sense and waiting until the wagon stops," Suzanne offered.

"Not my Jessie," Ruth said.

Ruth sat astride the smooth leather saddle where her brother would have ridden had he lived. She adjusted her felt hat—Zane's old hat—and squeezed Koda's side, urging him into a trot. It was probably the gnawing thought of how and when and whether she should tell Jessie the truth that bothered her more than anything, made her defensive about her responsibilities as a parent. The child was only five. Too young to know the bitter truths, and yet it might relieve Jessie to know that her mother still lived, even if it was a mother who'd never raised her, a woman she knew as "auntie"—which she was to the other kids. Mazy knew the story now. Ruth had finally told her. She'd been surprised that the woman had not held judgment in her voice. In fact, Mazy seemed to understand the ambivalence Ruth felt about Zane, a husband whom she still had feelings for, despite the truth of his having killed their son.

Ruth shivered. Those two thoughts in the same sentence sickened her. *What kind of woman was she?* she wondered as she approached the forward wagon.

"Jessie?"

"Watch this, Auntie," the girl said springing up from where she'd hidden in the wagon box.

Faster than Ruth could imagine a five-year-old could be, Jessie leapt up onto the seat, turned with her back to Ruth, spread her arms out to the wind and jumped backward—just as Ruth shouted, "No!"

What happened next came quickly. Ruth heard the thump of Jessie's body and the crack of bone as the heavy wagon lumbered over her left leg. She watched the shattered leg sink into sand.

"You shoulda let me ride Koda. You shoulda!" Jessie screamed at Ruth as she bent over the child, Jessie's face twisted in pain.

"We'll need to set it," Elizabeth said. "And it'll be a long way to Shasta City for you, little one, riding the rest of the way in the wagon. Wish we had some skunk oil."

Jessie was alert but shaking. Soon, wails began that increased to shrieks as Mazy broke a bed slat and Elizabeth laid it on either side of her leg to get it ready to bind. "Wish we had a stovepipe to spare," she said.

"I know, I know," Ruth said. She stroked the girl's face. "I wasn't thinking when I told you to go off and play. The wheels are dangerous. I should have made you stay away. Get Esther to stop the wagon to let you down." She was so poor at this mothering.

"Let's get her some laudanum, let her rest," Seth said. He'd ridden back at the first sound of the wail. "Set the bone at the next spring. Then rest the night."

"I think we ought to do it now," Ruth said. "It'll make her traveling easier."

"She's going to be miserable either way," Seth said. He'd remounted, his hands now crossed over the pommel of the saddle, his fingers relaxed as they held the reins.

Ruth stared at him. Tipton offered, "We have some laudanum."

"You have some left?" Lura said. "Best you save it for later, when we set the bone."

"Do it now," Suzanne said, the dog having led her beside Elizabeth. "It's best to get difficult things over with as soon as you can. The jostling could injure it more."

Seth continued to stare at Ruth, then nodded. "I'll check the hitching while you get her settled, give the laudanum a chance to work before we do it." He gazed around. "No crotch of a tree or nothing to yank it with to pull it into place. Few more days and we'll be in timber."

"We just need to get it set," Ruth snapped, "not imagine a dozen ways to do it."

It strained them all, this little one's wound. Jessie's eyes flashed terror even though Ruth held the girl's head in her lap and pressed her wet hair back from her eyes. Jessie wailed with each touch and arched her back, which hurt her leg more. Sometimes she screamed when Elizabeth merely moved the air over the broken bone with her hand.

"She's not hurting you," Ruth said, trying to keep the frustration from her voice.

"You don't know!" Jessie cried.

"Don't like giving a little tyke so much of this stuff," Elizabeth said, putting another three drops of laudanum on Jessie's tongue. "But she's got herself worked up inside like a coyote chasing its tail. She never will settle down. Sure wish I had thought to save some skunk oil."

"I've got some," Lura said, her voice tiny.

"You saving it for something special?" Elizabeth said.

"I was keeping it to trade. When we get to Shasta. It's not something people like to boil down, but they sure like to use it. I wasn't hoarding it. I got to take care of my Mariah, you know, case something happens to her."

"Go heat some up, and we'll rub it on this leg soon as it's set."

"It's part of my...investment," Lura said, hesitating.

"Ma!" Mariah said.

"Oh, all right. I'll get it. Mariah, you help me start a fire quick, so we can melt some down."

Finally the laudanum did its work and Jessie slept. Ruth's stomach lurched as her daughter jerked with the grinding of bone, but she and Mazy held her steady while Elizabeth and Seth moved the bone back into place. Lura carried a tin of the warm oil, using her apron as a hot-pad. The liquid reeked, but Elizabeth swore it would keep the leg from stiffening as it healed. Ruth dabbed at the smudge marks left by the wagon wheel, cleaning the leg. Then with huck-toweling Suzanne said had been a tablecloth, they padded the leg then wrapped the bed slats for a splint held with hemp rope. "That'll hold those old thigh bones together," Elizabeth said as she pushed herself to stand.

"It's a clean break," Seth said. "Lucky."

Elizabeth rubbed at her right hip, eyed the skunk oil left in the tin. "Be a couple of months before Jessie's ready to walk again. And she's not going to like being bounced around in the wagon, either." She looked at Ruth, patted her shoulder. "Now don't you be filling yourself with guilt, Ruthie. Be a good learning time for her. We'll find some things to make her giggle in time."

"It is my fault," Ruth said, slipping out from beneath the girl's head, folding a blanket under Jessie's neck for support. "I should have taken better care of her."

"I recall hearing you tell those kids to quit," Elizabeth said. "She could have fallen off your horse and broke her leg that way, too. Or any of a dozen other things that happen to little tykes. Don't let her put a corset of guilt on you." She dipped her hands in the water bucket, shook them in the air to dry. "She likes her own way enough as it is. If Jessie finds out she can get what she wants from you by feeding your regret, you'll have a monster on your hands. She'll be trying to convince you or someone else of all kinds of things, telling them they failed her by not bringing her buckets of joy whenever she thinks she deserves 'em."

They lifted the girl then, into the wagon, and Ruth tied Koda to the back, prepared to ride beside Jessie.

"I am responsible for her happiness," Ruth told Elizabeth. "That's the most important work a parent does—for their child," she added quickly.

"I've been thinking about what you said back there," Sister Esther told Ruth later as they stood next to each other in the necessary circle. The ring of women, their backs to the center, offered privacy in the treeless land. The Sister missed a front tooth and her *s*'s zinged when she spoke. "We are responsible for the...charges, the people, we take on. But I'm not sure providing happiness is the most important task. You must be a good mama to Jessie now that Betha's gone. That means loving her no matter what. But she makes mistakes. She's just a child. She needs forgiveness. You do too."

"It also means setting limits," Elizabeth piped in from across the circle. "And teaching a child how to look to her own self for the cause of her goodies and miseries 'stead of pointing that little finger of hers toward someone else. Lots of close loving will do that, Ruthie. You can do it."

"Goodness, Mother," Mazy said, turning to look over her shoulder. "I hope you're speaking of raising up Jessie and not referring to me!"

"If the corset fits, you best wear it."

They made the desert crossing that preceded the Sierras in "record time," Seth told them. Now at High Rock, they stood and talked a time before believing they could take the oxen and wagons through such a crevice.

"Seems awful narrow," Tipton said.

"Just walk in there and see the hub scrapes on the rocks," Seth said. "How we did it not a month ago. Tight, but negotiable."

Tipton leaned into the gap, then gazed up into the slit of sky. "No wider than the cleft in a sleigh bell. And so very dark." She rubbed at her arm.

"My mules will not go in there if it's unsafe," Adora said.

"The darkness is no bother," Suzanne told them, "if we trust our guide here."

"Thank you, good woman," Seth said and bowed slightly at his waist.

"He's curtsying, Auntie, ain't he?" Sarah said. "I thought only girls did that." The women laughed.

> "Sarah, Sarah,
> Pretty as a rose.
> Pink on her cheeks.
> Oh! So's her nose."

"Why, Seth Forrester, you're a Lord Byron," Mazy said.

"Are we gonna stand here and recite lines or are we gonna get this over with?" Ruth said.

Lura Schmidtke piped in, "I hate narrow places."

"I hate bad poets," Ruth said.

"Best we head through, then," Mazy said. "Either that or turn back."

"We'll go first," Adora told them.

"We will?" Tipton said.

"No need to be troubled, daughter. Your mother's right here, and if our mules say it's all right, then the rest of you can make it just fine."

Sounds jangled against her ears. Clayton's bell jingling. Mariah calling in the distance, the young voice in a singsong pattern. "I can see you behind that rock, Clayton. I can see you."

Suzanne heard her son laugh and felt a twinge of envy that just knowing he was seen could bring such pleasure to him. She wished she could do that for him, make him laugh and feel known. Would she ever?

It didn't seem he spoke as often as he had before that accident some months back when Mariah hadn't seen him wander up behind her horse. He'd been kicked in the side of his head. After that, they'd all agreed—he must wear a bell to be kept track of. Still, everyone said he was doing just fine, that it was just her imagination that he didn't speak as much. She felt patted on her head when she raised an issue about her children. Everyone acted as though they knew better, as though being blind made her dense as well.

She adjusted Sason in the cradle Elizabeth had fashioned for her to carry on her back even though Adora said it looked "heathen and disgusting."

"Just like that Pawnee Silver Bells had for her little one," Elizabeth defended. "Not so fancy, though. We got to use what we have. That shawl, some ropes." It allowed her to vary carrying him from the shawl at her breast. Walking felt less cumbersome with the boy on her back. Everything felt cumbersome.

Zilah's death had stolen her way out, her way to live without being inside someone's control. The Celestial would have followed orders, not given them, the way Adora did, telling her how to carry her child! Even Mazy's voice sometimes suggested Suzanne made less than admirable choices with her boys.

"Let me feed Clayton," Mazy'd said just that morning. "He's barely gotten a bite of biscuit. Can you tell? I think he's awfully thin."

The Wilson mules twitched their ears as they entered the narrow gap. Wary, Tipton thought. The walls seemed to close in on them. She could hear her heartbeat in her ears; her breath came in quick gulps. Her skin tingled. The clatter of harness and tongues, the crunch of wheels of the wagons behind them, all worked to distract her. Her arm was numb.

"Maybe I should drive. You want me to? I can drive," her mother babbled.

Tipton shook her head. She couldn't speak. The place felt closed in, the change in temperature from hot to cool made her hands clammy. The reins jerked, strained at the rig. The mules must have smelled the dampness, knew water was nearby. She had to hold on. A scraping sound, then, of wooden hubs against rock.

"Oh, oh," her mother wailed, the sound echoed. "We'll be stuck. We'll never get out!"

"Quiet!" Tipton ordered. The mules stopped then, backed up. She heard the "whoas" from those behind, the mooing of oxen and cows. She felt the wagon rock. "Whoa, whoa," she said. The mules stopped long enough for her to hold the lines with one hand while she wiped her damp palm on her skirt.

"What are you waiting for? Get us out of here!" Adora wailed.

You just got to keep going, Tyrellie, her fiancé, had told her. *Don't get scattered in your thinking when things get tough. You can do what you need to. Just remember, you aren't ever alone. Someone else can see what you can't. Just trust.* She mustn't get distracted. She must never tell herself she can't. She'd stopped dipping into laudanum as a way to escape. She could stop the rising panic now.

She'd head for Seth's tall hat in front. He was nearly to the edge of the chasm, nearly to the light. Tipton took a deep breath and pressed the reins so the mules moved enough to set the wheels straight in the narrow cleft. She focused ahead then, between the ears of the two teams of mules.

"Gee!" she shouted and slapped the reins. The wagon rattled forward while Tipton ignored the pitiful mewing sounds coming from her mother.

When the mules hit the light and the opening, they spurted forward, but Tipton held them steady, her arms aching with the strain. She wanted to shout for joy at the open space. She felt a huge grin forming on her sweaty face.

"Oh, thank the Lord, amen!" her mother said, fanning a handkerchief, dabbing at her throat. *Yes, indeed,* thought Tipton as she headed the wagon toward a spring Seth directed her to.

She nodded to him as they rattled past. And when he swept his white hat from his head and held it at his chest saying, "Ma'am," she took it as the highest form of praise.

The others came through the gap fine, and they rested that night at Granite Creek. Mazy said the bunch grass on the foothills stood long, and her Ayrshire milk cows feasted once again. Suzanne consented to Ruth's request that she play her troubadour harp.

"Wanting music to soothe the wild breast?" Suzanne said, forcing a smile onto her face. She was trying to remember to do that, to smile if she made some kind of joke.

"Something like that. Elizabeth says we can't give Jessie much more laudanum than she's had. I don't know what else might comfort her."

"Music can do it," Suzanne said. "Maybe Ned'll join me too."

Suzanne played and Ned sang, and the good camp spot along with their having come through a difficult place seemed to buoy their spirits. They always seemed to close with songs of missing what they'd left behind, Suzanne noticed, or a rendition of "Home, Sweet Home."

Ned sidled up to her later, when she fed the baby, sitting in the shade of the wagon. He pressed his round body against hers and talked softly, aware beyond what his years might suggest, that quick movements and loud voices startled the baby. He had a lovely voice, as pure as any she'd ever heard. Back in Ohio, she had instructed a chorus of young boys for a Christmas concert one year. They'd raised money for a new organ for their church and had even traveled to neighboring towns to perform. She'd only been married to Bryce a year, and she found the adventure a filling one though it took her away from her husband and her photography.

"Can I touch his hair?" Ned asked. She agreed, grateful that he'd had the politeness to request. Like Ruth's other nieces and nephew, Ned just needed a little attention. Ruth didn't really know what children needed, not having any of her own. Jason might be the smarter child, with a quicker wit and tongue, Jessie the more demanding, and Sarah as quiet as a breath. But there was something to be said for Ned, about kindness over cleverness.

The next day, they passed springs of water that smelled hot. Seth moved them quickly along as he said the boiling water would be bad for the cattle.

"Be nice to wash clothes with water already heated," Lura said. "I wonder if we could put this stuff in tins and keep it hot."

"My ma's got a million ideas, don't she?" Mariah said. Suzanne couldn't decide if her voice held pride or embarrassment. "Is it all right if Clayton and I walk off to the side, Suzanne? You can hear his bells. We won't be too far away." Suzanne nodded. The girl tried hard, that was certain.

They rested an extra day at a place called Deep Springs, then headed west. Suzanne could feel the hot sun on her face all afternoon. Seth said the land now was a large, hot, desert creek. "Not long and we'll be in the Smoke Creek Meadow," he said. "You'll smell the clover knee high to Ned. This day'll be the worst. Good to keep your eyes on what's beyond."

"You're very kind, to tell me things about what's here, what to expect," she said. "My husband used to do that. He was very good at descriptions."

"Don't know about the describing part, but I do like spending time with pretty women."

Suzanne wondered what he saw to say that. She wondered if she blushed.

Wheels crunched on by her, and Suzanne smelled the oxen, heard a bellow or two as they began a slow descent. She walked behind then, guided by Pig, and coughed with the dust, held Pig back a bit. She wondered what it all looked like, this country. How high were the mountains? As high as the photographs she'd seen in books when she could still see? Were they all snowcapped and sharp edged? Seth said these mountains were rounded, some with timber on them. "People say they look like a pile of dough with scattered trees like raisins dropped on them." She liked that image. A song formed on her lips, a silly song with her name in it. Others joined in and continued even when she stopped, all her concentration required to feel the tug of Pig keeping her on the trail and her younger son safely on her back.

She was grateful for something else, she decided as she listened to the voices: No matter what she'd face in this new land, she would have the memory of this—people who had become like family, if she could learn to let them. Tears came unbidden to her eyes. She'd been almost cloistered in this cluster of wagons and women, but they were also sheltered, sheltered by the loving of each other.

Seth announced a few days later that they'd need to start early for Mud Springs. "It's nine miles, not too much incline, but there are rough stones, kind of cobbled, that make it a slow go. After that, it's the Susan River we follow and, boys, we should be taking some trout when we hit that stream."

"Just the boys?" Ruth asked.

"We'll eat whatever's caught, I expect. Best we take an early rest. Ma'am," Seth said, tapping his fingers on his tall white hat and heading toward his horse.

"Is it still light out?" Suzanne asked Mazy.

"At least another hour," Mazy said. "It's hard to put children to sleep when it's light, isn't it? I can help put them down," Mazy offered. "Tell Clayton a story for you too."

Adora piped in. "Sason's little head's lolling, Mazy. Best you straighten that contraption. Wouldn't want him to get a stretched neck from neglect. Got to attend every detail of Suzanne's. Here, let me. Maybe you should take him out, Mazy."

"I think he's all right," Mazy said. "It's Clayton who—"

"Their mother is right here," Suzanne said. "Ask her if you might tend them. In fact, I'm going to take them...for a walk."

"You? Alone?" Adora squeaked. "But the snakes and all..."

"Yes. Me. Their mother." She felt her cheeks burn and her heart pound.

"Could you fix the board on my back, straighten Sason in it?" Mazy didn't answer, and Suzanne guessed she'd nodded.

"I'll come with you," Mazy said.

"No!"

Suzanne didn't wait for Mazy to object. She felt Mazy center the frame on her back, the sleeves of Suzanne's wrapper dress catching a bit on the slivers of wood, but she jerked away. "He's fine," she said, and called for Clayton. She heard his bell and Mariah puffing behind him. "Here, Clayton. Take my hand. We're going for a walk."

"I'll come with you," Mariah said. "Just let me catch my breath."

"I am going alone," Suzanne said. "Alone with my children."

"Golly," Mariah said, but she seemed to know Suzanne was serious because the girl didn't protest when Suzanne snatched her son's hand and with the other gripped Pig's harness. "Ahead," she told Pig, and the four of them retreated to the desert.

"Believe in English it'd be spelled *m-a-y-l-i-n-g*," Elizabeth said. They stood beside the Wilson wagon where an alphabet of brass tacks covered the sideboard. Once they reached Shasta City, Seth had told them, the tacks would be worth their weight in gold since things like tacks were luxuries in the northern mining towns. Everything had to be hauled in by mules from as far away as Sacramento City.

"I see name write down," Mei-Ling told Elizabeth. "Long time ago." She was practicing being insistent. Other women asked things. She could too.

She held her first finger up to the wind the way Sister Esther did when making a point. "Same like how I put in sand."

"You girls still don't get it, do you?" Adora Wilson told her, stepping in. Elizabeth and Mei-Ling both turned to her. "You've got to put aside those old ways, do things like they do in the States. You should keep the names the Sister gave you, the way Naomi decided. Help you fit in."

"I fit same like you," Mei-Ling told her, standing as tall as she could.

"Nothing about us is the same, if truth be known," Adora told her, brushing corn pone crumbs from her ample bosom. "You and Naomi are from a foreign land. I, on the other hand, am American born."

"You eat the same food nowadays," Elizabeth reminded her. "Liking those herbs and such, from what I hear."

"My sense of smell *is* coming back," Adora said, and then she began to chatter about herself and her daughter Tipton.

Elizabeth let the words drift into the hot desert air. When Adora stopped, Elizabeth said to Mei-Ling, "So you want the letters *e* and *i* instead of *a* and *y?*"

The Asian girl nodded once, certain.

"All right. That's how we'll spell your name from now on."

"What does your intended think your name is?" Adora asked. "Or have you told him something totally different?"

Mei-Ling's brows frowned over her almond eyes. She swallowed then, and her eyes blinked.

"That husband of yours may be waiting for an American girl," Adora said. "Did you think of that? Got to think of these things." She crossed her arms over her breast. "Might not take to a foreigner as his wife."

"We're all foreign in this place," Elizabeth reminded her. "I ain't never seen sand like this before or been surrounded by globs of rocks that look like hazelnuts rolled into cookie dough. Have you?"

"No. But neither do I have promises to keep when I reach California."

"Your loss," Elizabeth said. Then to Mei-Ling she said, "Don't you worry none, child. Your name means 'beautiful,' you said. So it's apt. Can't imagine a man not being happy with what you have to bring. Now all you got to do is tell the bees the new name you'll be using."

"Bees know. I tell them first," she said and walked proudly away.

Suzanne's heart beat in her throat, and she felt a throbbing at her temples. It wasn't fear, exactly, something else. Fury at their hovering over her, mixed with what? Her heart raced and her mouth got dry the way they did when she was asked to perform before an audience. There was no audience here—except herself. Her children and herself. She counted paces. *Three hundred fifty-one, three hundred fifty-two.* She fingered the cuts she'd had Mazy make on Pig's harness, each slice indicating one hundred feet. She wouldn't go farther than five marks before turning back. She'd be calm by then.

"Mommy?"

"Mommy can see you walking, Clayton. You're such a good walker."

"Mommy?" the boy said.

"You're pulling on my hand making Mommy walk really fast. Can you see the baby on my back? Is he smiling?"

"Baby?" Clayton said.

He should have been saying yes and no and two or three words together for his age, she was sure of that. She remembered being told that she carried on conversations with her mother when she was two, and he was nearly three. "Yes, the baby's there. On my back." She mustn't let her mind wander. Count. Talk. Walk. Calm.

"Back?" She felt Clayton tug on her hand.

"No, we don't have to go back yet." She could hear the women in the distance, a horse snort and the oxen chomp as they ripped at grass. Seth said tomorrow they'd see clover, red top, blue joint, bunch grass, all kinds of feed. And they'd have fish for dinner. Her mouth watered. She swallowed just as Clayton broke free.

"Clayton, come to Mommy," she said not loudly, not wanting to alert the women.

"I'll get him for you," Mariah shouted. She heard horse's hooves behind her then. *Would she never be left alone!*

"I'm fine." Suzanne turned toward the sound of the hooves, making sure she stood square. "You'll just make Clayton run faster. Stop, Mariah!" Suzanne heard the horse trot past her on Pig's side. She turned around and heard Clayton squeal. She felt her face flush with frustration. Then Mariah gasped. A grunt. A screech of hooves. Thumps. Then silence. She heard the sound of a horse trotting toward her.

"Mariah?" No answer. "Clayton?"

She'd have to let go of Pig in order to stop the big horse. Could she? Should she? Where was Clayton? She released Pig's harness and plunged her arm into the unknown.

"Whoa, now," she said. She imagined the animal, tried to remember where to grab. The horse bumped close, and she reached for whatever her hand could grasp. She held a clump of mane. She felt herself pulled along, her slippers skipping at the dirt. Pig barked. She hoped Sason stayed in the contraption. Dust billowed up to her nose. Dragged along, she pulled on the mane, yelled, "Whoa!" The horse stopped, so abruptly Suzanne's head jammed into its side. Sason hiccuped. "It's all right, baby. It is." She patted the horse then, found the reins hanging from the bridle. She held them. "Mariah? Pig?"

Silence. No bell sound. Her heart began to pound.

She should call for help. But she so wanted to tend things herself.

She heard a moan. "I hurt my ankle," Mariah wailed. "Got the wind knocked out."

"Can you see Clayton?"

"He's right here, patting my head," she said. "I'm all right." She started to cry then.

Sason made sounds in his cradle, and Suzanne felt her own shoulders sag with relief. "We'll be right there," she said and soon was. "Pig, stay," she directed, feeling in the air for Mariah. With her other hand, she held the reins of Jumper. When she touched Mariah's head, she said, "I'm going to help you stand and hold my hand so you can step up into my cupped palms, like a stirrup. Can you do that?"

"I think so. Oh, it hurts."

"Does it look broken?" Mariah must've shook her head. "Use words," Suzanne insisted.

"No. Oh, it's so sore. I think Clayton startled him. He shied away!"

"Last time, Jumper startled Clayton. Here. Take my hand. Ready? Up? Reach up now and take the reins. That's right." She felt Pig at her side.

Suzanne heard the girl's labored breathing, then her plop onto the horse's bare back. "Good work! Clayton. Take Mommy's hand now."

"If you can lift him to me, he could sit in front. And you could lead us back."

"So I could. Clayton." She lifted the boy at his ribs, pressed his right leg up and over the horse's withers. "Got him?"

"Yes ma'am." They started walking back toward the camp sounds. "Thank you, ma'am. I'm sorry I didn't listen to you. I didn't think you should be out here without help." She sniffed, her words thickened. "I'm the one who needed it."

"Nothing to be embarrassed about, asking for help, Mariah," Suzanne said. "Here." She stopped, dug in the sleeve of her wrapper for a handkerchief. She heard Mariah blow her nose. "All ready?"

She imagined the girl nodded as she stepped back away from the horse. "You're only thirteen, Mariah. You'll need lots of help yet to get you grown. Isn't that right, Pig?"

Suzanne shuffled along the desert floor, smelled smoke from a fading fire. "Clayton," she said. "I can see you riding."

"Mommy?"

A smile grew at the corner of her mouth, not one she put there consciously, but one that arrived of its own will. She kicked her skirts out a little higher.

5

God's footstool

Mazy and her mother walked up the twisting trail through tall timber. In his mouth, Pig, the dog that once belonged to her, carried an old sock he bumped at Mazy's knee. Absently, she tugged on it, barely hearing the dog's slobbery sounds. Ned called to him, and the dog bounded off. Mazy's hands smelled like fish when she brushed at a tickle of dog hair on her nose. They'd had trout for dinner and breakfast more than once in the past three weeks. Yesterday, Tipton surprised them all by catching the biggest and the most—so far. They'd marveled at the honey-colored lake and seen a majestic, white-topped mountain Seth called Lassen's Peak. Their tired eyes had gazed into valleys and ravines pocked with granite boulders larger than a stack of wagons. And while they'd puffed in the higher altitudes, the terrain had not challenged them as it had those months before. This was a gentle route to California. The only complaint Mazy had heard about the landscape lately had involved the water frozen in the wash basin that morning. Even Mariah's ankle didn't bother her. Elizabeth said it must have been Lura's skunk oil she rubbed all over that joint. Elizabeth dropped back then, to ask if she could put some of it on her own hip that evening, leaving Mazy alone with her thoughts.

Mazy felt like a dragonfly skimming the surface of her life, afraid that if she touched the water she'd be sucked in. Flying higher terrified her too. A wind could whip her into the unfamiliar. So she hovered just above the waterline, appearing to be part of the life of the pond, but she wasn't. She might never be again.

Seth had led them well these past weeks, and she'd relinquished guidance to him seemingly without effort. Relieved almost. But without the weight of deciding when to hitch up, when to rest, what to do, what was next, her mind was freed, emptier than it had been since Jeremy died. The weightlessness kept her hovering, unwilling to light for fear she'd be consumed by the churning inside.

"Getting on winter," Seth told Mazy. He led his horse now and walked beside her. She was almost as tall as him, but had to look up to see his eyes. "Got to hustle ourselves along, get settled before the rains start." He squinted through pines to a blue sky. "Could happen any time."

"You like doing this, don't you?" Mazy asked him.

"I like a little uncertainty," he said. "Maybe another train'll be willing to take the cutoff and I'll get another commission from the city fathers. It's an honest living. This trip's had a nice reward, bringing you ladies to a new land. I like my gambling time, too. All I need is just one good game with the right stakes and I can set my sights on more predictable things." He patted his vest pocket as though looking for his writing kit.

"Something inspire a poem?"

He shook his head. "Thinking to stop smoking."

"I didn't know you did."

"Don't now. Clouds my mind at the poker tables. Need to keep bright as a tack."

"I believe that's 'sharp as a tack,'" Mazy said. She smiled.

> "Mazy Bacon,
> Tall as a tree.
> Eyes like a wise cat's,
> Watchful and green."

"Poems I don't need writing tools for anyway. Especially when the inspiration's right in front of me."

Mazy blushed. "I don't feel particularly wise," she said.

"But you are. All you've had to contend with? Boys without their fathers, sisters without their brothers, wives without—"

"We've all had losses. I don't know that I've done anything wise to help us through it."

"Mazy Bacon. From the first, I liked your honesty, your lack of flashing eyes to get something wanted without asking for it up front. So I don't think you're expecting a compliment with that comment. But I'm going to give you one. And you listen to it and you remember it. Someone had to lead. Ain't no gathering of folks ever achieved a goal without someone reminding 'em of where they were headed, of what mattered, of getting 'em outside of themselves and thinking of others. Someone has to fill the holes left by the men. Got to inspire people to do more than they thought they could, to get back on the trail. They don't even know yet what they've accomplished. That'll come years later when they tell their kin. And, oh, the stories of all they did will grow bigger than a bullfrog's belly. They may forget what you did, but you best not. A good leader is ninety percent inspiration and the ability to spread it like a welcome blanket across people cold and scared and uncertain. You did that or these people behind us would never have been here, sassy and snappy as they are. There's almost no defeat in their faces. That in itself's a miracle."

Seth swallowed, and Mazy realized his face was red and his eyes were pooled.

She didn't think she'd ever had a man sing her praises so—or anyone, for that matter. "Why, Seth, I—"

He turned to her then. "Mazy," he said. His gloved hand pressed a lock of hair behind her ear. He brushed his lips against her forehead, light as a butterfly fluttering a blossom.

She had no idea what the rest of them would think. She wasn't sure what she thought herself.

They'd moved northwest, bypassing some tree-darkened buttes, but the rise through the Sierras felt gradual. The grass and water supply held steady. Around Black Butte, they turned at last southwest. At a slight incline, Seth suggested they lock brakes, but it was only for a short distance and the animals handled it fine.

They crossed creeks and watched clear, rushing water flow out of the sides of buttes. Yellow flowers bloomed, and the grass leaned out over stream banks like green waterfalls.

"It's beautiful here, isn't it?" Mazy asked her mother as she picked up a pine needle and used it to push some breakfast fish from the back of her tooth.

"It is."

They walked without talking, the silence broken by the wagon chains clattering and chatter of birds and the shouts of the children pushing Jessie in the little wheeled barrel they'd made for her, her leg sticking out in front.

"Do you suppose Sister Esther spoke with Zilah about...you know, what's beyond?" Mazy said.

"What made you think of that?"

"Oh, just all this splendor. It's like the Garden of Eden, I imagine. And I wonder if we're given places like this to remind us of what will yet come. I don't know. Just thinking."

"Don't know that Sister Esther's the only one assigned to talk of spiritual things," Elizabeth said.

"It seems like not just anyone should talk about heaven and hell. I'm not trying to avoid it. I just don't know how to say things right. I wish I'd known how to talk about...you know, when Jeremy died." She shook her head, remembering. "It couldn't have helped him to have me talking about cows and calving times and not the state of his soul."

"Comforted him, I'll ponder." Her mother put her arm around her daughter's waist, pulled her to her as they walked. "He'd made his own peace, from what you said, about his saying he was going on home, alone."

Mazy nodded, giving her mother's words some of that "pondering" she always advised. "But why wouldn't he have told me about his first wife? And that he had a child? Or that the cows might not even be ours?

Why wouldn't he at that moment of his life so close to the end, why wouldn't he have brushed the nap to lay everything right?"

Elizabeth bent to pick up a white rock. She pulled her arm back and threw it as far as she could. "Still throw one as good as the boys," she said. They walked in silence. "Don't guess we get the answers here," she said then. "Remember that old song? 'Farther along, we'll understand why.' We only get the wonder of the questions here."

"So I shouldn't seek answers?"

"Just meant your husband must have had his reasons. Might not be good ones, mind you. Not ones we'd understand if he'd said 'em out before he died. Maybe he was saving you, child."

"From what?"

"Your memory of him clouded with unhappy things. He didn't expect you'd read that letter. And if he'd lived, he probably would have tucked that thing away faster than a dog burying the first Christmas bone. Probably someday he would have told the story of this child, the other wife." Mazy looked at her mother and frowned. "He might have. Fact is, he didn't know he needed to leave explanations after him. He never knew that you'd be pondering the life he had before he met you—at least without him being around to provide the sorting of it."

"It does make me wonder. How old she is. Funny how I think it's a girl. And in Oregon. How did she get there? Don't you wonder? Maybe I should have gone north."

"We were wanting to be all together this first winter, and I think that was wise."

"I'd have to go to Sacramento this fall yet," Mazy said. "Before the snow flies. I don't think I'm ready for that. Too much to do, getting settled."

Elizabeth patted her daughter's hand, held it in her own. "Don't deprive yourself too long of something that might please you, just because you're afraid it won't."

"Maybe next spring we should go see what we can find out."

"Go where?" Adora asked as she caught up with them.

"Mazy's just thinking about the far future," Elizabeth told her.

"I'll just be pleased to arrive in Shasta City," Adora said. "Seth says they have bookstores there. Imagine that, in a little mining town."

"That was one of the worst things to leave behind, all of Papa's medical books and the others he loved," Mazy said.

"And your own," her mother answered.

"And my books. Yes." Mazy held her skirts out to the dusky breeze. She watched as Pig led Suzanne across the hard ground, followed by Sister Esther and Naomi carrying the baby, Sason.

"Maybe this journey'll inspire you to write a book," Elizabeth said, releasing Mazy's hand. "You've kept your journal pages, haven't you?"

"Folded over and creased," Mazy said.

"Writing's a good way to work things through," she said. "I see Seth carries a writing set in his vest pocket. You and him have things in common."

"Now don't you be getting her hopes up," Adora said. "If truth be known, I think my Tipton's got Mr. Forrester already smitten."

At a distance, Mazy heard Ruth's raised voice, and she let herself drop back a bit to listen. The walk had been steady but easy, and she'd spent the morning more focused on the past than the present. Mazy wondered just how many miles she'd put on her callused feet. She'd have to start wearing those thin-soled shoes just to keep her toes from freezing soon. She heard voices raised in irritation.

"Why are you talking about this without Suzanne here?" Ruth asked.

"We don't want to hurt her feelings," Lura said. The woman chewed on her clay pipe but didn't smoke it. "Keep your voice down."

"Wanting to avoid a sharp-tongued retort?" Ruth countered.

"She can't do things on her own," Adora said. "Even Pig's not enough to keep her out of trouble what with a baby. Yesterday Tipton took an earring away from Clayton—he could have choked. And that little one will be crawling soon, wanting out of that...thing your mother made for her to carry on her back."

"We've got to look after her and those children like they were all our own—or she'll never get them raised," Lura insisted. "Got to just tell her what to do with them."

"I agree with Lura," Adora said. "We should take turns riding in her wagon. And if truth be known, Ruth, you ought to stay with Jessie in Esther's wagon. Put less pressure on poor Suzanne."

"When did she become 'poor Suzanne'?" Mazy asked, unable to stay out of the conversation.

"Oh!" Adora said, her shoulders sinking in a way of shame as she saw Mazy. "Don't sneak up on a person like that. Now that you're here, though, you should consider moving Suzanne in with you in California. You have no children, and it'd be—"

"It would bother me if others made decisions for me," Ruth interrupted. "Without my say-so."

Adora opened her mouth as though to retort, but Mei-Ling interrupted, "Not good talk with no Missy Sue ears. Ear same like eye. Missy Sue need ear to see."

Imagine, the quietest one of them speaking up for the woman who had been the crankiest not long ago. There was a change in the landscape, Mazy decided. They all looked a bit guilty then, and Mazy suggested they have a meeting to talk of what they'd do—for each other—once they reached the new landscape called Shasta.

"That would be better than this gossip," she said.

Sister Esther joined Mazy at the morning fire, a shawl wrapped around her against the cool air. The world was awash with pink and purple as the sun lifted over the horizon.

"I'm sorry. I didn't hear you," Mazy said, looking up. The woman's hands were folded in front of her as though in prayer.

"God is indeed an author," Esther said, staring at the brilliant view. "Authors want readers to be...inspired, comforted, challenged by what they read, isn't that so? Surely God's writing should do no less." She nodded, her eyes scanning the sun as it struck the western slopes. Her lips pursed tight as though sewn. "This land was written by God's hand. Some deciphering is required, but the spirit of the author is present everywhere. In the consistency of the seasons and the reliability of the stars."

"In good things that happen for no reason at all," Mazy said. "Like the brass tacks promising us currency without our knowing it."

"Like that."

They watched the subtle light change what they were seeing, each thinking her own thoughts, and Mazy marveled again how this woman who could be so rigid and regulated had become someone she could confer with over words.

Esther sighed. "I do wonder, though, how far the money we get for those tacks will carry us, divided as it must be."

"Maybe your share will be enough for you to return the contract money," Mazy said.

Esther dabbed at her eyes with her fingers. "He never gives more than we can manage, Scripture says." She sighed. "Sometimes I do wonder why he thinks I am so strong."

Mazy waited to see if Esther would share more. In the silence, Mazy stood, straightened the shawl around the older woman's bony shoulders, and said, "It's God's landscape. Let's look for the pleasant vistas in it."

The water in the bucket had a thin covering of ice when Ruth pushed her hand into it that morning. She shivered. "What is it, Auntie Ruth?"

Sarah asked. The girl stood behind her, her narrow shoulders hunched beneath her shivering thin nightgown, her feet almost white from the cold of the ground.

"Get yourself dressed," Ruth said.

Sarah's eyes clouded over, her lower lip squeezed out.

"That's not a scolding," Ruth said. "I just mean it's cold here. Look at your feet. Guess we're higher up than we've been, and it's getting later in the year. So it's cold. Go on, now. Skedaddle. Get your jumper on and your wool socks. At least until it warms up."

The girl brightened some, pulled her thin shawl around her, and disappeared back inside the tent. Ruth shook her head. Pretty thin skin, that one, Ruth thought.

She splashed water onto her face, liking the numbing of it. She wiped her eyes with her fingertips, shook her head to dry, then replaced Zane's floppy felt hat on her head. Sarah was a fragile thing, so easily offended by Ruth's stark words. Today Ruth vowed to talk with Mazy and Elizabeth about caring for the children while she headed to Oregon to find her horses in Matt Schmidtke's care. She needed to give the women time to consider. The talk of what to do with Suzanne spurred her on.

She knew Mazy liked Suzanne and she might commit herself to the blind woman's care, leaving no room to look after Ruth's children. Elizabeth was good with little tykes, even demanding ones like Jessie, and for a brief moment Ruth wondered if Mazy might have been a demanding child. She doubted it. Mazy might be strong-willed and a bit stubborn, but Ruth couldn't imagine her being rude the way Jessie could be. How had Betha handled that kind of behavior? Ruth thought back. She hadn't ever noticed Jessie whine about her discomfort with Betha the way she did with her.

Yesterday, Jessie'd *demanded* a different quilt be put beneath her legs, had shouted so loudly Seth had ridden back to see if she'd been injured again.

"My leg, my leg! Put something soft under it," she said. "Get me your quilt, Auntie Ruth."

"Your Auntie Ruth needs that to sleep with," Elizabeth told the girl. "It's all she's got for a bedroll. You've got this nice cornhusk mattress that was your mama's. Now don't you be taking from someone else what little they got."

"She's s'posed to take care of me. My mama said she would if anything happened to her and Papa."

"And so she is," Elizabeth said, holding up a warning finger.

Jessie had actually struck at Elizabeth then, the action so quick and stunning, Ruth had jumped back as Elizabeth did. "I'll go get the quilt," Ruth said.

"Don't you be letting this girl herd you like a cow, Ruthie," Elizabeth said. "She ain't no general positioning her troops, either. You need your only quilt, and she don't need to be rewarded for her nasty behavior. She needs to accommodate. Yes, you do." She turned to Jessie, whose lower lip stuck out while her eyes were black as hard coal. "Best lesson a child can learn, to bend a little, tailor herself 'stead of waiting for others to make the perfect fit. Something the rest of us has to learn too. The world don't make many changes for us; we got to make it ourselves."

Ruth considered Elizabeth's words. Then later, as they'd made their way up a rocky swath of ground with Mazy exclaiming over black-eyed yellow plants she'd never seen before, talking about the maple tree they'd planted and carried now in a bucket, she heard Jessie complain again. She made her way to the wagon in time to hear her say, "These dolls are bad! Look. See the stickers they gived me?"

"The boys made them especially for you, Jessie." It was Suzanne's voice offering explanation. "They told me all about it. I suggested the dresses for them. I thought it was something you'd like."

"What do you know?" she sassed at Suzanne. "You got no eyes! You can't take my stickers out!"

The next thing Ruth knew she was ducking as the twists of pine needle dolls were hurled through the puckered canvas opening. Wagon wheels crushed them.

"Jessie!" Ruth said, springing into the wagon. "That's enough."

The girl cowered, perhaps surprised by Ruth's entrance, but just as quick she'd sat up, her arms crossed over her chest. "They make stinky things for me, and you let them. What kind of an *auntie* are you, letting an old blind woman take care of me?"

Ruth felt the blood rush to her face and her hands clench. It was one thing to be rude to her, but she couldn't tolerate it directed toward someone else. Ruth had wanted to slap the child's face, would have if Suzanne hadn't been there, she knew she would have.

A night of terror flashed before her, the night she'd been too rough with her son.

"I've got to go," she told Suzanne, racing from the wagon. She swung her leg over Koda's back and reined the horse around and let the wagons pass, trembling with the knowledge that the girl could so incite her. Farther behind, she dismounted, and felt the bile from her stomach move up. Fear and humiliation spilled out onto the ground. She wiped her mouth with the back of her hand, then laid her head against Koda's neck, still spitting out the vile taste.

Had Jessie been like that when Betha and Jed were alive? Ruth didn't remember.

"The girl could come in our wagon," Sister Esther said, the woman's quiet approach startling Ruth. "I was privy to what occurred back there."

Ruth shook her head. "No. She's just horrid enough she'd aggravate the bees. Then where would you be?" Esther nodded agreement. "Besides, Elizabeth says it's important that she learn to bend a little, not expect so much from everyone. She'll get along with other people better if she can do that."

"And be kinder to herself as well," Esther said. "We're almost always harder on ourselves than we are on other people, so just imagine what she must think of herself."

Ruth frowned. "You don't think her rudeness is from... I don't know how to describe it. Arrogance seems too big a word to describe a little person, but it comes to mind. Just like her father always was?" Ruth added.

"Not the word I'd choose, no," Esther said. "Frightened, perhaps. Lonely. Overwhelmed with the amount of influence she has. Imagine getting an important adult to do whatever you want. That's terrifying for a child. She may just think you can't take care of her so she has to do it herself."

Ruth stared at her. Scared? Lonely? The thoughts had never occurred to her. "That isn't the way I see it," Ruth said. "Bratty, that's what she is."

"You might be spending too much time living in valleys, Ruthie, and missing out on the mountaintops that living with children can bring."

"Whooee, look at that!" Jason shouted. He punched his younger brother in the shoulder, and the boys, who had walked out ahead, came running back, the thick and thin of them silhouetted against the blue sky. "There's a huge meadow and hundreds of deer over there."

"And a cabin," Ned said.

"John Hill's Ranch," Seth said. "Deer Flat, they call it too. And beyond is the Sacramento Valley. We're almost home, boys. Almost home."

Now they found the signs of civilization, of lumber mills where men came and ogled them, whistled and shouted to Seth about his "harem" as they crossed rushing streams. Hats were thrown into the air as the wagons rolled on by, and despite herself, Mazy smiled. "We're something of an oddity," she told her mother.

"They look the sort to celebrate most anything," Elizabeth said as she waved back. Something that looked like a cabin bore a sign that read "Shingletown." Three miles farther, they encountered "Charley's Ranch" and were offered peach brandy.

"Made it myself," Charley told them. "Heading back to North Carolina to bring out a couple of hundred more starts. This country has the best growing for peaches you ever seen! Ain't that good brandy, sir?" he said to Seth, the only one to imbibe.

"Good for medicinal purposes," Seth said, and he winked at Mazy.

"My mother was a great reader, enjoyed the classics," Seth told Suzanne. He had offered her his elbow, suggested a walk. It was the last evening before they'd reach the river ferry. "She liked language rolling off her tongue. She often said it was the true gift of slavery that she had help for the daily things, freeing her to do her quilting and raise her children as she wished. 'Course, other mothers paid the price."

"You left that life, to come west?"

"She always made sure the house slaves had their children about. They were my playmates." They walked in silence for a time. "But she sent them from the room when I'd push at her to read. S'pose that's when I knew that institution was wrong, no matter how my life grew rich from it. No matter how much my parents depended on the sweat of someone else's back. The work of holding hostages—and I saw it as work my family did—well, it tied them up too, kept them looking and watching their *holdings* instead of living their lives free. I wanted out from that. Thought I'd see what life looked like where people chose to be together, had equal chances."

"I'm not sure we do," Suzanne said. "Any of us." She reached to adjust the frame Sason bobbed in on her back. "At least California's a free state."

"Voted in April to keep free slaves out, send runaways back," he said, a tone of sadness in his voice.

"That's dreadful," Suzanne said. She stumbled, and Seth was quick to grab her elbow. She liked the touch of it, realized how rarely—except for the children—she felt another's warmth. "Don't people see we're all slaves needing to be set free? It's the challenges that differ."

She imagined Seth nodding in agreement when he added, "Those living in free States find ways to be held hostage too. You're right. Worse, they don't even know it."

"What will you do after you deliver us to Shasta? Or what did Charley call it?"

"Whoa Navigation," Seth said. "I'm a white-collared man, through and through. Like my risks. Keeps the blood flowing."

"So you'll head back out and try to lead another group in before winter?"

"Good chance of it. Like to see you women settled first, though. And I play a mean hand of poker, among other games of chance. You have some idea of who'll be helping you?"

"What makes you think I need help?"

"No offense, ma'am. Just that, with you not seeing and all, I—"

"I didn't think you were in on the conspiracy."

"Ma'am?"

"You call me 'ma'am' when you're caught in something," she said. "Yes, the conspiracy. To help 'poor Suzanne' who, by the way, does not need help from any of you."

She turned back then, feeling her way with her arm swept before her as though she held a magic wand. She heard Seth's "wait," but she moved forward, calling out to Pig instead. The dog barked and bounded toward her. "Good boy," she said, feeling the high brace still on his back. "Come, let's find Clayton and take care of him ourselves.

Another day and they passed Pain and Smiths ranch, rolled by a Dr. Baker's place on Bear Creek, and on to Fort Reading at Cow Creek, a hive of activity as men framed log and lumber buildings on rock foundations. "Nothing more than a mosquito-infested, marshy lowland meant to settle warring Indians, all who live too far from here to be a bother," Seth said. "Nobles said they just began building it last May. We won't stay. Malaria," he said under his breath. Then more loudly, for more of the women to hear, he said, "They give the men double rations, if that tells you anything."

"It doesn't," Lura said.

"Just means no one wants to be sent here, so they bribe them with twice the food."

"If they have a doctor, we might have him look at Jessie's leg," Ruth said.

"I wouldn't risk the malaria," Seth told her.

Suzanne heard Ruth's horse stomp against flies, the bit and rings jingling as he twisted his head. "All right. We'll take your advice. She seems to be doing well. I just wouldn't want it to cause a limp for her, later. Especially if we discover we should have acted differently."

"Your call," Seth said.

"Let's head on," Ruth said. "Maybe Shasta will have a doctor to take a look."

Four miles distant, they arrived at the Sacramento River. Suzanne smelled the water and mud and grasses before she even heard the shouts of men and others.

"There's a ferry," she said.

"How'd you know?" Seth asked, riding beside her. "I can barely see it."

"It just sounds like back at Kanesville and a few places since. The noises and smells give it away, the water lapping on the shoreline. The *thunk* of a wagon on waterlogged timbers." She listened again. They were surely crossing into something new.

A short distance farther, the women halted. Ruth watched the bustle of pack strings and ferries. Stagecoaches disgorged people and gobbled up others. The sun glistened on the river then hid itself behind a dark cloud. The wind picked up. "Rain in the air," Seth said.

They drove the oxen closer to the river, and then the three wagons pulled abreast of each other. Ruth scanned the activity at the water's edge, strangely anxious, but not sure why. The wagon wheels crunched to a stop. A river-washed breeze crossed her face, threatened to lift her hat. She shoved it down with her hand. Pressed at the whip she carried.

"This is where we can make our partings, then," Seth said. "Some of you want to head to Sacramento, you can do that from here easy as not. We'll cross on the Emigrant Ferry at the mouth of Cow Creek. Then there's a route south. Pick up a stage at Red Bluff, or take your wagon on in to Sacramento. If you've a wagon to take. Or catch the steamer if you want. We're just a day from Shasta. Those of you heading on in, tomorrow or the next one's the day."

There, it was said. Ruth's heart began pounding, and she looked over at Suzanne. The woman gripped Pig's leather harness so hard her knuckles were white. The dog growled low, as though aware of his master's discomfort.

"But I thought we were staying. All of us," Sarah said.

"We need a meeting," Jason said. "Like we used to. With a vote, isn't that so, Auntie Ruth?"

"We've been putting this decision off," Ruth said. She dismounted, patted the horse's rump. Mazy's cows mooed, and Ruth wondered if Suzanne could feel the vibration of the loose animals lumbering slowly across the ground, moving closer to the river to suck up the water dirtied by the slap of ferry and activity. "Guess we all knew that staying together wasn't all that realistic," Ruth said.

"I don't know if we have agreement about that," Mazy said.

Suzanne felt a clutching in her throat. She'd planned to ask Mazy what she thought she might do in Shasta, how Mazy planned to make a living there. She hadn't talked with Ned yet about his music either, or conferred with Ruth about allowing the boy to pursue it. Her hands felt damp, and she clutched her throat, circling her neck with her fingers—like she used to. Were they all going back to doing what they used to do? And what from the past was worth taking with them, and what just burdened them down?

Clayton took the moment to pull on his mother's skirt. "Go, Mommy." He pulled at his diaper as Suzanne bent to touch it beneath his little gown.

"Oh, can you wait, honey?"

"I'll take him," Mariah said. "I don't want to listen to this anyway." Suzanne nodded.

"We've got to decide. Time's come," Ruth said. "You've all been putting it off."

"And you haven't, I suppose," Adora snapped. "I haven't heard you say when you were heading up to Oregon for those horses of yours, or have you forgotten?"

"Hardly," Ruth said. "I've a few responsibilities on my hands right—"

"We should begin this momentous decision as we have before, seeking guidance and grace," Esther said. She must have followed her interruption with a bowed head because Suzanne heard a shushing that sounded as though it came from Ruth and had Ned and Jason's name in it.

Esther spoke her prayer, and at the "amen" a strange man's voice interrupted, "Well, lookee at all these ladies. Yessiree, you're quite the lucky one, Mister—"

"Forrester," Seth said.

"Greasy, recently of Shasta City. Heard you say something about heading that way. Good town," he said. Suzanne smelled garlic on the man's breath, though he stood a distance from her, judging by his voice.

"You been invited to this party?" Ruth said.

"Oh, an uppity woman," the man said, and laughed. "We California men are used to your types. Whatcha use that whip for? Snare yourself a man?" He laughed again.

Seth said, "These women are asking for some privacy, Mister, ah—"

"Greasy. Just call me Greasy, like I said. Some say my britches have more bear grease than thread holding 'em together." He laughed again, a high-pitched cackle that grated on Suzanne's ears. His voice was louder, as if he'd moved closer to her. "Ah, fine," he said. "I'll let ya be. Just being friendly in a new territory."

"I thought this was a state," Jason said.

"So it is, lad, so it is. And welcome to it." He whispered then, "Yesterday, I was a poor little hungry miner. Today, my pockets are full of ore. You're in California, all right. Where anything goes, overnight if you're lucky, long as you got the riches."

"Not anything," Sister Esther said. "Rudeness is still rudeness, no matter where you're standing. If you please?"

The man laughed his cackle again, but the scent of garlic left and Greasy with it as he shouted out, "Good-bye, ladies, see you at Goodwin and Yorks. Best place in town for ladies."

Seth cleared his throat.

"You don't agree, Seth?" Mazy asked.

"Not exactly a parlor." He cleared his throat again, and Suzanne thought, *He's uncomfortable.*

"Truth be known, you haven't decided yet, have you, Ruthie," Adora continued, "about going or staying? Sister Esther?"

Sister Esther took in a deep breath. "You all know we must go south. Mei-Ling to her new husband with her bees, Naomi to her husband-to-be, and me, to discover how to make up the losses. So yes, we will go. If we can arrange for a wagon without leaving one of you without shelter."

"Suzanne, you haven't told anyone what your plans are," Elizabeth said then. "Heading to Sacramento or staying on with us?"

"I haven't been...sure," she said, aware that an old habit of hesitation had just raised its head.

"And we need to settle on the brass tacks," Lura said. "Divide up the spoils. And the wagons. How will we divide three into what, eleven, twelve of us? I plan to buy chocolate, that's what I'm hungry for."

"The tacks are worth about sixteen dollars an ounce. Should be enough to buttress up your winter months," Seth said.

"Weren't we going to have a celebration?" Sarah asked.

"Yes. A fete, if I remember," Seth said. "For you women making it and for all those brass tacks."

Elizabeth said, "We don't celebrate enough everyday things. Gotta celebrate something...momentous."

"Like seeing a town with lovely springs coming out the side of the hill like a wedding veil, as Mr. Forrester so beautifully described to me over the evening fire," Tipton added.

"Described it to all of us," Jason said.

"And all those bookstores," Mazy said. "He talked of those as well. You have to see them, Sister Esther."

"The town and our making it together has been our destination for so long I believe we would fail ourselves if we did not celebrate the seeing of it," Sister Esther said. "We could wait a day or so, if you girls agree."

"Bees be happy wait a day, fly out. See town where friends soon live."

Seth scratched at the side of his bare chin, then pulled at his blond mustache. "How many of those bookstores did I say there were?"

"Four," Esther and Mazy said together.

"Hmm. Well then. I have a truth and a lie to tell," Seth said. He cleared his throat. "I hope I understand the rules in that little game you ladies played across the prairies. I'll make an alteration, though." He cleared his throat again.

"I lied about the bookstores.
Not their presence, just their number.
My optimism shades my judgment,
sometimes leads my mind to wander."

"Divide by two and subtract one from whatever you tell us?" Mazy said. Suzanne listened for irritation but heard only a tease in the woman's voice.

"Might be," Seth said.

"You lied about the bookstores?" Tipton said. "There aren't any?"

"There's one," Seth said. "Or was. Maybe by now there's more. I multiplied by hope. And four."

Mazy groaned. "What else have you told us that is optimism over truth?"

"Nothing. We're fifteen miles out. This is a good place to cross. Whoa Navigation is the fastest growing town in the north. Queen City is another of its names. Come spring, you'll have a garden fit for royalty," Seth said.

"Here," Mazy said. She dropped a handful of soil into Suzanne's palm, the grains damp and smelling of musk. Suzanne squeezed the clump in her palm. It held together. "What do you think?" Mazy asked.

Suzanne sniffed the rich loam, inhaled its lush promise. Then she let her tongue touch the wet grains.

"My ma said we wasn't ever to eat dirt," Ned said. His words held a scold.

"She ain't eating it," Jason corrected. "Just learning it."

"So what's it taste like?" Mazy asked.

Suzanne felt herself smile. "Like 'the footstool of God,'" she said.

"That's a tender picture," Elizabeth said. "From Isaiah, ain't it?"

Suzanne nodded agreement. "It's what Isaac Watts called earth, too, in that lovely songbook of his, *Hymns and Spiritual Songs.* You'd like them, Ned," she added.

"I'm going to try that too," Mazy said. Suzanne imagined Mazy touching her tongue to the earth, the scent of soil and new beginnings mingling as one.

"What's it taste like to you?" Suzanne asked.

"Like dirt," Jessie said.

"Like wet ground," Mariah countered, and Suzanne imagined them each touching their tongues to the earth.

"Like home," Mazy said.

And it sounded to Suzanne as though the words caught in her throat.

6

looking up

Sacramento City

Through the dirty window, Zane watched the rain drizzle, the drops slithering down imperfect glass. Puddles formed in the muddy streets, splashing red mud as a wagon or stage plunged through them at speeds fast enough to avoid getting stuck. Inconvenient if not dangerous to anyone standing on the boardwalk. Inside, the smell of wet wool, ale, and smoke caused a man with broken blood vessels across his nose to suggest they should all stand out in the rain. His comrades laughed, slapped him on the back, then picked him up as though to toss him through the window. The barmaid intervened, bringing another round of drinks.

Zane's eyes watered from the thick smoke of cigars and the iron stove puffing out as much smoke inside as out. He swirled his stick in the tumbler now half full of amber liquid. He heard a burst of laughter. A man with pants greasy enough to stand alone sat close to the stove and slapped at his thigh, hooting at some drivel another miner was telling him.

Zane wasn't sure why he stayed. He sat alone at his table, bigger and smaller men both giving him wide berth once he lifted his eyes and offered silence to their inquiries of "You needing this chair, mate?" or "Like some company?" They seldom repeated their question, moved on instead to the smooth bar or a table already covered with peanut shells and cards and cigarette ashes and men laughing and telling tall tales. Sometimes they looked back at him in the bar mirror. He liked being able to move people away from him with a mere stare. He liked perching like an eagle, scanning, watching, seeking prey with his back always to the wall. He liked that he did what he planned, alone, even in the midst of a crowd. He'd learned that in the Missouri prison too: how to be alone while in the presence of many; how to use others without being used himself.

He focused on the worms of humanity squirming in the smoky din but allowed his mind to reflect on the days just past. He'd stepped inside every livery stable, ducked his head at saddle makers, spoken with sooty blacksmiths, gone anywhere he could imagine a horsewoman might be found in Sacramento. His search turned up not one clue of Ruth.

His method of seeking never varied. He tipped his hat, used his most charming voice. Not too charming. He didn't want to be remembered. A big man needed cunning so he wouldn't be recalled. He casually inquired about purchasing a string of mounts. "Need a good mare for my wife," he told them, or "Considering buying brood mares." Sometimes he was given the name of a ranchero up in the hills or told to check with a place out of town. He'd done that, followed up on every lead. But most often he was laughed at and told that strings of horses were worth their weight in gold, so many being snapped up by miners heading into the gold fields, north and east. Few good horses made it across the plains. Mules could graze on the sparse grasses, but horses needed grain.

"Army's outfitting northern posts to keep the heathens in line," one blacksmith told him in between the slams of steel on his anvil. "Got to put your dibs on 'em long before you need 'em. Friend of mine has orders to keep him in business for the next five years."

He was told by more than one person that the only stock in greater shortage were milk cows and mules since those were needed for the miners and pack strings and freighters carrying everything from stoves to soap as far north as Shasta City. That was where the stage line ended. "One or two horses you can buy, but don't go looking for more than that 'less you want to add 'em two by two over time. What ya planning?"

Zane disliked men telling him what he should and should not do, and even worse were the questions. He rarely answered with more than a nod.

No one had mentioned any new animals recently herded in and none by a woman. He couldn't ask about a woman, of course. He didn't want to use Jed and Betha Bernard's name, Ruth's brother and his wife. That might well be remembered. Tomorrow he would check newspaper offices, to see if she had returned to her chosen work as a lithographer. He might even secure a position, look into banking. It would allow him reason to show interest in breeding stock as an investment and break through doors for pursuing Ruth.

He knew the note from that wrangler, Matt Schmidtke his name was, said he had Ruth's horses. He never knew his wife to be without them except when he had sold her favorite mounts. She loved horses above all else, certainly above him. Even the birth of the brats hadn't changed that.

Taut as whip handles, Zane and his wife stood in the living room of the estate he'd inherited from his father. Heavy burgundy drapes framed the floor-to-ceiling windows. Outside, rain poured, splashing on the veranda, obscuring the stable, now empty. They'd been married but one year.

"Hasn't Calle been of help to you?" Zane asked Ruth. His wife seemed defeated, he thought, and he smiled. "I had the agency check on her and she's quite qualified. If she's doing her job, I don't understand why you're so tired."

"I'm nursing them," Ruth snapped back at him. "The children need to

eat. A nurse can't do that. They need attention. And there are two children, or haven't you noticed?"

He walked to the sideboard, fixed himself a drink. "Of course I've noticed, dear Ruth. I'm their father."

"You were present at the conception, yes," she said.

He turned. "Ruthie, Ruthie. Why so hostile? We're accomplices in this."

Ruth sighed and sank onto the horsehair divan. "My body feels like it belongs to someone else. I had no idea the babies would take so much from me. I just can't seem to get rested."

"You sleep a great deal. Unfortunate that so much time spent in leisure allows you no rest."

He watched her eyes, looking for the old fire that had made her such a challenge to subdue. He'd been attracted to the fire, the streak of independence. And he'd watched with a mixture of excitement and regret as she'd allowed him to slowly strip it from her—quitting her lithographic work, wearing the clothes he chose for her, appearing at his banking functions draped on his arm just as he wished. It was his...creativity, he decided, sculpting this woman into just what he wished. He'd been so proud of his creation.

Now, blank eyes stared at him, and he felt for just a moment that he was looking at himself.

He licked his lips. "Perhaps a new steed would liven you up, give you something to...anticipate."

"I didn't think you wanted me to ride anymore," she told him, her voice still as dreary as the rain outside, her eyes staring at the Persian carpet. "Isn't that why you sold the others?"

"You were spending too much time with horses, dear Ruth. Why, I barely saw you. A man likes to have his wife waiting for him at day's end, and where were you? Off in the hills, off giving your love away to those creatures."

"Your days' ends had no pattern to them," she said. "Except expecting me to be here for you, waiting like a lap dog."

"Well, then, let's get you a new horse. Two, and see if we can change that. I'll come home at an expected time, and we'll ride together. How would that be?"

She'd lifted those empty eyes to him and pierced him like a knife. "I'd rather do without."

These past five years he had done without. Without a fair trial. Without freedom. Without control. Without even the hope of a dutiful wife waiting for him when he was released. As much as she loved horses, she had refused his gift—if his presence came with it.

"You all right, sir?" The woman wore too much powder, and her smile looked pasted on. "You're breathing like a horse rode hard." She nodded toward his empty glass. "You want another? Sir?" She shifted the tin tray at her ample hip, bent toward him. "Umm," she said. "You smell good. What is that?"

"Patience and revenge," he said and motioned her aside.

At the Emigrant Ferry

The river crossing consumed the day. Two loads of shingles and lumber from Shingletown took precedence at the ferry on the mouth of Cow Creek where it joined the Sacramento. Finally, the women had rolled their wagons, one at a time, onto the wooden craft. The sun had set by the time they reached the other side, so they'd circled there and stayed the night.

The next morning found them both eager and dragging their feet, Mazy thought. At least she was. Knowing that new decisions loomed ahead seemed to stumble them this morning. Oxen resisted their yokes.

Biscuits got burned at the fire. Mazy heard complaints of "hurry up" from Tipton followed by "wait for me" from Ned. It was all changing, and with it came the irritations. They were some twelve to fifteen miles out of Shasta, Seth had said, and they'd have creeks to cross. When they'd made a little more than half that distance by afternoon, Seth suggested they camp at a wide flat where the Sacramento looped east before twisting back south. "Only three, four miles out of Shasta there," he said. "You can rest, wash some duds if you want, then I'll take you in."

Mazy wondered if they'd dragged this day because they didn't really want this to end, didn't really want to make another big change.

Suzanne was glad they'd done what Seth suggested. They'd stopped earlier, and she could hear people chattering about what was in their trunks they'd forgotten about, not having seen items for months. A teapot still in one piece; a picture album. She heard tissue paper and knew dresses were being unwrapped. She'd given Clayton his top to play with, and Sason slept. She patted the mattress, making her way toward her own trunk. Her fingers found the earrings Bryce had given her, the ones she'd worn in that dream. She put them on, then joined the evening gathering, listening for Clayton's foot bell and the slobber sounds of Pig at her feet. They ate and then all settled around the campfire.

"It is the only way for us to take the bees south," Sister Esther said. She stood next to Suzanne, who could feel the heat of the low cooking fire made in the shelter of a cluster of oaks. The evening chilled. Smoke drifted up.

"Is it foggy?" Suzanne asked.

"Smoke flattens right out on top the trees," Ned told her. "Then it drifts back down. Look. I can make puffs with my mouth."

It must have been the misty fog that felt like rain.

"Placing them on a stage will not be safe for the bees. Is that not correct, Mei-Ling?

"Is correct," Mei-Ling answered.

Suzanne wondered if Mei-Ling resented having someone always telling her what to do, setting the stage for whatever came next. Or maybe she was just thinking of herself and the subtle but persistent comments of the others telling her how to do this and that. Just when she thought she had her own plan, everyone seemed to think she'd have to move in with one of them. She had money to pay her way—at least for this first winter. Bryce had been forthright about their expenditures and told her that if they were careful, they could claim land, live the winter, plant in the spring, and still have enough to start their photo studio business back up. But that had been *his* plan for Oregon. Here she was in California, without him. No free land to claim. No way she could run a photographic business. And two children, one with something wrong. She was sure of that even if the others patted her like a lap dog and told her it wasn't so.

Eventually she would have to find something to support herself and the boys—but at least she could afford housing and food for the winter. And she had a plan for doing that on her own.

"What about that?" Mazy said, the conversation with Esther continuing while Suzanne's thoughts had drifted inward. "Wait until spring, Esther. Then I might go with you, so I can talk with the solicitor about…my situation."

"Now there's a story, truth be known," Adora chided. "What do you suppose that husband of yours was thinking, keeping his other family to himself? Why, if my Hathaway had—"

"I hear Sacramento's quite a city," Elizabeth said. "Not like my Milwaukee and the lake, but it's got a bakery or two, don't it, Seth? A strudel sounds so good right now."

"Chocolate," Lura said. "Wish I'd a bought a block of it back at Charley's Ranch. Wish I could have bartered what's left of my skunk oil for it, that or a twist of tobacco. I wonder if skunks live in these parts. Seth?"

"Both two legged and four," Seth said.

"Couldn't you wait just a little longer, Esther?" Mazy persisted.

Suzanne heard Sister Esther clear her throat. She imagined the woman, her hands folded together over the belt of her apron, her shawl tight across her arms. That was how Tipton described her when she'd asked one time. "She's got large knuckles—so do I after driving the mules. They always look white when she clasps them to talk," Tipton told her. "She pinches her hands just like her words, looking all sour as they come out through her lips."

"She doesn't really sound…sour, though."

"That's just 'cause you can't see her."

"Oh, I see some things," Suzanne told her. "Maybe more than others because I'm not distracted by all the sights that others are."

Sister Esther's voice rose high then, almost argumentative. "We owe it to Mei-Ling's intended to go as soon as we are able. The drawing of her new hive design is completed, is it not, Ruth? It's been replaced. The dowry is still of value. The bees still live. Who knows what the winter will bring? Who knows if we will find suitable lodging for ourselves as well as the bees in this northern outpost? We have known trouble on this journey and we must learn from it, to not pretend we can make the inevitable wait. No, we can make a short journey into the town, but then I believe we must go south to Sacramento."

"Naomi, I wish you'd stay," Lura told the girl. "I've got a business proposition for you. I've been thinking about this and—"

Suzanne's heart throbbed in her head. Naomi might remain behind? It hadn't occurred to her that Naomi might be willing to give up her contract! Why hadn't she thought to ask? She'd just assumed Naomi would keep her agreement just as she'd kept the name Sister Esther had given her. She shook her head. Zilah's death must have grieved her more than she realized. She had gotten distracted when the one thing she knew she had to do was stay focused. Now Lura, the woman she often thought of as empty-headed, pressed her own enterprising case. She raised her hand as though to talk, but the words swirled around her, tangled with her thoughts until the moment passed.

"—so I figured you could be a big part of that," Lura finished.

"Thought you talked about a mercantile business back at Laramie," Elizabeth said.

"You dragged that knife sharpener all the way from New York, and now you aren't going to use it?" Adora said. "I could have brought another trunk had I known that 'stead of making space for that heavy old thing, truth be known."

"You didn't even know she had it until after we'd sorted things out," Mazy reminded her.

"I've come to like Naomi's herbs. That aromatic cooking this winter might be just the syrup for those miner's tongues," Lura said.

"Those herbs have helped get my smelling back. Tipton likes the flavoring too. Don't you, dear?" Adora said.

Suzanne needed to jump into the fray, press her own case. She would have to interrupt someone, Adora, Lura, Mariah—their words whipped around her, tangling the air the way fall gusts swirled dry leaves. "Could you—?"

"Naomi has a contract. A husband awaits her," Esther said. "And she has agreed to keep her commitment. It is settled. There will be no restaurant in Shasta City flavored with Naomi's herbs."

Suzanne felt herself relax. There wasn't anyone safe available for her to hire. She had to do this on her own.

"Actually ma'am," Seth said, "there are a few such establishments in Shasta already. Chinese have moved in pretty quickly. Have their own little Chinatown, working the mines, running laundries and eateries and such; sending money back home."

"Yes, well, they will do so without the benefit of Naomi's fine skills as she is going south. As is Mei-Ling. Will you take us, Mr. Forrester?"

"Yes ma'am. Said I would.

"Travel east.
Travel west.
Going south.
That's my best."

Ruth stood closest to Suzanne, and she heard a grunt of disgust from her. She wasn't sure if it was Seth's poetry that bothered Ruth or just his being a man.

"I'm hoping you'd at least take a day or two in town, though. Let the animals get rested and fed. Us too. But I'll take you. I'm a man of my word."

"Even if you do exaggerate it a bit," Mazy said. She laughed.

"Let us set the day, then," Esther said. "Two days to rest, get you all settled for winter, and then south. By mid-October."

"Bees need warm time," Mei-Ling said. "Air cool here."

"Then we'll cover them with quilts," Esther said.

"Take them to bed with us?" Sarah asked. Suzanne guessed the girl blushed when everyone laughed.

"Whatever we don't need for our own old bones," Elizabeth said. "A quilt's a treasure, that's sure. And we want to get Mei-Ling where she's headed in good shape. It'd reflect bad on all of us if she don't."

"Mei-Ling hope new husband as kind as this family," the girl said, and Suzanne imagined that she bowed then, to honor everyone. She wondered what Naomi thought. The girl had not spoken a word.

Sacramento City

He heard the words *blind woman* and *beauty* and turned even before he heard *horses* and *whip.* Zane Randolph dropped the eagles as payment on the table and stood, eyeing the crowd and the miner who spoke, huddled close to the stove. Smallish, the man had a beaked nose too large for his face. He chewed peanuts, exposing broken teeth and pelting the air with bits of peanut meat as he talked. His face seemed almost buried beneath an unkempt beard he pulled with his fingers toward his chest during the pauses filled with laughter. "Yessiree, she was a beauty. Gold hair piled up around the prettiest face. Didn't even notice she wore the dark glasses, first. Blind and beautiful. And smart, too. Kept a dog with her. She smiled even though she couldn't see my fine physique." He caught his breath in the laughter. "Fine addition to our State. Wasn't none of 'em bad looking. Oh, a few China girls I saw peeked out of the back. S'pect they're daughters of joy, welcome in most parts."

"You didn't take advantage of that, Greasy? Them with no men riding with them?"

"Didn't say that. There was one. Big, tall fellow. Seemed happy enough."

"With a gaggle of women to himself, why wouldn't he be?"

"First, I thought there was another," the man named Greasy continued. He rubbed his palms on dirty pants and lowered his voice so Zane was forced to lean closer. "Yessiree, she wore men's pants and a black floppy hat, made her look like a skinny boy, 'til I saw her eyes. Hazel and still as a hawk's. Wore a whip on her hip too. Don't guess any take her on easy. Riding a right smart horse too, and trailing a big gelding. Quite a sight, that many women at once."

Zane heard his own breathing, his mouth slightly open. He didn't want to ask where the man Greasy had seen the blind woman or where he'd encountered a woman with hazel eyes sporting a whip and trailing a horse. And she wore a dark felt hat. Zane wondered if it was his.

"Too bad you had to come south," someone said.

"Hitting the sale, then expanding my…interests," Greasy told them. "Besides. From the look of 'em, they was tired and beat enough to be staying on right there near Shasta City. I could find 'em when I head back. Might even take a bath first."

"She finds out you're sweet on her, she'll make herself disappear." The men roared again; one man slapped Greasy on the back.

"How hard could it be to find a blind woman traveling with one who dresses like a man?" Greasy said.

Shasta City

So here it was at last. The first separations. Most of the women had already set their tents and turned in for the night. Mazy tapped her pen on her writing book. She watched the sparks from the fire go up then flatten out with the smoke. No one but her had even tried to keep them all in one place, as though they all knew how it would end: Esther and her Asians heading south, the rest seeking their own homes. It did seem they were more cantankerous than usual, though, snapping and nagging at each other. She wondered if that was a phase people went through when they had to say good-bye, needing grumpiness to remember instead of the empty place in their hearts.

"Looks like you went to your saddle bag and found it empty," Seth said. He squatted down beside her, his white silk neckerchief hanging away from his neck as he poked at the fire with a stick.

"Does it?" She couldn't decide whether to talk further with him, not sure if it would imply an intimacy she wasn't ready for. But, she decided, she could talk with him as a friend. "It's just that I still resist change, even when I can see it coming and know it has to be. I can't seem to think about what good might be on the other side."

"Not everything around the bend is worrisome," Seth said. "May I sit?"

"Oh. Sure. I'm sorry. I should have said."

"You *shouldn't* have done anything," Seth said.

"I suffer from sorry-itis, I guess. A condition."

Seth laughed. "Old habits fade slow. Take my...anticipation of good things to come. Maybe not four bookstores yet, but I like believing good things'll happen up ahead." He took the writing kit from his pocket, inserted the pen into the tip, then pulled the cork from the bottle. From the inside band of his hat, he unrolled a piece of paper and spread it across his knee. " 'Looking for Hope' " he said as he wrote. "By Seth Forrester and Mazy Bacon. We've got a title, now what?"

"Oh, you," she said and tossed a piece of bark at him. The light from the campfire flickered against his face.

"Looking for the hope that Mazy will want Seth to return after taking the good Sister and her charges on to Sacramento. There's one hope I have." He looked up at her and smiled that engaging smile, his eyes with a question. She looked away, brushed at mud on the hem of her skirt. Seth poked at the fire again, and the sparks shot up into the night sky. "It's too soon, isn't it?" he said then.

Mazy nodded. "I haven't really said good-bye yet. I haven't gotten the old field put away for the winter, so I can't begin to think about tilling new soil and replanting." She pulled her shawl around her tighter, moved the log she sat on closer to the fire. A cow mooed, and beside the wagon where Suzanne prepared herself for bed, Pig slobbered in his sleep.

"It's a long time 'til spring," Seth said.

"I don't know if I can do it," she said, almost talking to herself. "Though I suppose I will. What choice do I have? But just the thought of where I'll get hay to last the winter for the cows and stock, of where we'll put up. Should I save that money? Use it to build a cabin? Stay at a hotel—there is a hotel?" Seth hesitated, nodded. "Where to live, how to live. Taking care of mother, finding out more about Jeremy, his child..."

"A bleak place you've come home to, that's how you see it?"

"A bleak homecoming. Yes." She shivered.

"Let me get a blanket," Seth said, and he rose, took his bedroll and unfurled a quilt of colored stars against a dark background. He draped it around her shoulders, the fibers molding over her back. She nodded her thanks. He sat back down, beside her. "I'd like to shoot a little hope into that bleakness," he said. "You're not alone in it, you know. Got friends."

She patted his hand. "I didn't have that many friends back in Wisconsin. Jeremy and the farm were my whole life. Well, and mother, too. Now half of that is gone and there's a pit of uncertainty in the middle of my heart: that I'll make more mistakes, spend my life looking back and curse myself for my stupidity. I almost want to stay cooped up inside this wagon and do nothing until I feel a little more hopeful about the future." She wondered if he could understand what she meant.

"Hope isn't everything coming out the way you want," Seth said. "None of us is assured of that. Still, what's the choice? Pretending life's a sack of misery or that nothing has any meaning at all? Is that what you want?"

"No. There's meaning. I believe that. There's a pleasant place waiting, if the Psalm is right. I just don't know how to get there."

"Some things are just worth doing, worth trying, even if fifty years from now we look back and say, 'That didn't work out well, now, did it?' But that'd be better than not doing anything at all. We're fashioned to risk, Mazy. The way I see it, God's a risk taker for sure, putting us here, hoping we'd not forget how we arrived. I'd rather have a saddlebag of mistakes to look back at than sitting in an old Hitchcock rocker with an empty mind because nothing worthy'd been risked. Memories are certain. Can't see what's ahead no matter how you try."

"But if you think a thing through well before you act, there ought to be no errors. If things fail, it must be because you didn't plan well."

"That's a high standard you've given yourself." He put his arm around her and pulled her to his side. "But it does make you responsible for everything that is. Guess I don't think that's rightly so." She rested her head on his shoulder, feeling the warmth of a friend. His jacket felt smooth on her cheek. "Lots not in our control. Can't see ahead, Mazy."

"Can't see behind you, neither," a new voice interrupted, and Seth jumped, "Oh, didn't mean to startle you, Seth." Elizabeth sat down on the other side of Mazy, who lifted her head and smiled as she felt Seth drop his arm and sit up a little straighter. " 'We look not at the things which are seen, but at the things which are not seen: for the things which are seen are temporal; but the things which are not seen are eternal.' I like to think that verse puts us all on equal footing with Suzanne."

"It does promise that same hope, I guess," Mazy said, "that we'll see through uncertainty if we keep our eyes looking high."

Ruth placed the buckwheat husks inside the flannel bag and held it close to the morning fire. The heat sent up a distant scent mixed with memories of Ohio farmers entering the newspaper office, the smell of corn and turned earth on their pants. Did buckwheat grow like grain? No, Naomi said it was a bushy plant with white flowers. It bore heart-shaped seeds that gave up groats for toasting. Naomi said they saved the hulls when the grain was milled and that was what she stuffed her pillows with. "It is ancient way," Naomi told her. "Old way, good way."

When the bag felt warm enough, Ruth carried it to the cart where Jessie sat, surrounded by goose down pillows and covered with a dark quilt.

"Can you raise your leg, honey? I'll put this under. It felt good before, didn't it?"

"It stinks."

"Jessie, please. Naomi took her own pillow apart to make this little one for you."

"It hurts."

"I know. But you've got to push a little, into the pain, or you'll never be able to use your leg again. Here, I'll help you lift. Elizabeth says it's healing well. You've got to get strong enough to try the crutches."

"They won't hold me. You want to see me fall." The child stuck her lower lip out—that act and the child's constant complaints flashed heat into Ruth's face.

"Jason and Ned worked hard to fix them for you," she said. "And Sarah padded the arms. You're being unreasonable."

"Ugly sagebrush. They smell. So does this," she said and tossed the bag of buckwheat husks toward the ground.

Ruth spun around, grabbed for the bag and walked away, shaking inside. She'd chosen this caring for the children, chosen this living with others. But she was no good at it. Fury came faster than fondness.

"Don't go, Auntie. I'll be good. Promise," the child wailed then. "Please, Auntie."

Was it her imagination, or did the girl drag out the word *auntie,* as though she said it as a tease?

"I've horses to tend," Ruth shouted to her over her shoulder. "When you feel like being pleasant, I'll come back." She fast-walked away. She needed to...leave, to go away, that was what she needed. To find a place where she couldn't injure others and where she could not be touched. Behind her, she heard Elizabeth talking to the child—Ruth's child—making her laugh. Ruth brushed at the hot tears that threatened.

"It's all right, Koda," Ruth said as she approached the horse, her hands moving along the animal's familiar jaw line, patting at his withers, then running her hand down his leg to check his foot. First one, then the others. She checked for nicks and scrapes, then did the same with Jumper, finishing with handfuls of grain for each of them from the packs she'd hung in the low branch of a pine. Here at least she was competent, could make things happen. The smell of damp ground and steaming manure, the mixture of horse scent and smooth hides always soothed her. She pulled the brush from the pack and began at the base of Koda's mane, pushing out toward his tail. She could stay with people, she decided, as long as she could spend a little time with horses.

"But I do have to manage the children," she told the horse. Koda nickered low. "Yes, if you could talk you'd tell me, what? What a fool I was to take them on?" The gelding nudged her.

"I could look after them, when we get into town."

"Oh, Mariah. You surprised me."

"Didn't mean to scare you. I'm good with children, really I am."

"Doesn't your mother need you for that business she talked about?"

"I know there was that time with Clayton, when I didn't watch like I could have, but..." The girl had picked up a brush and worked on Jumper, her eyes barely able to see over the big stallion's back. The center part in her hair was straight. Ruth looked at it as the girl worked.

"Everyone gets distracted," Ruth said. "I wouldn't hold that against you."

"Good." The girl stopped, came around, and stood with her hands on her hips, elbows out. Ruth smiled. It was how she stood herself, more often than not. "If you want to do a good thing, you have to concentrate. And I can do that. Keep my head now, I can. Ma says she's going to have herself a business and make bushels of money and make Matt proud of her when we meet up again. That's not me, though. I want to make Matt proud, too, but by being around horses. And children," she added in some haste. Jumper, the horse Mariah preferred, nudged her. "Keep your head up, that's what I'm finding I need to do. All the time. Look for chances. That's how we found the stock that time, not letting ourselves worry over whether we would or not or what we'd do if we didn't. We just looked for tracks and counted on making something happen. Remember?"

Ruth nodded. Mariah scratched at the horse's ears. The girl reminded her of herself those years before, all hopeful and bright with ideas. How could she have such an influence on this one and yet be so inept with her own child?

"I'm not sure what kind of an employer I'll be," Ruth said. "I do want things to happen my way. If you work for me, you'll have to remember that."

Mariah's face lit up. "But you're willing?"

"And there's the question of whether your mother will let you."

"If you asked, there'd be a better chance she would. I'm discovering that my ma and me don't always see eye to eye."

"I'll ask, then," Ruth said.

Maybe this could work. Things might be looking up.

7

knight of the whip

Sacramento City

David Taylor, jehu for the Hall and Crandall Stage Line, lounged against a post in the shade of the bakery's roof, separating himself from the crowd milling about. His homespun shirt stuck to him in the October afternoon heat, and he scratched against the trickle of sweat that threatened his back. Dust from stomping horses thickened the air. David tried to look relaxed, his booted ankles crossed over each other, his hat pushed back on his head. But he felt lost, away from his coach—the big Concord—incomplete as any jehu was without his whip and leather reins laced between his knuckles.

With his left hand—his near hand, as the jehus called it—he scratched at the day-old growth of beard on his chin. His mother would have clucked at him, "Always putting adventure before hygiene." He was only eleven when she'd said that first, as he'd tromped, full of spring mud, into their house. He asked her what the word meant—*hygiene.*

"Hygeia was the mythical daughter of Aesculapius," she told him, wiping dirt from his face. "In Greek stories. She was the goddess of health, and her father was the god of medicine."

"Who was her mother?" David asked.

"I haven't a clue," she told him, touching her nose to his. "Just a story. I only know that hygiene is the offspring of good medicine, which means you, young man, need more than a face wash if you're to stay healthy." And she'd sent him toward the copper tub, lifting a riding quirt from his muddy pants as he passed.

He needed a bath now, that was sure, and a shave, too. And he needed to braid the silk of his whip as he always did at the end of a run. He never neglected something on which his life could later depend.

But the scene spread out here entranced him. This mass of people pressed together beneath a sky washed almost white by the heat of a late afternoon drew him in. People, looking all curious and pushing and pretending they were bidding for horses or land instead of what they were. He ought to head for the home station where he could rest and wash his lanky, nineteen-year-old frame, complete his daily routine. He felt for the smooth hickory handle of his whip, then remembered it was with the coach, back at the stage stop. He'd go there shortly, he would. But for now, he studied the crowd, eyes just forward, as though catching another's eye would convict them for participating in such a vile event. Who would have the courage to look and nod while they did what they did? People hid beneath the shadows of their hats while sweat beaded on foreheads.

"One hundred eagles!" someone shouted, and David realized it had begun. His heart beat a little faster as he turned to the voice, so close to him. A number of others risked a glance at the big man dressed all in white, his eyes glistening as they scanned the crowd, his lips a thin line that masqueraded as a smile. The man sat astride a sorrel of eighteen hands who fought against the tight reins, moved its hindquarters about, and jerked its head up and down, the noise of the bit breaking into David's thoughts.

"I repeat. One hundred gold eagles."

"Taken," the auctioneer said.

Even from the distance, David could see the auctioneer's Adam's apple bobbing with excitement that the first bid should be so high.

David hadn't noticed that the bidder, large and sitting above them, had even been in the crowd, yet in seconds he consumed everyone's focus. His first bid was high, just to bring attention, maybe. Or perhaps he was the impatient kind, didn't like to waste time. Another bid came from somewhere else in the crowd. Necks craned to see who countered, but David kept his eyes on the rider. He thought he saw the white-clad man's one eyebrow flicker with the act of a challenging bid, noticed he breathed in through his mouth now.

"One hundred fifty," the auctioneer shouted back, pointing toward someone on the other side. Back to the large man. "Do I hear one seventy-five for this fine specimen?"

The big man ran his fingers at the edge of his hat. The auctioneer snapped at it. "One seventy-five. Do I hear two hundred?"

The man turned then, scanned the crowd, and when he did, he stared into David's eyes. David swallowed at what he saw there, sharp and hard and hot. He blinked and read *empty* before the man's gaze moved on.

Something about his intensity as he turned back toward the auction block, his tight control of the horse, his body rigid as a lamppost, the moisture at the side of his mouth, all brought fire to David's stomach.

Imagining things, that's what he was doing. From habit, David reached for the whip, felt the emptiness at his side. He continued to watch the bidders, the milling of men, the smells of human sweat fed by greed excused by the mob. And in the midst sat this big man as though above it all, yet driving it. He'd seen lots of men, big men like that, with a kind of presence, but they usually didn't attract his attention. Maybe because some folks said David was big and broad too. Maybe it was just this place on the Sacramento River and the yeast of desire raising the mass of men to do things they otherwise wouldn't do.

Not a good place to be, David decided. He rubbed at his jaw line with the back of his hand. Just being at this sale said something about him he didn't think he liked. His jaw ached from the clench, felt raw with his finger's rubbing.

The smell of fresh bread floated in from behind him and it nudged at him, reminded him again of his mother. This was his first free day in two weeks, and he was wasting it. A man was responsible for what he exposed himself to. That was sure. Why tempt fate further at this outdoor auction of flesh? David straightened his hat, uncrossed his legs, and pitched his back away from the post. If he spent more time, even just watching, not participating, not ever saying he approved, he could still be affected by the tentacles of stench. "Pernicious," his mother would have said, like a disease that rotted a person slowly over time even when they didn't know it was there. He'd had to ask what that word meant too.

He brushed the dirt from his pants, began to turn his back just as the Wintu woman on whom they were bidding raised her eyes over the crowd. They were brown eyes, deep and dark as good earth, and now, they locked on David's.

Zane Randolph, dressed in white linen, wearing a tapestry vest of cream silk, stared at the low-sided wagon set up as an open-air stage to display the merchandise near the river levee. He scanned the women who stood there, their eyes downcast, dark shoulders bent against the river's backdrop of dusky blue. A gust of Sacramento wind lifted tendrils of dark hair. Dust swirled. Men grabbed at their hats.

The women, girls, the merchandise all looked far away, as if wanting to pretend they were not here. He could see that, but it would not protect them. It wouldn't prevent the fate that these slobbering men had in mind for them as soon as they paid the price. The one or two he would successfully bid on were fortunate, indeed. They just didn't know it yet. He offered...opportunity for them. The other bidders, the lowlife miners and merchants and mountain men were nothing but greed-infested beasts massaged by the women's flesh enough to make their mouths water. They failed to see the larger picture.

He had seen the picture, perfect and clear, last night. After things quieted down, Zane approached the man known as Greasy, bought him a drink and chatted amiably with him, slowly bringing him around to a discussion of mining. Then horses. Then women.

"You say you encountered a blind woman, with a group of women traveling west? How long ago was that?"

The man's eyes were glassy with drink, and he needed sleep. "Just two, three days back," Greasy yawned. "Such a beauty she was, wearing blue and holding a baby in her arms."

"Where, again?"

"At the Emigrant Ferry, north. Heading into Shasta, that's what the man—let me think now—Forrester, that was his name. He's the one said they were going on to Shasta. I figure to see 'em again. I'm going back."

"They'd survived the journey well, these women?"

"Seemed like it."

"You didn't hear where they'd come from?"

Greasy shook his head. "Someplace back east. Where they all come from, ain't it? Wasn't about to have no conversation with the one dressed like a man. Didn't have no invitation in her eyes, if you know what I mean. Seemed more interested in her horses." Zane heard his own breathing as he sucked air in through his mouth. "Another said I was rude. 'Magine that. Thought themselves a little better than me." He leaned in toward Zane then, violating the space Zane liked to keep between himself and others. "I'm getting me some Indian slaves tomorrow," he said. "I'll be richer next year this time, and maybe those women'll find me a little more attractive."

"And Indians would have what to do with your plans for wealth?"

Greasy looked surprised. "Where you been? You just got to claim they're vagrants, homeless. Or buy one at the sales. Mostly Indians raided from northern tribes sold there. Law allows 'em to be sold within twenty-four hours of claiming they're without anyone to keep 'em. Any courthouse or sheriff can hold the sale. You buy 'em, you can keep 'em until they're twenty-one. Boys 'til they're twenty-five if you get 'em older, say fourteen or so. You can even take the grub you give 'em against their pay." He leaned back, hiccuped, and blinked. "Ain't that just the best law ever?"

"And what you'll do with these...boys is what?"

"Make 'em work the mines! Ain't you listening? File claims and set 'em to work. I got two, three streams being worked already. Need a few more workers. Might even buy me a woman to do some cooking and washing. Hate that laundering."

"And they stay?"

"Well, you got to train 'em the way you want," Greasy said. "But I do that. They stay. Even without chains or ropes. Guess they figure if they're fed good and not beat up once they learn your ways, it's better than being found by someone on the street and just hauled in again. Ugly as it is, they know what to expect at Greasy's mines. Must decide it's better than heading into what they don't know."

The smoke and the man's whisky-breath might have fuzzied Zane's thinking, but it cleared as the man rambled on about the Indian Protection Act and how the Wintus and Shastas were killed off by hostile tribes as well as the "locals." All the killing left women and kids ripe for the taking as vagrants. "Biggest sales are here in Sacramento and along the Columbia River in The Dalles."

"And you'll take them back north, toward Shasta," Zane said.

"Right back to my claims. At Mad Mule Canyon, most of them," Greasy said. "Resupply before winter and work the streams much as we can 'til snow drifts us out. Then make our way into Whoa Navigation."

"And your...charges?"

"My what?"

"Your...purchases, do they stay the winter in Shasta City too?"

"Naw. I got to get me a packer to bring in food for the snow months. Then come spring, if they're still alive, I'll be happy and put 'em back to work. Saves retraining new crews."

Zane had lain awake for a time after leaving Greasy, offering first to buy him breakfast in the morning. The man was lint off poor linen, but he was useful. He was sure Greasy spoke of Ruth. Zane must have just missed her somehow back at Laramie. And what a delicious twist that the beautiful blind woman had some connection. Forrester was the name of the man involved. He could find him and locate both women. He'd go north—just as soon as he found the auction Greasy spoke of.

He may as well sink some investments in California.

Now at the sale, Zane's eye caught a young man, jaw clenched, who had been holding up a post in front of the bakery. He'd bid soon. Zane knew that. Just a boy who couldn't wait to have a woman to call his own. Zane was above that, better than that. For him, this was strictly business.

His wide fingers with filed nails felt the silk ascot at his throat as he swallowed. He looked back, touched his hat brim, raised the bid again. He was aware of the attention he drew from the men around him, some near enough to push against his horse, brush his own legs. Zane disliked their closeness, but it was undeserving of anger. He reserved that heat for only one. The others were worms, challenging him only to imagine how he might use them or how long it might take them to squirm, to be pushed past what they said they stood for. Everyone could be pushed, despite how they preached or pleaded about principles, about being better than the rest. All men could be squashed.

Zane learned that during the years of his confinement. And he'd learned that the biggest, strongest, and least attached were the ones who survived.

Zane's horse stomped, lifted its back leg, and turned to bite at a fly. Zane yanked on the bridle, pulling the animal's head around. With his hat, he swatted at the horse's hindquarters. The martingale kept the beast from raising his head, but not from resisting. The sorrel sidestepped, forcing other men crowded close out of its way.

He would rid himself of this animal, once this sale was over. The unpredictability of him did not suit. Besides, it would give Zane the perfect reason to seek out a horse or two in Shasta. An investor arriving by stage needed a mount. Zane smiled then, satisfied he had a plan as he jerked on the reins, felt the horse tremble beneath his knees. He watched men scatter like cockroaches from light. His right hand reached for the short quirt, and he slapped at the animal's neck. The horse just needed a good whip.

That was what Ruth had needed too. Discipline. Control. Some beings resisted being commanded, but it was what they really wanted. He'd realized that too late. When he found Ruth again, he wouldn't make the same mistake twice. He would let her know of his control, but it would come to her in little moments he would plan, surprises. She would be his, a marionette, while he manipulated her strings.

The horse settled down enough for Zane to hear the latest bid. He'd picked out one or two girls he thought would suit his needs and bid on the one he favored most. Now his prize stared at that boy by the bakery. Zane lifted his hat to the auctioneer, smiled. The best part about this sale was that it seduced even the religious souls, the pious hearts who wanted only to "do good" for the poor heathens. They could rationalize, convince themselves of their clean nature, buy these unfortunate souls, make these people part of their families, give them homes. Homes! Zane smiled at the thought. Instead, they brought stench into their homes. They were sucked under "helping the heathens" before they even knew they'd entered foul waters. Some even asked the Indians to work thirteen-hour days on the very streams they'd lived beside for generations, now being ravaged by greed. And the poor Indians did it!

Well, that was to be expected. One had to be clever to keep from being used. One had to be of stronger character to withstand the demands of a superior being, a cut above the rest, a thinker who put others in awe.

He would enjoy the freedoms of this California he'd learned even more about at breakfast. Greasy had been both wordy and hungry. "Indians aid in their own downfall," he announced, his mouth stuffed with bacon. "They let us come in, we take their land, women, and kids, and then we spread the good news around by buying whatever we haven't done in. Yessiree, there's even bands of Mexicans stealing Indian women and children and bringing to sale along with other tribes. We're an international state, we are."

From what Zane could see in the faces of those being sold today, they had no fight left in them, except for the one he bid on. And if Greasy was right, there was no one left to fight for her. There was no escape. Perhaps she'd be wise enough to know that being owned was better than death.

Another raise to his bid, this time from the opposite side. Then another. Zane refused to look, not wanting to seem annoyed. Couldn't the men see Zane had unlimited funds? Probably not. One looked as if he'd just come in off the trail, dust all over a well-cut suit. Probably some Oregonian. Lots of them coming south, he'd heard.

Zane touched his white hat again, tired of it. "One thousand," he said.

A hush settled over the crowd.

"A thousand dollars?" the auctioneer asked. His voice squeaked.

"I find this a tedious ritual meant to be gotten over." Zane spoke loud enough for most to hear. He smiled at the stricken looks of the men, including the boy who had caught the woman's eye. Good. Let them remember this man who was impatient with protocol, for whom money was no object. It didn't matter if they remembered him as a buyer of chattel. It was associating him with Ruth he had to keep under wraps.

"Sold!" gaveled the auctioneer, his buck teeth formed into a grin.

Zane frowned. He would have liked to finish his pronouncement.

"She's all yours," the auctioneer said, pushing at the Wintu woman, who stumbled but caught herself before she fell. "Come forward and claim your prize, sir."

Zane reined the sorrel through the parting crowd as the woman—maybe fifteen or sixteen years old, he surmised—her eyes turned now toward him, watched him approach. Her arms were tied behind her back, forcing her thin cloth tight against her narrow frame. Did she gaze past him still to that boy? No matter. Now she belonged to him.

"She's carrying," the auctioneer whispered to Zane as he leaned toward the young woman, pressed his hands into the thin flesh of her shoulder, turning her so Zane could get a better look. "Hope that's not a problem for ya."

Zane leaned back from the man, who smelled of onions. "I can see now she's with child. You might have gotten more if you'd announced it."

"Not likely. Most of 'em can't do much work with a little one about. And she might die in delivering. Poor investment, some think, but I'm with you. Two for one is good business."

"I'm not with anyone," Zane told him, handing him a thick roll of bills the auctioneer began to count.

Zane leaned over and traced his finger along the woman's shoulder to her neck, watched bumps appear on her skin. "You're mine now, little orphan," he said. His finger lingered over her ear, down her cheek. He opened her mouth with the press of his thumb. "All her teeth. Good."

He wondered if she'd try to bite this hand that would now feed and clothe her, or if her love of her unborn child was greater than her hatred of being owned.

"I wouldn't, if I was you," the auctioneer said.

Zane forced his fingers to run across a row of bottom teeth while his thumb and fingers held her jaw still. "You're smarter than that, now, aren't you?"

She did not bite.

A part of him felt…disappointed at her compliance. He liked a challenge even when he knew he'd win. "Yes, little beauty. You're mine now."

"She don't understand no English," the auctioneer told him.

"Oh, she understands enough, I'd suggest," Zane said, removing his hands, patting her cheek. Her skin was soft as a baby's bottom. A smile eased across his face.

The woman parted her lips ever so slightly as she looked up into his eyes. He brushed the dark hair away from her forehead, pleased with her quick understanding of his power over her. The woman would have to work long and hard to recover Zane's investment, but he knew she would. And he'd enjoy the training of her, the breaking of her as he would break a good-spirited horse, the way he'd almost broken Ruth. He leaned in to loosen the binding rope, and Zane saw his reflection in the depth of the woman's dark eyes.

It was then that the Wintu woman spit.

David winced when the big man spit back.

The woman sneered, her head up now, not cowed at all. She had mettle, David gave her that, if not good sense. The crowd gasped, then broke into laughter.

She shouldn't have provoked the man. Had she no instinct to survive? Didn't she know that men like that hated to be made fools of? Couldn't she see he'd be likely to hurt her now for what she'd done?

Across the crowd, David saw the losing bidder laughing, slapping his leg with his hat.

The big man on the sorrel wiped at his own face, then scraped his fingers across the woman's mouth and nose, pinching off the spittle he'd just put there, leaving white pressure marks where he had rubbed her face. He grabbed at the girl, then yanked her up in front of him onto the big horse, sidesaddle, the slap of her thighs cracking against the pommel, her arms still tied behind her. With one arm, he pulled her neck into his chest. *Now she might bite him good,* David thought, but she didn't.

Instead, the woman stared straight out, never blinking, as the man in white, his own jaws clenched, breathing through his teeth, wove the horse out through the still-laughing crowd.

David stared at her. He wanted to drop his eyes, to disavow that he'd even been here to see this happen, but he couldn't. He thought for just a moment that she caught his eye, but it was as fleeting as a fawn's tail disappearing out of sight.

As the big horse moved to the edge of the laughter, Oltipa, the Wintu woman, thought of things she loved: the taste of acorn soup, sweet upon her lips, the memory of wind sighs soothing high in the yellow pine. Soft ferns pressed against her face, not the silk of this man's scarf. She smelled memories formed of scraped hides, not the scent of this white man's sweat. Through eyes set far away from here, she could see the yellowed grass, short now after spring's burning so there would be new grass for the deer, so the land would give no fuel to fire the trees if lightning struck in the dry summer, so the waters of the rivers would stay clear and the salmon strong. She let her imagination take her, her eyes gazing far beneath the oaks and pines. She would not let herself see this sea of men, would not let herself hear the laughs and jeers, would not allow herself to belong to the man who owned her body now if not her spirit. This man sat closer to her than any other man had ever been, except for the father of the child she carried. But he was dead. She blinked back tears.

She could not be owned, she decided, despite what some might have thought. As long as she held her stories in her heart, this man could not own her soul. This man could own her labor, her hands, even her body. But never her.

As they roped their way through the parting crowd, the men laughing and moving toward the building smelling of sweet scents of bread baking, she caught the gaze of the boy with kind eyes the color of spring water, eyes that did not approve of what was happening here, this ripping and tearing of spirit and soul. For just a moment when the bidding began, his eyes, as gentle as the father of her child's had been, those eyes had sent hope like an arrow over the heads of these drooling savages.

But in the time it took a hawk's wing to slice the wind above her, she knew he would not raise his hand, could not buy her and set her free.

The rider who held her jerked his hand to settle the horse, squeezing her with his arm. She grunted with the pain. Oltipa reminded herself not to accept blame for being snatched when the Modocs took her from her village in the shade of the big mountain, ripped her from the rushing sounds of Winnimem's Arm, the McCloud River, as the white men called it. Someday, she would go back to that acorn soup place where she and her baby could stay alive.

They brushed past him, the man with kind eyes staring. Her ragged dress stretched across her legs, cutting into her thighs, exposing her limbs. She heard the heartbeat of her captor, racing; smelled the horse's sweat. Her hope flew away.

David worked the braid of the cracker draped over his thigh, but he saw only the Wintu woman's eyes. He'd bathed and shaved and changed his clothes and bathed again, somehow not able to get the smell and grime from his skin the first time. He ate his supper at the way station, and now he sat beneath the sloping roof of the stable, bent over his work. He heard a few pelts of raindrops on the tin roof and smelled the scent of horses mixed with the smell of old straw and manure. The rhythm of the spans of horses grinding grain in their teeth soothed his thinking, helped him return to routine. He'd be ready for the trip north to Red Bluff tomorrow, rested and ready.

But he couldn't get the Wintu woman from his mind.

He couldn't have bought her, even if he had more than a thousand dollars, which he didn't, and probably never would have saved, not on a jehu's wage. A jehu. David smiled, then spoke out loud for the benefit of the horse. "And the driving is like the driving of Jehu the son of Nimshi; for he driveth fur-i-ous-ly." He always stretched out the last word of the verse from chapter nine, verse twenty, Second Kings, from which the drivers took their name. It was what the jehus were known for, driving briskly through rain-swollen streams or up snow-slickened grades, keeping their commitments, getting people where they planned to be.

Knights of the Whip they were called too, and sometimes "Charlie" if someone didn't know a fellow's name. But jehu fit them best, he guessed. They were paid in wild and furious adventure more than currency; in living at the edge, in wondering what washout might appear around the bend, what bandit might decide to hold them up if he wasn't alert to places along the trail ripe for ambush. They took their wages in wit and risk, experiences that massaged the senses.

The woman's eyes came back to him. Some knight he was, letting her go like that. And yet what would he have done with her? He didn't know any jehus who had ties, who were married. Most were orphans, like him, and the stage owners said that was what they preferred: no complications then when someone died, as they did pretty regularly, now that he thought of it. A Wintu...girl and him. He brushed the shock of dark hair from his eyes, leaving behind the scent of leather. He hoped to shake away the image of her. The oil felt slick on his fingers as he rubbed it into the bridle.

He might have taken an advance against his wages, maybe. And if he had, he might have found someone who would take her in, care for her. He looked down and realized he'd worn an open blister onto the pad of his thumb with his rubbing, something he'd never done. He put his finger in his mouth, aware of the taste of leather and oil mingling with the torn flesh on his tongue.

But if by some miracle he had bought her, wasn't that saying he condoned the practice of selling flesh? Didn't that make him just like the slaveholders his father had railed against before coming to California? Wouldn't his purchase just add fuel and fire up the tribes that took captives? And what good was helping one poor Indian woman anyway in the midst of so many who needed it?

"It would be good for her," he could almost hear his mother say. "No sense worrying about all the rest being too much to manage. You can just do what you can do."

Just do what I can do, David told himself. He tried that with his sister and had failed, hadn't had the wherewithal to bring her to him when she was left all alone. He hoped she was happy. The Wintu's face flashed next to hers; if he couldn't care for his own sister, how could he expect to care for an Indian girl? Well, he hadn't seized his opportunity yesterday, and now she was gone and there was nothing to be done for it. He should not have been there at all. He held the Wintu woman in his heart for a moment, not exactly saying a prayer, holding her in his mind. Maybe she would feel again the thoughts sent when she lifted her eyes, when he almost made a bid. Maybe she would feel a wash of kindness in a world lurking with sin.

David looked over the whiplash, turning it in his hands. A good driver never touched an animal with a whip, not once; but a crack of it beside the horse's head told the animals to make shifts and moves at rapid speeds, sometimes with just seconds to avoid a hole or rock that would otherwise tip the stage over. And the cracker, thin little rawhide strips at the far end of the whip, always needed rebraiding at the end of a trip. Hung out there at the end of the whiplash, the crackers took the greatest hit. "Like some of us," David said, "all frayed way out here at the end of things." Still, those tiny threads did good, strong, important work. He wouldn't have managed the big teams without them. They just needed daily tending, doing what they could do.

Light from the kerosene lantern glinted off the band of silver that marked his whip handle. He'd had it custom-made by a silversmith now in Shasta. That's where his jehu money went. A horse nickered low from a stall behind him. "I hear ya," David said, "I hear ya. Give me a minute and I'll come scratch."

The horse nickered again, and David stood, leaned the whip against the stall, and reached to soothe his friend. It was his mother who'd showed him where a horse liked scratching most, on that bone between his ears. His mother was on his mind tonight, reminding him of the things that truly mattered.

He was glad his mother wasn't alive to see western people turn to slaving. Even the so-called Treaty of Peace passed last year at Major Reading's ranch up north had resulted in not a single Indian being protected from the masses. So what was the good of it?

"It's a beginning," his mother might have said if she had lived to know it. "And sometimes just beginning a thing allows Providence to move it forward."

But to what end? What good did Providence do bringing him and his father south, consumed by the gold rush, only for his father to just disappear one day?

"We just don't always know what's in store for us," his mother said once. She patted flour into a ball that would raise and fill their little cabin with the scent of baking bread. "We just have to keep our heads."

Keep our heads. No one seemed to be keeping a sane mind when it came to the Indians. His mother'd always had a heart for them.

At least his mother had never seen such an auction or known such a despicable law even existed. It was the only good thing David could think of about his mother's death. That, and that she'd never suffered. The doctor said the arrow that took her had been swift and sure, and she'd never known what hit her.

Zane rode the horse hard out K Street, away from the river to Second and then beyond, away from the laughter and jeers. He rode until the horse tired at last, until he could no longer hear the taunts of the crowd. They were crows calling now, nothing more. As soon as he was out of sight in the dusky night, he set that purchase down, hard, tied her hands in front of her, then led her with a rope.

"Perhaps walking a bit will put you into a better frame of mind," he told her.

Knowing she was there pleased and calmed him. He controlled her with a rope long enough to let her to fall if she got too far behind, but short enough to make her wonder if the horse's hooves might hit her as she breathed in the animal's dust.

By early evening, Zane tired of talking himself through the episode—that was all it was, just a minor glitch in his day. If the crowd remembered him at all, it would be for the size of his bid, not the foolishness of the woman. After all, it was she who was the captive, not him. And he had a plan for her. That was what mattered, not the jeers of faceless men.

A light in the distance told him they were nearing the city again. A way station, two stories high with a wide veranda and white picket fence, was set off the road just ahead. He could rid himself of this horse there and take the morning stage with the settled-down woman.

Dismounting, he looped the reins around the hitching post, satisfied that the horse's head hung heavy with fatigue. Next, he untied the lead rope and pushed the woman up the wooden steps and inside, her hands still tied.

"That...person cannot be housed here," the innkeeper said, his eyes raised over tiny round glasses. "The diners..." he nodded to the side room where a few people ate a late supper.

Zane said, "Might I suggest the stable. Surely this...establishment has access to a livery."

The clerk hesitated, stared at the woman. "She sick?"

"With child," Zane added, deciding that even a heathen woman with child could be used to advantage.

The innkeeper's eyes softened. "Oh. Well. I expect Mrs. Barnes would allow accommodation then, of some kind." He looked thoughtful, adjusted his glasses.

"A locked tack room would be suitable."

The clerk nodded. "No latch on it, but you could rope the door tight. No windows. See she stays tied or you'll be billed for what's destroyed. Pay in advance for your room and hers."

"I've a horse to sell as well," Zane said, his fingers clicking gold coins. "Can I leave that in your capable hands?" He held the eagles above the man's fingers, just out of reach.

"You can board him here. Charge you little or nothing for the work of feeding him and sending on the bill of sale when I find a buyer." He snatched the coins Zane released, counted them. "Need a few more for the horse tending," he said. Zane sneered, then handed over an additional amount, which the man pocketed, swift as a ferret.

"Excellent. I'm also seeking the agent for the stage north. Would that be you?"

"Yes sir. You wanting for two?"

"This is not a passenger." He calmed his voice before he said, "This is chattel. Merchandise." He flicked the glove of his hand toward the woman. "Luggage," he said when the man frowned. "She'll fit just fine on top."

"Not the way Hall and Crandle see her," the clerk said. "Two tickets you got to buy if it's a living thing."

Zane grunted, handed the man passage for two. "I trust we will be of little bother to you," Zane said, "once this…package is stored."

"Tack room and stalls're just beyond. Jehu's working his whip," the clerk said, nodding toward the stable. "Just head to his light."

8

wide-eyed

David Taylor moved in and out of sleep, sometimes staring at the rafters of the bunkhouse, sometimes dreaming into his pillow, near the edges of awake. He'd finished his whip repair and turned in earlier than usual, noticing moisture sparkle against the kerosene lamp just as he stepped inside. He wasn't sure why he was so tired. Maybe the change in routine did it, maybe the thoughts of his mother, maybe the Wintu woman's eyes.

He was alone in the shedlike structure. The rope bed was a luxury after nights on just a board bunk. Hall and Crandall ran a good line, and he looked forward to seeing the drivers of the other two stages expected yet that night. "Three six-horse stages leave and return daily," ran the ads. "The public may rest assured that the arrangements of this line, for speed and comfort, are unsurpassed in the world. Neither pains nor expense having been spared in procuring the BEST HORSES, finest CONCORD COACHES, and the most competent and CAREFUL DRIVERS." It was a good company, a good life for a single man. The arriving drivers would catch quick sleep before heading on, but David still looked forward to the greeting, hearing about the road conditions north and any news of note. The other drivers wouldn't have a day to waste as David had, at least not for another week.

And he had wasted the day. He lay with his arms folded behind his head. He heard the scuttle of a mouse across the floor.

He was tired from trying to make sense of his inaction. He could respond quickly to risky situations on the trail. He anticipated places where a mud slide might happen following a rain, where the snowmelt could push high water, might shift the footing at a ford. Geography and the lay of the land—those he'd studied, and he felt he'd been a worthy student. It was in these human places where he struggled, the wilderness of relationship that took him down. The wilderness of the spirit challenged him too, he realized as he lay there, eyes cast toward the ceiling.

He'd failed in that realm the most by not standing up for the Wintu woman—or any of them at all—by not raising a ruckus against the treachery of the sales. He recalled a verse his mother sometimes quoted him. Something about doing for the little people—the least, she always said—being the same as doing for the Son of God.

Maybe this jehu term for him was more apt than he'd thought. The biblical Jehu had been a man who wiped out wrongdoing and treachery, all right, who was used by God to do it, but who never trusted God himself and had his own problems with morals and might.

Trust. What did that take? What about the drivers made them "competent and careful," trustworthy enough for folks to put their lives into their hands? Reliability, that was one quality. Integrity, being what a person said he was no matter where or with whom he stood. Well, he had room to grow in that one if standing at a sale of human flesh was any indication. What else, he wondered? Meeting people who were different, maybe, without looking down on them. He supposed his mother'd had the market on that.

"Unconditional love," she told him. "You just have to look and not be too quick to judge." Goodness surely reflected in her fair face.

And...honesty, David decided. A fellow blew his trust real fast if he stretched the truth. Why should God trust him to do a work if he wasn't honest with himself?

Then the thought came to him from nowhere and from somewhere—he was worried about what folks would think of him. He felt his neck grow hot with the admission. He hadn't acted to save the Wintu girl, not because he thought the task too large or too futile to take on, but because of what people might have thought. That he was a little daft or something, trying to rescue an Indian, throwing good money after bad. Or maybe that he'd be judged as wanting her for himself, as *that kind of man.* That could have reflected badly on him. Maybe even cost him his job. "You'll have to hit me upside the head when you want me to be sure to pay attention," he said out loud.

No wonder he was tired—wearing blinders took work. There was risk in learning to see.

He heard voices outside. One of the horses nickered low. A thumping sound or two followed. David walked to the door that opened onto the covered porch where he'd worked his whip earlier. His stocking feet felt the grit of sand tracked in as he peered through the square window. He didn't see anyone, but he noticed a shaft of light cut the river fog. It came from the tack room. The innkeeper must have been placing something there for shipment in the morning. It wasn't the usual practice.

David wondered if he should dress, see if the clerk needed any help.

Not likely, or he would have asked, David decided.

He yawned. He could sleep now somehow, knowing that if he had another chance, he'd take it, sure. God could trust him. He moved away from the window just as the light went out.

Shasta City

"Begin with the streets. Are they wide, narrow, straight, or are houses just plopped here and there?" Suzanne asked. She tried not to sound frustrated. "Go slowly. I'm trying to count and concentrate."

"Picture a teacup," Tipton said. "We're walking down the middle of it, headed west. Going uphill. Feel it in your legs? There are stores, one row, on either side. Maybe more at the end of the street. The road dips south. Looks like houses that way too. Hills just start right up behind the hotels, and smell the bakery? Pines, oak trees—they look like—and twiney shrubs and brown grasses surround all kinds of houses, if you can call them that. Just a hodgepodge of dwellings on rounded hills that had trees on them, but they're all cut down. Stumps stick up around. No streets, really, just trails twisting like tired snakes. Snowcapped hills above and beyond that." Tipton turned slowly in the street. "Wood houses and canvas tents farther up. Looks like maybe a spring coming right out of rock. Right here there are lots of stores, but you can hardly see the road for all the mules and horses and pack animals and dogs and wild-eyed looking people. Most of them look as though they haven't seen either women or a washtub for weeks." Suzanne laughed. "And, oh, there goes a whole string of animals heading out with no one leading them! Hear that? They're being chased now. The packs are slipping left and right, and the animals are kicking up a storm. Little birds are scattering after them. Must not have used diamond hitches. Tyrellie said those would hold no matter what kind of wild-eyes you faced."

"Mules or the men? They're both equally wild-eyed, no doubt," Suzanne said.

Tipton sighed. "Tyrellie would have liked this place, I think. I miss him, Suzanne. As much as if we were married. Despite what Mama says. It was real, our betrothal. Look out! Clayton!"

"What is it, Tipton?"

"You stay close! Your mother's hanging on to Pig, and she's got your little brother. She can't take you, too." The boy whined. "Don't be complaining."

Suzanne wondered if she should have asked someone else to go with her for this first trip into town. She hadn't wanted all the women with her. Adora went on and on about Suzanne "needing help," and she'd overheard Mazy and Seth talking about "taking chances," with Suzanne's name brought up as a poor example. She thought she'd done right well taking her children for a walk. And what if she did mix things up in the wagon? So did everyone else, she imagined. A wagon wasn't like a home where a person could put their things away and expect them to stay right there.

She wanted to experience the town so when she joined the others as they oohed and aahed, she'd be better able to keep up with their conversations. But Tipton troubled her now. She was just a child herself, her sharp tongue directed at Clayton. The girl described things well, but she was fluttery. At that moment, Suzanne felt as though she had three children to look after.

A horse with the scent of a hard lather brushed against her, shoving her into Tipton and the boys.

"Get out of the way. Are you blind?" a sharp-toned rider yelled.

"Hey," Tipton shouted after him. "She *is* blind. Are you?"

The man shouted something inaudible but kept riding.

"He couldn't have known, Tipton. It's all right."

"I thought Seth said they treated ladies with special dignity here."

Suzanne sighed. "Maybe it's because we're so early."

"You mean they might think we've been up all night? That we're—"

"No. We certainly do not appear to be women of negotiable affections," Suzanne said. "Not with three children in tow."

"I count two," Tipton said.

"Of course you do," Suzanne told her. She released her grip on Pig and pulled at the floppy bonnet that covered her face, tightening the strings.

"Well, he didn't need to be so rude."

"I don't have the strength to challenge every thoughtless phrase sent my way," Suzanne said. She adjusted her dark glasses.

"People ought to be grateful they can see," Tipton said. "Here's a step."

"Most of us aren't grateful until we lose something—or feel we might. Oh! Pig, wait! Where's he taking me?"

"Up the steps. Lift your skirts!"

"Pig! Wait!" Suzanne heard laughter, and once up the steps, the dog pulled her along a boardwalk. She brushed past people and smelled cigars and stale ale and the drift of fresh bread. She gasped, bumped against a railing, felt Sason bounce on her back and hoped his little head was secure against the pillow she'd fashioned. Clayton squealed. At least he kept up. Then the dog abruptly turned, slowed slightly as she felt a step then the dirt of the street. Tipton shouted behind her to let go of Pig and that she'd catch him up.

Suzanne did, chastising herself that she hadn't let go before. How stupid of her. She must have looked a fright. "What's wrong with him?" Suzanne called out. "Is Sason all right?"

"Leave that cat be, Pig!" she heard Tipton say.

It seemed an hour but was likely only minutes that Suzanne stood, Clayton's sweaty little palms pulling on her hand. With her now free hand reached behind her, she lifted the baby's board, moving it gently up and down. Breathless, Tipton came up to her. "Here's your dog. I've just sashayed around twenty men," she said. "Danced through lines of pack strings and mules' legs, past the door of a bookstore—I can hardly wait to tell Mazy—where your Pig chased a cat under another mule who leaped and bucked and left...well, something steaming in the street. Pig ran through it. But the cat's safe, and I've got him, Pig, I mean." Tipton took a deep breath.

"I can smell what he got into," Suzanne said. "Other than that?"

"He's fine. It was a great-looking cat. Has Pig never seen one?"

"He has now."

"Well," Tipton said after a pause. "We've acquired an audience, an admiring glance or two." Suzanne heard the crinolines of the girl's skirt swish, felt the breeze Tipton's bonnet made when she bobbed her head. "Hmm," the girl said. "Interest." Suzanne imagined Tipton fluttering her eyelashes, and for just a moment she replaced her frustration with the dog's actions with a wistful memory, of when she'd been Tipton's age. She'd enjoyed the attention of young men. The image of Bryce came to her mind. She felt an ache inside her, a longing for what was and would never be again.

She blinked, took a deep breath, adjusted her dark glasses. "What are you wearing?" Suzanne asked.

"A green woolen dress with a jacket. Saved for a special occasion."

"How did you know today would be that kind of day?" The scent of dried roses once stuffed into the folds of Tipton's dress drifted to Suzanne's nose as the girl apparently twisted and twirled.

"I didn't. But Elizabeth said we should celebrate little things more. And I think Tyrell would have made this a special day, my first trip into town. I'm smiling at a nice-looking man now, maybe twenty or so. Wearing a red plaid shirt. Oh, the old one next to him thinks I just flirted with him. They're bumping each other." She clutched Suzanne's arm. "Oh, Suzanne, I'm so glad you asked me to come. I like the secrecy, our doing it together without the rest of them knowing. Clayton! Quit grabbing at me! I'm letting go of Pig," she told her.

Suzanne reached for Pig's halter. The dog still panted from his run after the cat. "Clayton!"

"There's no reason to be sharp with him, Tipton. He's just a child. Curious."

"Easy for you to say. You're not responsible."

Suzanne flinched before she could stop it.

"Oh, Suzanne. I'm sorry. I didn't mean—"

"Yours is the larger responsibility," Suzanne said. She heard the coldness of her own words.

"But I didn't mean to, you know, say that."

Suzanne hesitated. "I know," she said. *Accommodate,* wasn't that what Elizabeth said they all had to do, not take things quite so personal and let hurt feelings keep them from being…focused. "Oh, what's that sound I hear, that rumbling? Is it a stage?" She swallowed, hoped they stood free of its run.

She felt Tipton turn. “It’s a tenpin alley. Listen! Bowling! Imagine that.”

Suzanne laughed, liked the feeling of relief. “My brother used to play that back in Michigan, until our father found out. Ninepins was illegal.”

“In Wisconsin, too,” Tipton said. “But this sign says it’s tenpins.”

“So the emigrants brought the game with them and changed the rules to make it legal. This is a fascinating place, this California.”

“You don’t think they’ll think Clayton’s my child, do you?”

“Anyone in particular you want to be sure knows you’re unencumbered?”

“What does that mean?”

“You’re young and free to flirt, Tipton. A single woman. And I suspect you’re lovely.”

“The men are smiling at us and adjusting their hats. Oh, one’s coming this way. I’ll just ask one of those fine-looking men,” Tipton said. Before Suzanne could stop her, Tipton had placed Clayton’s pudgy palm back in hers and left, the scent of dried roses leaving with her.

“Wait—” Suzanne started, then stopped. She was alone with her children. Wasn’t that what she’d always wanted?

Sacramento City

In the morning, David woke early, refreshed. He’d learned something yesterday, about being trustworthy, and he was up to the challenge. He spoke to the night driver about the road north toward Marysville at the fork of the Yuba and Feather Rivers. He would take the stage, mail, and passengers the fifty miles, exchange teams, then head up the red dirt road to Tehama. Another driver would take the route north to Red Bluff from there. David would rest the night and drive the next stage back to Sacramento. At least that was his plan.

"Got some additional...chattel for you, David," the innkeeper told him when he entered the hotel lobby to grab a final cup of coffee and gather up passengers.

"Thought I saw you out there rustling around in the tack room last night," David said. "Is that what I've got to load?"

The man handed David the mug of steaming coffee. "Ask him. Zane Randolph." He pointed with his chin to a man dressed in white, a cape draped over his shoulders. David looked up into the mirror behind the bar, feeling his heart pick up a beat. The man sat tall against the round-backed hickory chair. He sat alone, and David recognized his eyes.

"What's he bringing?" David said, not seeing any leather valise beside the man.

"A woman," the innkeeper said. "She's in the tack room. Or was. S'pect he'll be getting her out soon as you call the all-ready."

David felt a binding in his chest as though he fought for air. His thoughts raced, his hands shook. He'd never experienced this, not when his father turned up missing, not when he found the letter from his uncle saying his mother had died. Not even when he'd confronted a cougar once as he urged the Concord around a slippery edge. But he felt it now, the short breath, blood pounding at his temple. His head buzzed as if someone had hit him up beside his ear. He gasped. Was this the certainty he'd asked God for?

With a sneer on his face, the big man passed. David watched him go to the tack room as he gulped his coffee.

The Wintu woman was brought out, and now David could no longer tell himself there were no second chances, for there she stood, her eyes blinking into the daylight.

"You aren't getting ill, are you?" the innkeeper asked David. Then, looking concerned, he added, "We got six passengers. There's no way I can find a replacement."

"I'm fine," David said, setting his cup on the counter. He stepped outside.

"I thought perhaps we'd met before," the man in white said, addressing David. He didn't extend his hand, but his voice held charm in it. "You were the one my prize here found so fascinating. Didn't you, my dear?"

The Wintu woman's eyes rose to David's, and he felt a piercing at the broken expression he saw. "Ma'am," David said, and tipped his felt hat at her.

"So polite," Randolph said. "What did you say your name was?"

"David Taylor," he said, irritated by the squeak in his own voice. He had to collect himself. He had to make a plan. He'd been given a second chance!

He cleared his throat and said his name again.

"I'm guessing you want the outside seat," the innkeeper said to Randolph. "Good view from up there. We don't have a man riding as guard."

"There's room inside the coach for her," a male passenger said, coming out of the hotel. "It seats six."

A woman carrying a round wooden case stepped out next. She smiled absently at the Indian girl as the men parted to allow her to move through.

"The company will be more pleasant without her inside," Randolph told the man, his eyebrow raised in protest. "The weather's lovely." He gazed at the blue sky broken only by the dot of a seagull winging its way toward the Sacramento River. "And I'm sure our young jehu will find the company...admirable. Besides, the gentle lady would reasonably object to sharing seats with a heathen."

The woman opened her mouth, closed it like a hungry fish, then scurried into the stage.

"Not unless her hands are untied," David told Randolph. "She's not sitting up top with her hands roped. She needs to be able to hang on. We're going over some rough country."

The big man paused. "How far north are you taking us?"

"The rope," David said.

Randolph hesitated, then motioned to the innkeeper to loosen the rawhide that bound the Wintu woman's hands.

"Change drivers at Tehama," David said. He was breathing calmly now. He hoped he didn't look as weak as he felt. "I'll be staying there. Another will take you on."

"Until then you should have a merry time of it with this...girl. I think I'll call her...Hawk." Randolph lifted the girl's chin. "Fitting, don't you think? With those watching eyes staring at you. They hold a wish in them. To just fly away."

David pulled his gloves on slowly, forcing his mind to think. "Get 'em loaded," he told the clerk, who nodded, then hustled the passengers into the coach.

David walked around the Concord, the horses, checking one last time for any harness cuts, anything unusual in the tack or carriage. He spoke to the animals, looked at legs and feet, and then back to the luggage, loaded. He checked the passenger list the innkeeper showed him then, a finger and a nod toward the man. Zane Randolph, it was a name he knew he'd not forget. The man's body cast a shadow over the woman. Something about him reminded David of an animal, tensed and unpredictable.

"He won't go 'til all the luggage is secure and folks are settled in," the innkeeper told Randolph.

"Then let him load this last piece." Randolph pushed at the woman. "She's not so very heavy."

"You get on inside. Sir," David said.

"After the woman's loaded," Randolph growled.

The two men stared at each other. David nodded to the clerk, then, "I'll go up to the box." He stepped, pulled himself up onto the high Concord seat, then turned to reach for the woman.

She raised her arms, let herself be lifted up, helped by the clerk, pulled forward into David's arms.

She was light as a leaf. Her hand, brown as an acorn, fit into his and gripped it, offered no resistance as she stepped into the box. David looked at her, tried to tell her she was safe, and must have communicated something for she didn't turn her eyes away. Then in one fluid motion, his wide hands around her rib cage, he lifted her again across the box and placed her on the seat next to him.

"You can ride shotgun, Hawk!" Randolph called up to her. "Marvelous!"

"It's safer than on the luggage," David said to her, his voice low enough, he hoped, for Randolph to miss.

"Are you coming with us or not?" David shouted down. He heard activity below, felt the stage creak and ache with the weight of the big man stepping up and in. The innkeeper slammed the door, stood back, and signaled. David checked to be sure his whip was in the holder, tucked his pant legs into his calf-high leather boots, and adjusted the neckerchief around his neck. *Never forget love and faithfulness. Bind them around your neck.* He always thought of that proverb when he tightened his kerchief. This day, he said it as a prayer.

He inhaled a deep breath, loosened his neckerchief by two fingers to be able to cover his nose in case of a cloud of dust, straightened his dark bowler hat with a narrow nap brim, drawing it tight to his ears. Then he hooked the wide leather belt that would keep him on the seat if the road got rough.

"All set," he shouted down to the passengers. David tucked the lap pad around the woman's legs to keep the mud from flying up onto her. He reached for the lines from the right side, spread the reins between the fingers of his near and off hands, three ribbons in each palm. Then raising the whip with his off hand, he told the passengers, "Sit tight."

To the Wintu woman—just a girl, really—he said, "Hawk, is that what I'm to call you?"

"Oltipa" she said, patting her chest with the cup of her fingers. "Oltipa my name. It mean the same as *spring.*"

David stared at the girl's sable eyes. "Like the season or something to drink? Water?" he asked. She looked confused and he shook his head. "It doesn't matter. Just good you understand a little English."

"What's the holdup?" Zane Randolph shouted, his head leaned out the open window. "Let's get on with it."

"We're heading out. Hang on, Oltipa," David said so that only she could hear. He watched her grip the seat, noticed the red marks the rope had left at her wrists. She looked up at him and nodded once. He released the foot brakes, flicked the reins, and the stage lurched forward. The team knew the road north and they headed out, rattling their way through the streets.

All the while, David wondered, what could he do? When could he do it? And what difference would it make if he did set this young hawk free?

Shasta City

Mazy guessed things just changed when someone came or left—physically or emotionally. Children were not born into the same family as their brothers and sisters because the family shifted with each new arrival. A community did too, grew out in a different direction with each road carved, each building built. Even a marriage whipped itself up into newness—had to, she supposed, since its participants did. That was her marriage, all right. She'd be cautious about entering into that wilderness state again. Seth's apparent interest bothered her. She wasn't ready for that. She hated all the shifts. There were too many adjustments to make now, too many good-byes to say to be thinking of deeper hellos.

Mazy brushed at her hair, trying to get some shine that the months of alkali had stolen. Besides, Seth had a fondness for dice and racing. She'd already loved one man who failed to put her ahead of some hidden passion. She wouldn't risk that again. Seth even pointed out the

"Bear and Bull Baiting" sign at Charley's Ranch when they rode by it. "There's money to be made at events like that, money to siphon in a dozen different ways," he'd said.

"How could you engage in that? I'd give anything to have my dairy bull back, and in California they take the few bulls they have and put them against a bear?"

Seth had sounded wounded. "They aren't dairy bulls. They're beef stock, lots of them raised right here just for the ring, just like bulls in Spain. Guess I won't be inviting you out to Charley's anytime soon." His observation had ended the conversation but not her thoughts about the complexity of this man. So gentle and insightful and yet dense as a post at times.

Mazy rubbed the back of her neck. She'd be so glad to have her own mattress, under a roof where she could turn and twist at night without fear she would wake her mother or whoever else shared her tent. She shivered, then dressed and stepped outside.

Today they would all go in to Shasta. She looked around their encampment and saw Ruth, already up and dressed...in what? A calico dress and a shawl? Mazy waved at her and smiled when she noticed the woman's whip hanging limp at her side. She was a unique woman. Mazy knew a comfort wrapped inside Ruth's presence. She watched their patterns and habits developed over six months of joining. From having walked across a continent together, they created a basket formed of bonds that would never be broken.

Even Mazy's mother no longer seemed quite so eccentric. She supposed she should be wary of what new childish adventure Elizabeth would undertake next. First she'd tamed an antelope, then the antelope had bounded off at Deer Flat, forsaking the easy feed and comfort they promised for companionship closer to its own. She missed that old Fip. She guessed she just had a heart for animals. She missed Pig, too, even though she saw him daily. That would change too now.

Ned had sniffed a bit at Fip's departure, then in a day he became philosophical, remembering the fun the pronghorn had brought and saying he hoped Fip wouldn't end up as someone's stew. Mazy smiled. Children had such a fresh perspective on change.

Shasta forced another. She just needed to settle into a new routine. She had an idea of just what she wanted in her own brand-new little nest. And once it was truly her place of belonging, she'd let herself feel the anger, loss, and disappointment that she'd harbored all these months and finally grieve Jeremy's betrayal. Then maybe she could remember the good times, the joys they'd shared. And she could move forward to the pleasant places God had promised in the Psalms.

She must try to find some…joy in the shifting. She could replace disappointment with…discovering the sounds of the morning wind in the trees outside her windows, or smelling sun-dried, heat-pressed linens when she slept at night. There'd be pleasure in setting the few things she'd salvaged in prominent places: the hand-painted seed gourd filled with gift seeds, shell buttons made at the Cassville factory, the novel pin with a latch so she could safely hold the buttons to her wrapper, Jeremy's reading glasses, his Ayrshire book, cuttings of lilacs and the maple tree, some daffodil bulbs. She was grateful for them, perhaps more than she ever would have been without the trials of this journey. She would remember that. It might bring her comfort in her new home.

Suzanne's heart pounded, angry now that Tipton left her. Suzanne had bumbled into the tenpin alley, backed away from the smells of whisky and smoke, got turned around, lost count of the steps back to the street. She gripped Clayton's hand so hard he cried. Pig barked and yanked, and she hadn't a clue where she stood. If she could just convert this feeling of fear, she could take the next step. *Focus.* New things always carried a little fear with them. Focus, trust, step out, and do her best in this new setting. She took in a deep breath. "Pig. Forward."

Her voice must have sounded firm because the dog walked a step, halted, walked another, in that way he had of letting her stay beside him. When he stopped, she felt with her foot, found the stair and kicked her skirt out to step up, not letting go of either Pig or Clayton. She could either start walking back to the camp or—

"Can I help you, ma'am?" A woman's voice, spoken as Suzanne scanned the width of the step with her foot. "Not that it looks like you need much."

Suzanne turned her body toward the scent of tobacco mixed with something sweet at her right side. "I'm...looking for a land agent," Suzanne decided right then.

"That could be most anyone in these parts," the woman said. "Making a gold claim, are you? Buying a saloon? A house? What?"

"Just seeking a place to live," she said. "For me and my boys." A pistol fired in the background. Suzanne startled.

"That happens often. Nothing to worry over. You're not alone, are you? A woman like you shouldn't—"

"Can you direct me or not?"

A hesitation, then, "Sure. I think George King has a place to let. He owns the bookstore. But there's a land office on, well, you take a right at the end of—oh, never mind. I'll just walk you that way...if you don't mind."

"I don't mind," Suzanne said, her voice softened. "Thank you."

"My name's Estella," the woman said, patting Suzanne's hand at Pig's halter. "Friends call me Esty. There's a nice cabin. A doctor left it and headed home. If no one's taken it, you and your children would fit. If there's no mister."

"No mister. I'm Suzanne Cullver," she said. "These are my boys, Clayton and Sason. The dog's name is Pig."

"Clunky kind of dog, isn't he?" Esty said, but her voice was gentle and low. Suzanne felt Pig's wagging tail move his whole body, and she imagined Esty patting his head.

For a moment, Suzanne wondered if she should try to find Tipton. No, she could do this on her own with a newly found acquaintance. Isn't that what happened in a new place? Find a new home. Make friends. Learn to do things differently. Stretch a bit? She could surely do that on her own.

9

set free

Shasta City

Esty opened the door to the land agent's office. "Good," she said. "You're here early. Got a new acquaintance for you. Mrs. Cullver."

"Esty, not—"

"She's seeking housing. Nothing else."

The man's demeanor changed. "Then we can be of service."

"I'll leave you now," Esty said. "You'll be all right."

"Thank you." Suzanne reached her hand out to touch the woman, felt the ruffle at her sleeve. She had smooth hands, so someone else must have done her laundry, Suzanne thought. "I hope you'll come visit me when I have my home."

"Yeah...sure," Esty said.

"How will I find you? Your last name—?"

"The agent here can put us in touch. If you decide you want to be. Nice meeting you," she said, then the sweet smell disappeared.

So much of what people meant wasn't said in words, but in the look of their eyes, the placement of their hands, how they stood or lifted their chins. Suzanne wondered what she'd missed in this encounter. The photographer's eye had once captured all in the flash of the powder. Now she had only words and cadence and an occasional scent to tell her what was really being said.

"What did you and your husband have in mind...Mrs. Cullver, was it?"

"It's just me and my children," she said, turning to his voice. "I want a home. It doesn't need to be large, but it must have an area that's fenced, or can be. If it has some furnishings, that would be good too. I don't have much. Just came across on Noble's Cutoff."

"Without a husband? My dear woman—"

She held her hand up as though to stop him.

"Well...there's one that might work. It's up the street, kind of a steep little path to it. But the view is stupendous."

"I'm not much taken with scenery," Suzanne said.

He cleared his throat. "It's the fence I thought of. It has ironwork all around it. Built by a doctor in 'fifty. Only stayed a year there. His wife passed on and he left. Buried her right on the spot. I hope that won't distress you, a grave on the site. Now we have cemeteries set aside. Several." Suzanne shook her head. "Good. Seems she'd always wanted a large family, and they'd planned to fence it when the children came, to make a play place for them. They never had a one. He had the fence made anyway. Offered some healing for him, I suppose. Shortly after the gate was placed, he headed back to Massachusetts."

"Someone who grieved owned the house? I suspect it'll suit us just fine."

They looked like a bouquet of flowers, Seth decided. He might just miss their daily fragrances. Especially as they stood now, all decked out in their Sunday best for this foray into town. Even Ruth had donned a dress. Must have troubled her some to do that. She still stood off to the side, talking with her horses more than the women.

He'd picked a good spot for them to camp. He thought they called the place Poverty Flat, though he wasn't sure why. Looked to him to be an abundant place, creek water and grass here was tall as a tiger's tummy. Grass looked fed from some underground source of water. Beyond rolled out the Sacramento River, making a big bend east before it headed south. Low hills surrounded this bowl, and he noticed a couple of pack strings had come in already this morning, with forty or fifty head of mules mingling now and small campfires dotting the edges of the meadow. It was where Noble's first train had camped, then headed on in to Shasta City, some five miles down the trail.

He turned back to the women's camp. Everyone present and accounted for, except for Tipton and Suzanne. Funny. A later start than he'd planned for them, but they'd taken longer at their morning toilets. And it showed, all the colorful clothes he hadn't seen any wear before.

"Truth be known, I don't think we should just leave our wagons here, untended." Adora marched up beside him, talked as though she was sure when she did that everyone would listen.

Adora wore a bonnet with an ostrich feather held up by the stiff brim. Portions of the plume draped down. "I see others have come around and camped. We should post a guard, now that we're back in civilization."

Seth tipped his tall hat to her. "Figured I'd do just that myself, ma'am."

"Won't we need someone telling us about the town? I'm sure Tipton was hoping to walk on your arm this fine day. The Celestials might like to stay back."

"Suspect they're as interested in town as you. Fact is, they ought not be left alone," Seth told her. "Sometimes Asians get mistaken for Indians. Laws here don't favor either much. Wouldn't want anything foul to happen to them."

"Oh? And how is—?"

"Have you seen Suzanne?" Mazy interrupted. "Or Tipton?"

"Tipton?" Adora said, sweeping around, the ostrich feather fluttering in front of Mazy's face. "She slept in Lura's tent last evening. The two girls—she and Mariah—wanted some time, I thought. Isn't she there? Her good green dress isn't in the trunk."

Mazy shook her head. "She's probably just gone for a walk with Suzanne. And the boys."

"That woman has got to come to terms with her problems," Adora said. "She can't expect to be dragging my girl around—or others either—to be looking after her kin. People need to stand on their own two feet."

"Suspect that's her intent," Seth offered. He bent to his saddle pack that served as his night pillow and took out a telescoping glass. "I'll scan the meadow, see if I can find them. Don't see Pig anywhere either."

"The rest of us are ready. We shouldn't have to wait on Suzanne," Adora said.

"I thought we'd take one wagon on in, so Mei-Ling doesn't have to walk too far. Suzanne could ride, too, but…aren't you coming with us?" Mazy asked Seth.

"Not me," Seth said, the glass still to his eye.

"Nor I," Adora said, "at least not without Tipton. Suzanne needs to understand that what she does affects the rest of us, to detriment, I might add. I will simply wait here for her. Remind that woman of her obligations."

Seth lowered the glass. Adora could be as annoying as seagulls bickering over fish. Maybe this separating had its high side. "Can't have it both ways, Mrs. Wilson. Either she recognizes she's blind and sets her life to live the best she can, or she recognizes she's blind and waits around to be told what the rest of you think she should do."

"Well…I…"

"You go on ahead," Seth said. "When I find them, I'll send Tipton and Suzanne to catch up, put 'em on your mules if need be. You ladies stop at the St. Charles Hotel now. Make plans for that party Sarah's been wanting. Only got two days and this social club will be splitting up." It might be none too soon.

Mazy scanned the horizon, taking in the landscape. It felt so unsettled to be here. Would this be a view she would have every day for the rest of her life? Would this land of morning cold and drizzle which had turned now to a clear sky and a drying breeze become familiar someday? Oak trees, smaller than those back in Wisconsin, dotted the sides of the trail. She could see a good distance beneath the leaves—that looked glossier than those at home too. No heavy underbrush, just yellowed grasses that darkened near the earth, still wet from the morning drizzle. Black birds, lots of birds. And behind the oaks, rising like a dark mountain, stood tall trees, dusted at the top in white. Would her home be up the side of one of those? The wagon eased slowly down through a gully—a gulch, Seth said they called them here, the lower ends of narrow valleys where farther back in the steep hillsides, streams in the winter and spring ran fast and full of gold.

Their wagon lumbered back up and around the base of a butte. Little strings of smoke drifted across the lower ridges, and Mazy suspected that every steep, narrow gulch housed miners and streams and dreams. Would one of them hold her new dream? Would she eventually have a dream in this California place? She had to remember: She wasn't where she would someday be—at home. And she wasn't where she'd once been—at home. She was in between, and that could be unsettling, make a person want to stop if not turn back. But there was no turning back. The discomfort was just part of the journey toward making strange things familiar. She took a deep breath.

A number of dry creek beds challenged their way. Some with slender threads; others looking as though they had flowed once, but now ran empty. She must remember to ask Seth about that, about what happened to the water. And what were the names of those yellow flowers, and that leggy bush with red berries—*manzanita,* that was what Seth had called it near Lassen's Peak.

She and her mother walked on either side of their oxen, and she could hear the chatter of the women behind the canvas. Had they ever all been together in one wagon like this? Well, they were missing a couple, but even Ruth was inside, as though wearing a dress divided her from her horses, sent her to the same place as the women. She wondered why Ruth had done that, worn a dress after all this time. She'd have to ask her.

Mazy heard a burst of laughter. "What's going on in there? Speak up. We slaves can't hear you out here." She looked over at her mother and smiled.

Lura stuck her head out. "Just telling stories," she said. She'd laughed so hard she was wiping her eyes.

"Ruth's practicing sitting with her knees together," Mariah said, poking her head beneath Lura's.

"And Adora just told about Suzanne's diapering Clayton one day with a lace doily. Grabbed the wrong thing, she did, and you can guess what mustard-colored treasure squeezed out through those little eye-holes of Belgian lace. Set a whole new fashion."

"California style," Elizabeth said.

"Just one more reason she needs us, that woman," Lura said as she pulled herself back inside behind the canvas.

"Maybe as much as we all need her," Mazy said.

Jason then Ned leaped down, jumping far out from the wagon wheels. They ran out ahead. Walking backward, Ned lifted his tin whistle to his lips and played a tune. Mazy smiled and waved at him. Jason soon followed and skipped beside him. A pack string of mules worked their way up behind them, and Mazy directed the oxen to the side to let them pass. Farther on, a string moved toward them, carrying out gold, if what Seth said was true. The packers looked tan or maybe they were Spanish, but she heard another language, Portuguese? And she saw some children—Indian children, she guessed, with dark brown eyes that peered out from behind a tree above them on a butte. Soon she spied Chinese men, bent forward, their long braids black against blue tunics. She could smell new smells, of cooking and things she did not know, and she knew the town must be just around the bend. More riders appeared from nowhere, it seemed. Men tipped their hats, looked twice at seeing two women walking the oxen, not seeing any man at all. Most smiled.

Beyond Ned, Mazy thought she saw a dog, yes, Pig, and with him Suzanne and Tipton and the boys. Coming *from* town? That was a surprise. She heard laughter again, caught her mother's gentle smile, and pointed beyond the boys to where Tipton now waved.

Mazy felt the sun warm against her face and then she knew, she just knew—this moment would be a part of her forever. These women would be a part of a story she would tell throughout her life, a story of strength and flexibility, of fear and familiarity. They were but small pieces in this puzzle of life, this dance of coming and going, saying good-bye and starting over, but they were as precious to her as gold. They were part of each other, with all their aches and itches, all their hopes and wishes, all their mistakes and poor decisions. They were still connected—even these kind strangers whom she might never see again, these children staring, men smiling and moving past them. They were like some huge family, all brothers and sisters and children of God. A family that knew no beginning and no boundaries. And she belonged.

Her eyes watered, and she wiped at them with her fingers.

"Something wrong?" her mother asked.

"Nothing," Mazy said, tears wet on her cheeks. "Not a thing. I just feel...happy. It probably won't last, but I'll savor it just the same." And she breathed a prayer of gratitude for her arrival at this pleasant place.

On the Red Bluff Trail

"Faster than usual," the portly man commented, straightening his hat and helping his wife sit back up straight. Zane tried not to notice.

Instead, he allowed himself to enjoy this ride. The stage took him closer to Ruth. The girl sitting as luggage was merely an added tease. The jostling pressed these strangers against him. He deliberately did not brush himself off after they touched him. He didn't want them remembering him as rude, didn't want them remembering him at all.

Outside, he heard the jehu call out, the crack of the whip. He felt the horses move faster, then slow as they made their way around an outside turn. The wheels must have hit a rock then as the coach lurched, pitched left to right. Straightening himself with his hand to the side window, Zane noticed a tree-lined ravine whizzing by. A bank of rock-pocked yellow sand broken by tree roots appeared.

"Does the jehu know how to drive this road?" the woman asked.

The passengers bounced, and Zane hit his head, his hat knocked askew.

"Are you all right, my dear?" the portly man asked.

"Yes, Gabriel, I'm quite fine," the woman said, brushing at her skirts as the stage slowed for another corner.

"Perhaps you should sit on this side," the man with a cane offered. "I could take your place. Mr. Randolph, was it? Would you be willing to exchange with the woman's companion? It would give them both more room."

The stage slowed, hit another rock, pitching them again. They straightened.

"Not necessary," the portly man said, clearing his voice. "Is it, my dear?"

"No. But you're very kind to suggest it," she said.

"Prepare for another cornering," the portly man said as they braced themselves with the pitch and roll of the stage. It slowed.

"The road must be frightfully narrow here," the cane man said. "He nearly stopped."

Zane looked out his window opening in order to shout up to the driver, but suddenly the stage lurched forward and pitched the passengers once again.

"Oh," the woman said. Her eyes focused on something outside as the horses moved faster than they yet had.

"What is it, dear?"

She turned back to her husband, stared, her mouth slightly open. She cast a furtive glance at Zane. "Nothing," she said in a way that made Zane think she lied.

David had told her when to jump. Or had he? Could he claim with a clean conscience that he had no idea she would do what she did? No.

"You understand?" he'd asked her as he slowed the stage near the high inside bank. It was almost level with the stack of boxes and valises of the passengers riding inside. It was the best plan he could come up with while trying to manage the ribbons, maneuver the stage, think ahead to the best spot where there'd be confusion with the jostling yet slow enough for her to leap without them wondering, and still have an inside edge with some manzanita for cover. He was glad Randolph had taken the driver's side of the stage at the window, had yelled up to David so he knew where the big man sat.

She'd nodded once, her eyes speaking gratitude. He slowed the stage a bit more, almost pulling the team to a stop. His arms strained at the ribbons. It was a change for the animals; he could tell they were confused to be slowing in this unusual place.

Her hand pressed firm on his shoulder to steady herself. He hadn't dared look back as she made her way over the luggage. He thought now that the look she'd given him as she nodded had been one of uncertainty or fear instead of thanks. Then she'd jumped. David glanced back once to see if she'd slipped down or headed up or what she'd done. He thought he saw her dress disappear around the tree roots, but he couldn't be sure before the stage began the corner.

He memorized the landmarks. A large yellow pine pocked by the acorn woodpecker making a line of holes up the thick bark, the tree branded with dark rows of circles. Roots gnarled out like an old crone's hand, holding what was left of a gouged-out bank supporting the pine.

He turned back quickly, kept his eyes focused on the road ahead. He cracked the whip and the horses surged.

The space beside him felt empty now. He began to think of what he'd say, how he'd say it. The stage company would be liable for the loss of what the man would claim was luggage. He could only hope that would be the man's only response and not that he wanted to pursue the woman. David clenched his jaw.

What if that man pursued her? David hoped he hadn't underestimated him. Still, he could recover his investment through the stage company. A reasonable man would surely take that tack and not some vengeful action to bring the woman back.

David would convince Hall and Crandall that he would pay the man's loss from his own wages. No, it wouldn't cover the woman's "future earnings" as Randolph might point out, but maybe he could remind the man that she was a troublesome sort, spitting at him and all. No, he wouldn't mention that detail. Men like Randolph didn't like to be reminded of humiliation. He had to make sure that her disappearance didn't come out as humiliation, at least not Randolph's. David would claim he should have kept a better eye on the woman; that he should have been able to take those corners without slowing so much that she had a chance to jump.

Randolph would see that forcing the stage company to pay would be a good way to recover what he'd invested without having the trouble of "handling his luggage." Surely he'd be pleased to be relieved of that.

David snapped the cracker of the whip next to the ear of the near horse, preparing it to speed up the next grade. Scrub oak and yellow grasses sped by them. He might lose his job. Unless he convinced everyone that he didn't really have control over her. "She just took right off, leapt over the valises and headed for the hills. But she was my responsibility," David would add. He'd sound sad. "I lost a valuable. Have to make good on that, and I will, sir. I will."

That was what he'd say. It was mostly true. She'd taken the leap herself, he hadn't pushed her or helped her spring from the top of the coach. It was all her. She was her own free spirit. She wanted out—and who wouldn't?

He'd just leave out the part about his plan to come back to bring her food.

Shasta City

Suzanne heard the wagon approach and the women call out her name. She'd found Tipton after she returned from the land office. Tipton couldn't stop talking about the attention she'd received from the men, chatter that increased with the arrival of the others.

"You should have waited for Seth to go with you," Adora whined. "So headstrong, you are. I would have thought you'd learned. There are consequences to setting your course without regard to following a wise guide."

"Tipton is nearly grown," Suzanne defended. "Both of us took new—"

"I can be your tour guide, now, Mama. I can," Tipton urged.

Suzanne said little after that. She held Sason in her arms and nursed him, a linen spread over her chest and his head. She knew she had a smile on her face.

"You're looking like a canary-eating cat," Mazy said, sidling up next to her.

"You can hear me purr?" Suzanne said.

Mazy bumped her hip gently with her own while Suzanne wondered at her own decision not to tell them all just yet what she had found.

At the Kossuth House, a large hotel with a bakery and confectionery attached, the women pulled the wagon up. Ruth waited until all the rest had stepped down and out so only she and Jessie were left inside.

"We're going to go out now," she told the girl. "I'll help you stand, and I'll hand you these crutches. You'll need to swing yourself to the back, sit, swing your legs around and dangle your good one over the backboard. I'll be out there to lift you down. Ready? We're going to have fun."

"I want Mariah to help me. Not you," Jessie said.

"Mariah has already left. She's going inside to get some sweets. You can do that too, if you cooperate."

"No. I want Mariah. Right away."

Ruth didn't think Elizabeth knew one thing about rearing a child like Jessie. This girl liked being in charge. There wasn't a smidgen of fear in her face as she sat there, arms across her pinafore, eyes the color of cattails snapping back at her. Jessie, afraid that she could make adults do things? Not likely. She loved the power, relished the control.

"Jessie." Ruth tried again. "We have a long road ahead of us, you and I, if we can't find some way to travel amiably with each other. Now, either you let me help you, or we stay right here and miss the party. Those are the choices."

The girl stuck her lower lip out.

"It's one or the other." Silence. "Come on. I'm ready for a change, aren't you?"

"I want Mariah," the girl repeated.

It was how they spent their day.

On the Red Bluff Trail

At the first staging station, David Taylor stopped the team. Hostlers walking fast made their way from the barn to the coach, began unhitching the horses. They'd come thirteen miles, a good day's run for the team pulling the heavy Concord. It was only half of David's day. His heart began to pound as one of the agents opened the door and Randolph rolled out, brushing at his white suit, straightening his cape and hat.

David stayed sitting at the seat above, deciding height and distance might be a good position from which to begin.

Randolph looked up. His eyes narrowed, he stepped farther back.

"Where's my luggage?"

"Not here," David said. His voice cracked and he swallowed. "Couldn't bring the team to stop, they were so headstrong to get on in."

"I've little interest in your incompetent driving. Just tell me where my luggage's gone."

David cleared his throat. "Jumped right off a while back. That's what I was telling you. I couldn't stop the team to let anyone know."

"Send my property down. At once."

The others had stopped talking as they stepped out of the stage, aware of the intensity of the conversation if not the subject.

"She isn't here," David said. He called then to one of the hostlers. "We've got a passenger disembarked on route."

"She was no passenger," Randolph said, his eyebrow raised, his voice even and low. "Property. Chattel. For which you were responsible."

David wished the other passengers would go inside. An audience always raised the tension level of a disagreement.

"I'll have your job for this," Randolph said, "Maybe more."

"I believe you're the one who wanted her to ride atop," the man with the cane said, brushing at his arms, dust puffs deserting him as he came off the stage.

"He insisted she be untied." Randolph said, turning on the stranger.

"She had to be free to hang on, balance herself," the woman said. "The stage company isn't a penitentiary, after all."

"It surely is not that, madam," Randolph said.

"Just file a claim with the Hall and Crandall," the man said and tapped his cane on the ground. "They'll pay something for lost luggage. I'm going inside, out of this heat." Then he fanned his face with his hat. "Amazing for October."

As he checked his whip, David felt the stare of Randolph. He shouted down to the hostler, unhooked the leather belt, stood, then swung himself down. He landed in the dirt beside Randolph, aware again of the looming size of the man.

"You performed this deed on purpose, didn't you?"

"Don't know what you're getting at, mister," David said. "Excuse me." He turned his back and walked toward the team of horses, ran his hands over the rump of the near one, patted him. The puff of dust that rose made David cough, just as it always did.

"Misguided charity?" Randolph had moved close behind him, and David noticed the change from rage to smooth in his voice.

David turned, stared into the narrowed eyes, the stone face, the straight nose.

Randolph smiled then. "What you are is a thief, no different than a highwayman. You've set your own pattern. After I'm finished with you no one will hire you to man a stage or anything else. You're no man at all."

David blinked, his heart thudding in his chest.

Too quick, Randolph grabbed for David's neck scarf, then yanked at it, his breath hot, his wrist twisting, closing the air at David's throat. He pushed David up against the horse, who sidestepped as spotty lights flickered before David's eyes. From a distance he heard a sucking breathing—before his world went black.

10

see what I see

Ruth pulled the dress off and stuffed it into her bedroll. She jammed her legs inside Zane's old pants, and topped it off with a plaid shirt. She still wore the heavy boots she'd had on beneath her dress. Then picking up the floppy black hat, she pushed it over the twist of hair at the top of her head and stomped out across the meadow to the line of trees that skirted the grazing place. Dressing like a proper mother hadn't made a whit of difference in earning Jessie's respect. In fact, it seemed to make it worse.

The women had laughed at her "refreshing her ladylike ways," as Lura called it. She'd liked being part of the fun even if some of it was at her expense. She hadn't taken everything so seriously. She was trying to be less serious, she was. And they'd joked about every little thing—the condition of their fingernails, how the face powder felt strange after so many months without it. Nervous little chuckles, she thought, of excitement, floating around them like butterflies at a spring puddle. They told stories. They celebrated time without having to yoke oxen and miles to make.

But perhaps Jessie misunderstood it. She'd sat glum, her face unmoving. She hadn't even laughed when Adora told Ruth she'd better watch how she sat once she put hoops on or the residents of Shasta would see all the way to China. Maybe seeing her "auntie" enjoying herself gave Jessie just one more reason not to listen to her.

They'd spent the afternoon in the wagon. All they saw of Shasta was the view out through the oval of the canvas puckers. The child had not budged. Ruth couldn't leave her there alone, and the rest scattered, looking at shop windows, going into the bookstores—there were two, she noticed—and making inquiries about places to call home. They'd come back refreshed, excited. She had simply fumed.

She'd stick with men's clothes from now on—and her own plan. She'd find a place for the horses and farm the children out. She'd had time to think of that, at least. Jason might like to help Seth when he went back out to bring in another wagon train—though that might not be until next year. It'd be nice for the boy to have time with a man about. Ned might assist…Elizabeth, what with her bad hip and all. He could run little errands for her. He was a helpful child. Sarah? Surely Suzanne would be needing someone. Why not Sarah? Or maybe Lura and Mariah would make a good home for young Sarah. And then there was Jessie. Only Mazy would be strong enough—and kind enough—to take that one on. Ruth knew one thing for sure: They'd be best off with someone else. Jed and Betha would have understood. It wasn't as though she was keeping her own child with her. They all had to go. For their own protection. Hadn't her mother said exactly those words to her all those years ago?

"Just picking him up," Zane Randolph said to the agent who came up behind him and pulled on the boy's scarf until he sat. He had acted in haste. A momentary lapse. "Heat's too much for him. Perhaps you need another driver."

"David?" the agent said. "He's one of our best."

"He lost a valuable of mine, and now he appears to be unable to continue. If that's your best, this California is poor indeed."

"Just go inside and describe your lost baggage and catch yourself a bite to eat. Stage'll head out in fifteen minutes."

"That I doubt," Zane said as the man slipped past him, headed toward the jehu.

This could work out well. He could develop it into something lucrative. Pick up vagrants, set them on a stage as luggage, arrange for their untimely departure and file a claim. Yes, it had possibilities, something to add to his string of *investments* as he was beginning to think of ways of building up California treasure. The boy might not do it, but other drivers could be convinced—for a percentage of the profits. The boy would likely try to pay the claim back; he was that naive.

This piece of luggage had cost him, though. He'd paid high for her, and now she was gone, along with his plan to hire her out to a needy woman, take her wages while she cleaned and tended someone—like the blind woman. For that inconvenience, the jehu deserved something. A bad word dribbled here and there that the boy couldn't counter, like an untreatable cough turning into a fatal pneumonia. Soon, it would seem the boy had always been irresponsible, wasn't trustworthy. Zane knew how to slowly undermine a soul.

Once inside, Zane signed his name on the complaint with a flourish of the pen. He wrote his address down as Shasta, where he'd like the money for his loss sent. He'd be meeting Greasy near there in a day or two. Then, his appetite whetted, he ate a full lunch, remembered the delicacy of the blind woman, thought of Ruth and the way he'd chisel at her. Soon. He must be patient. He smiled, then stepped back into the stage.

Missy Esther beamed. Mei-Ling could see the older woman's broken tooth when she smiled large as a porcelain bowl. They sat around the fading fire, repeating little stories. Spoke kindnesses. Crises reached and crossed. It was late, maybe midnight, and still they hadn't found a way to say good night. Mei-Ling's thoughts fluttered like a butterfly lighting on a flower, beautiful yet soft. Soon, she would meet her husband. Soon, the bees would be home. This was their last evening gathering as a group of widows and women who came together across the plains. Mei-Ling had suggested Sister Esther look after her drawing of the beehive frame, once almost lost on the desert, once stained by Esther's ink.

"Despite my poor care of your patent drawing—and after I made such a fuss about *your* not keeping it secure—I find your trust in me miraculous and redeeming. Thank you. I will keep it safe until we reach Sacramento and you hand it over to your new husband." The tall woman bowed at her waist, enough so Mei-Ling could see the top of her little black cap, and then the strings, when she straightened, tied tight beneath her chin.

"I just don't like this, truth be known," said Adora, the whining woman who sat on a chair taken from the sideboard, the pointy toes of her feet facing the fire. Darkness as black as the dog named Pig surrounded them. The dog lay on his side, snoring.

Only the firelight danced across their faces. All of the women had pulled out capes and blankets and shawls to wrap around themselves. October came on wet wings, quiet, like a bat.

"We all went into Whoa Navigation and pondered the town. Had our fete at the confectionery, didn't we, Sarah?" Elizabeth spoke. "We knew we was all needing to split up. Celebrate what we have and then move on. Just hard to go to bed now and know tomorrow'll be all different."

"One of us found something worthy," Tipton, the girl with yellow curls, said. She nodded toward Missy Sue.

"I wish things could stay the way they are," Lura said.

"You're always wishing, Ma," Mariah said.

The whining woman wiped at her eyes with a lace-edged hanky. "When we turned around way back there, after the storm, I thought we'd all make our homes right together. We could live in the wagons 'til we got a house built big enough for us all."

"Adora, I can't believe you'd want to live with me and my brood," Ruth said.

"Well, I—"

"You come a ways, Adora, thinking we could all live in the same house. That's hospitality with a capital *H*."

"We can give that to each other no matter where we lay our heads to sleep," Elizabeth said. "We'll always be family, won't we?"

"Nothing stays the same," Mazy said.

"I'm just glad we had what we had when we had it," Elizabeth said, patting her daughter's shoulder. "What makes a home is not letting yourself get all distracted with what don't matter much, just remembering things to be grateful for. Pile up enough gratitude and it'll spill out. Then you get to give it away. That's when you're truly at home, when you got enough to give away."

"People could accommodate a little, and we could live in the same house," Adora persisted.

"Accommodation House," Elizabeth said.

"Sounds like a sign for a boardinghouse." Mazy smiled at her mother.

"The Warm Hearth." Elizabeth formed a square in the air with her hands. "'Friendly Accommodations and the Hospitality of Home.' It could work."

"Too long," Lura told her. "Won't fit on a sign. What the sign says is real important, Elizabeth. I'm pretty sure about that. Did you notice that one store in Shasta? 'Good Goods and Right Prices.' Now there's a sign."

"My Hathaway always said that too, about selling things." Adora blew her nose. "'Course selling in this California country might be a little different. Seems like everything has a little shading to it here. Even bowling. I guess that's another reason why I hate to see us separating. We all know what we are here, what we got and what we don't have. We know each other's little quirks and such. Now we've got to start again, with new people, new places." She sighed. "I don't know if I have the strength."

"We came to appreciate what each one had to give. It'll be hard to find that anywhere else," Mazy said.

Adora nodded. "Every one of you has become important to me. I never thought that would be so. Even you Celestials." She nodded at Naomi and Mei-Ling. "I just thought you were too different to ever be people I'd invite into my home. I mean, you still hardly ever sit. You just kneel, if truth be known. But now, I'll make sure I got a good pillow for when you come to visit me."

"Will we be invited to the wedding?" Sarah asked. "Yours and Mei-Ling's?"

"If husband consents," Mei-Ling said, "it will please me and bees." Naomi nodded.

"Still, you'll be finding your place there, and we'll be several days' ride away, right, Seth? So it may not be practical."

"If not, you'll know our thoughts are with you," Mazy said. "And you'll each stay in our hearts." She touched her chest with her fingertips.

"You think that's true?" Adora said, and she started to cry again. "I wonder if Hathaway will always stay in my heart." She wiped her eyes.

"I do."

"But aren't you scared?" Adora asked the question of Sister Esther now.

"The Lord has taken me this far. I must fix my eyes not on what is seen but on what is not seen. All else is temporary."

"Some faith," Ruth said.

"You could have it, child."

Ruth scoffed, pulled a blanket tighter around her shoulders, held it closed at her chest.

"Faith is merely 'the substance of things hoped for,'" Esther continued, "'the evidence of things not seen.'"

"I always thought of it as the distance between what you believed and what you had evidence for," Ruth told her.

Esther clucked her tongue. "How I wish I had more time with you,

Ruth," she said. "You have evidence that you are cared for here among us, that we see you as a loving aunt, a mother in the making. And yet you do not believe. Is it lack of faith that makes the gap so large you cannot cross it into comfort? Or do you just need a new set of eyes through which to see?"

"I hadn't intended for this to turn into a theology discussion," Ruth said.

"All life is that," Esther said.

"What better place to discuss it than here among kin," Elizabeth said.

A wind rustled the low branches of the digger pines. A few dried needles dropped toward the crackling fire. Mei-Ling had trouble understanding all the words and thoughts, but she could see the shine on Sister Esther's face, as she talked of words of *faith,* and she let herself be warmed by them.

"Perhaps we should do something to commemorate our time together," Mazy said then. "So, like Mei-Ling's bees, we will always recognize the home we've found inside the shelter of each other."

People sat silently around the fire. Even Seth leaned forward toward the flames with his forearms on his thighs, pitching peanut shells into the heat.

"What about making a sampler?" the wide-eyed Sarah asked.

"We could design it ourselves. Ruth draws and so do I," Tipton said, her voice sounding excited.

"What about something larger?" Missy Sue offered. "Something more...comforting. Like a quilt."

Mazy said, "Yes. Made of old pieces of wrappers and capes and blankets—"

"We could make squares about what this dusty old trail meant to us," Tipton said. Her blue eyes were sparkling as they had when she once walked arm in arm with the blacksmith she'd hoped to marry. Mei-Ling had not seen that brightness for a long time. She would have to tell the bees.

"Ponder that. Memories stitched by the hands of friends and placed over solid backing. A thing to keep us warm that we can set aside in the morning when we've rested but still be wrapped in comfort."

"Would we make a dozen quilts?" Lura asked. "Or a dozen squares or what?"

"No, no. That would take us forever," Adora said. "We'll make just one quilt and send it around. Each year, another woman will get it."

"And each year we don't have it, we'll get to anticipate," Mazy said.

"What about us? Are only girls allowed to have memories?" the sharp-tongued boy, Jason, said.

"Oh. Well. Sure you boys can do a square. Truth be known, Seth could make one up too."

"Ma said tentmakers had to make patterns and such," Jason said. "That sewing wasn't just a woman's task."

"The best tailors are men," Seth said.

"Only because women aren't allowed to earn the good money. They get to mend," Ruth said.

"Everyone should design their square and sew it," Esther said. "We'll put them together and once a year, maybe at Advent when we await the celebration of the Virgin Birth and prepare ourselves for a new beginning, then we'll pass it on."

"It'll warm us to our toes, all right. Remembering back to this night, when we thought it up, all of us together, that'll be warming. There'll be a sadness to ponder, but a hopeful place, too."

"If you want, you can give your squares to me," Mazy said.

"Why not to Suzanne?" Ruth asked. "It was her idea."

"I'm sorry," Mazy said. "Of course. It was her idea."

Missy Sue laughed. "The idea belonged to all of us," Suzanne said. "I certainly can't sew the squares together. But I'd be willing to help however I can. You could do it at my place."

"Your place?" several said in unison.

"Yes. I have a house. With a fence and a view—for those who visit."

"How'd you do that?" Lura said. "We settled on a boardinghouse. Nothing else seemed suitable. I didn't even see you searching!"

"I have my ways," Suzanne said, grinning as she patted Sason's back on her chest.

"Well," Adora said. "Well."

"Maybe my quilt square will be a house," Suzanne said.

"Anything you want it to be. The quilt will be our book," Mazy said. She looked over at Seth, who had taken the writing kit from his vest pocket and was making sketches on a crumpled piece of paper.

"The story of our journey home," Missy Esther said. "Reminding us of how we came to know what mattered to us though each of us came by what we learned in a different way."

Missy Esther's words fell into the silence, and Mei-Ling became aware of a hole in her heart, as large a fracture as when she left her own family, when Zilah began her journey home, when Missy Esther's brothers died, a hole made wider now by the thought of leaving, going a new and different way.

On the Red Bluff Trail

The moon rose over the curve of the hill. David rested the horse, letting the animal catch its breath. He'd been riding at a steady pace for the past two hours out from the staging barn where the passengers were bedded down for the night.

He'd driven another thirteen miles after his encounter with Randolph. When he'd come to, David had seen the back of the big man as he stepped through the door. He wanted to go after him, haul him down, shake him, but he couldn't catch his breath. He drank the water the hostler gave him, let the damp neck scarf almost dry on his face. Then he stood, climbed back up onto the seat. "Give them fifteen minutes more, then sound the all-ready," he told the hostler. "I just need a minute here."

He'd felt the tilt of the cab as passengers climbed in, imagined the smirk on Randolph's lips. David shouted the all-ready and snapped the whip, seething over his own inaction, his not standing for the girl. What he'd wanted to say was, "She wasn't yours to own. No human is. What you did may have been legal, but that didn't make it right. It wasn't. I didn't make her go just like I didn't try to make her stay. If you can convince Hall and Crandall that I lost your 'property,' then so be it. I'll pay them back what's owed. But I should have stopped it before it started."

He shook his head. *Coward. That's what you are.* The most he'd done was make it sound as if it was a quirk she leapt off. If it had been a bounced bag, he'd have stopped for it. It did look like he didn't take care of passengers' things. But she wasn't a *thing.* Why couldn't he have just said, "You'll never convince me she was luggage, nor Hall and Crandall either. She didn't belong to you. She belonged to no one."

Now, bone tired, his neck sore and red, David walked the horse he'd mounted at twilight. He'd ridden out on his borrowed horse as though for an evening ride. It was a man's right to have time to himself.

It was an early rising moon, just what he needed. He looked behind him. He saw nothing but the distant roll of hills and the tongue of road he'd ridden out on. David wasn't sure at all if he could find the spot. Worse, maybe she hadn't understood his plan to bring her food and water. She wore a blank face when he'd told her. Maybe he'd misread the expression in her eyes. Maybe she'd been terrified and hadn't wanted to jump as he'd motioned. What if she was hurt? He wondered what he'd do if he didn't find her.

Of course, she wouldn't be there, now that he allowed himself to think straight. She was a Wintu. She knew how to live from the land, how to take care of herself. What did she need him for? Why should she even trust him to come back? This whole trip was crazy, riding fifteen, sixteen miles or so one way to what, rescue a woman who didn't need it? And hope to get back before daylight to drive the morning run? He should just turn around then.

But he couldn't. If for no other reason than that he'd told her he'd be back. A man was nothing if he didn't keep his word. He carried food, a canteen of water, and a bedroll with a blanket and a piece of emerald green linen he'd bought with his first pay, had planned once to give his mother. Odd how he'd rolled the cloth into his bedroll and never taken it back out, even after he learned of his mother's death. It tucked beneath his neck when he slept. It would be enough to cover the Wintu woman while she made her way through towns, until...until what? David didn't know. He just knew he'd made this commitment to her and to himself, and he would keep it regardless of how outrageous or wasted a hope it was.

He felt the horse alert, saw its ears twitch. He twisted to look back. Was that a rider behind him? In this dim light of shadows, he couldn't be sure. He looked up. A strip of cloud speared the moon. He pulled the horse into the shadow of scrub oak lining the road. He watched for a time. Saw nothing. He leaned forward over the horse's neck. "Let's go," he said under his breath and squeezed his knees. The horse responded with a surge forward, a pace David hoped they could keep up.

That boulder. The moonlight polished it smooth, but David recognized it as the one he'd slowed the team for. So he must have already ridden past the spot where Oltipa had jumped off. He pulled up the reins of his borrowed horse, turned, his eyes scanning, hoping to sight something familiar. The gelding snorted once, his head low as he retraced his steps. The white pine tree with the acorn woodpecker's stash dotting the trunk, large roots hanging out over the side where the bank washed away, was it there? The top of the bank pitched out toward the road, as though it might topple over, pulling up a root ball larger than the Concord. Maybe there'd be a mark of her scampering up and over. She might have reached for the roots and missed.

It took courage to jump. David admired her for that. He'd looked back and had seen nothing in the roadway, so he assumed she'd made it. He hoped again that she hadn't been injured.

He wished she'd call out to him. Could she see who it was in the moonlight? Would she be relieved to know he'd kept his word or annoyed that someone had interrupted her sleep?—if she slept, if she was even still there. Returning was a crazy thing to do. He wasn't thinking well at all.

Then he saw it. The tall pine cast a shadow onto the road. With the cloud gone, he could even see the pine needles crisp against the sky.

"Oltipa?" He used a loud whisper. "Oltipa?"

There wasn't any way to stay on horseback and ride that ridge. He rode north again a few yards to where the bank began a slope to the road. He dismounted, picked a large rock and wrapped the reins around it. "Stay put, boy," he said, patting the horse at its withers. Then he untied the bedroll containing the food he'd talked the station cook out of and the emerald green cloth. He slipped his arm through the hemp rope that held the roll, hoisted it up onto his shoulder, and threw it up.

Tall as he was, David still had to jump for the tree root that stuck out like a gnarled hand from the bank. Successful, he soon straddled the thick root, then shimmied his way toward the body of the tree. He stretched his right leg around it, feeling his boots hit solid ground. He stood, his back to the tree. "Oltipa? Are you here? Anywhere?"

His eyes cast uphill, beneath the branches of a few pines, mostly oak. He heard an owl, listened for the night sounds. A branch broke off to his right. "Oltipa?" he said. He swallowed. Perhaps he'd been followed after all. Another sound. The hair at the back of his neck prickled through the sweat. He turned and saw it.

The animal was the color of wet sand, sleek in the moonlight. Its head was a round ball sucked into its muscled shoulders and neck. David couldn't see whiskers or eyes, so the big cat must have had its head faced away as its tail twisted down from the thick tree branch.

Something caught its interest other than David. He wanted to whisper Oltipa's name again, make sure it wasn't her the animal sought. A deer maybe? A fawn?

He couldn't take any chances. He had to bring the big cat's attention to him, just in case the woman was its prey. He reached for his ball-and-cap pistol. Its range wasn't that far and the accuracy questionable, but his rifle remained in the scabbard, back with the horse. At least he had six rounds. He kept the bedroll on his shoulder, making himself look as large as he could. His movements were slow as a winding-down clock. *Here, kitty-kitty,* he thought. The animal outweighed him, he was sure of that.

The pistol grip felt cold in his hand. He moved closer, grateful he was downwind and hadn't been seen. He took aim and shot.

David forgot how the pistol smoked and smelled each time he shot it. Through the powdered haze, he could see the big cougar fall, crashing from the branch and landing with a hard thud on the far side of the tree. He eased up, walked a wide swath around the cougar. He poked at the cat's ribs with his boot. There was no movement. He couldn't see exactly where he'd hit it, no blood anywhere visible in this shadowed light, but the ball would have pierced the underside. David stepped over the animal, his eyes beyond now, trying to see what had interested the cat.

He heard a whimper.

"Oltipa?"

He squinted toward the sound. Something moved, smaller than a fawn. A porcupine? A rat? Then it bounded toward David, black eyes peering out through a beard of scruffy hair. "What...?" David said just as the dog barked.

"Whoa." The dog pushed itself against him. "Wait, wait." He laid the pistol down and laughed a cracked-voice laugh as the rough tongue ran itself over David's cheeks, his eyes. With both hands, he held the animal at arm's length, the dog's back legs dancing in the air. "I got no time for you," he told the squirming mutt, smaller than a Christmas ham. The dog barked then, a yip almost. "You're sure a long way from home," he said. "That's certain."

The dog twisted itself from his hands, dropped to the grass then, and darted through David's legs, causing him to lose balance. "Hey," he said, turning to watch the dog run off. "Is that any way to treat your rescuer?"

David smelled the danger behind him before he heard the rustle.

He turned. "Oh," he said, his eyes locked on to another's. His heart thudded. He thought of his mother and his father as their faces flashed before his eyes. He never dreamed it would end like this, beneath a tree, the only witness an odd-looking dog. David eased himself backward like a wounded crab, his throat and stomach exposed as he shifted his hands and feet. He was supposed to make himself bigger, someone told him, when found by a cougar. Stare at them, make them think twice about taking you on. He could see the animal's tongue loll on one side. *It must be dazed.*

The scream ran cold fingers up his spine. The animal crouched low now, slow and deliberate, stalking. David should have shot again when he first downed the cat.

What happened next came quick. From the corner of his eyes, he saw a black streak. The dog raced between David and the cat, distracted the animal for no longer than the hoot of an owl, long enough for a shadow beyond the cat to rise, her arms raised. Then she plunged the rock with such force against the animal's head that the cracking of it echoed like thunder rolling through distant trees.

This California way of thinking proved…tiresome, Zane decided. Where was the challenge in setting people upon each other if it took no effort? A word dropped, a threat suggested, and the boy would be blackballed from the stage line, probably destitute within the month. And the

Wintu woman, with her dirty black hair stringed down over her face, would be an additional weight around the boy's neck if he actually did act to help her. Helping a person obligated a soul worse than hurting them, that was Zane's observation. It was a good lesson for the boy to discover. Perhaps he'd even helped him grow up, face life as it really was, hard and cold and cruel. Zane smiled. *Careful,* he thought to himself, *one wouldn't want to be obligated.*

The jehu, looking tired and red-eyed, had delivered them to the next stage stop and then driven back toward Sacramento. Zane had been assured by the next agent that his claim would be paid, and Zane had smirked at the unrepentant boy, then boarded the coach leaving for Shasta.

Now here he sat. He stirred his whisky with a rhythm to his wrist, gazed out over the tables of the Goodwin and Yorks Saloon. The tenpins threatened to be knocked about all night, along with card games where a fortune might be made or lost. He was surrounded by simple men, all so simple. Half were homesick, from the sound of it, wishing their wives and children were about. The other half had gotten what they'd come to California for—escape from the usual. Both groups worked their way to drinking down their profits.

Outside the window, a cold rain fell, filling the muddy holes of Shasta's streets. Tomorrow, he would file his gold claims, which Greasy would supply with working boys. He supposed there was some intrigue in that process, some fleeting pleasure in the look of their eyes as one stood over a sleeping Indian beside the road near Cottonwood, say, the Wintu or Yani waking up to his worst nightmare. The terror of being hauled off while his children screamed as they tried to cling to him like dust balls to a mop. Zane smirked at the pathetic image. Eventually, like all hangers-on, the families would drop off, desert and run, forget their men and boys. Women were fickle, not to be trusted, and children? As disloyal as pups. Best those native slaves discovered it now, before hope bit at them like a rabid skunk.

Greasy said the Indians were theirs for as long as they wished, though the law said at four months they were supposed to purchase their services again. He wouldn't bother. Greasy said no one protested. Oh, the Indians did, but the law forbid them to even speak against a white man in court. Once purchased, they rarely resisted. Amazing, truly amazing. If Greasy's Indians gave him grief at Mad Mule Canyon, he was his own judge and jury and could dispose of them as he did the other refuse that resulted from daily living. Zane brushed at a speck of lint on his cape. With resourceful men like him coming into the state, California might end up with no Indians left at all.

"Seth should have stayed until we were all settled in," Adora complained, shivering at the morning fire.

"He'd made a commitment to Sister Esther," Ruth said. "At least give the man credit for keeping it. Here, have some coffee. It'll warm you."

"Fancy you crediting a man. Any man," Adora snapped.

"I like men. In their place," Ruth said. She wore fingerless gloves and sipped from her own cup. "I just like horses better." *Was that actually true?*

"Better than anything," Sarah said.

"Not better than you, I'll bet," Mazy said. "Isn't that right, Ruth?"

"What?" Ruth said. "Look, this place is right, for now. Your cows and oxen can winter here at Poverty Flat. Your mules, too, Adora, if you want. Looks to be plenty of grass and water. Creek'll freeze over, but I can break the ice until I get a trough rigged from the Sacramento to it." She looked out across the flat where they'd camped this week while helping move people into their places in Shasta. "And if Matt and Joe Pepin ever get my letter and bring my horses and your bull to us, Mazy, this'll be the place they'll come to stop. Just off the trail as it is. All in all, it's a good spot. A pack string stops most every day, though I guess once the snow falls heavy, that'll end."

"Will you build a house?" Adora said. "There's no place to live, or haven't you noticed?"

"There is, actually. Back in the trees. An old barn and a small shack." She pointed. "I found it when Koda and I rode out yesterday. Pretty run-down, and the barn looks like it might have been flooded once, judging by the marks on the walls. But there's a stove left in it, still with a pipe. It's a little small, that's true. You children might find yourselves wanting to visit your other aunties sooner than you thought."

"Are there beds?" Jason said.

"We've got the mattresses of your mother's, quilts and blankets and tin pans and a coffeepot. It'll be...cozy. And we have a three-legged spider to fry up eggs—if we ever find some laying chickens."

"I saw some, riding a mule in town," Ned said. "A man with a long braid was arguing about them. Can we go calling on Chinatown, Auntie Ruth?"

"Maybe tomorrow." Ruth let herself imagine a day of just exploring with the children. "First we have to figure out which corner of the house you want to claim as yours. We've got to make repairs. Plug up some of the holes in the roof. Might be a skunk or two we can kill before it snows. Skunk oil's good for healing, isn't that right, Lura? Then see about buying and moving a haystack before the snows fall heavy. Your parents left you some money, but we've got to make it last. Girls, you'll be cooking and sewing; that's what you'll be doing. Jessie can even do that without using her crutches. Yes, there'll be a lot of work to do, no doubt about it. Oh, and we need to get Jessie up on those crutches. I'm not having any of you push her in that cart after today. We'll be needing it for hauling firewood, not a spoiled child."

Ruth watched the faces of her charges. Glances shifted between them. She was just helping them face reality and letting them see for themselves—in time—that living with someone else besides their auntie just might not be so bad.

"It's just up here," Suzanne said. "I've counted exactly one hundred and twelve steps straight from the digger pine at the end of that street. We should be right at the wrought-iron gate. Are we?"

"I'll be," Lura said.

"This is...great, Suzanne," Mazy said.

Suzanne's face could barely stop smiling. Her fingers fidgeted with the latch. She opened it, and Pig led her through the gate. "I know guests are supposed to go first, but I need to count to the porch steps and get Pig through too."

"Nice big yard, Suzanne," Tipton said.

"A little dark, truth be known," Adora said.

"Just shady," Lura said. "Kind of nestled back in here. No porch though, just one step, it looks like."

Suzanne stepped up, pulled the latch string, and pushed open the door to her house. She smelled the dampness and wished she'd remembered to ask the land agent to come ahead and start the fire in the fireplace. But it smelled clean. That was what she remembered when she first stepped inside. And there was a scent of...lemon, yes, that was what it was. The woman must have had lemons, the fragrance now permanent in the wood floor. Suzanne patted the walls, walking sideways, counting as she stepped. "The main room is about twelve feet by twelve feet. The bedroom's a little smaller." She turned to face them.

"Well? What do you think?" she asked as she heard the shuffling of feet as the women moved around to fill the room.

"Is the ceiling too low? Are there holes in the wall, what?" she asked. "Isn't it all right?" Silence greeted her. "What?"

"It's grand," Elizabeth said. "A little puny as you can tell by our shoulder-rubbing here. But it's dandy for you and the boys."

"Thank you for that, Elizabeth. Thank you." She took in a deep breath. "I know you all think I've lost my mind, wanting to be here by myself. And I should tell you now, that I want to do as much as I can without leaning on you as I have these months. I'm not being rude, truly, by seeing less of you."

"She can't see at all," Jessie whispered to Sarah. "Why'd she say that?"

"Hush!" Ruth told her, and Suzanne heard a scrape and shuffle, no doubt Jessie walking with a crutch.

"This is my new beginning," Suzanne said. "You'll all find yours, too."

"You'll have to get someone to build your fires," Mazy said. "I can't see how you'll make it without that. And to help cook. Look after Sason. I just don't—"

"I have a plan," Suzanne said. "Isn't that what you always said we needed, Mazy? I can do this. I found this place by myself, didn't I? All I need from you is help to carry what's mine out of the wagons. And your understanding. The rest I can do. I can."

Lura asked, "Where's your income going to come from?"

"Ma! That's personal-like," Mariah said.

"We're family," Lura told her.

"Not that it's your business...but Bryce left me in good stead. For this first year, at least. I'll be able to buy food and pay for firewood, even to have it brought up here. So you needn't worry. The boys will be fine. The agent gave me lots of information, and I've already met someone."

"A man?" Tipton asked.

Suzanne laughed. "Not a man, Tipton. That is not part of my plan. No, a woman. A very nice lady. She said she's a banker. I didn't know women did that, but she says it's how she supports herself. You'll meet her sometime."

No one seemed to want to enter the silence that followed, so Suzanne added: "It's the first time in my adult life I have lived...without being in the shadow of a man. I was married and went from living under my father's roof to my husband's. And good as they both were to me, I never discovered whether or not I could make good decisions for myself, recover from bad ones. I rather like the idea of being alone—with just my sons. In fact, I'm looking forward to the adventure." Still silence. "Can't you share my joy?" she said, wishing she hadn't heard the pleading in her own voice. "Can't you see what I see?"

"What do you see?" Mazy asked.

"Home," Suzanne said. "Just the way I want to make it."

Zane stopped by the Shasta post office to see if his claim had been paid. With a knife, he scraped at his fingernails, waiting, watching, listening. People hovered over well-worn letters from back home. He smelled pickles mixed with the cigars of shopkeepers, the lye soap aura of bonneted women, the horse and leather smells of homesick miners. A sorry lot, needing connection from what had been, hearing of things that happened months before. He watched their eyes light up as they read, some teared, even grizzled looking men bigger than him. They read of the death of a mother, the loss of a woman to the affections of another man. Wasted effort, the caring of another.

When he was the only one left, he asked for any letters for Zane Randolph. Still no paid claim. He should sue them for the delay—lawsuits always quickened people's feet.

Good fortune smiled at him already in the few weeks he'd been in Shasta. A few well-placed words—everyone gossiped about new arrivals—and he'd heard of a beautiful blind woman and of a "manish" woman with children settled out at Poverty Flat.

When he was sure just where Ruth was, he'd watch her from a distance. He'd let Ruth settle, feel safe and secure. It would be a good time for him to deliver supplies to the gulches Greasy told him of, then file some of his own claims.

He stopped at King's Bookstore on his way to the St. Charles Hotel, almost stepping on a long-haired cat. He browsed a bit, picking up a classic or two. He'd have time to read, practicing his patience, waiting for the proper moments. Tiresome but necessary. He paid for his purchases, including sweet-smelling cologne, just arrived. When he turned, he saw her.

His breath caught in his throat.

11

a golden spoon or a wooden leg

David Taylor dropped an armload of wood next to the hearth and looked over at Oltipa. Good, she still slept. She looked so small there, tucked beneath a blanket hide, knees pulled up like a baby. He fixed himself a cup of hot water and threw some wheat berries into it, telling himself it tasted like coffee. Snow fell harder now, outside, but the fire stayed strong. He shook his head, still amazed at how he'd arrived at this place of comfort with a wounded Wintu woman.

Four of Oltipa's fingers on her right hand were smashed when she killed the cougar with the thrust of the rock to its head. As he scrambled toward her, David patted for his gun, found it, and shot the stunned cat in the neck. This time, he was sure. Then he saw her wrist. It hung limp as wet wash. David held her hand in his and poured water on it from the canteen he retrieved from the horse. A twig formed a kind of splint he wrapped with his neck scarf. He tore a section of the green cloth to act as a sling. She never whimpered or winced even with the swelling.

He'd given her food then, ripped the cooked venison he'd brought from the stage stop into bite-size pieces. Her eyes clouded with...uncertainty, David decided, taking food from this foreign man.

"Yeah, I'd wonder too about how much help a man can be who lets a cat lay stunned and needs a woman to rescue him. She gets hurt in the process." She looked up at him, her face smudged with dirt and a smear of the meat, a blank expression. "Yeah," he said. "I hope those fingers aren't broken, just bruised bad. And I'm sure sorry about your wrist." She'd looked at her hand then, so he knew she understood at least some of his words.

The dog pushed against the woman, stepping its rounded toes onto the slinged arm, sticking his face into hers. "He can't be yours," David said, brushing the dog from her.

She reached out a small piece of meat, which the dog snapped up, scooting back under David's arm to eat it.

"Looks like a monkey sitting there, begging," David said. "Kinda cute with that beard. He's so dark, I can't even see his eyes."

The girl just stared at David.

Her hand must have been throbbing, and David made small talk about a mutt. He moved himself to lean his back against the tree, liking the feel of the rough bark against his shirt. He inhaled a deep breath, wiggled to scratch his back.

"So here's what I'm thinking," he said, handing her the canteen again while the dog plopped itself in front of David, licked its toes. "You can't go on far alone, not with that wrist and those fingers all smashed up." He scratched at the dog's neck. "So here's our options. You come with me now, and I'll hide you out, close to the station. That Randolph man has already filed his lost luggage claim, and he seems settled enough. He'll keep going north, leaving us alone. In the morning, I'll take the stage run back to Sacramento as I'm bound to, but I'll buy your passage. Pick you up on the way back out." He was planning as he talked. "Got to get you something decent to wear, though. Maybe I can borrow something from Mrs. Gant. Make up some story of why I need it. Or we can wrap the cloth around you, like I've seen some of those Argentine women wear. Serape-like." He nodded. "The dog with you will make you look regular," he said. "And we'll get the twigs from your hair, your face washed, and you'll get along fine in Sacramento, big city and all." She brushed at her hair, winced as she bumped her damaged hand. "All right. Let's see how we can get that green to wrap around you."

He unfurled the cloth, several yards long, and wrapped it around her shoulder, across her chest and then around her waist. He swallowed with the intimacy of it, of feeling the waist of a woman that wasn't his sister or mother. She held her good arm out so he could wrap the cloth beneath and up and over her shoulder, tucking the cut edge in at the waist. He stood back, gazing at her, and that was when he knew.

"Are you? I mean..." He made a motion with his hands as though he held a baby in them, rocking.

"Baby," she said and nodded.

"Yeah." he swallowed. The dog stood on its back legs, tugged at David's pant legs, then ran to the woman, snagging the cloth. Oltipa winced. "With a baby coming, city's no place for you, is it? At least not a big city. Thought maybe you could get work with someone and be fed there and all. But you'll be snatched up again, I'll bet. Declare you destitute. You need someplace safe you can tide over until spring, so you can have that baby and make it back to your people. You got people?"

She didn't seem to understand.

"Yeah," he said. He ran his hands through his dark hair, thinking. "We've got to find you a home for a while, that's what we got to do."

Streams of ideas ran through his head, mixed with memories and wishes and wants. He patted her shoulder as if she were a child. "It'll be all right," he said. "We'll think of something."

With his hands, he scraped up some pine needles to form a makeshift pad, then he laid out his bedroll on top of it. "Here. You rest now."

An edge of uncertainty worked its way to the surface, the craziness of what he was thinking of doing for this woman of whom he knew nothing. "I could take you to the cabin my father had, near French Gulch. Well, not far from Shasta City. Bring food enough for a month at a time, in case I don't get back from a run. I'd look after you like a brother." She stared at David, blinked once. "You'd be safe there through the winter. Until your baby comes."

David sat on his haunches, pushed his hat back and cocked his head as he looked up at her. "You don't understand a word of this, do you?" he said. "This thinking of mine, to take you to a safe place, be good to you and all. Not a word."

The dog barked its short sharp yip then, ran from David to pull again at the green cloth. The Wintu woman brushed the dog gently away with the side of her foot, stared at David as she did. "Sookoo," she said then.

"What?" David asked.

"Word for dog is *sookoo.* We take him, too?"

"You bet," David said. "You bet!"

Now here he was, his whole life a muddle of meddling. Mr. Hall, his former employer, had listened to his explanation of the missing "luggage," nodding his head kindly, the fat fingers of his hand grasping the lapel on his fine linen suit. "Fact is, David, the, ah, item was placed on the stage and did not arrive as scheduled. It was of worth to the passenger, and while we may disagree with the, ah, morality of this transaction, it is in fact legal and thus nothing to be done for it but pay the claim. I'm sure you see my dilemma."

"I don't, sir," David told him, his heart pounding, this whole situation pushing him into areas he hadn't imagined he'd go. "It's condoning slavery."

"Not the way it's seen, David."

David lowered his head, defeated. "I'll repay you from my wages." Even as he said it, he wasn't sure how he'd ever do it, pay and meet Oltipa's needs for food and shelter. His own, too.

Hall nodded. "And you're, ah, off the roll."

"You're letting me go?"

He gripped David's shoulder then, in that friendly way he had. "Perk up, boy. You're young. It's not the end of the world. California's a booming place. You'll make your wages—and your obligation to the line. It's just not worth the, ah, litigation that could ensue unless Hall and Crandall can show they took appropriate measures in this incident. The customer intends to, ah, take out ads, questioning our quality, our service unless we, ah, can assure him that our drivers are above reproach. You understand how it is."

David had misjudged him. Apparently he'd also misjudged the strength of that Mr. Randolph, a man who'd not only gotten his money from the stage company, but a pound of David's flesh, too. David guessed he was fortunate enough to get hired on with a rival stage line, Baxter and Monroe, before any word of his indiscretion reached them. Maybe this route operating farther north would be better for him anyway, good for Oltipa and good for him. Maybe it would all work out. A fellow couldn't always see what was around the bend.

He stoked up the fire in his father's cabin. It was a tightly chinked place. His father had built it to last, must have planned to come back, but he hadn't. Something had gotten in the way. David set his cup down, pulled the blankets up over Oltipa's shoulders, hoping she would wake so he could tell her good-bye. She didn't. He packed up some grub, then headed out. He hoped to be back before the week was out.

"Excuse me," Zane said. He was aware of his breathing. Steady. Patient. He was certain it was the blind woman from Fort Laramie, met all those months before. Should he suggest they'd met? No. The dog hadn't liked him. He looked about for the animal. Nothing. "Your boy there, the baby, his head has dropped to the side. May I…help him? He looks a little uncomfortable."

"Yes, please," the beautiful woman said.

He straightened the boy in the backboard. He even tucked the little woolen cap strings beneath the baby's chubby chin.

"Clayton, stand still, dear."

"Quite an ingenious...appliance," Zane said.

"They say the Indians use something like it," she told him.

Zane looked around, wondering where the dog was and if any of the other women were with her. The boy Clayton leaned from her, pulling her to move away.

"Would you like the boy to go into King's store here? There's a cat inside. Might interest him. It's warm there."

"So that's where the cat lives," she said. She was a portrait of loveliness, full lips, smiling now; a delicate nose on a porcelain face. Her whole form, perfection. He watched her feel her way through the doorway with a cane to assist. She stepped inside the bookstore. Zane followed and closed the door behind them.

"You're very brave to use something others might find crude or offensive," Zane said.

"The baby's board? Not really brave. I don't see the looks of others, so I'm rarely distracted by noses raised in disgust. It's one of the benefits—of being blind." She laughed.

"Excuse me?" Zane said.

"Oh, it just struck me as strange, finding something beneficial about being blind. I never thought of it before."

"So you are both brave and insightful," Zane said. "How admirable."

"Have we met?" she asked then, turning her body toward him. "Your voice..."

"Oh no. I would have remembered someone so lovely." He had almost said "delicious." He might have used the word in Laramie! Another habit he meant to change. "May I introduce myself. My name is—" He coughed. Why hadn't he thought of this? "Wesley Marks. Investor," he said as he clicked his heels and bowed at the waist. "I've just bowed to you, dear lady."

"I can hear," she said. "I'm Mrs. Suzanne Cullver. Not an investor."

"And Mr. Cullver, is he with you today?"

Suzanne stiffened. "I'm a widow, Mr. Marks."

The boy carried the cat to him, and Zane stepped back. "Ah, let's leave the kitty on the floor, shall we?" The cat growled with Clayton's squeezing. The boy's lower lip moved out into a pout.

"Clayton, put the kitty down. Too many things to get into here. Take my hand. We should be going."

The cat sprang over Zane's boot as Suzanne tapped her way around to the door. "May I walk you home, Mrs. Cullver?"

"I...we have a few items to get at the mercantile. Perhaps another time. Thank you, though, Mr. Marks, was it? It was delightful to meet you."

"Please," Zane said in his most charming voice. "Call me Wesley."

"Wesley. An English hymn writer bore that name. Charles Wesley. He had a brother named John who founded the church at Aldersgate."

"My mother knew of them," Zane said solemnly. "She told me often. As a result, I've always been a deeply religious man. May I call on you...Mrs. Cullver?" He waited, feeling his breathing change, hoping he hadn't moved too quickly.

"I think not, Mr. Marks. I'm becoming comfortable with making my own choices. Without a man about. I suspect such determination would trouble a deeply religious man." With that, she tapped with her cane through the door, holding the boy's hand.

"You're pretty quiet this morning, Mazy," Lura said.

"Am I?" She and Mariah and Lura sat on rough benches outside the St. Charles Hotel. A brief sun break felt like silk against their faces. Here they could munch their warm pretzels safely—men just stared and pointed at them in the hotel's eating area. It wasn't much of a hotel even if it was a board structure. There were no private rooms here, just one large open space for men to flop onto the cots when they'd tired themselves at monte or roulette. The provision for women at the St. Charles was a single room, for travelers and those who worked the casino tables. The Shasta was worse, no place for women at all.

"I'm just thinking about Suzanne's place," Mazy said. "The fence will be great for Clayton. But it's so far…from the main part of town. I don't think she realizes that. Or that it's so steep a walk. Taking Pig out daily…I don't see how she'll do that."

"Maybe one of us should walk him," Mariah said.

Mazy nodded. "That'd be me. I miss my old friend." She took another bite. "And the woman, Miss Williams, who's taken Suzanne under her wing, seems…odd somehow, to not come around to meet us."

"Maybe Suzanne made her up," Mariah said. "So we'd let her be."

"I hadn't thought of that," Mazy said.

"Well, I found out about that banker business this Esty's supposed to be into," Lura said. "I've got plans to be one myself."

"You don't have any money to bank, Ma. Not 'til Matt sells the cattle or brings them back."

"Don't need any for this banking they do here." She leaned in to Mazy. "It's handling the money in the saloons and gambling halls. That's what the banking women do there. Among other things."

"You can't be thinking of working in that kind of place," Mazy said.

"And why not? They're looking for mature, sober women who won't be taking advantage of the house, who can handle money and men who lose it. That's me," she said. She stuck her pointy chin straight out.

"But you'll get mistaken for those others and have to… Well, what will people think?"

"Who cares? It's an honest living. Pays five dollars a week and any gold dust I sweep up. Can't ask for more than that. No time at all and we'll have ourselves a house, Mariah. Besides, I can handle men thinking wrong about who I am. Grab their ears like their mamas would and tell them to hit their beds. Alone."

"What'll I do, Ma?"

"Well now, I thought you might like to help Ruth out at her place. You could sleep out that way too since I'll be working nights mostly. I'd see you on Sunday, of course."

"That's all? Sunday?"

"She said you wanted to help her. Don't you?"

"I just thought you'd be there too," Mariah said as she played with the frayed end of her braid. Mazy thought the girl would cry. What had gotten into Lura? This formerly quiet, bumbling, forgetful woman's thinking had seemed scattered worse than chicken feed on the trail. She'd even misplaced her money. And now she'd set her sights on something risky and moved toward it like a hungry hawk to a rodent. Would everyone change their ways in California?

"Not enough room for the lot of us in Ruth's little shack there. Four children, five with you and her, that's more than enough. I'll come get you on Sunday and we'll spend the day together. Besides, you'd be bored sitting in some old boardinghouse. I did think about running one of those. But I've no capital."

"I could loan you some. To get you started doing that," Mazy offered. The idea appealed to her. Doing something good for these two.

Lura frowned at her. "Best you figure out where that came from before you offer it," she said. "Besides, a woman's got to make a living much as she can on her own. In the spring, I hear, there'll be a school going, and Mariah can live with me in town again and go to it." She patted her daughter's hand. "That's what this West is all about, Mariah. Setting your own destiny and doing new and different things to get you through. Anything less and you'd be trampled by emigrants arriving. That's all Suzanne's doing. You best be getting into the swing of things too."

Mazy stared at her. She must have been the only one just treading water.

The snow melted quickly, then piled up again, drifted against the shacks, the tent houses, the boardwalks of the mercantile. Everyone talked about it being heavier up in the mountains, but even in Shasta, the piles shoveled away from the storefronts grew high enough a person couldn't see over them. Little alleys were shoveled through them so people could cross the street. From Suzanne's place, the lower streets boxed like a rabbit warren of tracks and trails.

Elizabeth and Mazy shared a small room at the back of Kossuth House where Elizabeth had taken employment, baking pretzels and bread for the hotel guests. Most were miners down from the gulches, ready to gamble for the winter. Shasta had more than two thousand people nestled in every nook and cranny. Shacks of canvas and wood sat pushed into hillsides, a flat place gouged out just wide enough for a floor. Men had little to do but gamble and eat and complain about the weather. Every kind of card game found its way into the saloons, and Mazy heard about women being more than bankers in the back rooms.

She pored over maps she acquired from the land office, spent time at the courthouse looking at land claims. When weather permitted, she bundled up in her wool dress and wrapped hides around her heavy shoes, then rode Ink out of town. She was looking for a place to call her own. It wasn't the best time of year to be looking to settle, not with the snow spitting and drifting and, in between, rain pouring down in streets turning to red mud. She thought she'd build a cabin come spring. Do it herself. She just had to find the perfect place. She wished Seth were around, someone to talk with about a potential building site, the lay of the land.

Now that's interesting, my wanting him around.

She hadn't seen Seth since he left for Sacramento with Mei-Ling and Naomi and Esther in October. *Coward,* she thought. *He never told us we could be drifted in for the winter. Must have been another of his "exaggerations" telling us this place was "the Queen City of the North."* If this was where the queen lived, she hated to think of the scullery maid's room. And he'd said nothing of the fires. Sacramento burned fast.

Then Shasta went up in flames. Despite all the snow, the miners said December was a good month to expect fires, what with the stoves burning day and night, sparks dropping on shake roofs, and the buildings so close together they could burn a block out in minutes.

Several people blamed its starting on Hong Kong, the Chinese area built right in the middle of the residential portion of town. But as Mazy rode the black mule through the burned commercial district, then on through the Chinese area, it seemed pretty clear that the fire had started in one of Shasta's saloons.

She and her mother, and other women she only caught glimpses of, had cooked and fed people through the night as others worked to put the fires out. Their backsides froze while their faces and hands burned hot from the cookfires. By morning, the fires out, the businessmen were already rebuilding, teams of horses and sleighs sent out to the mill at Rock Creek to bring in snow-covered stacks of lumber.

Mazy rode past Hong Kong. She liked the sounds of the Chinese talking fast, hands up and down, wide hats bent brim to brim as she rode past. Mostly men lived there; mostly men came from China to work the mines. A few had taken Indian wives. It did seem to Mazy that a lot of Indian women were widows. At least she rarely ever saw a complete Indian family, though to hear people talk of the Wintus and Shastas and a dozen other tribal names, she'd have thought them all surrounded by vengeful warriors. Yet she'd never seen a dangerous looking one. They all seemed defeated, to her.

At least in Hong Kong, the few children she saw looked fed and tended, not like the hollow-faced Indian girls and boys she saw sleeping beneath the back porches of the stores. Her mother started setting out leftovers for the packs of dogs to eat until one morning they watched a reed-thin boy wrestle for a breadstick with a skinny-tailed mutt. Mazy wished she could do something for them, but she couldn't imagine what.

At Suzanne's she dismounted, tied the mule to the iron hitching ring, walked through the gate, and knocked on the door. The huge sugar pines that dominated the yard kept the ground clear of much of the snow, at least near the house. She turned, waiting. The view from here was breathtaking. She could see the top of the St. Charles Hotel, hear the pounding of rebuilding going on. At least it gave people something to do besides gamble and drink. She turned back as she heard someone on the other side of the door.

"Thank you, Clayton," Mazy said when the little boy opened it. He was dressed warmly—maybe too warm for the fire burning hot in the fireplace.

"You really should ask who's there before you have Clayton let just anyone in," Mazy told Suzanne, stomping snow from her feet.

"I knew it was you. Pig has his little sounds he makes when you're about."

Mazy scratched the big dog's neck as he nuzzled her. Suzanne looked a bit disheveled, her apron caked with old flour, that tawny hair of hers in a braid, crooked and pulled off to the side. The house looked aclutter: a chewed shoe lay beside the door, clothes fell like snowdrifts in a corner. Into the back room, Mazy watched Sason playing with his toes while lying on the bed. He saw her, giggled, and began rolling toward the edge.

"No! Wait!" Mazy said, rushing to catch him. When she realized the bed had a rail around it, she stopped. "I thought Sason might roll off."

"Seth made that," Suzanne said. "It's awkward for me to get in bed with it there, but it works to keep him from rolling out. Sometimes I put Clayton there too. Just to keep him from the fire."

A wooden flute lay on what appeared to be a fine oak table—they were both new—and Mazy commented.

"A gift," Suzanne said, and blushed. "I was a little apprehensive about accepting them."

"Seth's a generous man," Mazy said. She let her hand linger on the smooth table finish.

"Seth? No, Wesley."

"Who's that?" Mazy asked.

"Apparently the man who ordered them at the mercantile left town or passed away," Suzanne continued. "So my new friend Wesley bought them. Along with that iron wagon, for the boys." Suzanne felt across the table with her hands, found the flute, and lifted it to her lips. She played a tune. "It has a lovely, haunting sound, don't you think?"

"It's beautiful. *You* make the haunting sound."

"Oh no. It's the craftsman. And the quality of wood." She laid it down, patting the table with her graceful fingers.

Mazy noticed other new items—a music box, for one. She wanted to ask if it came from this Wesley too, or perhaps Seth. She decided not to pry. Mazy bent to pick up the shoe. "Looks like Pig left his teeth marks on one of your shoes, Suzanne."

"Did he? Another one? He was a bit miffed when I left him in the house alone a time or two."

"You went somewhere, without Pig?"

"Oh, just downtown, before the snow got heavy. He chases that cat at the bookstore, and I can't seem to handle him then. I'm working on it. I have this cane now. But Clayton led us just fine. It was so...wonderful, Mazy, just going on our own like that, the way everybody does it, walking about with your children. And as a reward, that was when I met Wesley. He reads to me, Mazy. He has a wonderful voice."

"I'd like to walk him for you," Mazy said.

Suzanne hesitated, then said, "I know Pig would like that." Sason cooed from the bed, and Suzanne shuffled to lift him up.

Mazy pulled up a chair, brushing bread crumbs from the seat. "May I hold Sason? It's been so long." Suzanne released her son, and Mazy watched Clayton look up from his playing in the corner, then come to stand at Mazy's side. They looked...hungry, she thought, though fed. "So tell me about this Wesley. Will he join us for Christmas dinner at the hotel?" Mazy reached an arm around Clayton, who hovered in close. His hair was matted with mush.

"I doubt that. He travels quite a bit. For his investments. Oh, Mazy, I know I shouldn't feel this way, with Bryce not gone even six months yet, but it is so nice to have someone to talk to, a man someone. And he listens. He's so interested in how we made our way across the plains, who everyone is, where they are now. He really could fit in well with our little family."

"You're thinking of marriage?"

"No, no. I meant our family, we women. The way Seth fits in." Suzanne sniffed, waved her hands as she made her way away from the bed. "I need a clean diaper. Don't help," she cautioned. Mazy spotted a moldy piece of bread peeking from under a corner of the stove.

"I think Seth's avoiding me," Mazy said. "He told some pretty tall tales about this country. Mild winters. Ha. It's either rained or snowed every day since November first."

"He'll come see you when he returns, I'm just sure."

"Maybe. At least I'll write and invite him for dinner, remind him that he may have gambled one time too many, thinking he could convince me that Shasta is the perfect place."

"It's my perfect place," Suzanne said, taking her son to change his diaper. "And Wesley just adds to it."

"Suzanne," Mazy said, "the boys, you, it isn't...perfect. I'm worried—"

"Don't," Suzanne said. "Don't judge, Mazy Bacon, not while looking through your own uncertain eyes."

Mazy winced. "Looks like a good time for me to take Pig for his walk."

Tipton and Adora bent against the biting wind, Tipton wishing for the hundredth time that money arrived on the stinging sleet. She thought about money often. She dreamed about it—had almost every night since they'd arrived in Shasta City.

She'd hoped the brass tacks would carry them through the winter, but that dream had flitted away like a snowflake on her tongue. "Gold is worth sixteen dollars an ounce at the exchange in Sacramento. But only fourteen at these diggings," the assayer told the women as they stood hopefully with their pound of tacks.

"What does that mean?" Adora asked.

"A reduction of value," Lura told her. "Can't buy as much up here as we could in Sacramento or San Francisco. Gold is worth more in the city."

"It's pretty fluid there, too," the assayer said. "You ladies should know this country is unstable in ways. Not like back in the States where prices get set and seem to stay that way. Gold makes things shift and makes some people shifty."

"So this isn't the paradise Seth implied," Mazy had said.

"Just why running a business is the thing to do," Lura said. She smoked her pipe, but when Mariah scowled at her, she snuffed it out.

"It's not all easy being a shopkeeper," the man told them. "For instance, you got to order what's needed now, but it won't get shipped for weeks, maybe months around the horn or down from Vancouver. If your ship arrives, and doesn't sink, and if it gets unloaded first and it's carrying what everyone's been waiting for, well then you've got a gold spoon in your hand. If it gets unloaded last, or you know what's on it is no longer of interest, it may hardly be worth unloading. But still you got to pay and hand over the tax in coinage—not gold dust—or nobody unloads anything."

"People are that fickle with what they want to buy?" Lura asked.

"Yes ma'am. Your gold dust could buy lots or nothing. It just depends. As they say, it's a golden spoon or a wooden leg in California."

"So our little pound or so of carpet tacks brings us less than three hundred dollars," Jason noted.

"So it seems," Lura told him.

"We divide by eleven, then," Jason said. "I guess it's just you women?"

Tipton did the figures in her head. With flour at forty dollars a pound, that's about all they could buy with their share. A pound of flour.

"Don't count mother and me in," Mazy'd said.

"We should share and share alike," Sister Esther said. "You have contributed your tacks as did everyone else."

"Yes, but we have resources some of you don't have."

"They might not be yours, didn't you say?" the sister persisted.

"I may have to repay it with interest come next year. But for now, the money will help all of us survive. So divide the tack money by nine, Jason."

With that division, Tipton and her mother had eaten for two weeks and contributed to the "surprise" for Suzanne, though it cost them dear.

"I think we could ask Mazy, Mother. Repay her when we're onto our feet a bit."

"Truth be known, your father would have wanted us to do it on our own," Adora said. "He was proud that way."

"Then one of us must find work! Or we sell the mules. We can't afford to feed them through the winter, Mother," Tipton told her. "Please, couldn't we?"

"Ruth'll look after them. She owes us that much, giving two of them away to those Indians way back when. No, we'll hang on to the ones we have until the market improves. Come spring."

They'd found an abandoned shack that overlooked another, pigs rooting about both. Tipton took some pleasure in hanging the tent against the wall to hold out some of the cold near the bed. She planned to paint the interior when she could afford to. For now, her white shawl adorned the mattress, and the women sat on two stumps close to the barrel stove that heated their tea and potato soup. It looked...homey. If only her mother would stop complaining about her bad tooth, the cold, or whatever, Tipton might even have felt proud at their meager fare.

"Elizabeth's always got bread at the end of the day," Adora noted, and from then on, they "happened" to be near the Kossuth Bakery just as Elizabeth brushed her apron of the last crumbs.

Tipton'd put on a prosperous face and made up stories about her mother finding some currency. "Wasn't that lucky?" she told Mazy. "After all this time of worry over money. We'll be fine."

But they weren't fine, if truth be known. And on December twelfth, Tipton had put aside flirting with the young miners she passed in the street, stopped giving them promises with her eyes she didn't intend to keep. On that day, with the flour run out, with her dreaming now of food instead of money, with no woman needed anywhere except for banking or…unmentionable things, with snow drifting through the cracks of the abandoned shack they'd moved into, hoping the owner wouldn't come back, on that day, Tipton knew she would have to do something, or she and her mother would starve.

Perhaps if they'd arrived in the spring they'd have had more choices. Perhaps if there hadn't been so many of them, all needing shelter, or if the snow hadn't come so soon, maybe they would have…what? Looking back just didn't help.

On that December morning, a light dusting of snow covered the floor near the bed when she awoke. She shivered, cuddled closer to her mother for warmth. She'd have to scrounge wood in the snowdrifts. Most of all, she had to do something differently. Either admit how much they needed help or see if she could sell the mules and suffer her mother's displeasure.

"Remember the center of the wheel," Tyrell had told her. "That's what holds everything together so you can get down the trail." He'd been telling her about having faith, with God as the hub of that wheel. Today that faith seemed far away.

She wasn't much of a seamstress or mender. The miners all had their own needles anyway. Maybe she should consider what Lura was doing, banking in one of the gambling houses.

"You could do it for the interest of it," Lura told her. "People are fascinating creatures to watch. And so far the most dangerous thing is trying to suck in a good breath that ain't inflamed with exhaled whisky or cigarettes. The men pretty much leave me alone. I sass them right back if they try anything."

"I didn't think smoke would bother you," Tipton told her.

"I quit the pipe," Lura said. "Mariah didn't like it. Besides, I smoke just breathing now. You know, I figure every breath that's ever been breathed is still floating around? Got nowhere else to go. Ain't that a thought?"

"That I'm breathing the air my brother exhaled, yes. That is a vile thought."

She could ask again at Roman's Bookstore, just opened, but she'd had no luck with the others. Not the market, not the land office, none had need of a young woman—which was how she thought of herself now—for honest labor. She had even asked about cleaning stalls at the livery, but there were scruffy looking boys there who did that. And she had inquired about sweeping business establishments, but she'd been told either that their customers didn't care if things were less than tidy or that they could get Indian help to do it. She'd actually considered panning for gold. But that would have to wait until spring.

And always, lurking in the background were those women who wore pretty dresses, had plenty to eat and smelled sweet when she passed by them on the street. They didn't look hungry. They didn't look hungry at all. She shivered when she realized what she was considering. She could never sink so low.

Tipton shook her head. *Think of the center of the wheel. Then the spokes will hold well together.*

12

gifts given

Mei-Ling bathed in sandalwood perfume, sent to her by her future husband. Seth could smell the fine scent from where he stood next to Sister Esther and Naomi, the only *fan qui*—foreign devil—in attendance at the wedding. Mei-Ling had insisted, and in the end her husband had agreed to let Seth come at least for part of the ceremony. Mei-Ling wore red, a dress of silk with tiny gold buttons and the swirl of a dragon embroidered in green down the front. Her husband-to-be had it sent over for the occasion. Seth thought she shivered, but he couldn't be sure it was the occasion or the December cold.

Naomi told him what all the different colors meant, all the trappings of a Chinese wedding. Seth nodded politely, though he knew he wouldn't likely remember. He did well with figures and numbers but not details like what a headdress meant with all its height and beads and bangles. But the women would ask him when he got back, he was sure of that. And they'd probably wonder what had taken so long. Esther'd been busy with all the negotiations, giving him time for games of chance most days, and every night. Sacramento boomed.

Mei-Ling's skin looked as pale as the dried grass nodding beside the Joss House, where the marriage was held. He knew it was rice powder pressed onto her face. This was what she'd come across the country for, this marrying up, but he felt sad for her anyway. She looked white as death. Cymbals and tiny bells rang through the scent of burned incense.

"She happy," Naomi whispered to him.

"Fooled me," he whispered back.

"She give great gift to family, to new husband, to Mei-Ling. Now she go be wife. Very generous. Make very happy. Bees home all time now."

One of those little poems he never planned for popped into his head:

Mei-Ling's a wife now.
Her bees have found a home.
She begins a new life.
No longer all alone.

He shook his head.

"You say no?" Naomi asked.

"Just thinking a dumb poem," he said.

"Ah," Naomi said, nodding.

He watched as A-He, Mei-Ling's husband, took her hand when they finished saying the words he couldn't understand. They came out around a divider, stepped through a small opening, up over a step, and out the front door, all meant to fool the bad spirits, Naomi told him, who couldn't go around corners or up and over things and only traveled in straight lines.

Sister Esther sniffled. Seth wondered if she cried for losing a daughter, or that they were marrying in a Joss House and not in a church. He thought Esther said the husbands were supposed to be "poor but worthy Christian men." A-He didn't look to fit two of those slots.

Once outside on the porch painted red, the new husband handed Mei-Ling a white chrysanthemum he pulled out of his wide sleeve. "I wonder how he's kept that alive," Seth said. Naomi held her finger to her lips to shush him. He watched Mei-Ling take the blossom in her hand, bury her face in it, and inhale. She looked up with tears in her eyes and a smile across her porcelain face, and Seth said, "You're right, Naomi. She looks contented."

After the ceremony, Mei-Ling stepped over in her quick-quick way and pressed a red envelope into Seth's hands. "For help teach English," she said. "Husband very happy I speak."

"I think the custom here is for me to be giving you a gift," he said.

"No, no. You give gift by take this," she said and bowed, her hands together. "Someday come visit bees."

Inside the envelope, he found a golden eagle coin and something written in Chinese. "For give...crisis," she said, lowering her eyes.

"Crisis? What kind of crisis did I give you?"

She looked confused, motioned for her husband to come forward, spoke rapidly in Cantonese, showed him the characters she'd written. A-He bowed to Seth. "Wife say you help bring her through crisis. Word in Chinese formed by two characters: danger and opportunity. You help take from danger to opportunity. Help through crisis."

Mei-Ling had tears spilling from her almond eyes. "You and women. All together. My heart is empty for them already." She stood as tall as she could to pull him to her, her lips just brushing his cheek while he held her gift in his hands.

"There, there," Seth said, patting her thin back. "I just did what I could." He felt like a father, the idea passing through him with an ache.

"Looks to me like she's in good hands," Seth said later as they sat at the plank table of the boardinghouse Esther had located in Sacramento. Naomi had retired, and the other boarders were already asleep. Usually, he headed to the gambling houses to fatten his purse, but tonight that idea didn't satisfy as much as taking tea with Esther. "You did well, Esther. A-He's garden must be pretty lucrative. Looked like a man of some wealth."

"He sells to the hotels and such," she said. "He seems well respected among the Chinese here. And not disliked by the residents."

"Get Naomi married off as well and you can pat yourself on your back just fine and rest a bit."

Esther sipped her tea. "Naomi's husband has not responded to my inquiry, even after all this time," she said. "That's worrisome."

"Is he Chinese? Or some Californian who ordered up a bride, a miner or rancher living up in the hills?"

"I have to say," she said, straightening, "that those we hired to check these people out did a poorer job than I or my brothers would have done, given half the chance. I'm more than a little concerned that we undertook a cross-country journey with such poor information. A-He was the name given for Zilah's suitor. Yes," she said, nodding to Seth's raised eyebrows. "Mei-Ling's husband was a man of the soil, but he had found another wife, an Indian, I believe. He wished his money back, and Mei-Ling had no husband. It was a gift from God that A-He bought Mei-Ling's contract. Fortunately, both were men of the soil." She sighed. "Still, I must pay back the advance."

"Too bad Naomi can't stay with you. Once she goes, you'll be all alone."

"Don't wish another failure on me," Esther said. "It will be many years of my effort to pay back Zilah's contract. I don't want to have to pay back Naomi's, too."

"I'm gonna miss 'em," Seth said. "Been something soothing in this process."

"An obligation to be met, a promise needing to be kept. We usually are more at peace, we humans, with a commitment of some importance waiting for us. I suspect you'll find that out someday." She smiled.

He didn't smile back.

Ruth heard them whispering, probably about her. Scurrying sounds followed by silence. She should turn over, face them. They'd be joining Mazy and Lura and all the rest for Christmas dinner. A "family meal," Elizabeth called it. She wondered again why she'd agreed to go. Mariah joined her mother this Christmas, so Ruth needed to get up, stoke the fire. She grunted, prepared to push back the quilt, dress, and tend the horses and Mazy's cows. Sarah called out to her before she could leave.

"Auntie! Wake up!"

What now? Ruth thought.

She turned and was met with a crush of children pressing against her, pushing her down with Jessie scrambling behind her. "What are you—?"

"Time to get up," Jason said, taking one hand then and pulling her to sitting. Ned grabbed her other while Jessie slipped a ribbon over her face. "My eyes..."

"I won't hurt you," Jessie said. "You can't see your surprise."

They pulled at her until her bare toes felt the cold floor. Maybe not as cold as usual, as she felt heat shed into the room as they led her. She smelled something fragrant with lemon, felt Jessie's fingers against her back. Their touches tugged at her heart. Jason settled her onto something that felt rough against her flannel gown. A cold tin arrived in her hands. Then Jessie unfurled the ribbon.

"Oh," Ruth said, gazing. "When did you...how...?

"We been planning it for weeks," Ned said. "Do you like it?"

"I made the chair. From an old stump," Jason said. "Filed away the axe marks best I could."

"I folded the flowers. From paper. 'Lisbeth showed me," Jessie said holding up the rose on the tray Ruth held.

"Do you like the food?" Sarah said. "It's called Angel Pie. 'Lisbeth said we could have sweets for breakfast on Christmas morning. We did extra chores for Mazy so's we could get the lemons."

"I wrote you a song," Ned said. "I didn't write the music part. That's 'Morning Has Broken.' Suzanne told me the tune. *We need you, dear Auntie, to make us our home. We need you, dear Auntie, so we're not alone.* The words are mine. Well, all of us like the words."

"I love it," Ruth said, feeling a smile break onto her face, tears catch in her throat.

Zane could see if Suzanne was home by watching her house through his telescoping glass. He'd complained to the owner of the St. Charles Hotel that he wanted the same cot beneath the same window in the huge open-spaced second floor every evening and was willing to pay more than the usual five dollars a night for the privilege. Finally the little German had agreed. He even insisted that the Chinese laundry mark the sheets with a character indicating that they were his. Two hundred and fifty cots were set up nightly. Zane liked the anonymity of the numbers, something a boardinghouse with eight or ten curious bodies hovering close could never provide.

From his place at the St. Charles, he had a view out the small side window. He couldn't actually see Suzanne's door. The heavy pines shaded it. But he could see the gate and who came and went and when a horse was tied there. He knew whenever she was alone. He knew when she shuffled out with the children and the dog. That's when he would enter her home and leave things for her.

Once, she'd returned with him still there. The day he brought her the table. The dog had growled low.

He liked watching her for that moment when she knew something was wrong, liked staring as her perfect teeth pressed hard against her full lip, the rise of her chest as her breathing increased, her hand fluttered at her throat. It kept him in practice, this watching. When he'd had his fill of gazing, he'd tempered her fear by calling her name and leading her to the table, placing his hands over hers when she felt the smooth top.

"Oh," Suzanne had said, her fingers reaching for her throat. "You had me frightened."

She asked him not to do that again, not to come in when she wasn't there.

"It…it violates me," she said. "My home is my sanctuary. An extension of me. Your coming in uninvited…crosses a boundary."

He'd kissed the back of her hand. "But I love to surprise you with gifts, Suzanne. If you were sighted, you'd love it."

She'd pulled back, winced as though he'd struck her. He held her hand tight.

"You accepted the cookstove. From a perfect stranger."

"The former owner had paid for it. It belonged to the house. The way you give me things...invades me," she said, tugging her had free. "It would unsettle any woman."

He sneered, then lied, as he twisted the dog's ear. "In the future, my dear, I promise to honor your request."

Suzanne was home today. He put away the telescoping glass. He would ride toward his other prey instead.

He had seen Ruth. From a distance, through that glass. He knew where his wife stayed, taunting him with her presence. She lived there in broad daylight at a place called Poverty Flat. He'd ridden out before snow fell, nodded to travelers making their way from the Emigrant Ferry. His heart pounded in delicious anticipation. He skirted the meadow, stayed in the trees' shadows and waited, staring at the cabin, wondering how it would be to see her after all this time. She'd stepped out of the barn, carrying...a bridle. He might have known. Through his eye magnifying glass, he caught the concentration of her betraying face. She looked...content, peaceful. No worries. Just a woman walking, having tended her horses.

He heard his breathing, calmed himself. Let her be serene as a still pond. No need to rush. He would stir the waters slowly. He knew what it took to drown. He controlled the invasion of her life, the slow strangulation.

Today was Christmas Day. He was sure Ruth and the Barnard children and a Mariah—Suzanne said her name was—would head for dinner at the Kossuth House. Suzanne would join them, giving him two invasions in one day.

At the edge of the meadow where Ruth's animals pawed at the

snow, he halted. He heard his breathing change as he watched Ruth. Children piled into a wagon. His nieces and nephew, he guessed, the eldest boy having gone out to help yoke up the oxen. A girl with a limp. She looked to be he same age as his child would have been. Could that be *his* Jessie? She was the youngest, hopped on last, and they rode out giving him what he figured would be several hours of exploring time.

He left his horse a good distance from the cabin so as not to leave tracks in the snow. He wore skins over his own boots to cover his footsteps, made his way under cover of timber, looking out at the meadow where the road skirted in a wide arc before heading west into town. Then he simply walked through the unlatched door.

He heard his breathing change. The smell of her was there, a mixture of leather and horse, of homemade soap and liniment she might rub on an animal's sore leg. He could picture her slender hands, the hands he'd seen hold a lithograph she'd done with such perfection. He imagined those fingers running down the leg bone of her horse, lifting the foot in tender healing. Then she'd come inside, to this place, through this door, to wash her hands.

He looked for a basin, found a porcelain bowl set on the bench by the stove. A white pitcher sat near it. He took the hides from his boot, laid them by the door, then walked to the bowl. The water felt cool when he dipped his hands into it, dabbed some on his eyes, at the sweat on his neck. He swirled his hands in the water then, and smiled, knowing she would later splash the ripples he left, splash his scent on her own face without ever knowing. He would think of that back in his hotel, of how he touched her without her knowing.

He scanned the room. Sparsely furnished, which surprised him. She had liked lovely things, and Suzanne implied that Ruth had resources left from her brother's estate, the brother who had gotten what he deserved, to Zane's way of thinking. The lawyer brother who made the charges against Zane stick, who helped Ruth send him away.

Children's toys, a slingshot, dolls, writing material, the scratchings of a child; he found a harmonica still lying in its box, Christmas paper ripped open around it. A set of crude crutches leaned against the wall. Some underdrawers were draped over a stump acting as a chair. Beds with quilted comforters lined the back wall. Benches hugged a plank table. Ruth's whip hung on pegs along with a rifle. A photograph of the brother and his wife and…Ruth hung from a nail. Three children in that photo, that was all. None looking like the child with the limp.

He decided to move the frame. Just a small amount, setting it slightly crooked against the rough timber. He stood back. Yes, just enough to make her wonder if she'd bumped it herself. And something else. He must do something else.

He calmed his breathing, took a deep breath. *Patience.* He wanted her to slowly come to know of his closeness like a candle's light dimming, burning down, to first think forgetfulness or busyness caused her to misplace things or lose them.

Later, he would make the move that would leave her crying out, just as she'd left him. Today, he put the hides back over his shoes, scanned the room again, took one more item. He felt…delicious. As though he'd just consumed a holiday meal.

"Oh, my," Adora said.

"What is it, Mother? Your tooth bothering you again?"

"No, my tooth is fine today. Thanks for asking. It's that I've forgotten your birthday, Tipton, haven't I? Way back in October. I never even said."

"We had a few other things on our minds, Mother. I didn't remember it myself—until several days after," Tipton lied. She walked with her hands stuffed up inside her coat sleeves, a scarf tied tight beneath her chin. She noticed another place in her good green wool dress that needed mending. "What made you think of my birthday?"

"That brooch, back there." Adora nodded toward the mercantile window just passed. She stopped.

"We've no time to look now," Tipton said. "Elizabeth said she'd have supper hot by four. And I'm starved enough to eat our mules since you won't sell them."

"Prices'll go up in spring. It was done in silver with a blue stone, the brooch. Let's just peek."

Tipton's knuckles were red and scabbed from the scrub board that was as familiar in her hands now as a muff of fox hair had once been. And she had competition to worry over too: The Chinese people did the work cheaper and faster. Tipton constantly reminded her customers that she was an American they were supporting. She flirted with every grizzled miner, and she curtsied when they tipped her. This week, Tipton had a new customer—the St. Charles Hotel—who needed sheets and toweling washed. No tips to be found there, but the work was steady and she didn't have to go out and "solicit" men's dirty shirts to boil. She hated that part. But that was what a laundress did, and that was what she was.

It wasn't fair, her working so hard. More than once Tipton cursed her brother for having taken all their funds—and probably Lura's, too—and leaving her and her mother in this pitiful state. Other people had fared better. Suzanne had a nice place and a suitor, from what Mazy said. Elizabeth liked the bakery and living behind the kitchen even if her daughter still shared her bed. That Mazy must not have wanted to spend a dime of her money, or she could have had a house too. Maybe Mazy was waiting out the winter, like Tipton's mother was.

As it was, Tipton took the largest portion of her earnings just to pay for the back room of a shop where she could heat the spring water and do her scrubbing. Her mother did at least help her iron and sometimes delivered clean things back to the miners. The rest of what she made bought food and coal for their stove.

But she was always hungry. Tipton's stomach growled. She thought that strange when on the trail she'd refused to eat. Now she couldn't eat enough in her one meal a day.

It was not the picture she held when she set out for the West or even that first day in Shasta when she'd met nice fellows who laughed and punched each other as she blinked her eyes at them. Had that been only eight weeks ago?

Tyrellie would have been proud of her, though. He was a hard-working man who didn't believe in wasting time finding blame or pointing fingers. "Just keep your commitments," he often told her. "Every obstacle that gets in your way is just another chance to learn something you otherwise might never know. Something important to make your life have meaning." She wasn't sure what the laundry lesson was. Maybe that skunk oil stank, but it soothed her bruised knuckles too, or that she hadn't had to succumb to the life of "those women," even if their lives looked a lot more prosperous than hers or her mother's.

But she had committed to keeping her and her mother alive. She made her day-to-day pickups and washings and ironing and returned the items clean each evening. But it was not a commitment that inspired much. And there were constant setbacks.

Just last week, she'd been startled by a cat bounding across the street while she carried her day's work, and she'd dropped the pile into a muddy hole. She'd started breathing fast then, the way she had back on the trail; thought about just letting herself sink into dirty underdrawers and shirts and drift away, go back to living for the taste of laudanum on her tongue. But she'd chosen to "stay with them," as Mazy said. And something about being needed and wanted had helped her put one foot in front of the other. So she'd stood in the street, red plaid shirts and yellow britches soaking up grime and cried instead of dying, knowing her mother wouldn't survive if she didn't pick them up and start over. She'd hauled the huck towels and the shirts and carried them back to the room. Heated a new tub of water, and began again. That night, she'd dropped into bed just as the sun came up.

Who had time for dreaming?

"Just look at that silver brooch," Adora said, bringing her back. "It never hurts to look." Tipton let herself be pulled back to the shop window. Her mother pointed at items displayed behind the store bay.

"A place to live is more important, Mother."

"Money has been out of my mind, if truth be known."

"I do know. Ever since Charles left, in fact."

"Oh, don't let's start with that. Let's just look at this sapphire." She sighed. "How I wish I could get it for you. Doesn't sapphire stand for prosperity?"

Tipton allowed herself to grow a smile at the corners of her mouth. Once her mother had doted on her only daughter, but she'd changed coming across, didn't notice what a pretty young girl like Tipton might enjoy. Maybe she wasn't pretty any more, Tipton thought. She certainly didn't feel young. The afternoon sunlight hit the silver pieces. Nestled between them were bowls of lilies surrounded by quartz crystals, gifts every woman got from the Chinese at Christmas time. Tipton even had one at home.

"Mother, come on. They'll be waiting for us."

She grabbed at her mother's elbow. She hadn't meant to be abrupt. But she slipped on the slick boardwalk, stumbled and tripped, then found herself clinging to her mother to stand upright.

"Oh!" Adora said, losing her balance. "Oh, my!" And the next thing Tipton knew, her mother'd pushed Tipton from her just as her arm swung into the window. Shattered glass like snowflakes scattered at their feet.

Oltipa wondered why she stayed, why she didn't seek her band of people. Maybe she was just afraid to leave the safety of warm fires while the *yola* gathered in drifts outside the door. Maybe she'd been softened like a well-worked hide, by the tending of David Taylor.

David Taylor cared for her the way a kind brother served a sister. No need to search for food, no need to fish, to hunt. All that was needed was provided.

She had looked for signs of danger. She watched *eltee-wintoo*—white men. She could tell when their voices rose in anger, their fingers jabbed the air, how they pinched their eyes, held their teeth. The sound and speed of their words told her when to scurry out of sight. But in David Taylor, she saw only kind eyes, soft as the dog named Chance. He offered bags of bread and *chick-en* he called it, using words that made him sound like a chattering squirrel.

He slept on the floor of this cabin, covered with planks of wood, and he let her lie on a cloth stuffed with moss that smelled of summer, and he covered her with a hide blanket he said his father left. Too kind. Too good, this David Taylor. Yet she waited. For him to say she could *not* leave, that she was a captive, force her to do what she did not choose to. He had done none of these things. Yet.

She was not lazy. She stayed for the promise of her child.

David Taylor had come back for her, brought a horse, and together they rode through back country of oak then digger pine, up and down ravines until he took her here, a place he said his father built. The structure was nearly as tight as her husband's bark house had been. No rain came through this roof, and faded light came in through the bottoms of glass bottles laid up side by side to create a window. David Taylor gave her food, chopped wood enough so she could tend the fire with her good hand, and then he left her.

Through the winter season, when the trees slept and the sky cried tears of nourishment to raise the streams and bring the salmon back, she waited for him. Her wrist and fingers healed, her belly grew full beneath her breast. She set a trap for rabbits. Using the rifle David Taylor left, she put down a deer the dog had chased into the frozen creek, its leg broken from the fall. She dried the meat and spent days scraping the hide of hair. She made needles from the shards of leg bone, formed an antler into a handle for a knife she would give to David Taylor. In gratitude for what he had done.

Chance barked one night, and she found a porcupine and killed it with stones and rocks, then took the quills for decorations. She had to do none of this to stay alive—David Taylor had seen to that—but it served her, doing things to remember how. She filled the days waiting for her child to come, waiting for David Taylor.

Then in a cold dusk, he returned. Through silent white, on wide shoes made of deer gut and wood, he brought her new things to eat and a small package wrapped in string.

"But we got to wait to open it until I bring the tree inside," David said.

Bring inside?

David squeezed the small pine through the door, then tied ribbons of cloth like strips of venison hanging from the edges of the branches. He brought corn, and after heating it, they pushed white puffs onto strings, and they draped the corn on the tree like tiny butterflies settling on leaves. "We have corn to eat," she told him. "Put in stomach, not on tree."

David laughed. "This is special," he told her. "A celebration time. See? I even got Chance here a present." He put a ring of leather on the dog's neck that had four, five bells that jingled like ice thawing off the roof and dropping to the stones below. Then he handed Oltipa a gift.

Inside the wrapping lay a tiny silver spoon.

"It's engraved by one of the best in Shasta City," David said.

The spoon felt cool on her hands, and she smiled at the tiny picture of a hawk in flight, filling up the scoop.

David fixed food, and then he said he would tell a story.

"My people tell stories when *yola* falls too," she told him.

"Well, good," he said. "This is a story about a woman waiting, having trouble finding a place to birth her baby." Oltipa dropped her eyes. He touched her hand. His fingers were callused, his palms warm. "It's got a good ending. See, the baby was given as a gift from God, and God sent a man to tend her, care for her. When you tend somebody, that makes you kin. Guess that's why I came back for you."

"Because I will have baby?"

"A little hard to explain here," David said. He still held her hand. "Because that baby grew up and showed us all how to care for each other, our neighbors, family—like you and me—who might be different." David Taylor rubbed his face with his hands, scratched at his cheek. "I just didn't think it right, you being kept—like that spoon there. You're a human being, a woman. Family." He cleared his throat, looked away. "Like my sister."

She set the spoon down, reached for David's hand, held it in her own. "David Taylor is gift, like special baby. David Taylor's hands are His hands, taking care of this Wintu woman."

"Don't move!" A man shouted in irritation from inside the shop window. Tipton had no intention of moving, not a muscle. Not with the shards of glass on her wool dress and glittering at her mother's feet. She didn't see any blood. Thank goodness! Now if only the owner didn't threaten a lawsuit or demand immediate payment.

The man came out into the street, and his face looked less lined in irritation, and more noticeable for its pink flush captured by dark sideburns that swooped into a cropped mustache. He brushed at Tipton's woolen skirt, picked slivers of glass hung up on the buttons lining the skirt's front. Then he turned and squatted to brush glass from Adora's slipper. Tipton could see he did it gently, holding her mother's ankle as though it were glass itself. He stood again and wiped his hands on a leather apron covering his cream breeches. He took a deep breath.

Here it comes. It'll be months paying this off.

"I must apologize for the fragile nature of the window glass," he said then. "So pleased neither of you is hurt. Step over it gently and come inside, as my guests. I'll have chocolate and scones brought over while we wait on your husbands."

"We don't have husbands," Adora said sweetly. Was she flirting? Why, the man must be ten years younger than she. And why was he being so kind?

"I'm saddened to hear that. A mining tragedy?"

"A loss upon the trail," Adora said.

When they were settled inside, he introduced himself and Adora gasped again. "Nehemiah Kossuth, of the Kossuth House?"

"The same."

Adora sank against Nehemiah, who helped her to a stool. "Ernest," Nehemiah said to a young man who stepped forward. "Do a sweep, will you? While I tend to these fine women who were literally attacked by this poorly blown window glass." Nehemiah excused himself then, promising a quick return.

"What's wrong with you, Mother? Do you feel faint? Is it your arm? You're fanning yourself like it's August."

"He's of the Kossuth House," she whispered as Ernest swept. "We've hit the jackpot."

"We've hit nothing," Tipton scolded. "Except your elbow in a broken window."

"He thinks it was the window's fault, for being so weak."

Tipton rolled her eyes. "As soon as he gets back, we'll offer to pay for it and hope he doesn't accept or, worse, call the sheriff for what damage we've done. Then, we graciously remove ourselves. Christmas dinner is waiting." Tipton's teeth chattered in the cold. She wondered if there was a canvas to cover the window opening.

Adora pouted. "You didn't even get to see the brooch. You could look now. That real pretty one, there." She pointed, and Tipton paused to look.

"In his spare time, Nehemiah does silver work," Ernest said. "The work eased his mind when he lost his wife. Why he's working on a holiday—she passed on a Christmas morning."

"Can't imagine such a busy man having a spare minute," Adora said. "And he's a widower?"

"We really should be going," Tipton said.

"Oh, just look at them," Adora ordered. "Have you become such a work mule you can't enjoy a little silver?"

Tipton sighed, let her eyes drop toward the brooches. One looked like a spur and reminded her of Tyrellie. She blinked back tears. "Let's go, Mother."

"Can we see the one with the sapphire in it? Wouldn't that look good on my black dress?"

Ernest reached into the bay, picked up the spur, and handed it to Tipton. Silver surrounded the stone. "This one?" she said, holding it up in the fingers of her gloved hand. "It reminds me of Tyrell."

Several other pieces graced the inside glass counter, and the young man pulled them out, swept glass shards from around them, then rearranged the polished silver with his cloth. "I carry the finest work in the north here," he said. "Most of what sells has a nugget in the center. Nehemiah likes to use other gems. Unique things. Hand-tools the silver. I've done most of the rest."

Ernest Dobrowsky was "a gold miner, jeweler, watchmaker, and gunsmith," probably in his early twenties. "Been here since 'forty-nine."

Nehemiah returned then, carrying a basket with sweet-smelling cookies and breads and a green teapot shaped like a mushroom surrounded by several small cups.

"Are there mushrooms around here?" Adora asked.

"Indeed," he said. "In November usually."

"So we've missed them," Tipton said. "But next year. I'll tell Mazy. She loves mushrooms."

Adora smiled up at Nehemiah as he handed her a cup. Ernest came around behind him and poured. It seemed a little odd to have men serve, but pleasant. Maybe Tipton should just let herself enjoy the attention.

The scones tasted sweet, but increased her hunger instead of satisfying it. "We have friends waiting for us at the—well, your hotel, I guess it is," Tipton said. "Elizabeth Mueller?"

"Ah, my new baker. A dandy, that one. Her daughter, too."

"Mazy is a headstrong one," Adora said. "Not sweet-tempered like my Tipton here." The kind-faced man handed Tipton another scone.

"Thank you, Mr. Kossuth."

"Nehemiah. Please."

"If you'll tell us what we owe you, or is it Ernest here whose window we broke? I need to know how I can pay you back—over time."

"The window is my concern, as are you with injury so near," Nehemiah said. "It would please me, as small restitution for your troubles, if I could walk you to the hotel and—"

"It's right kind of you to offer compensation, truth be known," Adora said. "Windows like that, old and brittle, could do real damage to fragile bones, why—"

"Mother!"

"Were you admiring anything in particular?" Nehemiah asked, nodding to the silver piece in Tipton's gloved hand. His dark eyes never left hers, seemed to search her face, almost.

"We liked—" Adora began before Tipton interrupted.

"Nothing. Thank you."

Tipton tried to slip the brooch with the sapphire back into the window bay, but Nehemiah's hand reached over hers, holding the brooch inside her palm.

Warm hands. Gentle and strong.

"Please. Accept my work as small payment for your ordeal. It's Christmas. And your presence has been a gift that will surely bless my day."

An exceptional day. That was Ruth's description of the events from morning through the "family" meal with Adora's tale of injury and Tipton's talk of a silver brooch and their singing all the way home. Each of the women had found a simple gift to give one other. Ruth had done that too, braiding leather to decorate a picture frame; making charcoal portraits of each of them, the children included. Ned had opened up his harmonica before they left. She looked around. He must have already put it away. For Jessie, she'd had Mazy help her write a book, and Ruth had illustrated it. The girl had loved it and smiled and gathered up her skirts and pulled on boots when Ruth said it was time to go. The very first time. No nagging required.

The children slept now. The girls spooned beneath their comforter, curls mussed in sleep. The boys sprawled on their mattress. Ruth thought she heard them snoring. Maybe she could do this: raise them all together, let herself be loved. Maybe it was time to look forward instead of always looking back.

She picked up the bridle the boys had oiled for her. The scent of linseed oil and leather never failed to stir her, it was such a smell of home. She held it to her breast, then stepped to hang it beside her whip on a nail in the log wall. The picture frame beside it wasn't straight. She must have bumped it.

In the lamplight, something caught her eye. She looked closer. It was a picture of her brother and his wife, her and her nieces and nephews. She squinted, got the lantern and held it close. Her heart began to pound and her throat went dry. It couldn't be but it was—Ruth's face had been scratched completely out.

David Taylor rode in wearing a smile on his face. He looked at Oltipa as though she were a well-loved flower. Color rose on his neck when he saw her, then he turned quickly and tended to his horse and packs. Back inside, he handed her a bowl with a lily. "Chinese New Year," he told her. "Every woman gets one."

He stood far away from her after that and said little. She wondered if she had somehow offended him.

He whittled a sliver from a log and used it now to clean his teeth, threw the sliver in the fireplace and picked up his whip.

Something in the movement made Oltipa flinch.

"What? No, I'd never," he said. "Just oiling it, that's all. Here, I'll put it away."

Oltipa nodded once, forced a smile. The whip brought flashes of violent times, a burning bark house, her arms bound with rawhide thongs, her body tossed up behind the Modoc warrior as she watched the father of her child die. No. In this man's hands, the rawhide did good things. She must think of what was present, not past.

She picked up the whip, handed it to him. It was his work, and she had no right to keep him from it.

The smell of oil rubbed into leather with his fingers filled the air. She stirred up venison stew, added a precious onion he said "was the last one for sale in Shasta 'til spring. Guess nothing'll discourage people who can't see anything but gold," he continued, talking of white men's ways. He worked the leather, rubbed it across his thigh, looked up at her, then away. "Got some supper on, I see. I'll put this up."

Her back ached from bending over the andiron and lifting the heavy pot. David took it from her, said, "Careful now. Don't want to hurt that baby. Oh, almost forgot." He reached again into his bag. "It's a little painting of an eye like they do in France," he said. "Supposed to be your sweetheart." He coughed, pulled the small locket with a window that when opened showed an eye. "Lover's Eye, they call it. To remind you someone's thinking of you. Say, you look a little peaked. You all right?" He put the gift down quickly.

Oltipa winced and caught her breath. "Baby come," she said and watched as David Taylor turned the color of spring leaves.

Suzanne woke with a start. She'd been having a dream, not one with Bryce but where she was standing up in front of room full of strangers. She wore nothing but an old wash dress not long enough to cover her bare feet. People looked...expectant, as though she would perform some miraculous thing, and she could feel herself breathing fast, frightened, not being able to catch her breath. Then suddenly, she heard a raspy sound, as though she breathed through her teeth.

She sat up with a gasp, knocking the cane off the chair she had pulled beside the bed. She threw the covers back and, with her bare toes, patted around for the smooth walnut cane. Once found, she tapped it against the side of the bed as she shuffled her way to check on the boys. She breathed easier as her fingers felt Clayton's chest rise and fall in sleep. She gently reached for Sason's little back. He always liked to sleep on his stomach. She heard the intake and release of breath. It must have just been her own breathing in the dream, that sucking sound, that woke her. Or maybe Pig's dreaming. She listened for the dog's slobbery sounds from the corner of the cabin. She often left him out now, with the nights not so cold.

She tap-tapped her way to the table, bumped it, found the teapot. She would give anything for a cup of hot tea then, but she didn't want to wake the boys as she fussed with the pot on the warming oven. Her hands shook.

She heard—no, sensed—something out of the ordinary, but she

couldn't place it. "I'm just an old scaredy cat, aren't I, Pig?" she said, just to hear the sound of her own voice.

Back in bed, she lay awake, letting her heart calm. A dream, full of anticipation followed by fear all wrapped up in the previous afternoon.

She'd lost Clayton. He'd hidden from her—on purpose—and try as she might, she could not get him to come out of his secret place, wherever it was. Then he'd unlatched the door and slipped outside.

She could hear him giggling. "Come to Mommy, Clayton." She thumped with the cane, stumbled at the ironwork surrounding the grave of the former owner's wife. The metal felt cold and sharp with the little arrow designs marking the perimeter. Was Clayton dressed warm? Had he hurt himself? No, he giggled! She heard him scuffling near her. She grabbed for him but couldn't catch him. She was getting cold—he must be too. Sason was alone in the house. Why wasn't Clayton letting himself be caught? She headed for the house, counted, but she didn't reach it. She'd miscounted! She felt the cold air on her face, pulled her shawl around her, called again for the child, headed back to his giggle. She shivered, confused. *Focus. Think.* She sat down on the damp ground and wept. Only then had her son made his way to her, patting her back. "Mommy?" he said, and she grabbed at his thin little body and held him, making his shirt wet with tears of both relief and anger—at him and her own failure to keep him safe.

She carried him in on her hip, her other hand tapping with the cane. She sniffed the air for the smell of fire from her hearth. Yes, follow that! She prayed that she was walking in a straight line, and would find either the house or the fence and follow it. Then she'd bumped into a sugar pine, her nose bruised, she was sure, but she knew where she was then, and focused on the smell of the fire. Clayton's feet were cold, and she'd wrapped him in a quilt and held him close. Sason cried, needing her, and she wondered if she had what it took to raise one child let alone two.

Now she couldn't sleep for thinking of the bad dream, scared and exposed. Maybe she should ask Ruth to let Sarah come and stay with her. Sarah could tell her if the boys had slipped out or if Clayton had thrown cold mush under the table or stuffed his bowl still half full in the bed—which he'd done more than once. He was becoming a sneaky child, with no one to hold him accountable.

Sarah was kind and gentle with the boys and could help tend them—and give Suzanne straight answers. Suzanne would still make all the decisions.

She remembered expressing a similar thought out loud to Wesley near the Chinese New Year, about bringing someone in, no one specific. "Does that mean you're ready to surrender to the direction of another, my dear? I'm certain I know a candidate who would find that of interest." He'd touched her chin with his hand, with firmness. "Otherwise why ever would you want others pawing through your things? Now that would be a violation, I should think."

She didn't like the way he used her words back at her, or his presumption that she should surrender. She'd gone down the next day to Hong Kong, and when she picked up baked eggs, she also asked if there was a boy who might come to start the fires for her in the morning, maybe set soup on. Those were still her hardest tasks and the most worrisome. In February, Johnnie came. "Sent to serve lady," he said, bowing low.

She told him to make a grate of sorts around the fire opening, so Sason could not crawl too close, and put a latch high on the door, so Clayton couldn't undo it. Though she often forgot to latch it after he left. He bought food and prepared it so she had meals for the children. He took the laundry and brought it back.

Wesley had spoken as though through clenched teeth when he arrived, and Johnnie was already there one morning, fixing the fire, preparing rice.

"Having them around is risky, my dear. They'll steal from you, servants will." Had he spoken in front of Johnnie, as though the boy couldn't hear? "They learn your habits, where you keep your money."

"What do you suggest?" Suzanne asked.

"I could stop by each day and tend your fire. It would please me."

"And when you have to be gone, with your investments, what then? Doesn't that take you two weeks or more, you said?"

"Do what you've always done. Make do. Practice your independence."

"I am practicing my independence."

She remembered that Wesley said nothing for a time, then, "Don't blame me when things come up missing."

There'd been other pricklings of discomfort with Wesley. Little suggestions he'd made that came out threatening almost, as though if she did what she wished, she'd be unwise. She'd told him of her interest in photography and that she might set up a studio in the spring.

"My dear, you can't possibly have someone working *for* you. They'd rob you blind, the pun intended. Your best hope is to permit some loving man to treat you with the dignity and respect you so deserve. When you're ready, I know just who."

She knew what he wanted. And when he held her face in his warm hands and kissed her, she did think that surrendering to his care might be what she should do. Her boys would have a home, a life. They'd all be safe. It was selfish of her not to just accept.

Something held her back.

Maybe it was his reluctance to accept her invitation to meet Mazy or his always being unavailable on Sunday when she dressed the boys for church.

"It's probably my independent streak," she said out loud to the darkness. "Stubborn. If I squelch that, I'll wish I were dead. Just like back on the trail."

She heard scratching against the plank floor. She felt a gentle movement of cool air and assumed the dog approached, awakened by her talking. She reached her hand out into the darkness, moved it back and forth. She touched nothing. For a moment, she thought she heard the door creak, cool air again. She gripped the cane Seth had given her, swallowed. It was just the dream making her edgy, just the wind pushing through the cracks in her wall.

13

being kept

"I've been writing letters to the editor," Mazy told Ruth. "But he doesn't print them. I guess they don't want people to know that some of us think this Indian policy is appalling. You used to work for a newspaper, didn't you? Any suggestions for getting myself heard?"

Ruth shook her head. The two made their way through the spring-fed meadow, stubby grasses now spearing the March air. They carried buckets of grain out to Ruth's horses while Mazy checked her cows. "I never understood the politics," Ruth said. "It had to do with advertising. If you took out ads, they paid attention to your point of view."

"Maybe I'll do that, then," Mazy said. "Take out an ad. For the orphans. Then I want to find an old, abandoned shed, so they can get in out of the weather. Find real homes for them instead of people just taking their free labor." She pulled at a strand of oat grass and twirled it in her fingers. "They huddle in the back corners of buildings, sleeping next to garbage. It's dreadful."

"What about the elders?"

"They help as they can."

"No, I mean using the building. For an orphanage."

Mazy looked at her, surprise on her face. "That's a great idea. And maybe we could raise money to hire people to care for them. In Wisconsin we fixed pretty baskets with food and sold them. All it cost a woman was her time and a little bread."

"And spending an hour with someone you might dislike," Ruth said.

"Maybe some of the women who work with Lura could help," Mazy said. "Well, they don't actually work with her. They need help too. I mean—"

"I know who you mean," Ruth said. Sometimes Mazy's charity-talk could get on her nerves. She shook the grain, held the bucket up so the horses could see it. "They might not be attracted to the drop in pay, though, even if the working conditions were better. That hat Esty wore visiting last week must have cost a fortune, all feathery and wide."

"She made that hat," Mazy said. "Needed seven pins to hold it, she said. Esty has other talents. She just doesn't use them."

"You write with passion. Pen an ad about that—the orphans."

"I should." The ground felt damp and soft as they walked, and the earth smelled of spring. "Mother says I keep busy so I won't have to feel the old hurt. She says my 'causes' get in the way of true service."

"What do you think?" Ruth asked.

Mazy shrugged her shoulders. "I don't know. My mother has lots of advice. I'd forgotten how much. Not that I'm complaining, you understand."

"You could move out," Ruth said.

"I could." They stood watching as the horses made their way from across the creek running full with spring runoff. "Have you heard from Seth? I'm sure he's back, but I haven't seen a thread of him."

"Suzanne has, but she didn't say what he was up to."

"The pickings in the Sacramento gambling houses must have been pretty good to keep him south so long." Mazy snorted. "He's probably out at the amphitheater at the bull and bear fights."

"Thought you were wanting a little distance from him," Ruth said.

"He needs to make some changes before anything could really go on between us. I was just curious, is all. Mother says there's no sense trying to change a man. I've just got to accept him as he is. She thinks I'm looking for perfection. But my everyday life looks pretty boring to a man like Seth. Looking after orphans, milking cows, and planning gardens are tame things to do. I don't see him finding satisfaction in those kinds of things. I'm glad he looks in on Suzanne."

Ruth turned, wondering if Mazy was really that generous—or that unaware of her own longings. Ruth guessed Mazy really meant it. "She's being so independent," Ruth said.

Mazy laughed. "That's funny coming from you."

"All of us like to walk our own way," Ruth said. "I've gotten into trouble being strong-willed, even back in the States, but I wonder if the others were independent before. Tipton didn't seem the type, but she's come around." They walked in silence for a time. "Maybe Seth got an inkling of *my* plan, and he's staying away from all of us *but* Suzanne." Ruth laughed uncomfortably.

"Your plan?"

"To have Jason and Ned spend more time with him. And to get Sarah and Jessie into good homes. With good people. Competition for your orphans, Mazy." She laughed again but without humor. Koda and Jumper made their way running and bucking toward them. "I thought Jason could be a Seth helper. And that maybe Sarah could stay with Suzanne. Does your mother need help at the bakery? Ned would be good."

"Why deprive yourself of their company and of being that important person in their lives?"

A gust of wind came up, and Ruth turned her head against it, her long braid catching at her neck. "Wish those kids would tell me what they did with my hat," she said.

"That black felt one you like?"

"I don't really like it. It just fits good and it keeps the sun and rain out. And it isn't confining like bonnet strings. When I asked the children about it, Jessie just sassed, 'Your favorite? We'd never touch that.' The little scamp. I told her I was glad to see her learning about respect for other people's things, but none of them claimed to have touched it. I don't believe them one whit."

The horses munched on grain, and Ruth led them back toward the corrals, skirting the edge of the meadow. Mazy's cows grazed in the brush of standing grass, the last skiffs of snow piling in dips of land while the Wilson mules dotted the landscape in the distance.

"The oat hay here is abundant," Mazy said. "I've heard no one planted wheat. They were all looking for gold. We were fortunate.

"Horses had good pasture. I couldn't have picked a better place to winter, if I'd tried."

"You made a good choice," Mazy said.

"The house is small, though. You'll understand tonight when we bed down. And the privy needed lots of work. Cobwebs everywhere, and the stench. We threw some ashes down before Jessie would even go close. That child...I thought about talking Lura into another occupation, see if she'd be willing to take the children on if I provided the house. There'll be a school before long. They could all attend if they lived in town."

"If *they* lived in town, not *you?* It's hardly an hour's ride from here, and the walk in before school would do them good."

Ruth sighed. "Truth is, the boys hate doing anything for me, Mazy. I've given up trying to get them to clean the stalls. I just do it myself while they lounge around and play checkers, argue with each other, and the girls. I can't get them to work on the fence or fix the split rails. Wasn't bad during the winter, but with spring coming on, we have big jobs to do. And they misplace things, lose things. Why, I gave Ned a brand-new harmonica for Christmas, and do you think he took care of it? He couldn't even find it after we had our Christmas dinner with you all. It'll be a misery to get them to help with the garden, keep it up. I'd do better just by myself."

"I could do the garden. I'd like that. And I'd like to leave a section for wheat. We need the grain, and in all my wanderings looking for places to name as home, I've seen hardly any tilled fields."

Ruth nodded agreement, then continued. "Mariah can't get the boys to do much either, though she leads them in some studies. And she, at least, does what I ask her to do. She's a good little cook." They walked in silence, letting the horses follow, heads heavy, behind them. Ruth heard the swish of their legs pushing through the new grass. "And then I'm still hoping to hear from Matt about my horses. So I can head north. If he and Joe Pepin found a good place, I'll join them. If not, I can bring the stock back. Either way, the kids'll need someone else to keep them."

"You're not worried about that husband of yours anymore? What was his name?"

"Zane. Oh, he's out there somewhere. Sometimes I think I can feel him watching me, but I know that's just me, hanging on to how I used to feel. I'm as safe here as anywhere. That time on the trail helped me understand that. I can't be looking over my shoulder all the time, letting what happened before rule my thinking now. Isn't that what you said? Besides, why would he look for me in a California mining town?" They walked quietly, then Ruth said, "I wish I hadn't left that sign back on the trail, though. I was feeling my oats that day. Guess I thought that being surrounded by all of you would keep me safe from even the likes of him. That little spurt of bluff may cost me."

"We still surround you. You told him you went north, didn't you?"

"He may not believe me."

"I'll bet he's found a new life. Moved on, like you have, and should, with the children. You could be turning a little sliver of trouble from those kids into blood poisoning. Why not just say you're going to raise this family and stop wavering?"

"Look who's advising against wavering. You, without even your own home yet."

Mazy winced. "It's not easy setting down roots."

"Tell me."

"I don't think God wants us carrying around old miseries like that."

"Now you're talking to yourself," Ruth said.

"I'd let myself experience the joys of being a parent—if I had the chance," Mazy said.

"Hey. I didn't mean to hit a tender spot there," Ruth said, reaching to touch Mazy's arm. "Your losing that new life..."

"I would have had a baby by now," Mazy whispered. She cleared her throat, lifted her apron to dab at her eyes. "So now I have the orphans to worry over. And everyone else's problems." She forced a smile. "Maybe you ought to tell the children the truth, Ruth. Maybe that would bring your family together."

"And have the boys and Sarah know they're orphans but their little cousin isn't? Besides, Jessie wouldn't believe it anyway. She might really be unreasonable if she knew she *was* my daughter. Or that she had a brother I failed to protect."

"You did the best you could, I'm sure of it. And you sent her away for a good reason."

"You're hopelessly good," Ruth said. "But I'm not. And sometimes, when I'm honest to my core, I wonder if I wasn't the one who did the real damage. I can still see my boy's little face all pinched in terror, screaming, looking up at me like I was the face of death, his own mother! I almost threw him into that bed, Mazy, to get him out of my hands. Because I wasn't sure I wouldn't...do him harm. And I've been so frustrated with Jessie I've almost struck her." She shook her head, let loose her grip on the bucket. "Jessie might just see through me into what I am."

They walked in silence for a while and put the horses into the barn. "Won't be long and there'll be another bunch of pack trains coming that way," Ruth finally said. "Is Seth still going to take you south, to meet with that solicitor?"

"Someone will. When I'm ready. Right now I want to get the calves born, start milking and selling it. There's a great market for milk. A dollar a glass, in most places. I can support myself and start doing what Jeremy thought we would. Sow some wheat. Farm. Make a living. Hopefully have some left to help those orphans and those...unmentionable women."

In the manger, Ruth dug a hole in the loose hay. Mazy poured the rest of the grain from a bucket into it, for the horses to eat later. As was her habit, Ruth swished the grain around a bit, pushing it deeper. When she did, she felt something cool.

She thought maybe it was a forgotten egg, now frozen. She pawed around, pulled it out. "Well, look at this, she said, and swallowed. "It's Ned's harmonica. Inside my felt hat."

Zane made his trips into the surrounding gulches each month, meeting up with Greasy as they'd planned. A tedious but necessary task. Greasy said Zane "rode his trap line" as though Zane gathered up beaver pelts instead of gold, as though Greasy spent time with rodents instead of prodding vagrant boys to dig at distant claims.

Each little claim had a wormlike man Greasy had picked to make the vagrants build diversion ditches or assemble troughs known as Long Toms for splashing water through to filter out the gold.

Zane might have found the landscape beautiful, once in his life. Fast-moving streams spilled out of brushy ravines with wind-felled trees and wildflowers, now in spring, standing as quiet sentries. Now he saw it as mere resource, a richness ripe for exploiting. He wondered if the Indians mourned the loss of their fishing streams, or plotted how to regain their hunting grounds overrun by miners, trees chopped down for fuel, game shot or scattered. They probably didn't even notice.

He unloaded rice and flour from his pack animals at each stop, picked up ore, and left. Zane didn't like paying for food for boys just lying around in shacks, keeping warm all winter. It allowed them too much time to cook up schemes to leave come spring. But there was no other way.

"They worked good until the heavy snows," Greasy reminded him. "If we feed 'em through the snow months, they'll be ready to go first sign of a thaw. Easier than finding new ones I got to break in again. These are like little scared rabbits when I take their leg chains off. They don't even try to run. You just keep bringing in stuff for panning, sluicing, hydraulicking, dredging, and these here rodents'll work their backs off soon as they're able," Greasy assured him. "Spring comes, yessiree, we'll make up for lost time then."

Zane grunted and nodded toward a black, scruffy-looking dog. "No sense to feed that ratlike thing." The dog growled and snapped at Zane when he walked toward it, dark eyes staring out through tight curls. Zane kicked at it and missed.

"He's just a little old dog. Came around a month or so ago. Entertainment for us. He don't eat much."

With quickness, Zane picked the animal up, saw a wound, and felt the grease someone must have put there for healing. "Don't go wasting good lard on such as this," he said, dropping it and wiping his hands on one of the boys' thin shirts. "Get rid of the mutt," he said. "He's got a collar on. Someone might come looking."

The off weeks, when he came back to Shasta, Zane watched and planned. Suzanne and Ruth had things in common. Both did things in their own way. But Ruth had eventually broken, let herself be resculpted by Zane. How long had that taken? A year? Nearly two, before she realized his thinking for her was best, before her high spirit had been split the way that whip of hers had once split fat oak leaves. But then she'd turned on him, drawn strength from somewhere else, and sat before him on that witness stand in accusation. The brother must have goaded her. And Suzanne said he was gone, had died on the trail. What he deserved, Zane decided. What Ruth deserved too.

Suzanne, the softer and more beautiful of the two, offered special intrigue. Despite his objection, she'd invited the Chinese boy inside. Zane had removed an item or two from her home when he visited Suzanne and the boy wasn't there. A pair of earrings she was attached to, then a necklace with a chain of interlocking silver squares. "Why don't you wear the necklace with the amethyst?" he asked her then, holding it in his hand as he spoke. "Shall I look for it for you?" And when she nodded, he would paw and make noises as if he were searching, then cluck his tongue. "I'm so sorry, Suzanne. I can't seem to locate it. I fear it's that boy again, taking advantage of you. Probably sold it for extra money." He'd slipped the gold chain and jewel into his vest pocket, thinking to have a watch fob made of it.

Then the girl came. The child was Ruth's niece, had to be. Older than in the photograph at Ruth's, but not old enough to remember him. He intimidated her with his looks, and she stayed off in the corner when he came. But she watched him. And it meant someone was almost always at the house now. Even when Suzanne put the ill-tempered dog outside. What he wanted was for Suzanne to see that she needed him. He wanted for her to finally succumb, rely only on him.

He wished he could see Ruth come to visit her. Suzanne spoke of all the women as though they were…sisters. And looking through his telescoping glass, he'd seen one or two come by. An older woman and a tall one with auburn hair. He smiled to himself, imagining Suzanne and Ruth in the same room—women on their way to knowing who truly controlled their lives. Wouldn't that be lovely? To have both of them in the same place at once? He stopped midway in pulling on his cream-colored vest: Perhaps he could do something to bring Ruth to Suzanne, and he would join them. Hold them there. He imagined the fear in Ruth's eyes, the confusion on Suzanne's face. He wiped his mouth with the back of his hand, a new plan forming.

Elizabeth liked her life. The smells of baking, rising early to send the scent of yeast and flour drifting across the town. The previous baker had quit when the rains came and had headed back to Piety Hill or Mule Town or some other strange little gulch defined by a stream, so she had latched onto the employment and the little room that came with it, not much larger than the wagon. But it had a window covered with white lace, a chamber pot, a cot wide enough for two, and a little table and two chairs. And it had a view—of the rock wall behind the bakery that sported green and tiny white flowers. Elizabeth caught water from the spring for washing and put the leftover in the bucket that housed the thriving maple tree she'd set in the corner. The plant wasn't very tall, but it had buds on it. That was a sure sign of spring.

Mazy would soon be spending days and nights at Ruth's, what with the calving. That would make life better. Not that she didn't like having her daughter share her bed, but she liked to spread out, and this little hamper of a room didn't allow much of that. Mazy'd be needing to milk twice a day. Elizabeth hadn't tasted milk since...way back on the trail. For the new year, Seth brought back a round of butter he said came by ship all the way from Vancouver. It had been iced and tasted sweet as summer. But it was soon gone. Her mouth watered, thinking of fresh dairy—though she hadn't missed the work of churning.

"You ought to build yourself a little place next to Ruth's. That way you'll have your privacy but be close to your cows," Elizabeth suggested to Mazy.

The girl leaned over the seedlings she'd planted inside a box fashioned out of wood crates. They lined the perimeter of the tiny room, making the air smell of good earth. "Maybe I will," she told her mother.

Elizabeth handed her daughter a cup of chrysanthemum tea she'd picked up in a Hong Kong store. Chinatown was a great place for shopping. She especially liked the candies. "You afraid settling in will say Jeremy was right about us leaving Wisconsin?"

"Maybe I'm not ready to say my life is better because we left, not with him dying. And not telling me his whole truth."

"Seems a waste to keep yourself from sitting on God's footstool. You said the ground around here tasted like home. Are you punishing Jeremy, or yourself?" The girl sipped and sat, lost inside herself. "Maybe you should hurry and talk to that lawyer fellow. Maybe that should be your goal come spring. Clear the air for good so you can begin again."

"Maybe."

That girl was more maybe than not. She could put off deciding longer than anyone she knew. Why, Elizabeth had found this room and a purpose in less than a week. Mazy was still looking for the perfect place. Oh, she was a busy woman, her daughter. She'd been working on the town fathers and the church elders to consider ways to help those orphans. She hadn't yet brought up her plan to get the women of "negotiable affections" to feed and tend the wee ones. "I don't think they're ready to know my entire plan," Mazy'd laughed.

So in nearly six months of their being in the Whoa Navigation city Mazy had navigated greatly around the area, but all she seemed to say was "whoa!" To Seth, too.

Seth was a good man. But Mazy had to find that out for herself—and a home first, Elizabeth guessed. 'Course, avoiding that journey south with Sister Esther and her girls *had* decided two things for Mazy: no alone time with Seth and no unsettling news about Mazy's former husband's life. Maybe her daughter did know that she made decisions by choosing not to.

Elizabeth dressed herself by candlelight that March morning. She splashed cold water on her face, dabbed it dry with a linen, tied her shoes on, and thought to herself that it would be nice if someone cobbled a shoe that fit each foot separate, wasn't interchangeable. She'd soaked the callus on her right foot and scraped it with a knife, but it always came back. Soon as she could get a lemon, she planned to soak some of her fish-bone buttons in it. The lemon would melt the buttons to a salve she'd heard would work to rid the callus of its hold. She'd given the last lemons for Sarah's little Angel Pie they gave to Ruth for Christmas.

Breakfast came after she heated up the bakery ovens, well before daylight. Then she kneaded and rolled dough, patted it, watched it rise. She moved the big pans of pretzels and biscuits so they had just the right heat, just the right amount to brown. She could hardly wait until they had milk again. And fresh butter. How that would change the flavor of her strudels.

She did love the joy that flour could give, first in the making, then the eating, watching others smile and be filled. Mr. Kossuth paid dearly for the flour, too, what with so few fields planted last year. Mining distracted even farmers.

Once a day, Elizabeth walked to the post office even though she never expected to read a single letter addressed to her. She liked to hear the names called out, of people waiting for news from somewhere else. That was another nice thing: Her whole family was right here. It was enriching just to howdy people, lend a listening ear. Pack trains arrived two, three, even four times a day now with the snows melting in the mountains and runoff pouring down the streets, turning them to mud. Stages rumbled in, got stuck, got pushed free, and rolled on south again. There was talk of a new stage road north into Oregon Territory. This town was growing. And the roar and rumble of tenpin games and gambling houses going day and night never bothered her. She found the noises soothing as a waterfall, lulling her to sleep.

If she needed quiet, she'd spend an evening with her daughter, reading, or taking a bath, while Mazy worked on the quilt pieces she'd gathered up so far.

"This mining town may be a crazy place to call home, but I love it," she told Mazy as her daughter poured hot water into the copper tub, over her shoulders. The smell of rose hips floating in the water came to Elizabeth's nose. "A dozen different languages, people rushing about. Makes me remember when your father lived and he brought folks home. Just like your Jeremy. But I didn't do so good a job letting that husband of yours in," Elizabeth said.

"Jeremy said things weren't always as they seemed."

"True enough from him, having a wife and child somewhere else. Hand me that towel, will you?" Mazy did, then sat down on one of the two grandmother chairs they'd managed to bring with them. Her skirts fluffed out around her like a mushroom.

"These are good." Mazy held up a popover her mother had saved back for her. "Thank you."

"Be even better with your home grown grain, come fall. Still, a mother likes to think she can see a wolf showing up at the door, looking like a lamb. And I didn't."

"You let me make my own choices. That's what a good mother does, even if sometimes the results aren't what she wants."

Elizabeth grunted. "Always were a forgiving child."

Nehemiah Kossuth was an accommodating man. The rooms he provided for Tipton and her mother were larger than Suzanne's whole house. A smaller room off to the side held a copper tub, their lingerie, and the irons that pressed them. The main room was both a bedroom and a sitting room, furnished fully. When she'd first seen it, Tipton took short, quick breaths until her arm tingled. It was like a fairy tale, this room, this hotel, this encountering of Nehemiah. Even after three months here, Tipton wasn't at all sure how she felt about accepting it. Or what attachments came with the receiving.

Her mother had no doubts. "He thinks you're a princess, come right out of a book. Oh, we are so fortunate to have found him, so lucky to have fallen into that window." Her mother threw herself onto the bed, her arms spread across the gold-and-rose-colored brocade cover. Adora stuffed a lace-covered pillow with ruffles beneath her head.

"He is a nice man, mother, but I don't know—"

"Of course you don't. You're young and inexperienced. You just trust your mother. Let him soothe his conscience." She sat up, rubbed her arm as she talked.

"Your elbow is fine."

"Well, I know that. But truth be known, it does ache more than it did before I fell. It does!"

"It needs exercise, like ironing."

"We don't have to do that now."

"I only agreed to stay here because it's better for you."

"Nothing bad has happened since he let us have this room. He isn't making any demands, is he?"

Tipton shook her head.

Adora went on, "I didn't think so. It's just a gift. Hospitality. You could quit that laundering—if you just would."

"People count on me. And Tyrellie always said that was the best thing to have in a day, knowing it mattered whether you did what you said you would or not. Just staying here, in this fine room all day, it's like I'm being—"

"Tyrell was a fine man," Adora said. She stood, untied her bonnet, hung it on the high, turned walnut post at the foot of the bed. "But he is gone. He is never coming back."

Tipton's eyes watered. "I don't like this, Mother. I don't like this mixture of feelings, of liking Nehemiah's dinners and visits and now providing a room. I feel obligated. I don't like working so hard my knuckles bleed, but I'm not fond of charity, either. You wouldn't let us accept help from Elizabeth and Mazy."

"This is different. You're helping that poor man with his grieving."

"If only Charles hadn't taken our money and left us. It's all so unfair."

Adora motioned Tipton over to sit beside her on the huge bed. "You can help each other, you and Nehemiah. Let him keep looking after you. You might find yourself enjoying his company. Keep scrubbing if you must. Set aside the money for a room and offer it, though I doubt he'll take it."

"We could still sell the mules. Use the money for the room."

"Those mules are the last of our legacy, our money in the bank. Don't want to use that up foolishly. Besides, Nehemiah looks to me like he's got enough to give away. Isn't that what Elizabeth said hospitality was?—having gratitude enough it spilled over and you could give it away. Nehemiah Kossuth is grateful to have met you. And you're letting him be kind, so you're being generous too."

"I thought Elizabeth said hospitality grew out of being grateful for your home," Tipton said. "Your place of belonging. This doesn't feel like my place. I don't feel like I'm giving anything to Nehemiah."

"Because you won't spend a nickel to put something here that's yours." Adora patted her daughter's shoulders then stood and swirled around the room. "You got to spend a little to feel at home."

A boundary existed, Mazy thought, between Hong Kong and the rest of town, and there were unwritten rules about when it could be crossed. At the Chinese New Year, the Asians gave every woman a good-luck gift, a "Sacred Lily of China," sometimes an embroidered scarf or two. The men got cigars, and everyone laughed and clapped at the parade with blasts and pops of firecrackers and gaudy paper dragons winding their way through town to the sounds of cymbals and drums. Even children ate the nuts and ginger and candy and the doughnuts without holes that were fried in special oils that made them the color of pale carrots. Then the next day, those same spectators and recipients of lilies talked of how troublesome the Chinese were and that Governor Keating was right about having them shipped back to China and making them pay a special tax on any gold they mined.

A woman's life had strange borders here, too. She was presumed a lady but had to work as hard as men. She thought of Tipton's red knuckles. Most of the miners treated the widows like fragile flowers, tipping their hats at them, stepping aside when they met them. Then they turned around and...well, used some women like property, as though they weren't someone's daughters. They seemed to accept Ruth with her pants and her hat. And they acted hopeful they'd have cow's milk soon, assuming Mazy'd be successful at building her herd.

The rules weren't laid out nice and clear, here. That's what seemed confusing. They were each responsible for their own boundaries and overcoming their own barriers, by themselves. While Adora thought it grand, Tipton hadn't blossomed as Adora thought she would under Nehemiah's attention. Suzanne's friend, Esty, seemed a pleasant sort, but Adora was sure she did more than bank. She had told Suzanne, "You might be risking a tarnish on your stellar reputation by associating with the likes of her."

Lura, however, said Esty and her friends kept to themselves in the casinos. Some of them, like Lura, had just found ways to support themselves as independent women. "Then there're others who do what they will."

"How sad they've chosen to let themselves be used that way," Mazy said.

"People got to do what they got to, to survive," Lura defended. "Don't be thinking you're better than them, Mazy, just 'cause you got a man's money in another way."

Her words irritated Mazy, made her think about being a "kept woman." Was that what she was in part? Allowing Jeremy's money—money that might not even be his—to define her life now? What was that definition of a virgin Ruth had told them? "A woman not dependent on anyone and complete unto herself." Perhaps it wasn't possible for a woman not to lean on someone.

She wore a scarf around her neck and pulled it tight beneath her chin. The wind was cold, though the sun beat warm against her face. She kneeled and dug with her spade, working up the soil for the herb section. She wasn't exactly doing good things with what Jeremy'd left her; but she would. Didn't that make her different than those others? She was still mourning, that was all. She'd keep walking through that landscape, and then she'd recognize the perfect place to call home.

Mazy pushed against her knees to stand. Come spring, she'd have the milk to sell. Come spring, she'd plant the seedlings in this patch of ground back by the water hole, fence it from the pigs that wandered here and there. What she and her mother didn't use, she planned to harvest along with other people's summer overflow. They'd serve up big stews at the church. One good meal a day for the orphans. She'd gotten the elders to agree to that at least. She wasn't sure how she'd get the children fed next winter.

She could recognize six or seven of the children now who came out at dawn to put their brown hands inside the white linen of the breadbaskets. People said that a growing town like Shasta served its children well, even planned a school. Yet here were dozens, maybe hundreds of children made orphans by those same "good people" killing off their parents—encouraged to do so by the editorials and letters from the legislature. Grabbed and thrown into slavery in the gold streams, in people's houses, working off their indenture as though California carried with it a bit of old England or the South.

She'd written about that in her ad, but the *Courier* editor Sam Dosh had toned it down. She guessed she'd crossed some boundary of "properness." Well, so be it. A woman was allowed that kind of fence crossing, here in California.

Suzanne could be pushed into needing him. Zane could create a crisis, a little chaos that would make her come to him and ask for his assistance. Something about Clayton, perhaps. He might come up missing, and Suzanne would ask for Zane's help. Or perhaps the baby could be injured, not badly, but enough for her to see how damaging it might have been if he hadn't been there to intervene. He'd insist she move into a home large enough for him and her children so he could keep her safe, manage her day, provide daily what she needed.

And Ruth would come to visit.

Yes, he must create a crisis, be there to pull her from it. He'd think of something. It was like a new trap line being readied.

Mazy and Ruth bent to their tasks, cleaning the stalls in the barn. The milk cows, curious, found them in the old building, the June light coming through the roof slats to catch the confetti of dust. Both of Mazy's cows had had calves. One heifer and a sturdy bull calf, both with reddish spots and deep, brown eyes. On spindly legs they'd stood, their mothers licking them to life.

Mazy'd stayed on at Ruth's after the March arrivals, waiting three days before beginning to milk the cows, all of them then celebrating with a drink of "white gold." That was what Seth called it when Mazy lifted the tin of milk cooling in a nearby stream. Foam fuzzed at their lips. They talked of fresh, sweet-tasting butter. But something in Seth's eyes said he'd prefer another subject.

"Now that you have your herd going," he'd said to her, "I'll never get you to myself."

"You have plenty to occupy your time," Mazy said. "Always have, as far as I can see. Didn't even hear from you since December 'til now."

"Giving you room in this house of cards you're building. Poor use of words," he said and grinned. "What would it take?" he asked her, taking the tin from her hand, wiping the foam from her lip with his finger. He let his hand linger, wiping at her lower lip when she knew it held no drops of milk.

His touch had startled her, warmed her more than she cared to admit. "To what?"

"Allow me to officially come courting."

She bent to place the larger milk container back in the stream, put the cover on the tin she was taking back to Ruth's house. "We're so different, Seth. You like...excitement. I like...calm. You like fixing things. I like to keep them from being broken."

"There's joy in taking a little risk," he reminded her. "Look at Suzanne. She's lit up like a new candle, being on her own. Who would have thought in her blindness she'd be the one to see that?"

"Last time I was there, I saw a house riddled with danger," Mazy said. "She needs routine more than anyone, and she's got three kids running around, four with the Chinese boy, so nothing is ever back in the same place. I'm not sure what Ruth was thinking of, sending Sarah off to Suzanne. She isn't sorting the dirty clothes from the clean any better than Suzanne did. Johnnie must be doing all the washing and cooking, but it still isn't safe."

"Tipton does some of the laundry. Suzanne told me."

"Well, then you've been there, seen it. Food scattered all over the floor like a fete for roaches. I worry about her, I do. Her independence just may cost her more than she wants to pay."

Seth smiled. "Led you right into a change of subjects, didn't I? I'm not very good at this." He stepped in front of her. "Mazy. Let me be a part of what opens up your life. Give us a serious chance. There's something special between us, I know that." He pulled her to him.

"Oh, Seth, I—"

She still held the milk tin between them, but she let herself sink into the strength of him, felt herself melting like warm butter, her heart like the thumping of a fast churn.

"Maybe," she whispered into the leather of his vest. His finger touched her lip as she stepped back. "What'll it look like, your courting me? Different than what you've been doing?"

"We'll talk of us. Of what we hope for with each other, not just about the cows." With his thumbs, he pushed wispy strands beneath her kerchief.

"So that means I can talk about my hope you'll find a more...respectable occupation?"

Seth smiled "Not exactly the hope I was hoping for."

He bent as though to kiss her, but she raised her hand to halt him before he crossed a boundary she wasn't sure she wanted crossed.

14

clouded eyes

Zane smelled smoke through the windows open to the June night. He heard the rip and crackle of the flames he couldn't place at first. Then someone in the big room he shared shouted, "Fire! Next door!" Despite the confusion, Zane still grabbed for his telescoping glass.

He slid it into his saddlebags pouched with gold dust as the first sound of the fire alarm clanged the town awake. He took the rickety back steps two at a time, pushing off smaller men from the St. Charles making their way bootless to the water wagons. The whole street blazed. Zane headed for the livery where hay stored in the back already burned. Horses reared, screamed, eyes wild with fright. He grabbed a rope, and in the guise of helping pull horses out of the building, yanked at the nearest bay, led him out, then tied the gelding to an oak. Raced back in for a saddle.

He could hear shouts and cries, a fire wagon clanging. The whole town flamed. The St. Charles Hotel, Washington's Mercantile, the bookstores, the silver shop, Kossuth's. From roof to roof the fire moved like squirrels, carrying the flame to the residential area. It was light as day, black smoke rising high into a dark sky. He yanked the bridle onto his horse, threw the saddle, tightened the cinch. He swung up, then kicked the animal. Chaos, that was what he called this. A fortune could be made in chaos, if a man kept his head. He pulled up the horse. Yes, if a man kept his head! This was it, what he'd been waiting for!

Suzanne woke with a start at the sounds. Pig, scratching? One of the children up early? "Sarah? Is that you?"

The girl moaned, still inside sleep. It wasn't the boys. She heard their sleeping noises. The branches of the huge pines outside, brushing against the shake roof, that was what it was. She calmed herself. She'd ask Johnnie to chop off the limbs. Surely he was large enough to do that. She might ask Wesley. No, he'd think she was relenting, giving in to his constant conversation about her need for him. Bryce had done many things for her, but he'd never made her feel as though she couldn't do them herself. Something about what he did for her felt temporary, as though in time she'd learn the new routines and eventually take over again. But Wesley's tending cloyed, like the heavy scent of flowers at a funeral.

She'd ask the boy. Or maybe Seth. His assistance didn't come with hidden obligations either. He was a friend. Perhaps she'd get Seth to sweep the needles from the roof, at least. Squirrels, was that what the sound was? The little things racing from branch to roof and back. Did Shasta have squirrels? No one had ever said. Raccoons. Maybe that. She should get up and serenade them with her troubadour's harp, sing a tune. That would drive them away.

She heard a sound like someone crunching nut meats. *Squirrels. It must be.* She smiled, felt herself snatch at a moment more of sleep.

Mazy and Seth had sparred weekly, for a time. They'd argued about where Mazy might live and about the wisdom of Seth's new plan to invest in a lumber mill or build a warehouse near the river. "Still speculative," Mazy said.

"You think only dairying is stable," Seth answered. He thought she put too much time and energy into her "feeding and reforming" activities, and she thought he didn't care enough for human causes. Now he talked of going out to meet the first wagon trains in a month or two, taking Jason with him. "Maybe we both need time to think," he told her. His visits had been fewer since then.

In the June warmth, the cows pushed at Mazy with their noses, tipping their big horns so Mazy could scratch at their heads. She patted Mavis, the sun warming the heifer's fat side. The smell of cows and earth punched the air while red-winged blackbirds dipped then disappeared into grasses close to the river. The last of the orange poppies faded on the side hills.

"I've no grain for you," Mazy said. "Soon as I want to touch your babies, you turn on me." She wore gloves with no fingers that circled the fork handle. "At least the winter here was nothing like Wisconsin," Mazy told Ruth. "The cows handled the cold well."

"Cold? Are you cold?"

"No. I swear, Ruth, sometimes I think you can't hear. I'm always repeating half of what I say. I was remembering the winter and thinking that the snow is less wet here, not as cold." She pushed Mavis out of the way, went back to her shoveling. "Go," she said when Mavis stepped closer. She watched the cow amble toward its calf, barely visible in the leggy grass.

In the distance, Mazy watched Ruth's horses, their heads down as they ripped at grass. She heard the boys laugh near the swing they'd hung in a tree and saw a stray cat make its way across the muddy paddock, stepping close to the new calf's nose. Not intimidated by the calf's larger size, the cat stood its ground when Bumper startled backward. Mazy smiled. She liked this place. Liked it a lot.

"I'm an easily kept woman," Mazy said. "Fresh air, cows, and open space is enough to make me feel wealthy, setting my feet to firm. Even being around people is growing on me."

"I think you ought to take this place, Mazy," Ruth said.

"I thought you liked it here." Mazy braced the fork handle on her chest, retied the scarf at the back of her neck. "Besides, I'm still looking for a place closer to Shasta. This is a good four miles out. Traveling back and forth with the milk, it gets hard on the oxen and on me, too. And don't tell her, but I miss my mother."

"Nothing of mine fills the cupboards here, not really," Ruth said. "I could leave."

"But you'd take the children with you."

"Ah yes, the children," Ruth said.

When she woke again, Suzanne dressed, then fed Sason. Johnnie hadn't arrived yet, and the two other children slept, so she felt for the cast iron pot, swung it back on the andiron and into the hearth. Stew kept bubbling there. The pan for tea warmed at the stove. She patted for the stick Sarah left for her each night before she went to bed. "That way if I want a cup of tea in the night, I can poke the fire and get the pot hot." She did that now and lifted the kettle with her apron, carefully dipping her finger into the cup set on the table as she poured so she wouldn't overfill it. She dropped the peppermint leaves into the mug, put her hands over it to feel the steaming heat. She could do this, on her own! Waiting for it to steep, she counted steps toward the bedroom, picked Sason back up, and was burping him on her shoulder when Pig started his barking.

"What is it, Pig?" It was his warning bark. She sniffed the air. Had she stuck the stick back in the right place? Did something burn?

"Pig?" He barked in his biting tone that grated on her ears and forced her to pay attention. "What is it!" She set Sason near the bed, hung on to the side rail, then turned square. Pig pulled on her arm now, his teeth sharp. "Ouch! That hurts." The dog barked again, tugged at her until she moved toward the door.

She heard the clang of a fire wagon in the distance then, not in the residential district. The sound moved away from her. She could neither hear nor smell anything wrong. What did that dog want? She heard a scratching sound. No. Crackling like dried leaves.

Suddenly, she felt a rush of air. *What was it?* Then she knew. Her heart pounded in her chest.

"Sarah! Clayton! Get up! Get up! Fire! Fire!"

She tried to localize the smell, the sounds. Was it at the back of the cabin, the side? She stumbled toward the bed where the children slept, shook Sarah, pulled on the girl's quilt. Sarah started to cry. She coughed.

"Get up! Don't cry. I'm not mad at you. Can you smell the smoke? Get Clayton. Hurry!" Pig barked, pulled at her arm again. "I've got to find Sason!"

Suzanne swirled around. Grabbed for her cane, felt herself sick with the taste of smoke. Where was she in the room? She'd moved too fast, not turned square. Where was the door? Where was the smoke coming from? Where was Clayton? "Pig! Find Sason. Sarah!" She was just a child herself!

"Clayton," Sarah wailed now. "Fire!"

"Sarah! Come here!" She felt the girl's hand. "Take me to him, lead me, quick!" Pig pushed at them. She reached for Sason, snatched him into her arms before thrusting him at Sarah. "Go! Follow Pig. Is there fire between us and the door?"

"No," Sarah cried.

"No time for tears. Go to the door. Now!"

She was coughing now; they were all coughing. She scratched at the bed with her hands, her arms, pulled on the quilt. It resisted, the boy must have been there. She could hear coughing. The smoke was heavy, and above her she heard crackling. Her throat burned. She felt heat. "Clayton! Come to Mommy." She made one final grab for the child, prayed it was him on the quilt.

Pig barked, standing by the bed, she thought. He should have taken the other child out! She heard her son cry. At last, she held him, felt the flames singe her hand as she rolled him in the quilt. The dog grabbed at her arm then, yanked with his teeth. She followed him, her eyes stinging, her throat tight. She felt the weight of the blanket dragging as she held her son and stumbled where Pig pulled her toward a coolness she hoped was an open door.

She heard a breaking, splintering sound, like timbers crashing in at the back of the house. "Sarah? Where are you?"

"I'm here, my dear," she heard Wesley's voice say, then. "Let me take the boy."

Ruth wondered if her mother had agonized when she'd sent her away.

Her mother wouldn't have described it as sending Ruth off, never saw herself as a mother who abandoned her daughter. She'd have said it was to keep Ruth safe, words Ruth used about Jessie, too.

The fever took so many that year. 1832. Ruth's mother pleaded with her father to send both her and Jed farther north, but Papa held firm. Jed already pored over legal books at the university, and her father saw no reason to disrupt his life. Ruth's, however, was another story.

Ruth begged to be allowed to stay. She told them she wouldn't get sick, pulled on her father's arm, her fingers gripping into the thin-striped lines of his sleeve.

"It's for your own good," her mother said. Her hands shook. She pushed up her tiny glasses on her nose. "You'll be safe, out of the city, away from this plague."

"You don't want me," Ruth shouted at her, the force of the words causing her mother to blink and lower her chin as though struck. "There's nothing wrong with me. I'm not sick. You just don't want me."

Ruth swallowed, the memory choking.

Then finger by finger, her father pulled Ruth's hands from the grip of his arm. "You have wounded your mother deeply. You will apologize."

It was the first time Ruth really saw the hardness in his eyes. She planned to apologize, of course. She hadn't meant to say it, though she believed it to the depths of her soul. It was a moment of defiance. She stuck her lower lip out and crossed her arms instead.

With a handkerchief, Ruth's mother wiped perspiration from her own wide forehead, stood, and turned her back. Ruth watched her narrow shoulders leave through the carved oak parlor doors without even a backward glance.

It was the last time Ruth ever saw her mother. She succumbed to cholera that night.

"Where'd you go?" Mazy said, touching Ruth's arm.

Ruth shook her head. "Sorry. I have a habit of drifting away." She turned then, picked an egg out of the pile of grain sacks stacked in the corner. She handed it to Mazy, who tied it in her apron. "My mother was an artist. Did I ever tell you that? Quite good. A perfectionist. She used to say, 'My eyes just aren't what they used to be. My hands either,' after she drew a lovely piece that people raved about. I tried my own hand at the replica of a horse one time, wanting to please her. She patted my head and said, 'You'll master it in time, dear. In time.' I was always a disappointment to her."

"That sounds like something encouraging a mother might say. Not disappointing."

"Does it?"

Ruth bent back to her work.

"Maybe, as a grownup, you're looking at your life with the same critical eye you think belonged to your mother. Maybe that's the cause of the dance of demand between the children and you."

Ruth didn't respond. She watched Mazy throw another forkful onto the manure pile, making the pen that held her cows and calves all tidy. Mazy's shoes had burlap bags tied around them.

"Why don't you just buy yourself a pair of boots?" Ruth said irritably. "Sometimes, you hold back when going ahead would be wiser."

Mazy stared at her. "Manure'll cure scratchy feet," she said, "and peeling hands. A little seeping through my shoes is nothing to worry over."

Ruth shook her head. Mazy bent her back to the muck, pushed the wooden fork tines with her foot, then pulled back on the handle, bent her knees to lift the load. The layer of hard crust made her grunt with effort. It gave with a second push of her fork.

"Since I'm already standing in muck, so to speak," Mazy said. "And seem to be annoying you anyway, I may as well share this thought, too. Those boys ought to be out here. We could show them that working together can be a good time. That we like their company."

"It's soothing without them about. And I can do it better anyway."

Mazy carried the mix of old straw and manure to a pile they would come back to later, to fertilize the garden plot next to the cabin they'd planted. "It may not be my place to say this, but your nephews need to learn to be useful, that others are counting on them to do their parts. Jessie is at least churning butter now. If you don't give the children important tasks and let them know they're important, they'll grow up expecting others to meet their needs. Maybe even lazy. Worse, they'll learn to think they have no value, not even to themselves. It's hard to hold a family together when people think their not being there won't even be noticed."

"Jason wanted to be paid," Ruth said sharper than she intended. "They never have owned up to losing the harmonica and taking my hat. And there are other things, almost eerie. Things moved. My whip twisted differently than the way I hung it. And they deny it, that's what rankles. It's like they're teasing me, Mazy. I even found a photograph… My face had been scratched out." Ruth shivered. "Maybe if I'd had one child at a time with room to get to know them, maybe I'd feel more secure about this mothering thing. Maybe if I had made a better choice in who fathered my children, or left him at the first sign of his...ways. Maybe my son would still be alive, maybe I wouldn't be living with his father's shadow over every part of my life."

"There's no wage in finding blame," Mazy offered. "Not of others and especially not of yourself. What's done is done. It really is."

Ruth nodded then wiped at her eyes. "All I can do now is figure out how to react." She looked past Mazy toward the road then. "Wonder why Seth's got his horse all lathered up."

It was like taking milk from a baby, Zane decided, holding Suzanne as she shivered. He draped the smoldering quilt around them, her and the boy. Sarah carried the youngest one on her hip. Both children cried, their faces red with tears and snot, coughing up the smoke.

"Johnnie, is that you? I hear someone."

"Yes. He's here," Zane said. "Probably started it with his clumsiness, getting your fire going. What is he bringing out of the house? Your harp," he added with disgust.

"No, Wesley. Don't let him. The things don't matter."

The boy had almost caught him, as he set the blaze low and slow, he thought, at the pine needles dusting the ground behind her house. He hoped the flame would eke its way into the cabin, with smoke awakening her and then his rushing in. But he'd seen Johnnie shuffling up the hill. Maybe it was his usual time to come, or he'd heard of the hotel fires and was looking after Suzanne's gold purse. His presence forced Zane to slip out behind the house and come up from the opposite side. By then the flames had bitten into the logs. He'd stood watching at the window until the smoke clouded his vision. Then he'd come around and been there when the dog pulled her to the door. That Chinese interloper had arrived at almost the same time and had rushed in, hauling trunks and just now that wretched troubadour harp Suzanne insisted on playing and seemed to gain strength from.

They might have lost everything.

"Let me take you to a place I have," Zane said. "You'll be safe there. Nothing's left in town. Not a thing."

Suzanne's teeth chattered as she talked. "Just get Elizabeth for me, will you? She's at Kossuth's Bakery if it still stands. She and Mazy will help us. She and Mazy, my family. Get my family for me."

"You're being naive, Suzanne. Hurtful. Putting your children at risk. You need to come with me." He'd pressed her head into his chest.

"Tipton's friend's coming," Sarah said.

"Is he? Oh, good. He knows Elizabeth. He can get her."

"You should come with me, Suzanne. I can take care of you. And the boys. Just look at what your irresponsibility almost caused."

"I need to see how the others are." Her voice sounded tense, strong. "We're family, Wesley. That means something to me."

"Good then," Zane said, dropping his arms from the quilt. Suzanne lurched a bit when he stood back, caught herself from stumbling, her arms outstretched now. He watched her weave her hand to find him. "I need to be helping fight the blaze," he said. "You're all right here, then, with your *family.*" He thrust the child at her. Clayton cried.

"It's gone," Seth said, his face flushed as he rode his big sorrel up, reigned up just outside Ruth's barn. Puffs of air shot out through the horse's nostrils as Seth stepped down. "I've never seen anything like it." He lifted off his hat, ran his hands through his yellow hair.

"What are you talking about?" Mazy asked, the pitchfork still in her hand.

"Shasta City. Whole place went up in flames. Weren't enough buckets to stop the spread."

"Mother—?"

"She's all right. But most everything you had in your rooms, it's gone." Mazy gazed at her feet, her dress pulled up between her legs and tucked into her belt, then looked up at Seth. "Except for what you brought here. And Suzanne," he said. "She'll need you two. Nehemiah brought her down to Tipton and Adora's while I headed out here."

"Sarah?" Ruth asked.

"She's fine. They're all fine. Scared. Just a kid."

"Go in and get coffee," Ruth told him. "We'll hitch up."

He nodded. "The Wilsons want their mules and wagon, so we've got to harness their team, too," he shouted after her. "Get the boys to help."

Mazy walked out to gather up the Wilson mules, using a bucket of grain to lure them in while Ruth called the boys already heading toward them at the sight of Seth. They hitched up the wagons, saddled Jumper and Koda, then headed inside. Seth faced a sea of faces, answering questions put to him by Mariah and the children.

"Kossuth House, too. And the St. Charles. The Shasta. Your bookstores, Mazy. Seventy houses, all the rest of the businesses on either side of the street, and half the buildings in the alleys. Even the church. Everything. Mackley Alley, Two Foot Alley, they're all just rubble."

"Were you burned out?" Mazy asked.

"Didn't have much, but I've been staying in a tent with a wood floor I put up myself far enough from Main and Second. It's fine. Spending most of my nights at the hotel working." He winked at Mazy, and she bristled, her shoulders stiffening. "Guess there won't be any games of chance there for a while."

"The St. Charles got singed in the fire last December too, didn't it?" Mazy said, filling a tin with milk from the pitcher.

"This time it went. Town looks like a mouth of black and broken teeth."

"How'd it start?" Jason asked.

"They don't know exact," Seth said. He took the refilled cup Mariah handed him and drank, looked up over the top. "But it spread a long way fast to get as far as Suzanne's."

He sat on the big bay and watched the town burn. The second story front of the St. Charles once painted yellow fell blackened into itself. Licked with flames shooting a hundred feet into the air, it would all be gone in minutes. The residential section popped and burst with canvas and wood, and oak leaves slick with oil spread the flames faster than a lick of the lips. People ran and scattered like rats, some carrying water buckets in long lines hopelessly trying to save a home, a church, a store. All without success. Rebuilding would consume them when it was over. And in the rebuilding, there'd be a fortune to be made. Maybe with less work than running his "trap line."

He pressed the reins against the horse's neck, turning it northeast toward one of Greasy's shacks. He'd wait there, let things settle a bit, consider what rich opportunities lived inside this danger.

Partway out of town he had another thought. Ruth surely would be heading in, to see about Sarah. Perhaps he should make a visit while she was gone, leave something of himself at her abode. Yes, this would be a fine time to raise her heart rate, something delicious to do before he decided to check his traps. He'd set new ones.

"You stay here," Ruth told Jessie and Mariah. "Ned too. Jason, you're old enough to help."

"I want to see Ma," Mariah said. "Is she all right? Have you seen her?"

Seth nodded. "She had a couple of the other banking ladies in tow," he said. "She told me to come on out and bring in what we could, for you not to worry. I'll bring her back soon as we're able."

"Don't want to be left with no girls," Ned complained. He kicked at the dirt in front of him and looked so glum that Ruth relented. "All right. But you stay close. This is no picnic we're going to. Mariah, you and Jessie are better off here."

They loaded quilts, extra food, and any clothes the children had outgrown and Ruth's one dress. "So many people burned out," Mazy said. "But Mother's all right? You're sure?" Seth nodded.

"At least it isn't winter like the last fire," Ruth said. "No one will freeze to death."

They rode at a fast pace toward Shasta. From a distance, Main Street looked like an ant colony, people moving here and there, carrying shards of burnt boards, people standing in clusters, the scent of wet wood and smoke still punching the air. Chinese locust trees—the ones the Celestials planted and called Trees of Heavenly Light—stood with blackened trunks along with the oaks that once promised shade.

Mazy felt anxious, nervous. Not the loss of things she feared, but for her mother. Her mother, who wouldn't be in Shasta at all if not for her.

They rattled the wagon to a stop in front of what had been the Kossuth Hotel, Confectionery and Bakery. The sound of hammers pounding greeted them.

"Can that be? They're already building?" Mazy asked. "Things are still smoldering."

"'Coming back' is ground into a Californian like dust," Seth said.

Bent over a small pile of burning embers, Elizabeth stood with a shawl around her shoulders. Hers was a planned fire, and her shoulders shook as she dried out small pieces of cloth in its heat. She turned, her face smudged with soot when Mazy called her name. Tears pooled in her eyes and streaked her wide face as her daughter held her. "I'm glad you wasn't here," she said. "It was awful." She held her daughter with her elbow, not her hands.

Mazy held her close, then said, "What's wrong? Let me see."

"I saved these snippets of quilt," Elizabeth said, turning away.

"They're not looking too good. Got fired and scorched, and then I dumped them in a bucket. Just trying to dry 'em out now."

"Mother, you're hurt. For heaven's sake, let me help."

Elizabeth's palms were scorched, the skin already turning black.

"Butter," Mazy said. "I brought some in."

Elizabeth groaned. "Waiting all this time for sweet butter and it ends up on my hands. Wish we had some of Mei-Ling's honey." She let Ruth spread the white gold—as Seth called it—on palms Mazy held, chattering as the women worked. "I went back after the Bible and your lawyer letter, Mazy. Saved those. Glad you took your writing with you out to Ruth's. Happened faster than an otter hits the river. Never saw anything so fierce or hungry. Oh, I saved the currency too, but not much else. Not your Wisconsin seed gourd. Our vegetable patch is trampled worse than when the cow brute did in yours back home. I'm sorry, child," she said.

"No need to be," Mazy said. "You did better than most would have. I wish I'd been here to help." She patted her mother's back, then bent to gather the quilt pieces. Touching her elbow, she led Elizabeth to the wagon. "You get in," she said gently. "Put this blanket around you. You're so shaky." It felt strange to be tending her mother. "We'll go find Suzanne and the Wilsons, and Lura, too, and see how they've fared. You'll get practice now, Mother, in letting someone else help you."

Zane skirted the meadow, coming from around the butte as he'd become accustomed to doing. He pulled up the horse, less edgy now that they were away from the noise of the fire, though the smoke hung like a layer of fog above them. Bits of ash rode with the stench of it, dropped on the pines. The slick leaves of the oaks and the thickness of pine needles would fuel the fire and—chaos, maybe for days. He watched the cabin and barn to see activity. Milk cows grazed, their calves close by. He noticed two mules and a horse were gone. The wagon he'd seen next to the barn was gone too. The house looked deserted. Good. They'd all headed in. He'd simply step inside the house.

He wondered if she had felt his presence there yet, or if she had told herself the little things were all the children's doing. He liked the pace of this, a slow building up to knowing someone else controlled her thoughts. He wanted her to feel the confusion, a tiny tendril of foreboding that would grow until it was a rope of fear, tightening until it choked.

Zane had wanted to run himself, once. In that moment of lost control with his own son, he had wanted to run. But he'd stayed, for her sake; she had seemed so needful with the child's death. And then she'd turned on him, her and that brother, and his life had been ripped and whipped at the whims of others—sheriffs, then wardens, then inmates and guards. It sickened him, that powerlessness. The pain had nearly killed him, made him want to take his life until he'd found a purpose, a reason to get through.

The raspy breathing brought him back into this tree-lined meadow. He swallowed, calmed himself. He'd have to leave something of himself in the cabin this time, something she could not blame on the brats but that would puzzle her. He liked to imagine her uncertain, waking in the night wondering. He'd liked finding the photograph. Felt a kind of lightness as he scraped away her face. To move her like a chess piece. Soon, he would take her to the place he'd come to all those months back, that decision place, where ending his life or someone else's had carried equal weight.

The house looked still. A striped cat sunned itself beside the door and didn't move when he pushed the plank open with his foot. He ducked his head to enter, let his eyes adjust, then scanned the room.

"You better say your prayers," a girl's voice said behind him.

He jumped, his heart pounding, his face hot in an instant.

"Don't turn around. Just put your hands...on top of your head."

"Now, young lady, no need to be alarmed. I'm here to find out about a horse," he said.

"Where we come from, people knock before they enter." *It was a second girl's voice.*

"I should have. You're absolutely correct. It's just that it was so still I assumed I'd arrived when no one was home." He had a flash of brilliance. "I'm a friend of your Aunt Suzanne's. She lives in town? She's blind." He turned.

"We know." The first one seemed to do most of the talking. "Picks poor friends."

He laughed easily, used his most charming voice. "I would have left a note. May I?" He motioned to his vest pocket. "I've a pencil. I can still do that. From Wesley Marks. Or perhaps you could leave your mother a message from me."

"She's not our mother," the girl without the pistol said. She didn't look like one of Jed's kids, too tall and skinny for that. He wondered who she was. The other one was smaller and had familiar looking eyes. Jessie! The child was his, and she didn't know him! She hadn't claimed Ruth was her mother!

"Just someone interested in horses," he said.

"We don't have many," said the taller girl. "Not 'til my brother trails in Auntie Ruth's."

His heart skipped a beat hearing her name spoken right here in her house!

"And when will that be?"

"Ain't none of your business," the little one said.

"Jessie!" the taller one cautioned. "If he wants to buy a horse…"

"Oh, I do," Zane said. "I do. Perhaps I'll wait until then, when your Aunt Ruth, is it? When she has more horses to choose from. I'll just be backing out now. You be sure to tell your aunt. Tell her a man stopped by. Suzanne's friend."

The taller girl nodded. The little one just stared, as though she looked right through him. She never wavered, though the pistol looked heavy.

"Pig barked and barked," Suzanne told them. They stood all together next to a pile of clothes, toys, some tins of tea, a mattress, quilts. Pig panted at her feet, and Sason slept on a blanket placed in the Wilson wagon. "I could smell the smoke. I couldn't focus. I knew it was close, but I couldn't find Clayton. I'd just fed Sason. I had him on my shoulder then laid him down. So stupid! I heated water for tea. Pig barked and barked. I had to wake Sarah. She's a sound sleeper, Ruth."

Mazy thought she told her story rapidly the way people did when they were relating a disaster and their own escape from it.

"He didn't have his halter on," Suzanne went on. "I'll have to keep that on him all the time. I swung my arms trying to find Clayton, trying to get Sarah to take Sason. She's so young, but you did all right," she said, turning her body to where she thought Sarah stood. "Once she got going." She swallowed. "Then Wesley came. I thought the house must be gone, but Johnnie, my Chinese boy, started pulling things out. A gift from God. He was wonderful. He shouted in Cantonese all kinds of rushed things. I could hear him slapping at something then dropping things next to me, breathing hard, coming and going. Then I really smelled the smoke and a roar, almost like fire going up the chimney when the wind draws, and my face was so hot." She coughed. "I thought Johnnie might be in there."

"How lucky he happened along," Tipton said. "And your friend, too."

"Not luck, Providence," Suzanne corrected. "He got most of my things out. No furniture, but the important things." She felt the pile next to her, lifted the troubadour harp. "See?"

Adora said. "Did the fire start from the cookstove we all worked to buy you? Explode or something?"

"You bought the cookstove?" Suzanne said. She frowned.

"Mother," Tipton chided. "That was a secret."

"I thought it went with the house," Suzanne said.

"You can be blind as a bat sometimes," Adora said. "Who would have ordered a stove when he was leaving town?"

"What happened to Wesley?" Mazy asked, changing the subject.

"He...left to help fight the fire, of course," she said, irritation in her voice.

"Maybe it's a sign you should stay with one of us now," Mazy said.

"Why would I do that?"

"Might be tempting fate too far," Seth said, "trying to do this all on your own again."

"Imagine that comment coming from a gambling man," Suzanne said, "and from people who claim to be my family but who keep secrets from me."

"Now, Suzanne," Mazy said. "We had good intentions."

"That's not how they arrived," Suzanne said. "I did fine running things myself. I can rebuild by myself, just like everyone else."

"That's what friends are for, helping out," Seth said. "You don't let us do that much, Suzanne. It's all right to admit when you're beaten."

She turned her body toward him. "I feel blessed," she said, emphasizing each word, "not beaten."

Adora snorted. "Standing here with little more than what's on our backs and she says we're blessed. Warped religion. The whole town looks like when we came across all the discards on the trail. Look at my Tipton here."

"I look like a toss-away?"

"No, no. Just everything around us having to start over, find out what's essential. Again. And poor Nehemiah, losing his hotel, everything. Probably a pauper now."

"We'll think on the good things. That seems to have worked in the past," Tipton said. She said it lightly, but she rubbed at the crook of her elbow as though it ached.

"Were you hurt?" Mazy asked, nodding toward her arm.

Tipton dropped her hand. "No," she said. "I'm fine. I think maybe I strained it when we pulled the trunk out. Didn't expect our hotel to go. Everyone worked so hard…"

"Now your Nehemiah'll have a dozen directions to go and he'll have no time for courting. Who knows how long we'll wait for a marriage proposal. We needed him—or someone—to be looking after us."

"You've been needing help?" Mazy said. "You haven't asked."

"We don't *need* anyone, Mother," Tipton said. "We still have the mules. And I'm not exactly sure how I feel about any proposal of marriage."

"Of course, you're sure," Adora said. "What if Nehemiah spent his time and what money he has left on rebuilding? You'd be disappointed then, truth be known."

"Mother, keep your voice down. I'm not interested in Nehemiah for his money, I'm not sure I'm—"

"That's the best news I've had today," Nehemiah said, making his way with Johnnie from the rear of what was left of Suzanne's house. Removing his hat, he slapped ash from it against his thigh. He put it back on, brushed at the dust on his red beard. Tipton blushed, fidgeted from foot to foot. "I lost my hotel," he said, "but as long as I have you considering me, Tipton, I'm wealthy indeed." Nehemiah put his arm around her shoulder then and squeezed. "And I'm not headed for the pauper's prison just yet, Adora."

"My baby'll be waiting just as long as it takes, won't you, Tipton?"

"The mules look good," Tipton said as she stepped away from Nehemiah and patted the neck of the nearest. "I'm glad we didn't sell them before. We'll need that money now."

"What're your plans?" Seth asked Nehemiah.

"Rebuild," Adora answered for him. "Has to."

"I've been considering that," Nehemiah said, walking to the other side of the mule. "But maybe Shasta isn't the place for us." Tipton looked across the neck of the mule at him. She smiled a little, and he grinned as if she'd given him a drink of water on a hot and thirsty day. "I've been thinking to take a new wife—if she'll have me—and if her mother'll let her marry before she turns seventeen."

"A proposal of marriage! Truth be known, this is a fine, fine day!"

"Why not rebuild right here?" Tipton asked, flashing her mother a look to silence her. "Couldn't you take a loan to rebuild the hotel? People will be counting on that."

"Place'll burn again, is my bet. Town's burned twice in six months. That's not a good sign."

"They'll widen Main Street. Heard already they want rebuilding with fireproof buildings," Seth said.

"It's always been my belief that a door doesn't close that another isn't opened. Nothing says it has to be on the same street. I'd take you both," he said, speaking to Tipton then, as though they were alone. "A young girl might like having her mother with her, farther west, in Humboldt County. That's where I'll head. That's where my father always said I should settle, near the coast. Cattle country."

"The coast? That's a little…out of the way," Adora said.

"First white woman arrived there last year." Nehemiah never took his eyes from Tipton's. "I suspect she'd like a little company by now. I served with General Taylor in '47 when we defeated Santa Anna. There's talk of a Bounty Land Grant for us old soldiers." He grinned at Tipton. "That comes through, we'll have quite a spread. Even without, we'd do all right. Together. I've got some holdings there." He moved around the mule and lifted Tipton's hands in his. "Wasn't what I'd planned for you, Tipton, but circumstances being what they are, will you accept the change of venue I'm suggesting and become my wife?"

"What do you say, dear?" Adora asked, hovering close. "Mother will be with you." Tipton bit on her lower lip.

Nehemiah should have known better than to put the question to her in front of others, Mazy thought. The fire must have rattled him more than he realized. Rattled them all. Suzanne felt blessed by surviving but hurt by their offers of care. Elizabeth worried more over Mazy's losses than over her own wounds. And poor Tipton was getting a marriage proposal surrounded by ashes and eavesdropping ears.

"I love you enough for the both of us," Nehemiah whispered to Tipton, but they could all still hear it.

"Maybe she needs more time," Mazy said. "Or privacy."

"Now you just stay out of this, Mazy Bacon. This is Wilson doings, and unlike you, we don't need wallowing time before we come to a decision."

15

the devil's mill

"Hey, look at this!" David Taylor reached down to lift the dog, one hand on the bucket, the other trying to manage the squirming black body whose front paws grabbed at his pant legs. Its tongue now licked his face, his ears, the feathered tail wagging, the little bells rusty on the collar. David took it off and scratched the dog's neck. "Oltipa! Bring the baby and come see this! Our little mutt's come home."

Oltipa, dressed in a blue-and-white calico dress David had given her, came to the doorway, a child on her hip. When she recognized the dog, she set the boy down. He leaned forward, rocking with delight, his face full of laughter. "Chance comes back," Oltipa said.

"Hey, Ben, look at him." David called the boy Ben, his father's and his own middle name, but Oltipa used a name she said meant boy—*Wita-ela*—telling David that when he was older she would give him another name that was only his. "Well, my tongue doesn't wrap around that word too well, so mind if I call him something easy?" David had told her that cold February day of the child's birth.

"Call him what you wish," she'd told him. "*Wita-ela* lives because you care for me." David's stomach ached with the memory of that time, his worry and wonder at the arrival of this child. His eyes had gotten wet as a girl's at a wedding with the sight of Ben arriving on this earth, fully ready with his thick black hair, alert brown eyes, and all the other expected parts. Oltipa had told him how to tie the cord and to put the baby on her stomach. She did all the work, but he was the one who danced the jig. A click of his boots as he jumped in the air—after the baby safely arrived, after the baby turned to his mother's breast and nestled there as though he'd always known just what was expected. Later, when Oltipa slept, the baby stayed watching him. He'd talked to the boy, holding his gaze, and he knew then he'd done a good thing those months back. Any risk would have been worth this. Who cared what people thought of him? What some man like Zane Randolph had done to get him fired? This was what mattered, the tending of another. He'd meant it for harm, that Randolph, but God had turned it to good.

Today Ben's smile formed in full, round cheeks surrounded by a head of hair as thick and black as the dog's. Oltipa looked...happy. David had wondered if he should buy her white women's clothes, or any dress for that matter. But she accepted the calico and a small mare, a pony almost, to keep her company when the dog ran off. He wasn't sure just why he wanted to give her things—he just knew he thought of her often on the stage run for Baxter and Monroe, his new employer. He thought of her most of the time.

"Where do you suppose he's been?" David said, petting the dog. "He looks fed. Lots of stickers and burrs on him though. He's been around some streams." He turned the paws over and saw the scars on one leg, the tended healing that must have allowed it. "You came back just in time. Keep Oltipa and Ben company, while I head out. Maybe I should bring you into Shasta," David said to Oltipa.

"This good place," she told him.

"Yeah...just with the fever against Indians growing instead of getting better, I worry about you being way out here, other cabins so far away."

David lifted the boy onto his shoulders, the dog scratching at his legs. "Way the *Courier* tells, it doesn't look good for your people. Talking removal to reservations, but they're acting like they don't want any of you left to move. Worries me, someone coming and just taking you when I'm not here."

She nodded once in that way she had, took the boy and set him on the floor with the dog now licking his face. She turned and finished putting food into a sack, and David realized again how much he liked knowing her, what a gift she and the boy had given him by allowing his help. With the horse, she could leave anytime she chose, but she hadn't. He didn't think she'd ever ridden the eight miles or so down from this claim in Mad Mule Canyon into Shasta. Maybe she knew it wasn't safe out there for her. She was safe at home.

Home. He wondered how his father had ever left his mother in Oregon and come south, thought to make a home *for* her but without her. He didn't think he could do that.

He lifted Ben to her, felt Oltipa's hands brush his as he did. Her eyes met his, and he felt filled to the brim, warm to his fingertips, knowing someone waited for him at the end of a run, even if it was a woman whom he'd never even kissed and a fat baby who wasn't even his.

He kissed Ben on the head and held him out to his mother. He planned to pick up his saddle pack. But Oltipa changed that. She held the boy between them, then shifted him to her hip. She moved herself closer to him, nothing but her calico dress and his plaid shirt separating them. She reached up on tiptoe and kissed him. "Come back, David Taylor," she said.

"Well, sure, I'll do that," he told her, his face feeling hotter than it ought.

She smiled at him then, and in that instant David knew why he bought her presents, why she always filled his mind.

While Wood and Tomlinson won a six-hundred-dollar bet by being the first to rebuild their burned-up store—Tipton planned her wedding. Two weeks it took those men to put up two stories of bricks, roof it, build, then stock the shelves. The rest of the burned district wasn't far behind, a clear message to all in California that with money as the motivation, anything could be accomplished.

Tipton developed a headache the day of the fire that hadn't gone away. Elizabeth suggested pepper on a slice of potato wrapped around her forehead. It didn't do a thing. That morning, she found Seth's stash of peach brandy and sipped some, just to settle her nerves. Medicinal.

It was all happening so fast, so many people around all the time, so much planning and changing and leaving, all pushing forward without really much of her needed at all. She wiped her mouth with the back of her hand, felt steadier. It certainly wasn't something she needed, Seth's brandy. But it did help, with the wedding just hours away. She slipped the flask back into his pack, then walked a short distance from where the men had been sleeping under the line of trees. The garden was over that way, at the lip of the meadow, just beyond Ruth's house. Pig chased at birds near the creek. They'd all rendezvoused at Ruth's. That was what Nehemiah called it, as though they were all beaver trappers coming together for a celebration. She wondered if he realized those events were centered around trapping more than celebration. She looked at her nails. She'd been chewing them, and she pinched her fingers into her palms, hoping no one would notice. She bent as though to check on the garden's growth. Mazy had latched onto one of the first pack loads to arrive after the fire. Sure enough, there'd been seeds and starts aplenty, and she'd planted them the same day. No sign of activity in those rows yet, but there would be. She wondered if there'd be a garden plot on their land, the land Nehemiah said they'd go to. She'd never lived outside a town—except for the time on the trail. She wasn't sure where she fit in. Wasn't sure she wanted to. "Think on the good things," Tyrellie always said. She was helping her mother; this marriage would surely help her mother.

"You're looking like a waiting bride," Lura told her, meeting up with Tipton beside the house. Lura walked with her arm at Tipton's waist. They moved slowly back toward where Ruth bent, helping Elizabeth put food on the planks of lumber set on sawhorses that made up the outside table. "Won't be long and my Mariah'll be putting on that dress of marriage." Lura sighed. "Got any advice for her, something I should tell her? What to look for in a western man? You're the first of our little trail to take a western husband."

"Mei-Ling and Naomi were first," Tipton reminded her. "Though Esther said it took extra time to locate Naomi's husband. I guess I liked Nehemiah's hands best," Tipton said. Everyone laughed.

"We are attracted to strange things," Lura said. "Now me, I like a man with a sense of humor. My Antone, he could make me laugh. He didn't do it much, mind you, after we married, but it was his laugh I noticed first."

"Marriage isn't a laughing matter," Ruth said. She set a platter of biscuits near the edge to keep the breeze from lifting the tablecloth. Mariah brought out pitchers of sun tea.

Elizabeth said, "It can be."

"And I like his beard," Tipton added.

Lura nodded, chewed on a smokeless pipe.

Tipton knew she spoke of meaningless things, as though those were all her mind could hold. Maybe it was having nearly everyone right there all the time, all mushed into Ruth's house. Maybe it was knowing that this was the last day of her life as a...girl, as a woman not dependent on a father or brother—not dependent on herself. A sudden tightness seized her chest.

She had hated the work of the laundry, but now what she'd done there took on bigger proportions. She'd taken care of herself. It made her want to cry, the changes. Everything made her want to cry. The smell of the pines, the sight of the calves, the scorched quilt pieces Elizabeth kept piled in the corner. No one understood it, least of all her mother. They all just looked at her with big cow eyes, as though this was what happened to a woman on her wedding day, the bride got all addled and strange. She had to button up, to pull herself together, to be firm about this decision. It was done. It was made. She had made it. She ran her tongue over her lips, remembered the strength she could draw from the taste of the peach brandy.

"Tyrellie had wide hands too," she said. Her lower lip quivered.

"A craftsman's hands," Elizabeth said, patting her shoulder. "A good thing to remember."

"Not necessarily a good predictor of a husband," Adora said. "And you better be thinking of your new fiancé 'stead of your old one."

"It was a year ago last week he died. He could make things—and made things happen," Tipton said.

"A year passed," Mazy said. "So long ago and yet it feels like yesterday."

"Don't go getting morbid, Mazy. Can't think about back then. Nehemiah'll make things happen. He did here in Shasta," Adora said.

"Don't you miss Papa?" Tipton asked.

Adora looked away. " 'Course I do. Too many years together not to. But life moves on. You need to too." She fussed at the tucks on Tipton's dress, gave her daughter a peck on her cheek. "It'll be all right."

Tipton nodded, straightened, and took a deep breath. "I have a secret to share," she said.

"Won't be much of a secret if you tell all of us," Ruth said.

"Nehemiah won't mind. He's going to run for senator in a year or so. First from the district to the state legislature but then eventually, from California, to the United States of America. That's what he told me. He said he'll need a wife to stand beside him."

"Should be a lawyer or a judge first." Lura said. "Or a sheriff. That's the election to win. Sheriffs appoint the jurors." She jabbed the air with her pipe. "That's why lawyers do so well. They get to know the sheriff, stack the jury, and they always win their cases."

"You'll have to share him with a lot of people if he becomes a senator," Ruth told her. "Are you ready to stay at home alone while your husband travels and mingles?"

Tipton's voice quivered as she continued, "I'll go with him." She clasped her hands so the heavy ring she wore glittered in the afternoon light. "I know how to deal with strong feelings. I've grown quite a bit at that."

"With your mother beside you, there'll be lots to do when Nehemiah isn't about, won't there, dear?" Adora said. "A mother just never loses her influence."

Reverend Hill and Nehemiah arrived along with a copy of the *Shasta Courier* carrying news that Main Street was now widened to one hundred ten feet. "Paper must be operating out of a tent to get an issue out so fast. Look, Ruth," Mazy said. "The editor's used a lithograph. Do you ever miss doing that work?"

Ruth shrugged. "Sometimes. It was my first love. Well, after horses."

"Oh," Mariah said. "We forgot. A man came by, Ruth. That day you left me and Jessie here. The day of the fire. He was looking for horses. And he came right inside the house. Jessie pointed your pistol at him 'til we knew he was safe."

"You promised not to tell."

"You shouldn't be handling my pistol," Ruth said.

"I didn't like him," Jessie said. "Even if he was your friend, Aunt Suzanne."

"My friend? Wesley? How odd."

"He said he'd come back when your other horses got here." Mariah bit at the edge of her finger. "It was scary, him just walking in."

"It's the bride who's supposed to be shaky," Adora said. "You getting sick, Ruth?"

"If I ever leave you alone, any of you again, you bar the door from the inside, you hear? Didn't I tell you that? Didn't I? I'm just no good at this, I'm just not!" She walked backward, then turned and ran to the barn.

Tipton said, "I don't think I've ever seen Ruth cry before."

"Oh, people always cry at weddings," her mother said. "You will too."

Nehemiah also brought the mail, and in it came a long-awaited letter from Sister Esther.

"Should we read it before or after the ceremony?" Mazy asked.

"Ernest isn't here yet with the ring," Nehemiah said, looking toward the road. "So we can't begin. Go ahead and read it."

"She'll tell us all how Mei-Ling and Naomi are," Sarah said. "And look, a quilt square. Oh, two." She picked up what rolled to the floor when she opened the package. "Shouldn't there be three?"

Esther's quilt square was the obvious one. An "appliquéd piece," Mazy called it, cut out patterns stitched on top of each other. "She's placed two graves under a circle of sun," Tipton said.

"Her brothers," Suzanne said quietly.

"Could stand for all we've lost," Elizabeth said.

"But she also has tiny women with bonnets bent over the graves, and a dog lying next to one headstone," Mazy said. "It's really quite well done."

Mei-Ling had composed a square of bees made with French knots of black thread. They flew over a green bowl with a red dragon sprawling around it.

Mei-Ling wanted the bowl to be for Naomi as well, Sister Esther wrote. *She always kept her herbs in a green bowl. Green is the color of prosperity, though I am not sure I approve of such pagan thinking. The tiny "v" in the corner is for Zilah–Chou-Jou. It stands for a bat, which she said means good luck and wisdom, too.*

A murmur of reminiscing filled the June air. Mazy read ahead. "Oh," she whispered, her voice hushed, which stopped the women's talking like a hand over their mouths.

"What is it?" Seth asked.

She blinked up at him. "Just mention of some trouble with Naomi's new husband. Esther's had almost no contact. Apparently he...mistreats her." She glanced at Tipton. "I'm sure it'll be fine."

Mazy read on. "Esther's working as a cleaning woman in a performing theater late at night. She works days, too, putting all she can into repaying the debts of the lost Celestials."

Lura said, "She might make more cleaning up in one of the saloons. The gold dust catches in the floorboards. Little nuggets do too. I did right well, 'til the fire, sweeping up in addition to the banking."

"Sister Esther treated those girls like her own family," Mazy said, looking up. "It must be awful for her. And to work around actors and musicians."

"Those folks got paid right well too," Lura said. "Especially the women. There's lots of choices for enterprising souls. Nehemiah, if you ever mistreat Tipton, she can—"

"Oh, thank goodness. Here's the best man," Mazy said as she redirected the girl's startled look.

Ruth knew she should rejoin the group, but the sense of "family" gathered out there pierced her. That Jessie. Handling her pistol. And Suzanne's choosing a friend with such poor judgment. That troubled her too. What worked best was to live alone. That was what she'd done the years Zane was imprisoned, and now she knew why.

But there they all were. In her yard. For a wedding. She sighed and walked back from the barn. Mazy met her and squeezed her shoulder with one arm, pulling her close. She filled Ruth in on what she'd missed as Ruth dabbed at her red eyes.

"My daughter needs to have a joyous time," they heard Adora say as they approached the group gathered in the shade. Blue and white lupines dotted the low hills around them. "If truth be known, such a day is every mother's dream from the moment a daughter is born, isn't that so?"

Heads nodded, and Ruth wondered again what was wrong with her that when she gave birth to her daughter, the last thing she thought of was planning the child's marriage. She had never been a proper mother, never would be.

"Ned, you're going to sing for us, I hear," Mazy said, a little too cheerily for Ruth's ears.

The boy nodded. "Morning Has Broken," he said and smiled at Ruth. *How could they be so sweet and yet be so difficult to raise?* Ruth wondered.

After he sang, Preacher Hill—whose church had burned to the ground—cleared his throat, and everyone moved forward to circle the marriage couple. Tipton had asked her mother to serve as her attendant, and Nehemiah's man was Ernest the silversmith.

Tipton Wilson became Mrs. Nehemiah Kossuth, saying the vows and hesitating only once—on the word *obey.* Ruth wasn't the only woman who smiled wistfully at her stumbling. Then Nehemiah placed a silver band on her finger.

Tipton wore a white dress with a ribbon of blue at her throat and ivy Mariah had woven through the yellow braid of her hair piled high on her head. She carried a small white Bible with a blue ribbon marker she said later was set at Corinthians.

"Where ever did you find it?" Suzanne asked her, her graceful fingers lifting the layers of lace after the brief ceremony. "Who did you get to make something so intricate so quickly?"

"Mama sent it with me when I left Wisconsin," Tipton said. The girl gazed at her mother in a look Ruth would've described as adoration. "She made sure it was one of the...essentials when we had to sort things on the trail." She touched her fingers to her mouth to cover a giggle, the way Mei-Ling often had. She hiccuped.

"Kept it in the trunk that got carried out first from the fire," Adora said. "If truth be known, I'd rather we saved it than any other thing. Nothing's more essential than a daughter's wedding day."

Elizabeth—despite the throbbing of her hands—had earlier in the day directed the other women in preparing the wedding feast. And then she herself had stirred the white cake, the brown age spots on the back of her hand looking like a single fluid line from the speed of her stirring. After the couple was married, they cut the cake and served it with glasses of milk—compliments of Mazy's cows.

When everyone had eaten, Suzanne said, cake crumbs scattering down her front without her notice, "In Michigan, a couple is shivareed on their wedding night. People ring bells and blow horns and whistles and hit pans and kettles," she said, "and keep it up until they're invited in for cake and lemonade or whatever is left to drink."

"Won't be necessary here," Ruth said. "The bride and groom are sleeping on the floor surrounded by all of us. And these kids and Pig'll keep the noise up all night without whistles being blown."

"I think we'll take a spot beneath a tree," Nehemiah said. "Let the sky and coyotes shivaree us. In the morning, Tipton, we'll head home."

"Let's have one last song," Elizabeth said. She dabbed at her cheeks with a linen napkin. "Send you off to music. Suzanne? I'll get your harp."

To Suzanne's accompaniment, Ned sang "Home Sweet Home," and people slowly joined in the way stars fill up a night sky, taking empty dark to a corner of comfort. Jessie came to stand beside Ruth. The child looked up as she dabbed at her eyes, and then leaned against her. The touch of the girl both startled and soothed her. What was she going to do with this child?

"What did you think of the wedding?" Seth asked Mazy. They walked through the meadow, Seth and Mazy and the children, even Jessie, herding the cows toward the barn for their nightly milking. Considering his question, Mazy watched the older children raise bugs in the meadow grass.

"Women usually put that thought to men," she said. When he didn't answer she added, "I thought it was lovely; Tipton did seem a bit distracted. Maybe the unhappy talk about Naomi…I shouldn't have read that part out loud."

"She's been into my peach brandy," he said.

"Why'd you bring that with you?" Mazy asked.

"Medicinal," he told her.

"I'm sure."

> "Mazy turns the tables,
> Faster than an otter.
> Talk about a wedding,
> She'll tell you what you oughter."

"That's a terrible rhyme," Mazy told him.

"But true. Look. You've had time to settle in, put down roots, and you haven't. Now with your rooms gone to fire…" he coughed. "I'm not doing this well. Why don't we just get married?" He stood in front of her, lifted her chin to him. "We'll build ourselves a place. On a good chunk of ground. I've been thinking I'd like that. Now as ever. I might even learn to milk."

"Oh, Seth. I…" She couldn't look at him. Wouldn't. Her eyes searched past him toward the cows. "Mother needs me more…and I still have to find out about Jeremy's business."

"Then let's get that over with. Maybe that's what holds you back. Go now, before I head back to bring in another train."

She pointed to the cows they herded. "These. Twice a day. Milk deliveries. Especially now with people not having much. Who would I get to milk them?"

"Ruth?"

"I could ask. But I think she has other plans. She's been after me to take the house and...for you to take on Jason."

"Me? I'm not fit to raise a boy."

"Well, thank you very much for the proposal of marriage, Mr. Forrester, coming in the same paragraph with the news that you're not fit to be a parent."

"No! I mean yes! You know what I mean."

She poked him in the ribs, then started walking faster. "I'll work on it, Seth Forrester."

"The marriage part?" he called after her.

"Asking Ruth to milk the cows," she shouted over her shoulder from a safe distance.

Suzanne stayed in the wagon with her boys while they napped, just as she had on the trail. She thought of the ceremony, Tipton a little nervous, putting on this great change in her life. She sensed a hesitation in the bride but none in Nehemiah. He loved her enough for both of them, she'd heard him say. He would keep her in the safety of his heart.

She was glad Wesley hadn't been there. She didn't want to have to explain his...ways to others. She couldn't explain it to herself, his walking like that into Ruth's home. Being here without him, she felt...relief. She'd been thinking of something Lura had said about the entertainers, and knew he wouldn't understand that at all. He'd...find fault. He said the right things, but the words didn't ring true. In the presence of the women she could see clearer, it seemed.

Esty had told her once that some of the groups traveled from camp to camp, receiving pay in gold dust. "Many are women and children, and they put on little plays. The miners cry like babies when a child sings. No one has ever been harassed. If I had a single talent, that's what I'd do."

"You made your hat," Suzanne said. "Ruth said it was lovely, and she doesn't hold much for fashion, I'm told. So you do have a talent.

"Not for performing," Esty said. "Not like you and your music."

She'd been given the gift of music and voice. Suzanne agreed. Was it pride to recognize that? She didn't think so. It was being honest with her gifts. If God wouldn't return her sight, she was still sure he would provide a way for her to see what she needed to do.

Her confidence grew with that thought. She and her boys. Lura and Mariah. Ned might come with them too. He sang like an angel. "Papa took us to see Jenny Lind," he told her when she expressed admiration for his singing at the wedding. "I was little, but I 'member taking her voice inside me. Mama always cried when I sang. I sang for her today. Is that all right, you think? Even if it was Tipton's wedding?"

"I'm sure you didn't cheat on Nehemiah or Tipton one whit when you sang," she told him. He'd leaned into her as he had when they'd sat around campfires back on the trail.

They could travel together, give a more respectable occupation to Lura, allow her and Mariah to be together, and let Suzanne's boys be raised by their mother. It would serve the others right, too, for lying to her about their gift of the stove—she'd survive this fire on her own terms.

"Really?" Lura said when Suzanne laid out her plan later that evening. "They make five hundred dollars in gold dust for a single performance?"

"Esty said if the song sang was 'Young Ladies, Won't You Marry Me?' you can get even more."

"I could take my knife sharpener with me. Tend to knives and such during the day and then what, you'd sing? Play? What?"

"We could put together little dramas. Ned too, if Ruth will let him. Maybe you could play a part. Mariah could help with the boys if she would."

Lura cackled in delight. "We travel to camps. We sing and dance. They throw money at us? Suzanne, I like the way you see things."

California was a strange place, Suzanne thought as she listened to the wind pop against the wagon canvas. She hoped she wouldn't get blindsided by something she hadn't seen. Even sighted people could be caught unawares though. She had to be twice as clear to make sure she wasn't being led astray in some way.

Something Bryce had told her once came to her mind. He'd talked of the devil's mill. "In Irish lore," he said, "the devil builds a mill. It looks promising, inviting, as secure and safe as home. But it lures people in, Suzanne. And before they know it, bad things happen to them. Unfortunate events that whisk away their happiness, love, and wealth. To trick the devil is never easy once one succumbs to the mill," Bryce told her. "You have to remain true to your heart to avoid that seduction."

She'd thought her plan through. It used her talents. It was no devil's mill. She wondered why she'd even thought of that.

She saw it as a way to stay true to her heart.

Ruth slept in the barn that night, listening to the crunch of the cows chewing their cud and the gentle slurp of calves bunting their mothers as they suckled. Coyotes howled in the distance; her horses stomped as they shifted their weight in sleep. She couldn't sleep. She knew why.

That Wesley person. It seemed odd he would come out to buy horses on the day of the fire when everything was so chaotic. A serious suitor would have stayed behind to help Suzanne. She hadn't been thinking right herself, she guessed, leaving the girls, not reminding them to bar the door. She just didn't think like a mother, didn't act like one either. It put those children at risk. She worried over Suzanne, but what about *her* inability to take care of those she said she loved?

And she did love them, truly she did. But her mother had done the right thing in sending her away. More and more, she knew that was what she needed to do too. She would make it look as though it was best for them. If she had…an occupation, then they'd have to be cared for by someone else. They wouldn't feel shoved away. They'd see that with Auntie Ruth working, they wouldn't be safe, left home alone.

So what might she do? She pulled the blanket around her. Shoe horses? She'd done that once or twice in her life. But there were plenty of blacksmiths around for that. She was no good at cooking or laundry. Maybe helping rebuild. Carpenters made twenty dollars a day. She might paint portraits. A horse snorted in its stall. She could draw. She could make lithographs. Return to what she knew first, and maybe it would tend to her soul. She turned over in her bedroll, calmed by the grinding of the cows' chewing. She knew what she had to do.

If only she could get Mazy to agree to stay at this place. The boys could help her with the cows. That might work. Maybe keep Sarah on with Suzanne—wherever Suzanne ended up in town. That left Jessie. She'd have to think about that one.

Maybe sleep would give her an answer.

In the morning, Ruth stood and stretched, achy and unrested. Adora was already out by the bedrolls of the newlyweds, hovering. Nehemiah said something, and Adora scurried to the house. Ruth shook her head. Family. She thought of the wedding. She wished Tipton well in her new life. It did seem that she'd found a man who adored her, someone good and kind yet willing to be strong when needed. That was what Tipton said she always wanted. She'd need someone strong enough to love her yet not so much he smothered who she was. Smothering could easily happen, especially with someone so young.

It was good that Adora would go with them. Grown up as Tipton thought she was, sixteen was young, and the girl was still forming. Best to have a mother close at hand. Jessie's face came to Ruth's mind.

It would have been a perfect day of celebration, she thought, if they'd waited to read the letter from Sister Esther. Who needed the reminder on their wedding day that more than gentle laughter and good wishes might fill the marriage bed ahead?

Ruth started toward the house to fix the morning coffee. Then saw something from the corner of her eye.

The man's face was lifted away toward the sun, but Ruth recognized him instantly, even before he turned.

"Well, Ruth Martin," he said, pulling at that clipped place on his ear.

"The prodigal son returns," Ruth said.

"It's such a lovely morning." Charles Wilson grinned.

"Until you arrived, it was."

Tipton stood with a blanket around her, not yet even dressed. Though the morning air had already warmed, she shivered. She shivered the first moment she heard her brother's voice as he bent over her and Nehemiah's bedroll. "What do you want?" Tipton asked.

"Why, to wish you well," Charles said. "And maybe to warn your husband that you have a history of bad luck with those you love." Tipton noticed her mother approaching like a mother cow discovering her lost calf. Why hadn't Charles gone to the house before rousing them from their marriage bed?

"Her first fiancé turned up dead," Charles said, leaning in to his new brother-in-law, who was pulling on his woolen pants.

"With a question over how he died," Tipton said.

"Was it an accident or...suicide," Charles said. He held his hands out as though weighing ore.

"No suicide. An accident, maybe. Or worse. But not suicide. That much I know. It's taken me a year, but I know Tyrell loved me and would have married me if he had lived. The rest, that's all your doing, Charles. That's in the past."

"Which we've no time for," Nehemiah said. He tightened his arm around Tipton's shoulder, then said, "Why don't you get dressed?"

She shook her head. "I'll wait. I don't want to leave mother alone with this...person."

"Oh," Adora purred, breathless. She opened her arms as though to inhale her son. Charles leaned into the embrace. "If truth be known, I did not know just when or if we'd ever see you again."

"I was always looking to find you, Mother."

"Were you?"

"How dare you spoil my wedding day," Tipton said, her voice lower and shakier than she wanted.

"He really didn't, Tipton," her mother said. "You were married yesterday."

"And I missed it," Charles said. "Still, I see the flavor of your celebration. Tables of food, a beautiful wedding dress worn, I'm sure. And a lovely nightdress."

Tipton's knuckles were white where she held the quilt tight around her. She wished she were dressed, wore something to give her strength. "Come on, Nehemiah, let's finish loading what little we have and leave. Coming, Mother?"

"We have to take a little time with your brother, find out how he's been." She took his arm. "Where did you winter? How did you find us? Oh, we can talk of that over a great big breakfast. I'm just sure everyone will want to hear your stories once they're up."

"Mother. After what he did to us, to all of us?"

"He's family, dear," Adora said.

"Come on, Tip," Nehemiah told her. "You and I are family now. Let's get dressed, eat a bite, and then hitch up."

Adora linked her arm through Charles's. "Are you living near here? Surely you're hungry. So many questions."

"Had a string of unfortunate luck, Mother." He patted her hand. "But that's changed now that I've met up with you. Oh, Tipton, you'll like hearing this. I know father would have wanted me to do out here what we did back in Wisconsin. Run a store. Shasta's as good a place as any to do that."

Adora put her hands to her mouth, her eyes filled with tears. "Oh, Charles, that's so wonderful. I knew you'd come to your senses."

"Good time to do it with the whole town rebuilding."

"And you have capital for this venture?" Nehemiah asked.

"You probably still have some of the money you...borrowed, don't you, Charles?" Adora asked.

"Truth is, Mother, I used that all up just staying alive. I had to live in a tent all winter near Sacramento. Got my feet frostbit in the mountains. I'll have some trouble standing on my feet all day tending to customers, but I just think it's what we should do."

"We? You have a partner?"

"Why, you, Mother." Tipton gasped. Charles went on, "I felt sure you'd want to be a part of Father's dream. Didn't figure on Tipton being married, or she'd be welcome too."

"Right here in Shasta. Imagine that," Adora said. Her face was blotched with reddish spots. A light breeze fluffed against Adora's flannel gown.

"And you got a loan and all, to start to build?"

Charles turned to gaze across the field where Jason and Ned led four black mules toward the Wilson wagon. "Our mules, Mother. I was hoping you still had them."

Adora turned, their arms still linked. "Whatever a son needs," she said. Charles smiled at Tipton over his shoulder.

It was too much for her. Tipton brushed between them then, her face hot, her eyes blurred by tears that spilled as she ran. Behind her, she barely heard her mother say, "And they'll bring a good price this time of year too. I'm just so glad we waited."

16

tearing down the devil's mill

Zane planned to give Suzanne time. Let her flounder with those women and discover what she'd given up in refusing his offer. Yes, he'd give them time. Both of them, he thought as he rode south toward the Middletown camps, then west, and finally ending up northwest at Greasy's camp. He expected to hear the sounds of working boys, picks and shovels, and shouts. But the diversion dam had not been set in Whiskey Creek that ran through Mad Mule Canyon. And no one stood in the water shoveling ore into the Long Tom sluice box.

A sliver of smoke came up through the chimney of the shack, so someone was there. Zane eased off his horse a distance from the cabin. The door stood partially open. Stupid Greasy. The Indian brats had probably outwitted him.

Inside, Greasy lay sprawled on the floor. A gash at his head bled, forming a pool beneath it. "Help me?" He coughed.

Zane stared, looked around. No gold stashed. The boys had been smart enough to take that after they took Greasy on.

"When'd it happen?" Zane asked.

"Not long. You. Catch 'em." The man's beak nose looked broken, his face already bruised. "Help. Me?"

Zane reached over him, pulled a bottle of whisky and set it beside him. Greasy reached for his pant leg, and Zane moved quickly back. No sense getting blood on his suit.

The ankle irons might hold those boys back, he thought as he spurred his horse. Those and the weight of the ore they carried. He picked up their trail, slipping and sliding, so close to the thickness of the timber, then through it. He noticed handprints clutching at rocks, bare feet gouging the earth. They couldn't be far ahead. Branches still moved from their passing, and he thought he caught a glimpse of one or two. Tendrils of long black hair hung on low branches.

Zane zigzagged the horse up the side of the gulch, crossing over their tracks, once or twice picking up where one split off from the others. The footprints he followed sank in deep—they'd be carrying the ore. Not much loss, the boys. The war fever against them would tend to them soon enough anyway, so Zane had no fear of complaints if they turned up wounded. Or worse. They couldn't even bring a charge against him. But he wanted his gold. He had earned it.

He rode now, just below the top of a ridge, through manzanita with its glossy leaves, around large boulders bulged out from streaks of red and sandy earth. Once, he thought he lost the trail, but then he found it again, and this time it worked its way down over the side of the hill, and then something from the corner caught his eye.

They'd dropped the ore pack. Must have decided their lives were worth more than the gold. Zane smiled, rode over to the spot on the steep side-hill where the canvas lay. He dismounted, scanned the area, then lifted the sack, securing it behind his saddle. The horse stomped, twisted its head back to bite at a fly. Zane wiped his brow of sweat with the back of his arm. Something moved in the distance.

Another rider, headed out of the ravine, up and over the next ridge. Zane eased himself over to his saddle bag, moved slowly, got out the telescoping glass. A single rider. Where had he come from? He scanned the horizon, moved his gaze down through the trees to the base of the ridge. He stopped when he saw the cabin hidden among the pines. A small open space of green spread out from it toward a fast-moving stream. He moved the glass. He saw a woman and a child.

The woman looked up then, stood staring in his direction. She put her hand at her forehead to block the sun, and he thought perhaps there'd been a reflection from his brass. He quickly pulled it from his eye, but not before he recognized who she was.

His breathing sounded raspy, his thoughts clanging as he rode back to Greasy's cabin. He found the man dead. Inconvenient. He considered digging a hole in the gravel and dragging the body to it. Instead, he set the structure on fire.

A new focus twisted with the old one, as he watched the flames. The shack burned hot and fast, leaving little but ashes to drift across the gravel bar.

July came on dry and hot. There'd been no rain since April except for a sprinkle in June. The temperature had risen along with tempers as Shasta sprouted tendrils of streets and alleys, no letup in sight with rich new diggings being uncovered. Main Street resurrected itself. Running east and west like a trough between the hillsides dotted with shanties and cabins rose buildings of sturdy red bricks and heavy lead doors and shutters, no one allowing fire to ravage the "Queen City of the North" again. On the side streets, the smell of fresh-cut lumber and sawdust tickled the nose. Seth's anticipation of four or five bookstores looked to come true before long. Two already lined the new, widened street. A third was planned. Farther down, but on the main road toward the coast, the route Tipton and Nehemiah had taken from town, rose Chinese quarters, Koon Chong's store, his competition—Quong Sing and Company—and simple houses facing west. Their presence made it easier for Shasta housekeepers to buy their imported fish and oil and nuts, and easier for Mazy's mother to fetch the Chinese candies she'd come to love.

Right down the street rose up Charles's Mercantile financed in part by his mother's mules. Mazy heard them arguing with packers over supplies one morning when she delivered the milk tins to Washington's Market. She could hear Adora screeching from the covered walk.

"You brought me more Dutch ovens? I ordered three-legged spiders. What about the Lover's Eyes? By the time you get here with them, the fad'll be over. People will paint their own eye for a locket. And what about that piano?" she said to the packer's back as he unloosed diamond hitches to unload his tired mules. "We ordered that first thing, didn't you, Charles?"

"I left that to you, Mother. My gout..."

She halted and looked at him, eyes soft. "Your gout. Only old people are supposed to get that," she said. "My poor baby. I'll check the orders. See if it's there. It isn't something I'd be likely to forget, though, a piano coming in. You bring those bolts of cloth?" She was back at the packer. "And maple candies? I'm tired of Hong Kong getting all the market for sweets. You take better care of those Chinese than you do your American customers. Oh, hello, Mazy. I didn't see you there."

"I've got to get my foot up, Mother." Charles walked on his heel, limping in a way Mazy thought exaggerated.

"You should ride out to Mazy's and wait until one of her cows makes a pie. Stick your foot in it while it's still hot. That works," she said. "For gout. Elizabeth told me. Doesn't it, Mazy?" she said as she fast-walked after her son inside the store. "Charles?"

Mazy shook her head. The last thing she wanted was Charles Wilson putting his feet in a cow pie while she was anywhere around.

She had enough chaos in her life. Much as she planned, nothing seemed to happen easily. She milked her cows—but Mavis would stick her tail in the bucket, ruining a day's work. One morning, Jennifer got into clover next to the creek and bloated. It had taken her and Jason and Jessie as well to get the cow up, put a stick to hold her mouth open, then yank her neck tight toward her back, trying to release the gas. They'd walked her then, for more than an hour while Mazy frantically read in

Jeremy's old cow books to see if there was anything more they could do. *If all else fails, seek the highest point of the bloat on the left side. With a butcher's knife, puncture the cow's stomach at the top to release the gas. The cow may not survive this procedure.* One of Lura's sharpened knives had done the deed, and Jennifer survived. But now Mazy had to clean the wound daily to prevent infection. Always something to break up her plans.

One day she'd churned the butter for placing into new wooden molds. But the cart for hauling the milk broke, spilling white gold into the thirsty dirt. She planned, all right. But she must not be doing something essential or she wouldn't be having so many problems.

"If I do things right, if I plan them out and work hard, then they should work. And if they don't, it must be my fault," Mazy told Ruth one day as her friend arrived home from her new job as a lithographer.

Ruth was thoughtful, then said, "If you tell yourself you've made a mistake or done something stupid every time something happens, you'll soon be afraid to do anything, won't you? I would be."

Ruth pulled seven-inch hatpins from her wide-brimmed hat and placed it on a hook. "I can hardly wait to get out of this corset," she said.

Mazy still found it strange to see Ruth wearing a skirt and going off to work.

"Maybe God's telling me to make a new plan," Mazy said. "I just haven't been listening."

"Do you have need of Sarah?" Ruth asked Elizabeth. "She's a good little worker."

Elizabeth motioned Sarah away from the tent front she called the Popover Bakery where she'd been kneading bread and strudels since the fire. "We grownups just need some time to talk here. Why don't you see what Ernest is up to? His saddle shop is almost rebuilt. My bakery is next for boards."

"I see what you're doing, Ruth," Elizabeth said when the child was out of earshot "It's hard enough to see Ned off with Suzanne and Lura on their 'entertainment circuit.' You've got Jason and Jessie working with Mazy. Just seems like you, young woman, are walking on a crooked road. 'Course Lura's traveling there, too, and she's old enough to know better. No helping her see different, though. But you—"

"Please," Ruth said. "Mazy's already said I'm asking for more trouble than a barrel full of snakes. But this is best. The lithograph work isn't so bad. I can put up with Sam Dosh's tirades, too. For the children's sake. Besides, everyone says Ned has a voice like an angel. He promises to bring his weight in gold dust come winter, if their touring is successful. He'll see some of California, too."

"That's a reason to deprive yourself of him? For the money?"

"One look at California prices should answer that. But no, it isn't for the money I let him go. Suzanne can nurture his music. I can't. And you can teach Sarah to bake. I can't. And Jason and Jessie, well, Mazy's got a way with tough little kids. I don't."

"You sell yourself short, I'll ponder. Seem to me—"

Ruth held her hand up to stop Elizabeth's next thought.

"The Popover'll be inside a building before long," Elizabeth conceded, allowing herself to consider Ruth's request. "Out of this cooking tent. Not a brick building, mind you, but we ain't on the main street, either. The strudels and pretzels'll lure them in. Sarah could run errands." She turned her hands over, followed the palm lines with one finger. "These're better, but sometimes they still tingle and ache. I guess I could use another pair of hands even though it worries me, Ruth, that Sarah'll be serving me instead of you. I have to say, Ruthie, seeing you in a skirt with them feathers in your head and seven-inch hatpins 'stead of your whip makes me wonder what your running is really taking you to, or if you're standing still."

Essential. Mazy's husband Jeremy had used that word often as he gazed over the top of his round glasses, frequently sending a withering look his wife's way. Scorn might have better described it. Or disgust. Oh, Jeremy would smile that lazy smile of his, even run his hands through her tousle of auburn hair and call her "his pine of sturdy stock." Now with a year since his death, it was his looks of disgust that kept more gentle memories distant.

"Stand back," Mazy told Jessie as she poured water over the ashes in the pit behind the house. They were making soap. That was an essential she thought Jessie should know about. They'd made the molds first, greasing the wooden rectangles with butter. Then Mazy'd found a broom handle. Soap handles seemed to get shorter through the years, the lye formed from the ashes and peppermint tea-scented water eating away at the wood. In the blue-sky afternoon, Mazy stirred, keeping her head twisted away, coughing, then taking in a good breath. She told Jessie what she was doing.

"Put your hand over the top, like this," she said. "Don't touch it. It'll burn. Now hold your breath so you're not breathing in this stuff. All right. Feel the heat of it? When it's just right, we'll dip in the crock and slowly pour it over the tallow. Until it's like honey, creamy-like. Stir now," she told Jessie, "for a half hour or more, or do you want to do something else?"

"Got nothing to do," the girl said.

"Gather up the eggs, then," Mazy told her, "or make yourself a special mold, something that'll be just yours." Jessie's face lit up, and she headed toward the house.

The stirring gave Mazy time to think. Today, Jeremy just seemed on her mind.

Sometimes she wondered if her marriage could have survived had Jeremy lived, respect so essential in a marriage and its absence such a ravage on theirs. A frightening thought. Maybe that was why Seth's suggestions of closeness found their way to a category she labeled "later" in her mind.

Honor, that was another essential. She had promised to love, honor, and obey him, and she had. It was he who'd worn deception. Seth showed up in that thought too. Could she honor a man who liked whisky and widows? Could she trust him to be what he was and accept his good qualities without letting his other ones keep her pushing him away? What was essential in a marriage anyway?

She had wondered over that. After nearly a year here, she still didn't know what it was that kept her deceased husband more on her mind than the friendship and love offered by another. At twenty years of age, Mazy knew how to be a daughter. She'd been what she thought was a good wife. She had no brothers or sisters, so being a sibling wasn't asked of her. Maybe her relationship with Ruth fit that, a sister in spirit, at least. But this morning, when Mazy pressed at the dark circles under her eyes—eyes Jeremy had once called "fern green"—she'd called herself a widow. A young unmarried woman. She still didn't know how to be that.

Maybe that was what Suzanne was trying to discover by heading into the camps as an entertainer, trying to find her way as a woman not dependent on someone else. She hadn't even asked for Mazy's opinion, just worked it out with Lura, and suddenly they were gone. It would have been easier on the rest of them if Suzanne had allowed assistance. Even while staying during Tipton's wedding, she'd insisted on dressing her children herself, putting the dog's harness on, even if it meant the rest of them twiddled their thumbs until she was ready. She'd even told them that when she got back from their "entertainment tour" she'd be getting her own place again, without moving in with any of them. "I don't want to hold you hostage," she told them. "So don't be planning for me." She'd turned her head to where Mazy stood—it was almost as though Suzanne could see who would be planning the most.

"That's foolish, Suzanne," Mazy had told her. "The fire could have been disastrous."

"But it wasn't."

Even Seth condoned Suzanne's plan. At least he located props for their show, costumes and such, before they left. Apparently he had "friends" from Sacramento who performed in saloons too. Mazy wondered if Seth's shadow-life was as unknown to her as Jeremy's had been.

After they waved good-bye to the Schmidtke wagon filled with entertainers, Mazy told her mother she was thinking of building a house large enough for Suzanne and the boys, too, when they got back. "I know she doesn't see she'll need one of us, but I think I can convince her."

Her mother had shook her head. "Haven't you learned yet that Suzanne's got her own way of seeing things? And you, you're putting off seeing what you need to, just focusing on other people's problems. Might just ask yourself who you're really helping and what it is you avoid like it was a fragrant skunk."

Her mother's willingness to let things be, to just accept things as they came without attempt to alter made Mazy wonder sometimes if she hadn't been an orphan child picked up after being abandoned at her mother's door.

"Think of why you're always giving advice," Elizabeth told her, patting her daughter's shoulder. "People got to solve their own troubles, Madison. You can't always be 'Mazy fix-it' even though it's natural to you."

She had felt her face flush. This, from her mother who would offer hospitality to a stranger from her own deathbed.

"You do too much for someone, Mazy, and they start to eat the idea that they can't do it for themselves. They wonder if you're maybe wanting something back from them. Or worse, they accept it, come to count on your giving. Then they just wait and open their mouths like baby birds expecting others to do for them. Then folks resent it if you don't. What we intend ain't always what arrives."

"Oh, Mother," she'd protested, but a flicker of recognition came wrapped within Elizabeth's words. Mazy didn't want to end up as the period of a sentence that always read: *You couldn't do it without me.* She'd resent that herself, she guessed, which was probably why she spent so much time making her plans, making sure no one ever had to help her.

On the trail, when she'd miscarried, then she'd accepted help. But the trail wasn't life. The journey west was a pause, a hesitation, nothing more. All of what she'd learned along the way—like looking forward just a bit to the pleasant places God had in store for her—was more difficult to apply in everyday life, harder to hang on to in any new moment. She wondered if that was why she spent so much time in the past or in other people's lives and couldn't seem to settle on what she should do about her own.

Jessie interrupted her reverie. "Is the soap ready?" The girl puffed as she rolled a heavy stone, stopped it at Mazy's feet. The center had been smoothed out into an almost perfect oval several inches deep.

"Where'd you find that?"

"With some baskets and stuff. Buried off over that way," she pointed to an area in the tree line. "I dug 'em up. *Auntie* Ruth says they're old Indian things. This'll make a round soap, won't it?"

Mazy nodded, kept stirring. Ruth was right. The girl did have a funny emphasis on the word *auntie.* "Help pour the lye and tallow mixture into the mold," Mazy said "Keep your head to the side so the fumes don't sicken you. Looks about right," she said then. "We'll stir in a little sugar. Makes the soap lather."

Together they lifted the pottery crock and poured the creamy substance into the wooden molds making sure there was enough left for Jessie's stone one. "After it sets for a bit—no, don't touch it. It'll still burn you. After it sets, we'll use a knife and cut lines for breaking it later. That'll be the size we get. Then we let it dry in the shade. In a month or so, we'll wrap them and have a daily treasure that makes us clean and smells nice, too. Good work, Jessie," she said.

The girl beamed, and Mazy squeezed her thin shoulder. "Your mold has the most interesting shape. You have your auntie's eye for art."

Jessie looked at her, cocked her head to the side, and opened her mouth as though to speak. She didn't. Instead she bent to push the stone into the shade of the back of the house.

Making something practical out of discard, that was how Mazy saw making soap. Maybe it said something essential about the remaking of her life.

They gathered for a meal at the newly built St. Charles Hotel, as they'd agreed after the fire to do weekly. On Sunday, the widows worshiped together at Reverend Hill's Methodist Church, continuing "stedfastly in the apostles' doctrine and fellowship," as the verse in Acts said to do, "and in breaking of bread, and in prayers." On this Wednesday, the fellowship had broadened from the wagon train women to some new additions.

"The St. Charles still has the best food in town," Adora said.

"My baked goods and candies are much improved with Mrs. Mueller's charms," Gus said. He owned the rebuilt St. Charles, along with the Popover Bakery Elizabeth ran. He sat next to Mazy's mother, his short, fat fingers covering the dots of brown that speckled the backs of Elizabeth's hands. "I am sorry Mr. Kossuth did not rebuild. Competition is good for the soul."

"If that were true, this country'd be made of saints instead of all these sinners," Mazy said. "Present company excluded—or almost," she said.

"One can't live on bread alone," Adora said.

"No, you need sweet things, too," Elizabeth said. "That's why I'm so proud of Mazy's cows. Cream makes such a difference in cooking."

"I don't suppose I could talk you into selling your milk through my store," Charles said.

Mazy still found the sound of his voice jarring, thinking of the hurt he'd given to his sister and his mother. They'd just been healing of it too, looking forward to a new adventure when his finely etched face with those tight Roman curls showed up, chopped ear and all.

"It's mostly spoken for," Mazy said. "Until I expand my herd..." She raised her hands as if to say it was out of hers. "Maybe you can drive one or two cows down from Fort Vancouver," Mazy said then, aware of the chill in her voice. "You being such a well-traveled man."

"Now, Mazy, my Charles is just taking care of his mama," Adora defended. "With the money I got for the mules, we didn't have to borrow any to stock our shelves. Unlike some folks building a herd on borrowed funds. We're contributing to the community, Charles and me."

"And what he could have had in Wisconsin, if I remember right," Mazy said.

"Well, we had to follow dear Tipton now, didn't we?" Charles told her, sitting up quickly enough that Mazy blinked and moved her head back. Charles sucked on the stick he used to stir his gin-sling, eased back into his chair.

Mazy couldn't understand how Adora had simply let him slither back into her life, shatter the fragile relationship she'd restored with her daughter, and then act as though this was what was always meant to be. She'd hated seeing the tears pool in Tipton's eyes as she hugged her mother good-bye. Nehemiah had borrowed Mazy and Elizabeth's oxen to haul the wagon, leaving the mules behind. Mazy hadn't even had time alone to talk with Tipton and couldn't imagine the betrayal she felt.

But Mazy ached too, seeing Adora treat her boy as though he were the prodigal son returning. He was hardly that. He hadn't a repentant bone in his body. And his return, riding high on a good horse, his shoes polished and his hair cut by a barber's scissors, told them all he'd done well, despite what he said, while his mother and sister had suffered terribly from their losses on the trail. He would do anything, Mazy suspected, to achieve his ends.

But who around here wouldn't? she decided as she and her mother walked back to Elizabeth's new little two-story bakery after their St. Charles meal. Everyone in Shasta seemed engulfed in the drama of becoming rich overnight, regardless of the cost. Seth wasn't unique in that either, she guessed. And who was she to say she wasn't just like them, in her way? Thinking about how much money she could get for milk, how she'd expand her herd once the cow brute arrived, what alternative she had if it didn't. Oh, she provided food for the orphans, had placed a few in worthy homes. She tried to offer a way out for the women like Esty too. She'd even invited two or three to tea, but they'd declined.

And she'd had no help from the press with her concerns, even after she took out ads, even after Ruth began work there. Instead they'd printed an article rousing people to more killing of any remaining Wintus and Shastas. Mazy cut the article out of the *Courier* and showed it to her mother.

"Well, ponder that," Elizabeth said, pinching her nose with her fingers, shaking her head. "What have we come to, then?"

"It isn't the kind of place I hoped to make my home in," Mazy said. "Not a very pleasant place at all." They sat for the evening on the porch at the Popover, shaded by a spreading oak that had survived the fire. Smells of ginger drifted from Hong Kong and dogs barked in the distance. Mazy missed Pig anew. Sarah worked on her samplers, and Mazy would soon head back to Ruth's, making the early evening ride on Ink, taking less than an hour to do it.

"This can be a pleasant place," Elizabeth said. "It's all in what you make it. I like the mix of Celestials and Portuguese and trappers and loggers and sweet-smelling women, stagecoaches bringing in new folks and wagon trains heading this way more now. And miners coming in with nuggets, listening to others soothing the wounds of those who've spent their last dust. The swirl of things don't have to be all you see of this place. It ain't the landscape so much as it's your eyes, the way you see. Why—"

"Reverend Hill said people actually justify their accumulation of wealth through this hostage-taking and slavery, by giving a tithe! Can you imagine?" Mazy said.

"Everyone's looking for ways to soothe their souls," Elizabeth said.

"Coveting's a fever, I'll ponder, with healing a long and wandering process. 'Specially if what you're seeking promises just more empty hunger."

Greed. That was the word Mazy'd written in her journal that morning. It overwhelmed this California land. There were laws against greed, scriptural laws, yet here she sat in the midst of people driven by it, and she was powerless to stop it. The opposite of greed, what would that be? *Generosity,* a characteristic of God she'd "pondered" more than once.

"I don't understand why Adora didn't go with her only daughter," Mazy said. "Like you did. Was she trying to be generous to Charles at the expense of Tipton? To just throw in again with that rascal son of hers seems so shortsighted." Mazy spoke out loud as though her mother'd been part of her thoughts. "He'll just take advantage of her. I can see it already."

"Hard to know how to help a child—send 'em away, take 'em back, loan 'em money, make 'em pay. How to forgive but not get caught up in the same old ways of doing things." She reread the newspaper article Mazy had given her, then handed it back. "Most folks don't realize that getting money ain't the same as keeping it. They get blinded. Don't find out how the gold and the seeking of it holds them hostage. All the while they think they're hanging on to something, it's choking the air outta them. Same thing happens to anything we hang onto too tight. Keeps us distracted from what God intended."

Mazy stared. Was her mother talking of gold or…

She bit hard on a piece of maple candy, rubbed at her cheek. "I think I broke my tooth."

"Let me look," Elizabeth said. She motioned for her daughter to open her mouth. "Your tooth looks fine." Elizabeth sat back, wiped her forehead with the back of her hand, patted her neck with a silk hanky. "It's hotter than a highwayman's pistol," she said. "Or maybe older people just sweat more."

Mazy looked over at her mother, reached to fluff a graying curl back behind her ear. "You're surely not old, Mother. Why, you even have a suitor."

Elizabeth smiled. "We ain't never too old to love."

Her mother was like an acorn, Mazy decided, bobbing along in a rushing river, believing that God would plant her where he wanted in his time and she'd eventually become the oak that he intended, shading the place he had chosen.

Mazy hoped she'd live to become so strong an oak.

Zane spent the time gathering up ore from the other traps, the other cabins on his line. He had time to think, to plan. He dreamed now of what he'd do, how he could use each of them to finally get to Ruth. He was ready. He'd given Suzanne enough time to become desperate, needing him. And it was time to step up his pursuit of Ruth.

He rode back in to Shasta, surprised at the brick-and-lead buildings, the activity. More pack strings, more stages spitting out people. The trees still stood with blackened trunks, but the smells of beefsteak drifted to him as he rode past the St. Charles.

Find Suzanne. That was his focus now. Find her first.

As independent as Suzanne was, he knew she'd rebuild, make her own place. But chances were she was still at Ruth's, waiting. Stores and hotels would take precedence over some blind woman's whim.

He stopped first at the saloon and located Esty, telling her he was a friend of Suzanne's.

"If that's so, you'd know she left town," Esty told him. She squinted her eyes in suspicion.

"I've been...unavailable," he said, his mouth dry as he breathed through it.

"She's with a traveling group," Esty said after a time, watching him. "They're going to the camps and entertaining. You might check with

Mrs. Mueller over at Popover. She kept pretty good tabs on Suzanne and the boys."

He found the bakery, and using his most pleasant voice told the large woman with flour up to her elbows that he was a friend of Suzanne's. "Zane Randolph," he said before he realized what he'd done.

"Where you know her from?"

"Back in Missouri," he said. "I've just arrived and I'm most anxious to see her. She sent a letter telling me she was here. I...have failed to find her."

"She's singing and playacting and probably having quite the time. Little scary, but then most all life is at some time or another, wouldn't you say, Mr. Randolph? That's what you said your name was?"

He nodded. "And you have no idea at all where she might be?"

"None. Expect her back come August, maybe later. You might ask at the *Courier.* A friend of hers works there, Ruth Martin. She might know just where about Suzanne and the troupe were headed. One of her kids is with her. You just got here in town, though? Huh. Your name sure sounds familiar."

"All right," Elizabeth told Sarah after Zane Randolph left. "You can come out now. I see your feet hiding behind them flour barrels. What're you doing back there?"

"Staying safe."

"From who? Me?" Elizabeth turned now, alarmed by the sound of the child's voice.

"That man. Why'd he say his name was Zane Randolph? His name's Wesley."

"Suzanne's Wesley?"

Sarah nodded. "I seen him there."

"Ponder that." She tapped her floured finger to the side of her cheek.

Not back until August? How dare she be difficult. He should not have to wait. He was tired of waiting, of playing her games. A blind woman with no more sense than to turn his proposal down and set herself for the pawing-on of slobbering miners. She used him, did this on purpose, coming and going, pretending weakness, just as Ruth had done. Ruth probably knew where she was.

Ruth. She had done this! Her refusal to be herded as a woman should, spreading like disease to Suzanne. Ruth, luring him west, just to humiliate him using a blind woman. She was evil, Ruth was. Deserving of what she would get. Never mind Suzanne. It was Ruth who needed tending. He should go to the newspaper, see her sitting there, holding a lithograph. Was this now the time to take her, to make real his image of her dressed in white inside her coffin? She was so sure that he would follow, so sure she was in control. That was why she lived out in the open, in her old ways, drawing pictures on stones. His breathing rasped. He had to calm himself, to think. She had done this to him.

He could take Ruth. She probably knew he was watching her, had known it all along and didn't care. He hadn't made her weep and wonder. She laughed at him, talked with Suzanne about him whenever she had the chance, talked with the baker woman, too. Hadn't she said his name was familiar? Ruth made this happen, lured him here, made him come after her with her lies, her tricks, her judgments, then deliberately got in his way. His mouth dried from his breathing. He swallowed.

Ruth had to pay now. The time had come.

He wanted it over. Not at the newspaper office. He would have to do it on the road between the meadow and town. Five miles to find the perfect place to take her. Close to home, so she'd think that she was safe.

Zane spurred the horse, headed east, rode to the tree line that surrounded the meadow. He found a higher, well-hidden place, and there he pulled his telescoping glass from its leather holder. He scanned the road behind him, then turned to Ruth's farm. He saw the privy. Nearby, someone stood on a stump, throwing clothes over a rope. He could see feet beneath the sheets and towels. He couldn't tell who it was. A child. The cabin stood partly shaded by oaks and a smattering of yellow pines. He moved past the house, the barn, to the meadow.

He saw milk cows. A black mule. Some oxen. A long-horned bull. Two horses. A herd of deer. No! Not deer. He counted—ten, fifteen horses. And Durham cattle. More than he'd ever seen there before, still coming, being pushed by drovers.

Someone rushed out of the barn now, running like a woman, but wearing pants. Ruth! He was sure it was her. He could tell it was Ruth as she bounded up to one of the drovers, patted at the lathered horse. The man swept his hat, held it to his chest, bent forward to her.

Zane removed the glass. His eye caught another movement. He looked again. A woman kicked up her skirts as she ran. A boy whooped and shouted, then looked up at a skinny man riding a good mount near the back. Behind him rode another and another. Too many men. Dust and the milling of horses and cattle. The men all smiles. Ruth's stallion and gelding kicking and whinnying at the presence of so many mares. And there came Jessie. Zane's Jessie. Limping a bit as she hurried from the back of the house. She must have been the one hanging clothes. Ruth pointed at the girl. The child stomped back toward the house, toward the clothesline, throwing more garments over the rope. The towels and skirts on the line formed a perfect barrier between the activity in the meadow and what Zane now had in mind.

Suzanne knew it might not have been best idea she'd ever had. But how else could she bring up two boys without a father—one of whom hadn't said much more than "Mommy" for the past six months? She'd taken a gift and turned it into a way to be responsible for her family—and she was having the time of her life. They were well treated by the crowds. Was it wrong to have a fine time and still serve her family well?

"We're almost ready," Mariah told her. "Can you hear them pounding? I think it's their gold pans. They don't seem to go anywhere without them."

Hear them? The stomping and pounding was music to Suzanne's ears, salve to her soul, misplaced as their adoration might have been.

"Your hair looks like twists of gold dust laced with the night," Mariah said. She was a sweet child. "Even if I did fix it myself. The little tin stars we made catch the lamplight." She pressed her fingers against Suzanne's hair. "They'll love it out there."

"Thank you."

Suzanne reached out and, with the palm of her hand, gently cupped Mariah's ear, brushed her cheek with the flesh of her thumb. Her skin was smooth as a piano key, and she imagined it as white. She felt the girl's face smile. Suzanne could localize sound well enough that she could imagine where her face was, could "see" Mariah's ears and eyes and the brush of her hair, so that when she reached out for a familiar person now, she was certain and sure. Like the photographer she'd been, she could aim, focus, then touch.

She remembered a psalm Sister Esther read once at one of their Sunday stops: " 'Great peace have they which love thy law: and nothing shall offend them.' Psalm one-nineteen, verse one hundred sixty-five. Peace, greater than any we might know of our own effort, a completeness," Sister Esther told her. "It's what God offers with him and his laws as the focus." Suzanne liked the image of not being offended as much as the picture of peace and God's law as the focus.

"I wish you could see yourself," Mariah said. "You really are beautiful."

"Thank you," Suzanne said.

She felt the curls the girl had twisted with the hot iron then pressed braids of black thread through them to set off the blond hair now piled high. The tin stars poked upward like a crown. Mariah described things as she worked, not as fully as Tipton had, but with her own flair.

Pig whined, pressed against Suzanne's leg. "Looks like everyone's getting impatient," Mariah said.

Suzanne heard bursts of laughter, foot stomping as they called out her name, and the patter of their hands on their knees, slapping for her presence. Tobacco smoke tickled her nose, and she felt a breeze lift the crack at the flaps of the dressing tent Lura, Ned, and Mariah had set up beside the big one. Suzanne pushed her round dark glasses onto her face, smoothed the skirt at her hips, the linen cool despite the August heat. Then she felt for her troubadour harp, picked it up. She grabbed Pig's harness and took a deep breath. "All right," she said. "Get Ned and Clayton ready. They're on next."

Suzanne stepped through the opening. She smelled the smoke of cigars, the pounding got louder, and she heard appreciative applause, a sound she never imagined she'd ever hear for anything she did. Pig led her to a chair. She seated herself, and with the first strum of the harp and her clear soprano voice lifted in song, the room hushed then exploded into applause as she completed the old Irish hymn, "Be Thou My Vision." As she bowed, Suzanne marveled again at her choices. A body had to ache and stretch a bit to see just what it could do if a person wasn't too frightened to step out onto a cloud of faith, believing she would not fall through.

17

sharpening

"Matt Schmidtke!" Ruth beamed at the lead drover. "You made it! I can't believe it! It's incredible, just incredible!"

"At your service, Miss Martin," Matt said. "With apologies for the delay." He held his hat at his chest. "Ma'am," he said. He still had that shock of white hair against the black. Ruth blinked. Had he been that big a man when he left a year ago? No, he'd been merely a boy. A nice boy, a thoughtful boy, but still just a boy.

Joe Pepin, the string-bean drover who she thought was in charge of bringing her horses and cattle and Mazy's bull west, rode up now, his Adam's apple bobbing. "Good to see you, Miss Martin, Mrs. Bacon," he said. "Glad you made it."

"Oh, we made it fine," Mazy told him. "It was you we were worried over."

Ruth smiled at the sight of the sun on the brood mares, the sounds of whinnying so welcome. "You did well," Ruth told him. "Thank you. Thank you, Joe, very much."

"Don't thank me," Joe said. "Matthew there's the one who did it. Got us through things I never woulda. Yup, he's the one to thank."

"Now, Joe, don't be modest," Matt said. "It was a team effort. Hired on some boys to help us bring them south. What took us some time was wintering in Oregon. Worst ever, they said. Fed the horses tree moss, snow was so deep. Had to earn us some wage money. Sorry about not letting you know. When we got your letter, we decided to beat the postman south and just show up."

"And here you are," Mazy said. "Marvel give you any trouble?"

"You ever know a bull that didn't?" Matt laughed. "Kept our cows busy."

Ruth thought he had a nice laugh, full and deep. And Joe had called him "Matthew" not "Matt." *How old was he, anyway?* Ruth thought. She looked away.

"Is my ma around? My sister, Mariah?" he asked then.

"They're...working," Mazy said. "Your mother is quite an enterprising soul."

"Ma?"

"We have some stories to tell you," Jason said. "She's in the gold fields."

"Ma?" Matt repeated. He put his hat back on, held the reins lightly in his crossed hands. "My quiet little mother?"

Mazy laughed. "Your sister's with her, along with Suzanne Cullver. Remember her? They're entertaining in the gold fields. People change in a year. Your mother sure has."

"And you've grown a foot," Matt told Jason. Ruth thought Jason stretched even taller with the boy's, no, the man's notice.

"I'm helping Mazy with the milking," he said. "And I might get to go with Mr. Forrester if he brings some wagons in next month."

"Good for you. Looks like lots of changes." He smiled at Ruth, then twisted in his saddle to scan the meadow. "Good choice, Miss Martin. Good stack of grass hay you put up, too."

"It's Ruth," she said. "Ruth Martin." She looked away, almost shaky. *What was this about?* "Let's get you men something to eat. You must be starved what with all that time on the trail."

"For a lot of things," Matt said, looking straight at her.

Too many people. Too many. Zane felt a thudding in his head. He pinched at his nose. This must not unravel. Not now. He had to make a plan. He'd take the girl when Ruth was at work at the paper. Yes. When the others were milking, he could go into the house and get the child. He'd have to chloroform her to put her out. And he needed to leave something behind—the perfect thing to let Ruth know that Jessie had gone with her father. Ruth deserved to know, so her confusion could twist and turn into a paralysis of fear and powerlessness. He knew that progression. Had known it, over and over again.

"He wasn't a nice man, Ma," Mariah told Lura. "We can't be letting people come back here with Suzanne and the boys. Not safe." The evening cooled the hot day, and the women stood outside the wagon, letting the still air dry their skin.

"I didn't *let* him. He pushed by, said he *had* to see Suzanne, couldn't live unless he personal-like gave her his gold nugget. Don't you be telling your elders what's what, missy," Lura said, then, "What was I to do? It was the size of my fist."

"Keep him out," Mariah said. "Suzanne spent almost two hours talking to him. I told him to leave. She did too. Pig growled every time he got too close."

"Well, see, Pig took care of her."

"But he could have shot Pig, hurt the boys. Hurt Suzanne. He only left when he was ready, didn't care what we wanted." Mariah hesitated. "I was scared, Ma, not just for them but for me. For you."

"Some of these people forget they're human," Suzanne said. "There's no law anywhere near. They know no one can make them account for what they do—they have to be gentled out."

"And the whisky—"

"It's all right," Lura told her. "We'll get you a gun."

"Mariah's right. We've got to prepare better. Not be letting this happen," Suzanne said.

"Did he give it to you, then?"

"What?"

"The nugget, of course."

"Yes," Suzanne said. She was too tired to manage this argument—one of many between Mariah and her mother. "He did. But I gave it back."

"What?"

"It came with conditions," Suzanne said. She sank into the chair, wanting to take her corset off, get out of the powdered wig she wore for this latest performance. She was tired. Too tired. She'd been so happy before going on stage. She'd sung, then declaimed from Elizabeth Barrett Browning's poems that Mariah had helped her memorize.

Then this intrusion, this violation, happened. Almost as it had occurred with Wesley—someone violating a boundary she'd put up, walking right through it. She took a deep breath, felt herself biting her lip. Pig pushed his head against her, and she scratched his ear. "You're tired too, aren't you?"

"What conditions?" Lura persisted. She helped Suzanne lift the wig from her head.

"Marriage," Suzanne said. "He proposed marriage."

"Oh. Well, that's nothing new."

Free of the wig, Suzanne reached for Pig's halter, turned and stepped inside the wagon.

Suzanne heard shuffling. Someone followed her. She smelled Lura's perfume, heard her move as though she looked to clear a place to sit. "He was good-looking," Lura said then. "You couldn't see that, but he had a good tailor. And money. Nugget tells you that. Want me to help with your dress, there?"

Suzanne nodded. "He was also very persistent. He didn't listen to what a lady told him, which was 'no, thank you' in as many different ways as I could. "

"But it could be your way out," Lura said. "Listen, you can't keep this up forever, Mariah's right about that. But you could…betroth yourself to one like that. Not marry, of course, but accept money. For wedding plans. I heard about a woman who did that. Maybe even accept the interests of another someplace farther on. Wouldn't really be cheating."

"Ma!"

"You still listening? Go to bed, child," Lura told Mariah. "A woman's got to use what she's got, to survive," Lura continued. She lifted the dress from Suzanne, untied her hoops at the waist. "All I've got is my business sense. So I'm putting that to production, here."

"You have cattle in Oregon, Ma," Mariah reminded her. "That might be a better life."

"Shush. This is a bird in the hand." She turned back to Suzanne. "You, you got your looks and talents. Why, you could even marry and divorce if you don't like them. Mariah? You still out there, Mariah? Go get your ma a glass of water," she said, and Suzanne heard the girl leave. "Now listen," Lura said. "I've had a few proposals myself, so I know it's not hard to get them. You got to work them right, though. Think on the grounds for divorce in California. There's six or seven. We could find one that'd fit when the time came. And you'd get half of what he had."

"Lura…I…my mind is as soft as a pretzel right now. I don't have another ounce of energy. Let's talk in the morning."

Lura handed Suzanne her nightdress. She felt the thin chemise cool her shoulders. "You just think about this. Couldn't happen anywhere else but in California, right now, with all this gold and hardly any unhitched women about. Timing's everything. Don't want to hold out too long. You'll need a lacier nightdress if you're getting married."

"Lura, please."

The woman left, and Suzanne wondered if it wasn't performing that tired her but this Mad Mule Canyon that just made everyone mad.

On a day in early August, Mazy let her mother know of the plans she and Seth had to ride to Sacramento. "I'll take Ink," she said. "He's a surefooted mule. If you've no objection." She wrapped a bedroll, rolled it in waxed canvas, then tied it with a piece of rawhide. She sniffed at one of the soap molds she'd brought back from Ruth's, pressed her fingers to it. "Not hard enough to cut yet," she said.

Elizabeth sipped on a cup of tea with four chunks of sugar. Hot or cold out, her mother did like sweet tea. Simple things, Mazy thought. Her mother was nurtured by them: sweet tea; fresh-cut flowers in a milk tin adorning the whitewashed table next to her bed; that pair of newly cut-out underdrawers hanging from a nail. "I'm going to make me a new pair every fall," Elizabeth said as Mazy eyed the underthings. "One of my traditions. You sure you don't want me with you in Sacramento?" Elizabeth asked then. "I can tell them that Jeremy received money from the sale of my house as well as yours, so it ain't surprising he had a thousand dollars cash extra with him."

"I hope that's what it's from. But he had to have money for the bull and cows, and after outfitting us to head west—buying your wagon, too—I'm not sure there should have been that much left unless he did have an advance from his brother."

"Well, time you found out so you can let go and start living again," her mother told her.

"I've been living, just fine. I like milking the cows, Mother. I always did. But with Matt—Matthew, he calls himself now—and Joe Pepin agreeing to milk my two cows, Seth and I, I mean, I can do what I need to do. About putting Jeremy's past to rest."

"Your past, too," Elizabeth added. "You deserve that. Seth'll like time with you without the usual interruptions of milking."

Mazy smiled. "It does seem every sweet and intimate moment between us has had a milk bucket in it. But he has 'interests' in Sacramento well beyond spending time with me getting there."

"Don't you be lying to yourself, now, child. He feels something special for you, and he's been waiting like a gentleman to tell you, I'll ponder."

Mazy remembered his pulling her close, his proposal, her own difficulty in even acknowledging it. "Maybe I should clarify for sure why he's willing to go with me," Mazy said.

"He is a good man, child."

"Seth loves to wander and he's a gambler. That's just who he is. Even if he gave up cards, he'd still take risks somewhere else. I'm looking for predictable and routine."

"Taking a chance is what makes life interesting. You got it in your head it's quiet that brings peace. Need something more to fill you up, though. But you got your dicey streaks." Her mother grinned at her. "Take those bloomers. Why, you were the first real person I knew to wear them. And I see you got yourself a new pair, too. Your own fall tradition?"

"They're practical. And you gave that first pair to me, so you were the risky one."

Elizabeth leaned back and closed her eyes. "You were never more alive than at your marriage. Getting all ready to leave with your new husband to a new farmstead, a place of your own. I remember that, watching you go, leaving Milwaukee for Cassville. Nice to ponder that."

"And see what it got me," Mazy said.

"It got you to doing something new and bold and telling yourself you could. It got you heartache, too, I know. But that's part of living. Finding meaning in life don't relieve us of that."

"I'm just planning to be cautious in courtship."

"Tell me something I don't know," Elizabeth laughed. "I hope you ease up in time. You have a heart for loving—loving living things. I'm not pushing you on it. Just want you to know that I see sparks in that man's eyes when you come into view. And I wouldn't want you to be blinded by it when your ol' mother ain't around to lead you through it."

Mazy laughed and felt the urge to hug her, spilling the tea as she did. Elizabeth set the cup down, brushed at the darkening spot on her apron, then opened both arms to her daughter. "Come here. I'll take a real one."

Mazy felt her mother's elbows narrowing into her, palms kept out like wings, still tender from the burns or perhaps now a habit. She smelled lavender soap, felt the softness of her flesh, and noted a fragility, too, in shoulders thinner than she remembered.

Mazy released her. "We'll probably leave tomorrow if things work out with Ruth. And I'll talk to Seth about his intentions."

Her mother smiled. Her fingers lifted Mazy's hair at the back of her neck, letting the air bring coolness. "You do that," she said, "though it's not *his* intentions I'm worried over."

"Otis and Truett have the lumber," Mazy told Seth, "and I can start building. All I need is to give them the thousand dollars for a thousand feet of lumber."

Seth whistled. "Whoa. There's the gold mine to be into. Looks like all those limitless trees'll yield more treasure than gold panning." He walked with her from the bakery to the livery where Ink was kept.

"Now that I've found the perfect place to build, I've decided to construct it myself. It'll only take a week, and I won't have to pay carpenters sixteen dollars a day. I want to make it big enough...for Suzanne to have a choice when she comes back. Is that intruding?"

"Pushy maybe. Suzanne's a grown woman. Knows her own mind. Seemed pretty excited about this latest venture, not that I blame her. Imagine doing something you always wanted to, not letting your lack of sight get in your way."

"She's always wanted to perform?"

"Likes music. Found a way to share it."

"You didn't waste any time helping her find costumes and such. You are a resourceful man, Seth Forrester."

"She likes making people happy with her music. I understand that." He walked quietly beside Mazy for a time. "Gonna build here, huh? Find someone else to join you?"

She sidestepped his insinuation. "I think I've procrastinated long enough anyway. I've been rattling on about people taking advantage, about the lawlessness, the lack of care for the Indians and Chinese, everyone seeming to be driven only by money and how much they have and how to keep it. And as I fretted about my house, I decided I'm no different."

"Pretty different, I'm saying," Seth said.

"Thank you. I appreciate that. But I'm not sure it's true. It won't be until I find out if the money I've been living on this past year is really mine to have. And if not, if the bull and the cows aren't mine either, well, I need to begin to pay it back. Find a way to do that. Otherwise, I'm no different from those I'm judging."

"So when will you go?"

"That depends on you," Mazy said. "I'd like you to escort me, if you will. To be sure I'll get there in good shape."

"Is that sarcasm, Mrs. Bacon?" Seth said. Mazy almost didn't hear him, for the cicadas filling the evening air.

"I'd feel safer with you, what with the reports of raids and all. And you know the area. Thought we could stay where Sister Esther is. Maybe get some better news about Naomi." His shoulder brushed hers as they walked. The smells of roast duck and pork rose from Koon Chong's store. They mixed with the hint of opium lifting from Quong Sing's back room where Mazy'd heard that fifty or so men smoked away their loneliness near the narrow bunks they slept in.

"How soon do you want to leave?"

"I'm ready. Matt, I mean Matthew, has agreed to milk the cows. Jason said he'd help. I was so pleased at that. They'll bring the milk in, too. That last pack train brought in iceboxes, did you know that? And ice blocks wrapped in sand and straw. I want to buy one of those, keep milk fresh and cold, even in heat like this." She stopped herself. "See how quickly I think of *possessing things?* When this trip is over, I may not have a dime except what those cows have made me—and I may not get to keep much of that."

Her slippers caught on a tree root reaching out onto the twisting path they walked. She tripped and Seth caught her, held her. She looked up at him. His eyes moved toward hers, and then he kissed her forehead, gently pressed the back of her neck with his wide hands and pulled her to him. His lips barely touched her eyelids—one after the other—forcing her to close them. He smelled of leather and fine cologne. She felt her palms grow wet, her breathing shift, and she almost allowed herself to sink into the safety of his arms, let something new begin.

She leaned back from him instead. "I'll tell them what happened, the lawyers and Jeremy's brother—if I get to meet him. Give them as much information as I can."

"I'm sure you will," Seth said and he stepped away, brushed a tendril of hair from her temple. She saw him smile, wistful almost. He took her elbow and turned her so they walked again down the street.

"Maybe Jeremy's brother is a kind man," she said, aware now that she rambled. "Maybe he'll understand that his brother didn't always tell his wife of things that mattered," Mazy said. "Maybe what I discover won't surprise me at all. After all, I already know he had a wife and child in Oregon. What more could I discover that would surprise me now?"

"Maybe nothing about him," Seth said. "Maybe something about yourself."

It was dawn. A red-tailed hawk lifted and dipped above him. He had waited. Now he watched Ruth ride off down the trail, west, into town.

He saw the boy herd up the milk cows, watched as the other two men moved them toward the barn. From his two days of watching, this was the routine. The other woman had ridden out with a man. There were no other children about.

Jessie would come to the privy before long. She would stop either on the way or coming back to look at something spread out on a board. In odd containers. This morning, he would be waiting, close to the privy so he could surprise her with the chloroform on his silk handkerchief. Silence her.

He eased his way through the tree line, leading his horse. He held himself still behind the privy. He heard Jessie walk out, her feet swishing through the grass toward the little house. Good. When she finished in the privy, she would leave, then dawdle at the containers. He could take her then. His heart thumped. He heard his own breathing and slowed it.

The leather hinge squeaked as the door opened. He heard her little feet clomping on the wooden floor. He waited. The hinge creaked again. She was walking out. Steady, steady.

He stepped out from behind the privy. He thought of himself as very small now, smaller than a boy, smaller than dog or bird, small enough to drift toward her, pull her with one arm and push the silk into her face with the other. He heard a cat squeal, the girl jumped, said, "Out of my way, you lazy old thing," and then she turned and saw him.

The cat! He lunged for her, hoped he could keep her from screaming. Her mouth open, she backed from him toward the containers. She grabbed at a stone, round and heavy, too heavy, he thought for one so little. He had her now. She lifted the stone up over her head as he grabbed her arm trying to stuff the silk at her nose. She struggled, wiry and strong for someone so young. She tried to bite him. He could sense her sinking, sinking. Then with what felt like one giant effort before she eased against him, she kicked him and broke free. She hefted the stone and slammed it with a thud on his foot. He smelled a whiff of tea-scented soap just as the pain shot through him.

"I guess they have entertainment coming sometime this week at that strip of stores they call a town," David said. He lifted his whip, turned it over to check the repairs he'd made on the cracker. He stepped outside, tied it onto the saddle's front rigging ring, came back inside. "You might hear it from here, the music at least. Funny how sound'll carry in these ravines. Sometimes I can't hear you calling me from the other side of the cabin, but I can hear a man shout about a strike that must be a couple of miles away."

Oltipa tilted her head, the way she told him she didn't understand all that he said, and he smiled, picked up the baby again in one arm and the dog in the other. "Wish I could be here to take you. Might be nice to step out with you, listening to a tune. Maybe if they're delayed, we could do it next week. A day will come when I don't have to work so long a haul. Claim'll be paid off and I can take you dancing. Maybe."

He wished they could hear the entertainers. They'd have a pleasant outing he could follow with a proposal.

He gentled the baby into Oltipa's arms. As she nursed the boy, David felt a fullness inside him. He loved them both. There, he'd said it to himself. If only he could say the words to her.

Oltipa looked up at David and smiled, then brushed the backs of her fingers at the boy's chubby cheeks. David swallowed. "Let's get me something to eat," he said. "Then I best be on my way."

Ruth wore the same dress, the only one she had. *Why was she wearing it?* She shook her head. How silly. At least she hadn't sunk to riding sidesaddle again. She would never do that. And she wasn't even sure why she decided to keep the lithographer work. It had been hard to leave Jason and Jessie that morning. She'd found that odd. She'd enjoyed the chatter about horses with Matthew too. Then, here she rode to work for a man whose editorial policies she detested. Now that she had her horses back, why did she stay on at the *Courier*? When she could begin the work of breeding and selling and making her living.

It was ridiculous, that was what it was. She'd be pleased when Matthew left to find his mother. "There're dozens of little mining towns," she told him. "Some with actual theaters for performances and some with just tents, from what Esty tells me."

Matthew had leaned on his elbows at the table that morning, and behind him Ruth could see the hearth. For the first time, she noticed how bare the house was, how unlived in—except for the clutter of the children. It was almost as if *she* didn't live there. All the things that were personal to her had been somehow moved around, taken down, or altered. She thought about telling Matthew. Telling him about the scratched face on her photograph, the cuts made on her whip with a sharp knife. Telling him that none of the children would own up to it, that she felt all alone. But she hadn't, the thought of sharing it making her weepy or worse.

"And my ma learned about this by just listening to people talking at the post office?"

"Your mother listened while she worked as a banker at the casinos," Ruth said.

"My ma, in the casinos." He shook his head, his wide hands around a tin coffee cup.

"She was just doing what she thought best. Supporting herself and your sister after Charles Wilson took off with her money."

"You know that for sure?"

"Adora said she lost her purse somewhere, and so did your mother. They noticed not all that long after Charles left us. Now he's back, and that store cost more than what the mules brought. Adora swears they built it with no borrowed money. Might actually be some of your mother's lost cash."

"I'll go looking for Mariah and Ma soon as Mazy and Seth get back. Milking cows isn't something I'd want to do for a lifetime, but I guess everybody has to find their own way of living. Me, I like beef cows. And I grew kind of fond of your mares."

Ruth felt herself blush. How childish. She'd poked pins into her new, broad-brimmed hat and left for work. Wearing her only shirtwaist dress.

It was all so confusing. Matt couldn't be more than eighteen at the most and she was what, nearly twenty-four. He was just a boy. He'd done a man's job in bringing the horses back, but he was still just a boy.

It was best she remembered that.

Suzanne folded her son against her breast, cooing to soothe him, the wound of his hand made worse by the guilt of her own neglect. She felt the stickiness. Blood.

"You didn't say I had to watch him, Ma," Mariah said. "You said Ned should. You sent me pawing through your things for a tobacco twist."

"Don't correct your elders, missy," Lura said. "Ned's younger than you, gets tired easily."

"I should just let you keep smoking and listen to you cough all night. You keep us awake," the girl said.

"How did we get from your bad behavior to mine?" Lura said.

"He should have been in bed," Mariah said. "All of us should be asleep."

Suzanne listened, holding her sobbing child in her arms,

"Don't know how he managed to get that knife out anyway," Lura said. "He had to climb on the trunk and balance to reach it."

"You shouldn't have left the knives where he could see them," Mariah told her.

"Listen. Just put a bandage on it, and it'll be fine," Lura said. "Just one of the cuts and scrapes of childhood, all this is. Go ahead, Mariah. Get some water and we'll wipe it off good. It's hardly bleeding, Suzanne. He's just scared, is all. It's all right, Clayton, it is."

Suzanne said, "Pig, get cloth."

"What?" Lura asked as the dog came back with a rag drooping from his mouth. "Well, I'll be."

"I've been teaching him. To help me, even in the wagon, or to do more than just lead me around," Suzanne said. "He picks up things and brings them to me. Surprised me the first time." She patted Clayton's back, and his sobs lessened into deep gulps of air. She had to stay calm so the child would quiet. She could tell by feeling his palm that it oozed blood, but the wound felt like a poke rather than a cut.

"We might work Pig into your act somehow, Suzanne. Charge even more for a dog that does tricks." Lura dabbed with the cloth at Clayton's palm. "Spencer's built a big hotel at Horsetown. Got a concert hall with raised seating for three hundred. We could do a big show there, with the dog. Maybe even dress little Clayton up. Or"—her voice dropped as though to share a secret—"maybe this'll be the time to show a wealthy one you really need his tending, Suzanne. A lot of men like looking after helpless women, with pitiful kids. Makes them feel bigger themselves. Here you are blind, with a wounded child and a baby. Think of the possibilities."

Zane cursed at the child, his foot throbbing from the crack of the stone. Jessie lay in a heap on the grass. He stuffed the chloroformed cloth into his vest, felt "Ruth's surprise." He must leave it, place it somewhere Ruth would find it and know that he'd been there. She must know. The cat hunched on the table, its tail twisting over the wooden soap containers. He brushed at the cat, laid "Ruth's surprise" on the soap. Then he lifted *his* Jessie and limped toward his horse.

He had a dozen back ways out. He decided to skirt Shasta completely to not risk meeting Ruth until he was ready. His toe throbbed, pushed against the top of his boot. The brat lay like a rag across the pommel of his saddle. He'd put her out again before they reached the Wintu woman's cabin. He bumped his toe against the horse and groaned out loud. *No! Never cry out not for pain, not for humiliation, nothing, ever!* She'd done that on purpose, hurt him. Just like Ruth had. Mothers and their brats. Like that Wintu wench and hers.

He'd watch. He'd ride to the area above "Hawk's" cabin, wait to see when the jehu's horse was gone, and then he'd take her, take her and his Jessie north.

And Ruth would know who had her child. He imagined Ruth's terror, her helplessness, her life out of her control. No way to find him. No way to respond. Now she would know what he had survived during those years in the prison. Because of her. He calmed himself by breathing deeply, sucking air in through his teeth. His Jessie moaned. "You're going north with me," he said. "You and the Wintu." He'd forget about Suzanne for now. She'd beg to find him someday. He must focus on Ruth, on her slow demise. He smiled, placing another dab of chloroform over the girl's face. Let Ruth shrivel, knowing that her only living child was now with him.

18

journey into purpose

Ruth had worked at the *Courier* a month now. Plenty of time to get a feel for things. And still, she resisted being under someone else's reins. Oh, she'd met and liked Madeline, the correspondent said to have coined that "Whoa Navigation" name for Shasta. But the editorials of Sam Dosh bothered her. She'd kept her tongue bridled. But today, she felt strong enough to speak of what she saw as injustices. Justice coursed through her blood. She guessed she shared that with Mazy. That and a hard time coming to decisions.

"You have a responsibility," Ruth told the editor that morning, knowing as soon as he looked at her that she should have picked a better time. She'd already stepped into it now. "To set an example for how people might be, could be, should be. To use the press to…inspire all of us to better things."

Sam Dosh's black eyes narrowed as he turned from the type table. He ran ink-stained fingers through flowing black hair. "My dear woman," he said. "An editor reflects the attitudes of his readers. He can't shape them as you suggest." He looked over the top of his glasses at her as though she were a bug. He reminded her of someone she preferred to forget. "I only print the news."

"Sensationalizing, that's what you're doing. Just to sell papers," she charged. "You make the worst of humanity seem reasonable and ignore the facts of decent people doing decent things. You barely gave an inch of copy to the women who raised funds for Father Schwenninger's benevolence efforts for the orphans."

"You actually measured the copy space?" he said.

"Don't change the subject. Why not inspire people to clean up the legal system at least? Change laws so people can be proud of their town. Investigate the jury stacking. Haven't you noticed that rich lawyers never seem to lose a case, and poor ones end up hauling freight or dealing monte no matter how just their cause? And I've yet to see any Indian found 'not' vagrant when that claim is made." Her heart pounded and she felt her cheeks burn. "You could expose that."

"Actually, the judges earn five dollars more when they find for the plaintiff in the cases involving the return of Southern slaves to their owners. Did you know that?" She shook her head. He smiled now. "I suppose I could report that some enterprising soul collected the Chinese miner's tax all winter but kept the money for himself. Enough to build a warehouse or a mercantile. Now is that exposing fraud or celebrating some entrepreneur in our fair city?"

"Do they know who did it?" Dosh shook his head. "Expose it as fraud. That's what it is, and it would be a better story than printing the governor's wretched address, inciting people to storm into Indians' homes."

Dosh bent again to his typesetting, that half-hat on his head keeping his long hair out of the way. *Was he just going to ignore her?* He looked up again. "What you should do is put your passion into women's suffrage," he said. "Cady Stanton and her Seneca Convention and all that chatter about equality. Then you could be a juror. Set the world straight. Suppose you think that large hat you wear symbolizes your...equality, equal to a man. Imagine. A juror with a plume and hatpins."

"I wouldn't stop at being a juror," she said. "I'd become a judge."

He laughed at that. "Not worth holding out for," he told her. "You have a fine gift for lithograph work, Ruth. Best you just stick to that. Beginning right now. We've work to do."

Ruth kept her fume as she accepted his dismissal. There was no changing another's mind. She could only change herself.

Seth and Mazy made the journey without incident. They talked easily as they rode, pulling the horses up to step aside for fast-traveling stages. They met a few riders, several walkers, wagons loaded with lumber, freighters burdened with treasures arriving from San Francisco and shipped up as far as Red Bluff by steamer. Very few Chinese, Mazy noted, or natives, those people more and more seeking shelter from any who might be incited by the calls for their elimination.

"It bothers me, not seeing any Indian people along this road. They must fear for their lives. Everyone's gone crazy and blaming them for it, acting like they stand between them and their riches."

Seth nodded agreement, stayed silent. Mazy supposed he tired of a subject discussed often between them but with no resolution. The Indians couldn't fish the rivers much, the salmon runs were all confused, and the streams were torn up by the dredging and water diversions, the silt and the sand swirling the once clear streams into murk. And when the Shastas or Pitt River or Wintus retaliated by stealing beef cows or pigs or chickens, they were hunted down like murderers, rarely brought back, justice handed out right there, while the fire roasted beef taken just to feed themselves. It was condoned. It was the law, published in the paper.

And she was part of it. Even the house she planned to build would rise near a meadow she learned had once been a place where Indians had camped. And all the deer that nibbled there would eventually go away with her presence and the mules and cows.

"Mother has a heart for Indians," she said as they rode.

"Your mother's an accepting sort. Sees the good in everyone no matter who they are. That's a quality that gathers friends."

"I'm sure that's why we were blessed by those Pawnee back along the Platte River. They rescued us from a certain death as I think on it now. We could have tried to walk back to Wisconsin, but we'd have run out of food long before we got there."

"Glad you didn't try."

"Strange, isn't it? How we can't know what's ahead or how what's happened in the past will be woven into the present. It's a little like reading a book. You hope the author knows there'll be a satisfying ending, but by reading along, you've agreed to trust that, not knowing if the difficult things faced will ultimately lead to something good."

"Doesn't always have to be good to be a satisfying read," Seth said. "Some of my best lessons have come from making mistakes."

She smiled. "No, but there has to be hope. Some meaning found inside it, something that says we had good reason to trust in what we could not see until we got to the end."

"Guess that's why we're not supposed to spend much time bemoaning old memories or speculating about the future," Seth said. "Can't predict what's ahead."

"Yes," Mazy answered, her gloved finger raised to make her point. "But there's something more in life—there has to be—than just how much gold a person can gather up no matter the cost." She looked at Seth, his eyes never having left her face. "I think that's part of my anger yet at Jeremy, that he risked our relationship and all we held dear for an unknown treasure."

"Might have just been the challenge that lured him, Mazy. Maybe he was feeling…stifled back there. You said he hadn't always been a farmer."

"I don't know what he might have been. He had that coughing whenever he worked around the animals. The dust, I think, which would be an odd thing for a man to have and want to stay with farming."

"See there. Maybe he was wanting to just try something new, is all I'm saying. Something he could set his teeth into, really hold onto."

"But he chose the Ayrshires and getting into a dairy herd."

"He might have thought your marriage could survive that kind of change," Seth said. "And it did. You came with him though you didn't want to."

"Yes. And I've found things out about myself I wouldn't otherwise have known. I'm grateful for that."

"You'd have made the best of it with him. Just as I'm hoping you'll be willing to make the best of it with me." He pulled up his horse, reached across the saddle horn to take her hand, held it.

She felt her face go hot. Here it was. Why had she even brought the subject of Jeremy up with Seth? It opened the door to the intimate, a place she hadn't intended to go. She sighed. Maybe it would all be easier if she just gave in, let herself be tended by this good man.

Instead, she cleared her throat. "Seth," she said. "I don't..." She slid her hand out from his. "This isn't a good time. I've got lots on my mind." He nodded and pressed his horse forward.

She did make the best of things, but she wanted more. She wanted to celebrate, to feel real joy. It might not be as a wife and a mother. Maybe as a friend, and in that way she cherished Seth, for helping her see that a man and a woman could be friends and be blessed by it. But she sensed that her passion would come as a woman who made her own way, stood for something, stood for herself. That was what had filled her up on the trail. That was what she wanted: deep-down passion, more than making the best of it. Seth deserved more than that too. "Seth," she said. He turned to her and smiled. "About making the best of things..."

"Wouldn't you? Have made the best of it with Jeremy?" he said. She saw a sadness now in his hazel eyes, a knowing coming through them.

"Yes," she said. "I would have. Those were my vows. But I know something now I didn't know then."

"About his not filling you in on everything?"

She shook her head. "No, about what I'm willing to wait for, what I'm trusting will be there to fill me up, even though I can't see what lies ahead."

The day at the newspaper moved slowly. Five more minutes and she would tell Sam Dosh of her decision.

She finished filling the oil decanter—for whoever would work on the lithographs next. She set the inked rollers in their tin trays. Dosh spent considerable money on good Bavarian stone for the lithographs, allowing her to use hard, gray blocks as though each of her drawings might be as much in demand someday as Currier and Ives pieces were. She surveyed the room, her work. She could have found a worse place to work, easily. If it weren't for his news slants. Maybe if she remained, she could influence him, over time. Maybe she should give this decision one more day.

Finished, she brushed the powdered flint used as an abrasive from her skirt, dipped her hands into the wash basin. She waved them in the warm air, then reached for the hat she'd ordered from Esty after Tipton's wedding. She wasn't sure why. Maybe Dosh was right about the hidden meaning of a hat, its placing women at a different level in the world with men. She poked in the hatpins over the twists of her hair. She stood tall, checked the hat's placement in the hall mirror, and reached for the brass doorknob.

It opened, startling her. The bell above the door rang, and Dosh yelled from the back room, "We're closed."

"I've got it, Mr. Dosh," she said when she saw it was Matthew Schmidtke. He held his hat in his hand. "Ma'am, Ruth. I sure hope little Jessie's been with you all day. We've been looking since noon. Didn't miss her this morning. Jason says she stays to herself, so I didn't think anything was wrong...checked the creek, the river. I...Jason says she troubles you some. Troubling us, too, today. I'm just hoping she followed you in. Should have ridden in sooner. Just kept looking for her there."

"Jessie's missing?" Ruth tried to make sense of it, all thoughts of work and wondering fleeing from her mind. She thought only of her child.

Zane waited most of the day. Finally, he watched the man he assumed was the jehu ride away. He gave him a good long start. His Jessie sat groggy, and he held one arm across her chest, holding her as he eased the horse down the steep draw. They brushed through manzanita, pushed against pines. Once he stubbed his foot against a tree, the horse scraping too close. The jolt of the pain at his toe surprised him, but this time he didn't groan. He was in control now. Everything was under his control.

At the cabin, he flung the door open. He tossed his Jessie inside; the sound and surprise set the baby to crying. The Wintu woman dropped the pan of cornbread she'd been stirring. Zane slammed the door shut, limped forward, the terror in the Wintu woman's eyes almost enough to make him forget the throbbing in his foot.

The Wintu woman picked up the child, pushed him onto her hip and eased back toward the window. His Jessie lay in a heap, barely moving. The woman glanced to the girl then to Zane. Beads of perspiration formed at her forehead. He watched her take in huge gulps of air, and he knew cold knives of fear must have been scraping up her back. Outside, a dog whined.

"Open the door," Zane told her. He took out a pistol now, motioned her toward it. "The mutt wants to be seen, let's see him."

She opened the door. The dog scampered in. As it passed by Zane, he kicked it with the side of his boot, sending it with a yelp back out into the yard. He saw it stand, shake itself, then start back in. Zane stood awkwardly, favoring his foot. The dog barked. Zane took aim and fired.

The baby screamed at the shot. His Jessie woke up.

Ruth fast-walked to the house, Jason nearly running beside her. "We looked everywhere. Thought maybe she took a picnic or something. Or went with you."

"That scamp, that..." Ruth's dress kept catching between her knees, threatening to trip her. "Cantankerous dress," she said, stomping into the house.

It was still and warm inside, despite the shade trees. Ruth walked around the room, looking for some clue, some hint of what this child had come up with now, meant to drive her crazy. *She couldn't hide all day. She must have gone exploring. But where, why?*

Ruth walked out the back door, toward the privy. The cat sat curled on the board with the soap, the grinding stone Jessie used for a mold lying on the grass. "How'd you knock that heavy thing off, Miss Kitty?" Ruth said. Ruth squatted down to retrieve the stone, set it back on the board. She gazed around. Nothing, no hint. Had the child run away? Did she believe no one cared for her? Maybe she interpreted being stuck with Ruth as a punishment while Sarah got to go away.

The cat stood, arched into a purr. Ruth absently stroked its striped back, running her hands out to the end of its tail. She heard it mew, looked down.

When she saw it, her face turned hot and her heart sank.

"Well, Hawk," Zane said. He pivoted awkwardly on one foot. "This is a rare moment. Sit over there," he directed then, quick with his words while his hand pointed with the revolver. "You've made a difficult day for me, my Jessie."

"Not your Jessie," she said.

"Oh, but you are, you are. And you'll have to do a bit more for me since you've broken my toe." He turned to the woman. "A lost possession returned is more treasured than when originally obtained. And today I have two such treasures." The baby cried.

Zane's eyes moved quick to the sound of the boy, noticed the lamp stand, a book or two, things brought in by another. A rocker moved near the baby. The Wintu woman was being kept—but not against her will. "David Taylor's managed my baggage well." The woman's eyes shifted ever so slightly with the stage driver's name. "So you aren't keeping yourself, then? I was right. Ah, this is sweet revenge indeed." He sighed. "I'd love to spend the evening with you basking in this domestic scene, but I fear that gunshot just might bring someone back. And so I suggest we ready ourselves."

He grabbed at the boy the woman held at her hip. He ripped him from his mother's arms. The child screamed, his face reddening as he wailed.

"You," Zane said, pointing with the gun to the woman as her hands reached for her son, "get the rope from my saddle." He pushed her from the child, who shook as he wailed. "Go!" he shouted, then almost sang out sweetly, "You come right back, or I'll be forced to deal with this child the way I know how."

She tried to touch him, and Zane struck her. "Still a bold one, aren't you?" Now he pushed the boy's head, his fingers like long snakes pressing against the boy's face, close to his eyes.

"Ello, ello," she whispered, her fingers to her lips. "No, no." She pulled herself from the floor and scuttled past Zane through the door.

He knew David Taylor might be back, and he debated about waiting, anticipating the pleasure in watching the jehu's face when he came through the door and saw him, this woman again under his control. He wanted him to see that. But he wanted something else more, liking this taking and retaking game better than dealing with mindless men like Greasy managing the claims. He liked this...and imagining Ruth's terror.

He ran his tongue over his lips, decided. "You, my Jessie, find what food you can and put it in a sack."

"No," Jessie said.

Despite his toe throbbing, he lurched toward her and struck her with the back of his hand. "You do what I tell you," he said. Tears filled the girl's eyes, but she held her sob, pressed her fingers to her cheek while she dug in the cupboard for cans.

When the Wintu woman returned, rope in hand, he told her, "Find me something to scratch a note on." He motioned for paper. "I want to be sure when that jehu returns *home* he knows who it is that's intruded."

David carried the payment with him, the monthly installment owed to Mr. Hall. He'd thought about quitting the Baxter stage line and trying to work full-time on the claim his father had abandoned, maybe locate a dry digging where the wet ones hadn't paid. Placers not far away had proven rich, the gravel giving up color enough to support one man at least. Maybe there'd be enough to support him and his family. He smiled. His family.

He could have worked the streams more when he brought food and milk out each week for Oltipa and Ben, maybe pick up extra to repay Mr. Hall faster. He did usually take a pan out and swirl the water up, almost over, the slanted edges as he squatted, watching the boy as he sat in the mud and splashed. Once or twice they watched a raccoon washing itself on the other side of the creek, and the boy pointed. He was quick to notice things.

"It's a raccoon." A person would have thought he had fathered the boy himself.

Yes, he could have worked harder to find some hidden bar or coyote down some random hole hoping it would lead to his fortune. But when he came over the rise at the end of his run, when he dropped down into the gulch where the cabin sat, digger pines and live oaks draping over the roof, when he rode around to the front, saw lilies shooting up green beside the door, the last thing he wanted to think of was working a claim.

He wanted to ride low in the shy glances Oltipa gave him when he handed her the sacks of food, feel the weight of the boy when he lifted him and know that here was something good he had done, something that had made a difference, even if tomorrow they left him, even if they never came back. Here, he had left a mark.

He was pleased about the dog, Chance, coming back too. The little thing kept the rats down. At least after the dog disappeared, not long after the baby was born, they noticed the rodents seeking shelter in the heat of the cabin. David spent more time than he wanted stuffing holes with rags and shakes that the rat would eat through before he returned. He'd have to chink it good before winter—if they were to stay there through another. It was one thing with just Oltipa there. She was tough and sturdy. But with a baby, a long winter might be too much even with all the wood he had chopped and stacked.

He felt the currency in his vest pocket. Maybe he should work on Hall's sympathy a bit more. At least that's what he thought he'd experienced when he'd paid him last month. The old man had coughed and cleared his throat and said something about "not really necessary, David." But he'd taken the money. He should try to negotiate the debt. It would be nice to have the weight of it from his shoulders.

Still, he'd made an agreement. He'd been well paid for that decision despite losing his job. Oltipa's look and the boy's laughter were more than enough compensation. He shook his head, wishing his work days went as quickly as the days he spent with Oltipa and her boy.

Dusk approached. He'd be taking the stage run leaving that night and wasn't far now from Shasta, the trail nearly all downhill coming into town from the northwest. He pressed his knees into the horse, thinking to make up a little time. He was always lagging when he left, he noticed, and hurrying fast coming home.

He pulled up on the reins. "Sorry, boy," he told the horse. He twisted in the saddle. "Thought I heard something." Then, "What're you doing all this way, Chance?" he said when he noticed the dog.

He stepped down off the horse, thinking as he did that he'd have to take the dog with him now or be too late for the stage run. He had no time to take him back. "Tongue all hanging out. You've been on a hike, little one, haven't you? Why'd you chase me?" He picked up the dog. When he did, he felt the ooze, blood seeping from the little dog's side.

The monster kept them bound. My Jessie—the name Zane Randolph called the child—rode in front of Oltipa. He'd wrapped another rope around them both, had that rope attached to his own horse. He could feel any effort they might make to shift or slip away. Oltipa felt the coldness of the child's back through the ache of her own hands, the coldness of her own heart. He had killed her child. He had killed Ben.

Oltipa could hardly stay awake now, but to sleep meant losing a chance for escape, for revenge. It meant betraying her child, her now lost child.

Zane had first secured the girl's hands, then led her to the horse tied outside, his body sideways in the door. "Be civil and stay right there now," he had said and smiled. Always a smile. Then he stepped back inside, grabbed Oltipa, tied her arms behind her. He must have thought they were secure because when he stepped close to the baby on the floor, Ben pulled on the man's pant legs, screaming, each scream piercing through her. Then Zane kicked at him. He grabbed Ben with both hands then, lifting him by the shoulders, his fingers sinking into the smooth flesh of her son who was raging now, screaming, jolted as though dragged across a rough road. Zane shook him, yelled at the boy. "Silence or I will silence you! What I should have done already." A twitch in the man's eyebrow, strange breathing, like a wounded deer, made Oltipa fear his mind had gone away, could not stay with the challenge given by a small, frightened child.

She'd felt a surge of fury then, so powerful and full of protection that she slammed herself into him, jammed her hands against his side using all her force, sure that if he dropped the baby it would be safer than if he shook the child to death.

Zane lurched forward with the blow, one arm letting loose the baby to swing at Oltipa, the other pinching Ben's little arm as he dangled. Zane missed her. She struck at him again with her body, and this time he released the child, who landed on his bottom, the sound of flesh hitting the floor a crack like a shot. Ben screamed while the back of Zane's hand struck her, the pain of the blow to her face nothing compared to the pain of her child's cries, cries she could not comfort.

Zane headed for the child, who was sitting, leaned over into his sobbing, shaking with each new raging scream, his legs straight out, his hands stiff before him, his eyes a thin dark line of terror.

"Leave him," Oltipa said then.

"What?" Zane turned, the sound of her voice breaking into that distant place. "What?"

"You cannot travel with the child. Leave him. Take us. A child's death brings trouble you do not want."

The man scowled as though she'd put new fire into his rage. Oltipa feared it was this that may have saved *their* lives, but not her child's. He stared at the crying baby as though far away, as though remembering another time. He breathed like a gut-shot deer, raspy and sharp. Then quick as a weasel, he twisted back to Oltipa and grabbed her. He pulled the tie that bound her arms until she whimpered, then led her out, lifted her onto the horse behind Jessie, and bound them together with the rope. He returned inside, carrying a lantern and a sack of food. He caught up Oltipa's horse and saddled it, then forced the women onto the mare's back. He tied his own horse to them. His last act before mounting and leading them into the night was to set the lantern back in the cabin.

It went dark inside. The baby whimpered anew, sobbing and screaming a high pitch Oltipa had never heard before, of terror and confusion and rage. She longed to go to him, grateful he still lived enough to cry, powerless to make it stop.

Then the baby quieted, a knife slice to her heart.

Oltipa prayed he might bring the child out, let her take him with them now that he was quiet. She heard nothing, a final silence as the monster pulled the door shut.

David pushed the horse hard, back toward the cabin, the dog tucked into his shirt. He wished there was a way to tell Baxter what had happened, why he wasn't there to take the stage. He'd lose this job sure, gain a reputation for being irresponsible. If she was all right, if the boy was safe, then it would be worth whatever any might think of him. He shouldn't have left them. What was he thinking of? He should have brought them into town. Anyone could have found them, taken them. California had become a breeding bed for madness, crazy for blood and blame.

He'd hang on to the hope that since the dog lived, she and Ben did too. He wondered how long the dog had taken to catch up to him. It looked as if a bullet had grazed his side. He might have been out for a time, then wandered, sniffing at squirrels, following rabbits before he came to David. How much time had elapsed?

He imagined a dozen things: She was dead. Ben was lost. There'd been a fire. A claim jumper had found them. He shook his head and pressed his knees to speed the horse. "Sorry, boy," he said, "but you got to give your all." The horse broke into a gallop and David tucked down in the saddle. At least the moon was up. And the horse did know the way.

"What is it, Ruth?" Matthew Schmidtke stepped up beside her. Jason hung back closer to the house.

She handed him a rectangle, a limestone plate.

"What is it?"

"A lithograph," Ruth said, her voice flat and low. "Of Columbus, Ohio. I made it five years ago. For my husband. He has her. On a trail cold for following. I don't even know where to start."

When David arrived at the cabin it was dark. His heart moved into his throat, and he felt the pulse at his neck throb. The dog squirmed and whined. "No," David whispered, petting Chance. "You've got to wait. This doesn't look good." He dismounted, tied the horse a hundred yards from the house. The end of the whip brushed his face, and he thought to take it, but pulled his rifle from the scabbard instead.

For the first time in his life, he wished he were a small man, able to tuck and bend and slide quiet as a cat without being seen. He still carried the dog under his arm, but when David crouched, the dog squirmed out and scurried toward the cabin.

David eased his way around to the door that faced the stream. The dog whimpered at the porch. Then before David could approach, Chance pushed against the unlatched door. David held his breath, listened. He breathed again when he heard a baby cry.

"Oltipa?" he said. "Ben?"

The crying that had been a gasping sob now broke into a wail as Ben recognized his voice, the dog licking at him where he lay on the floor.

"Oh, thank God," David breathed when he saw the boy. He said it as a prayer, spoken in his soul as he rode back, pounding in his heart as he saw the darkened cabin, a song to cool his parched throat as he heard the baby cry. "Ben, baby," he said and lifted the child to his chest. Ben's muslin shirt was covered with dirt and damp from his tears. "Oltipa?" David called, looking around. "Where are you?"

He lit a lamp, still holding the child, the light spilling over a room he hoped would show him Oltipa, safe, just asleep, perhaps. But he didn't see her, just the baby's face, caked with snot and dirt, his eyes puffy from the crying. Small purple bruises the size of a man's thumbs appeared on both forearms, even on his pudgy fingers.

The baby's arms were wet with sweat, and they wrapped around David's neck, so tight, so tight now, as though he gripped for breath, for life. David patted his back. "It's all right, Ben. It's all right, fella. You're okay now, you're okay. It's not happening now. You're all right." He repeated the words, saying them as much for himself as for Ben. He patted the baby, walking and walking around the room, scanning for evidence of what had happened, where Oltipa was.

A tin cup sat on the table.

The fireplace was cold. He could see that. She'd been gone a long time. At least the baby hadn't crawled into hot coals. He picked the cup up, saw the paper beneath it. Ben began a new burst of crying, as if fearing David thought to put him down. The dog barked, scurried around as though looking for Oltipa, too, inside and out. He left little dark spots of blood where he walked.

David found a dry cloth and changed the boy. He wiped his eyes and face, all the while trying to piece what could have happened, why Oltipa wasn't there. He lifted the boy. His eyes fell again on the paper.

I've reclaimed my possessions. It was signed, *Zane Randolph.*

David's ears rang, he felt his face grow hot. His stomach ached as though struck by a post. That man, who had tried to ruin his life, who saw human beings as baggage, had struck again.

David hadn't kept her safe. Again this vile man had found a way to bind him. He slammed his fist into the table, and the child screamed anew. David held the boy closer to him. Poor child. What had he witnessed? How deep were *his* wounds?

Oltipa, how she must be grieving having left her child behind. What could he do?

He stepped outside, wondered if the moon was bright enough for him to track them. He checked the corral, Ben still on his hip. Her horse was gone. She was probably alive, then. He could go after her, but what could he do with Ben? He couldn't take him along, at least not while he searched for this man so lethal, so without feeling. He'd have to take the baby into town, the dog, too. There might be someone there he could leave the boy with.

He packed Ben into the basket Oltipa'd made for him, one she carried on her back. Ben sat up, his little knees tucked up inside, the bow of the reeds keeping sun from his face during the day. He strapped Ben around the middle, tucked the green cloth he'd once given Oltipa as a gift over the boy's legs. He tied the basket at the saddle's horn. He hung a bag of food behind the saddle, then walked to the stream and pulled up the tin of milk." May as well take this, too," he said.

He picked up Chance, checked the wound. The bleeding seemed to have stopped. He put the dog back inside his vest, then mounted and headed out, talking quietly to the boy until David was sure he'd fallen asleep.

They'd traveled a mile or two when he heard the music. A voice so clear and clean with notes like an angel singing with a harp. And he remembered—the entertainment in Mad Mule Canyon, all this week, at different camps. Three women and three children is what he'd been told by a passenger on the stage who'd heard them. "Sing like angels." They might be up to looking after Ben, and he could gain good time, not have to head into Shasta. Maybe they'd been provided by God, perfect timing.

At least he could ride there and assess them for himself. If they looked like people he could trust, he would. It might be crazy, but if it would get Ben's mother away from that man sooner, it was worth a little risk.

He reined the horse and headed toward the harp.

Suzanne couldn't remember a night like this one. She lay on the mattress stuffed with cornhusks, thinking when she got home—wherever that was—she might try what Naomi had suggested, using buckwheat hulls. The husks pressed dust out through the linen. Did that make her cough? No, probably the strain on her voice, singing so long, so many nights and often afternoons, too, in a row. She felt Clayton's gentle intake and release of breath beside her. She brushed his head with her hands, remembering the color of his hair.

Clayton's bandaged hand lay on her stomach. He slept hard. She wished she could. Even hours after the performances she'd lie awake, partly still taking in the adulation; partly from the raucous noises that kept on through the night, card games and arguments she could hear in the distance. If a town had no tent or structure they called a hotel, they always pulled up and camped at the outskirts. Not so far out as to invite trouble. They were, after all, just women and children. But far enough out to feel safe.

The fatigue must have been adding to her restlessness, she decided. Without sleep she couldn't regain what she needed for the day, gave up too much, and then couldn't get refreshed. When had she last felt refreshed? At Tipton's wedding, when everyone was there, together, and she felt a part of something worthy and worthwhile. A good mother who had kept her children safe despite a fire, despite her blindness, who had a new goal. She'd listened to Ned sing. She'd shared in Tipton's joy. What had she done to empty that fullness?

She lifted Clayton's arm with her hands. She heard him moan, then settle back into his sleep.

Suzanne eased her way out from beneath him, stood, checked Sason, too. He slept still in an overhanging hammock. He'd passed his first birthday. Soon he'd be just too big for that swing. Pig must have lifted his head because she heard his collar jangle. "It's all right," she whispered, smoothing the silky head with the back of her hand. She heard the dog's tail pound against the wagon's floor. She patted for the troubadour harp. The playing—just for herself—would be soothing, the song a soulful prayer.

It was what she was doing when she heard the sound of a horse, a rider, coming in. She stopped, her heart moving faster. That persistent miner? Who? Whoever it was pulled up, called out just as Pig bounded out of the wagon.

"Hey, there! Whoa, Chance, no! Wait."

Pig slobbered and barked low. Another dog barked and growled. The snarl of struggle over territory enough to wake the dead

"Call off the dog! Please, I need help," a man shouted. "I have a baby here. Chance. No!" A baby whimpered.

"Pig! Down!" she commanded from behind the wagon's canvas. The commotion finally came to a stop. An infant cried, then rustling sounds from Lura's tent where she and Ned and Mariah slept.

"Please," the man's voice said. "I'm looking for the women, the entertainers. Was that you, playing the harp? I need help. For my boy."

"Whatever are you talking about, young man?" Lura said. Suzanne could imagine her in a nightcap and gown, a lantern held high to see what was happening before her.

"My boy, Ben, something's happened to his mother. I've got to find her. I can't take the boy. Can you look after him? My name is David Taylor. I'm a driver for the stage line. I'm reliable, you can check on me. I'll come back for him; I just need a safe place for him. Now."

"What is it, Ma?" Mariah awoke.

"A crazed one wanting something for nothing," Lura said. "Kind of a yappy little dog you got there. Your boy looks Indian. You kidnapped him?"

"No ma'am, no. I can pay," he said.

"How much were you thinking about?"

Suzanne interrupted the negotiations with her command. "Pig.

Come. Step." She heard scraping, hoped the dog pushed the box with his nose so she could step out of the wagon onto it. She felt with her bare toes and stepped down, the dog close by her side now.

"Sorry for the intrusion, ma'am," he said as Clayton awoke, came crying to the back of the wagon box. That caused Sason to begin to wail and the man's baby, too, and then the man's dog began his yip-yip bark. Pig growled low.

Mariah darted past her—she could tell by the scent of the girl—and went inside, apparently to comfort Sason and Clayton. Suzanne turned, patted the wagon box behind her for Clayton, touched him though he still wailed.

"My boy, Ben," the man said, desperation in his voice.

"Of course we'll keep him," Suzanne said.

Suzanne felt movement beside her and she reached out, expecting the man to hand her his child for safekeeping. Only cool silence filled the space between her arms.

The man almost whispered, "You...you're blind, ma'am? Out here with little ones? Oh, I can't..."

It was in that moment of an empty place inside her arms that Suzanne truly accepted, truly understood her limitations.

"We'll look after him," Lura said. "Just what were you thinking would be fair?"

"You can't charge the man when he's in such need," Suzanne said. "We have the ability to help him, and to make him pay for it—when it would be easy for us to give—that would be sinful."

"Listen," Lura said. "Mariah can't be looking after all these kids without compensation. You're not able to do it for yourself. Now, you know that's true. You pay with your earnings, so this man's being treated same as you. Not sinful at all. You won't even give us a figure?" Lura said. "That's what gold country's all about, bargain or bribe or do without."

Suzanne blinked back tears. She felt Mariah step into the wagon box, heard Clayton's little feet pat back inside. "Let me help you," she said to David Taylor, "please."

She so hoped he heard generosity offered, not pleading in her voice.

"Ma'am," he said. "My thanks, but this isn't the best place for my boy. It'd be a crime, me adding to your troubles."

She could tell he was Mazy's height, and the worry in his voice told her he was desperately in need and not unkind. And yet his words cut her as cleanly as one of Lura's newly sharpened knives.

His voice sounded as though he'd turned away. "Got to get help for Ben. Get help."

"Wait," Suzanne raised her voice to him. "I know someone. In Shasta. She runs the Popover Bakery. Elizabeth Mueller. You look for her. Good with children, kind. You can trust her. She has a helper named Sarah who once helped me. Your boy'll be safe. Trust me. Tell her Suzanne Cullver sent you."

Silence met her act of generosity. He would never know how much it cost her to send him to someone more...capable.

"Thanks," he said at last. "Elizabeth Mueller. Thanks a lot."

He rode off, and Suzanne listened until she couldn't hear the hooves. He'd known in an instant what it had taken her months to discover, and finally accept: she could not help him until she truly helped herself. She could not care for *his* child when she could not protect her own.

Ruth missed them. She missed seeing Ned's little cowlick early in the mornings, watching him try to flatten it with spit and his hand. She missed the splash and squeals as Sarah stepped into tepid water in the bath barrel, always the last one to use up what little water her siblings had left. Even Jason she missed, having squelched his questions and sent him to spend time with Matthew or Joe, Seth and Mazy. She was in their lives, but had never really been present.

Most of all, she hungered for Jessie, for her sass and challenge. Jessie was just curious, as curious as a raccoon left alone in the cabin. She had her thoughtful ways, she did. Like her care for Miss Kitty, the striped cat, and her nudges to Ned to lead the table grace they'd begun singing after they moved into the cabin on Poverty Flat.

She wanted all of them around, even if it did make life less than ordered, did challenge the meaning of *harmony.* Didn't harmony have something to do with *balance?* Her life was out of balance, that's what it was. She stood in the middle of the cabin she'd kept from becoming a home.

Mazy was right. How could the children realize how much she valued them? She'd held back not because of their bad behavior but because of her own—her own fears of unworthiness, of being sent away. And so she'd left first.

If Jessie came home...no, when she did, she'd tell them the truth. Jessie had to come back. She had to! To keep torturing her, Zane would dribble information to her, pound at her powerlessness to make her insane. To become what he was, had become. And when he did, he would leave clues. Just one clue was all she needed to find her child. She combed the backyard for clues, rode a wider and wider circle, reading tracks or signs. But nothing.

And yet Ruth believed she would find Jessie. Her friends would help, and the children. And when she did, she would tell them all the truth. There would be no secrets. Secrets just ate away at a family, chewed on the core of things, kept people distracted from what ought to matter, the loving and care for each other. It had taken her this year to see that, maybe the arrival of Matthew—a man who adored his sister, who loved his mother. It had taken that to change her vision; that, and the disappearance of her daughter.

Ruth, who liked justice and truth, didn't like to put a slant on things, was doing just that with her very own child, with all of *her children.* There would be risks in the telling. Jessie might scream at her to go away, that she didn't want her to be her mother, that Betha was the mother she loved. And Sarah and the boys could hold her accountable for their parents' deaths—coming west to help her stay ahead of a husband just released from jail. That was a risk she'd face, stepping into this wilderness of relationships.

She would tell them anyway. And let them know that their parents had loved Jessie enough to risk all for her, to keep her from someone dreadful. Families did that for each other when they saw danger. They listened, they grieved, they sacrificed, and they acted. That was what their parents had done, and that was what she had done for Jessie all those years ago.

And out of that grieving and aching, came meaning. Out of those stories that she had stifled when the children asked, out of those memories came meaning.

She'd tell them and then they'd have a real family, a real settling in. She'd add on to the cabin. Maybe Matthew would stay on to help. They'd make a life here, not just drift through it. She would tell them, the firmness and focus of her decision giving her relief, filling her up almost as much as the ride on Koda did each morning, rides that since Jessie's disappearance left her empty and hungry for more. She looked again at the lithograph.

She'd been a fool to think she could run from her past. She needed to face it.

What had Sister Esther said *hearth* meant? From the word *focus,* the center of the home. It wasn't only lineage that bound people, but experience and walking together, building a hearth, having a focus, together.

She'd tell them all when Jessie got back. Jessie just had to come back. Her child just had to come home.

Ruth headed for the barn then, mending her heart with that prayer.

19

unbound

David Taylor knew his eyes looked red. His face felt drawn and haggard, and he hoped he wouldn't frighten Elizabeth Mueller when he knocked at the Popover Bakery's back door.

He hoped Elizabeth Mueller had kind eyes, compassionate, too, and was curious without being a gossip. The kind of older person not yet willing to let down and just wait to die.

The word *die* made him press the horse faster. The animal had done well even though now its head hung low. Travel back to the cabin then to the entertainers, and then here, had taken its toll. What if Oltipa was dead? He couldn't let himself think that. Randolph wouldn't have left a note. He'd sell Oltipa, be losing money if he didn't. The auction! Sacramento was the closest. That was probably where he was headed, south. But he might choose The Dalles's auction block just because it was farther away. He had to find her trail. Just as soon as Ben was settled, he'd go back and check the tracks, see if Zane and Oltipa headed south. That was his plan, and it kept his head clear, forced back the bile that rose in his throat each time he let his mind say how hopeless this was, how he'd probably never see Oltipa again. He shook his head, spoke out loud to himself: "Don't think that. Just keep your head. Just keep your head."

If only the entertainers had been more satisfactory. The blind woman was kind enough, he could see that, but she looked as tired as he felt. The way her shoulders sagged when her arms went up for Ben and he'd refused to hand him over made his heart ache. But the younger girl was doing all the running after the babies and it seemed to him her mother was more concerned about adding to her purse than what her daughter was about. He hated to see how the kind woman interpreted his decision, but he couldn't leave her with yet another child. The boy had a bandage on his hand, both of them sobbing. It just wouldn't be safe. "Would it?" he said to the dog whose head panted out from his vest.

The sun rose as they came down the Red Bluff road into town. People were already up and working. Packers unloading, masons stacking bricks and rocks. Expanding, more people moving into Shasta than anyone ever imagined. Why, they had so many people now they'd set aside plots for cemeteries. They were up to four, not counting the Chinese one. David heard the Chinese kept the bodies there just until they had money enough to send the bones back to China. Even in death, people wanted to just go home. Even in death. He shivered, not liking the train of his thoughts.

He tied the horse at the hitching rail, then picked up the basket with Ben. "You stay here, Chance," he said and walked around to the back. The ground was wet, the springs that had first caught the founder's attention seeping out no matter the rainfall or the weather. A butcher shop next door had expanded a cave and kept the meats there, cooled by the water and rocks. He eased the baby over the sluice-box-like arrangement taking fresh water into the hotel next door.

He jumped over a muddy spot and took the steps two at a time, Ben still in tow. He wiped his boots on the backs of his calves, smoothed back his hair. He took a deep breath, knocked on the door, opened it.

"Mrs. Mueller? Are you in here?"

From a small room that must have been a pantry, the woman came out carrying a clay crock. She set it down on the floor with a grunt. "Kraut," she said. "I love it."

David moved the basket carrying Ben from one hand to the other.

"What can I do for you? Fresh bread?"

"I'm David Taylor."

"And this is?"

"Ben," he said, lifting the basket to her eye level. "Suzanne Cullver said you'd help me, with my boy. Look after him. Just a short time."

"Well, he's a cutie, all that black hair and those pretty brown eyes." She leaned toward Ben, but not too close or too fast.

"He's a little over six months old. He's an easy keeper. Likes balls and dogs. His dog's outside. I could bring him in." He set the basket on the table.

"Why would you want to do that?" she asked, eyeing him with curiosity.

"Just to make it easier for you to keep him, Mrs. Mueller. Elizabeth." His words rushed now, he couldn't slow them. "I need you for more than just an hour. Might be weeks. His mother, something's happened. She's a Wintu. A man bought her last year at one of the Sacramento auctions and I, well, I helped her escape. I'm paying it off, so it wasn't like I cheated him. But he isn't a good man. And he's taken her. He left Ben, just left him at the cabin. If the dog hadn't come after me, I wouldn't have gone back for a week. Ben'd have..."

He swallowed, his nose stung with welled-up tears at the thought of the slim and fragile distance between life and death, between turning back and keeping on. The image of Ben left alone squeezed at him, threatened to take his breath. "He's not my boy, Mrs. Mueller, just hers, but I signed on to help her out those months ago, and I'm responsible now. They're like my...family. I didn't find a good way to deal with the man."

Elizabeth came to him, patted his hand. He realized then that his shoulders had dropped with the ache of fatigue and worry and wondering if this woman would be right for Ben, do right for them. Elizabeth put her hands, palms out, to the boy. As she did, he saw that they were pink as a baby's tongue. Smooth, too. He wondered why he noticed. Maybe to keep from letting what he felt come rolling up and out.

Ben kicked in his basket chair, cooed and babbled, reached out his arms. David bent to loosen the tie that held him in, lifted him out. Good. The boy felt safe with her.

"Been through a wilderness, have you?" Elizabeth said, lifting the boy from his basket. She bounced him gently, ran her hands through his hair dampened in dark strands stuck to his forehead. "Maybe it's all a mistake," she said. "Maybe your mama stayed out later than planned and—"

"She wouldn't have left him alone. Not crying, sobbing on the floor like he was. Not unless she was made to. And my dog was shot at too. Will you keep him?"

Elizabeth nodded.

"Thanks. Thanks. Look, I've got to get back, to pick up their trail."

"Any idea who? Why?"

David pulled the paper from his pocket, used the move to wipe at his eyes with his thumbs. He handed it to her. "He left this."

Elizabeth read the words. "He says 'possessions,' like he had more than one. Know what that means?" She handed it back to David, still patting Ben's bottom. "Did he mean to take the baby and then change his mind?"

David shook his head. "I don't know. I only know he took her and if he doesn't hide her in some remote place, then he's headed to a major auction site. Sacramento, San Francisco, or The Dalles."

"Be good to change that law." She turned to the baby then, wrinkled her nose. "And we've got to get *you* a change too." She lifted his hair with the back of her fingers and frowned. "That's an ugly swelling forming at his temple there," she said. "I know for certain babies won't bruise on their own."

"You see the kind of man I'm dealing with here? Ben needs a safe place. I'll pay you back, I will."

"No need to worry over that. You just do what you got to."

He bent his head to the boy's and rubbed. "You be good now for Elizabeth. I'll be back just as soon as I can."

He squeezed the boy he thought of as his son, then held the woman as well, briefly, the smell of sauerkraut rising around them.

"Two hugs in one morning," Elizabeth said. "Sarah? You up, child? Come see this little one. Go now. Ben and I'll hold your hands in our prayers."

David backed out, waved at the boy, whose face suddenly turned from the happy smile to the bubble of a lower lip, his eyes widen.

"Go on," she said. "He'll be all right."

David opened the door, picked up the dog. He'd take him along. He could help find her trail.

Elizabeth called out as he pulled the door shut. "That name, on the note. What was it again?" He told her. "I don't know why, but it has a familiar ring. I'll have to ponder that."

"I'm going home," Suzanne said.

"You got the wagon most of the time, now. It's pretty much your home the way you want it," Lura said. "I tried to make it right for you. The three of us are sleeping in the tent."

"I understand. And I know you've meant well and that my coming along was my idea. I pushed you to accommodate the boys and me. And you have."

"Listen. We're a team. We've made twice what we would have with just me sharpening knives, so I'm not complaining."

Suzanne sighed. She and Pig had made their way to the shaded tree beneath which Lura worked with her whetstones and knives. Lura had shown her once, how one hand turned the crank and the other set the blade in just the right place for grinding. She smelled something hot and earthy and imagined Lura's hands working, the swishing sound loud enough to make Suzanne wait before she spoke again.

"There," Lura said. "Sharp as a diamond. Just as shiny, too. Move, Pig."

"I intend to make a home," Suzanne said. "But not in the wagon and not traveling on with the boys to mining towns."

"Your playing and singing, they're gifts from God. I heard Sister Esther say that once and she ought to know. Can't misuse those," Lura told her. "I'm sure that's some kind of sin to not put talents to work. Isn't there a Bible verse or something about using gifts and all?"

"I won't forget the music. But I've been given other gifts, too. My children, and the responsibility to raise them as safe and sound as I can. I need help to do that, much as I hate to admit it. I do. And I need to make better choices about where and what I expose them to."

"Mariah's been good help."

"Yes, she has." Suzanne petted Pig's head as they stood, the stillness broken only by Lura's work. When the sound stopped, Suzanne said as gently as she could, "It isn't fair to her either, Lura. She should be in school herself this fall, learning and laughing and just being a child. Growing up, having fun. It's not fun to be watching after my boys. And me. To be up half the night fending off miners."

"They're just being appreciative."

"It's dangerous," Suzanne said. "Even a blind woman can see that."

Lura grunted. "So what'll you do?"

"Go back to Shasta first. Then head south, to a larger city, maybe, where I can get help for Clayton. I need to see a doctor. Find out why he isn't speaking more and what I can do about it. And then," and here she paused to take in a deep breath, "I need to hire someone to take care of...all of us. All the time. Someone who will care about my children but not try to take them from me because they think a blind woman can't raise them, or shouldn't."

Suzanne heard the sound of the crank winding up, the whetstone zinging against another knife. Lura stopped. "Get married, that's what I say. Put up with someone controlling your days so you can be sure your kids are safe. We could find a good prospect if we put our minds to it. And he could travel with us."

Suzanne shook her head. "I'm going to Sacramento. I'll stop by Sister Esther's and have her help me find someone—not to marry, but for the children. I'll pay them to look after my children. And me, hard as that is to say out loud. I need a keeper same as them." She sensed Lura's sadness, wanted to soothe it. "All this gold dust will help me find a worthy person I can pay reasonable at least through the winter. I'm grateful to you for that."

"Can you wait to go back until maybe October? We've got lots of good towns to head into. Fact is, Ruth won't want Ned staying on with me without you around to keep him safe."

"That's ironic. A man desperately in need would not hand a baby to me, and you think Ruth sees me as safe."

"You lend...dignity to things, give folks the belief that they've entered into royalty almost, that pretty blond hair, the way you stand so straight, the backs of your hands making gestures while the rest of us just point. Ruth won't let Ned stay, I'm certain of that. Not with the likes of me."

"I don't want to ruin your business plans, but I have to go back. Tomorrow."

"Listen," Lura said. "Mariah won't stay out here with me either without you around. Maybe we should all head south. Visit a few camps along the way. Maybe I could be that person for you."

Suzanne didn't know why, but she thought this might be the first test of her true commitment to her new focus. She took in a deep breath. "I know your offer is given with great care, Lura. And I thank you for it. Still, I believe we've learned things about our differences while we've traveled together. I need...a person able to devote herself to my children and to me. And you already have a child and a dream for a business, and when Ruth heads north and catches up with Matt, you'll have your son back and will want to be free to be with him. And who knows, *you* just may fall in love with one of those miners yourself and marry. Then where would I be?"

"I'd never kick you out," Lura said. "You're kin."

"We see the world differently."

"Difference is what makes life interesting," Lura persisted, and Suzanne recognized in the tone of her words a small child, bargaining, trying to imagine saying what this other person wanted to hear so they could get their way.

"What did you say the law of this land was?"

"Bargain, bribe, or go without?" Lura rattled her knives, sniffed. "Guess I'm going without," she said. "Well, you do what you want then. It won't bother me."

Suzanne felt a twinge she wasn't sure what to call. Irritation, relief?

"I need for you to drive us back," Suzanne said.

"I know that," Lura said, blowing her nose. "I was just trying to bargain for when."

David Taylor had changed horses, left his payment with the hostler whose eyebrow rose with irritation. "You'll likely lose your job, Taylor. Not showing up isn't taken lightly. We had to roust the whip who brought the stage in, and he wasn't none too happy about taking your long run."

"I wouldn't have done it if it wasn't life and death," David told him.

"Yeah?" the hostler said. "So can you take tonight's run?"

He shook his head. "I don't know when I'll be back." He ran his hands through his hair, dirty with sweat and dust. "Do what you have to."

"Getting a reputation, Taylor, and it's not a good one."

David nodded, swung up on the horse. He stopped at Washington's and filled his saddlebags with food, filled his canteen, then headed out of town. *Not a good reputation.* All because he acted on his belief. Would he do it again? Yes, he decided, he would.

He rode with a prayer of "help-her, help-her, help-her," as though it were one word, his wish that Oltipa would live. He was so grateful the boy was all right, that Elizabeth would tend him, that David had a next step. His mother always said not to get caught up waiting for faith enough to finish, only to find faith enough for that next step.

He wondered whether Oltipa thought the boy was dead, whether she knew the dog had gotten to him. He was grateful too, for that. And that he and the dog might just pick up their trail at the cabin. He patted Chance's head, his paws resting on the saddle's swell.

He just needed to find some small sign of their direction once he reached the cabin. Two choices north: the old Sacramento Trail into the McCloud River area or the Yreka route, better traveled, over the Scott Mountains. Two other choices: south to Sacramento skirting Shasta or west toward Weaverville and the coast. Chances were slim he'd know for sure. But *ye have not, because ye ask not.* He thought that was the verse his mother quoted.

He smiled. He didn't realize how memorizing those verses could spur him forward like the good crack of a whip beside a horse's ears: telling him the direction, telling him which way to go and that he wasn't alone.

At the cabin, he tied his horse near the corral then began circling, wider and wider with each walk around the structure, watching for any excitement from Chance. Either the ground was so hard and bare or the breezes had laid flat the grasses, allowing no distinct tracks. Up the ravine, the rocks and water showed no signs they'd headed west. But no signs any other way, either. He thought he'd head south. Something about the man's enjoyment watching that first auction months ago made him think of Sacramento.

But he might imagine David would second-guess that and deliberately turn north. He found nothing to tell him either way. He was about to choose, just trust, when he heard the dog bark.

The dog panted and yipped, ran forward, came back. Chance's little tongue hung out, the size of Ben's palm and as pink. It stood out, surrounded by a black curly mustache and beard. "Show me," David said, and Chance bounded out north. David mounted his horse and followed.

Ruth paced the room. "He had to have been here before. Do you think he might have hidden Ned's harmonica and my hat...?"

Her eyes grew large.

"What're you thinking?" Matthew asked.

"The photograph...he scratched out my face. For him to just...to take her...right out from under me! If only I hadn't taken that job. If only I'd gone ahead and tried to find you, Matthew, find my horses, left this place. Gone to Oregon."

"He still might have found you," Matthew said. "Looks like he's been on your trail for a time."

"I'm going to scratch his face," Ruth said, "on a lithograph. Sam Dosh will let me print some, I know he will. And I'll put them up at the mercantiles in the region. Maybe of Jessie, too."

"We could ride out and show it around. Give it to the postman too," Matthew said.

"That could work. At least it would be something." She heard Jason shout outside. She stood, went to the door open to the August dusk. "What? Who is it?"

"Looks like Elizabeth," Matthew said. "She's got Sarah with her, and they're pushing their mounts. And they got a basket full of something."

Within moments, Elizabeth was pulling up, huffing hard.

"It just didn't come to me right away, it just didn't," Elizabeth said after she told them she'd explain in a minute about the baby named Ben. Sarah took the basket, barely able to carry it inside. "But then Sarah, bless this little cherub, she remembered the name. Zane Randolph. That's it, ain't it?" Sarah nodded.

"What about Zane?" Ruth said. Her shoulders stiffened. Her hands clenched at her side. "Have you seen him and Jessie?"

"Jessie? No, well, see, he come into my bakery a week or so ago. Said he was a friend of Suzanne's—"

"Suzanne's?" Ruth gasped. She'd brought danger to Suzanne, too?

"Said he knew her back in Missouri or Michigan or wherever she was from. And that she'd wrote to him to come visit. But after he left—"

"You didn't tell him how to find her?" Ruth felt her chest tighten, and her hands grew sweaty. She wiped them on her skirt but couldn't seem to get them dry.

"Don't know myself. But I told him you was working at the *Courier.* I didn't know. I thought you might know where she'd be singing. Well, then after he leaves, Sarah says he lied, that his name was Wesley Marks."

Ruth blinked, sat, trying to weave it together.

"Shoulda told you before, but I forgot. Didn't tell Mazy either. That ain't the real trial. Today a stage driver comes in with this baby. Says someone has taken his Wintu wife, claimed her as a vagrant, he thinks, and he's off chasing them. Then he shows me the note left by the one took her. Says he has *possessions* with him, like he had more than one. And Zane Randolph signed it."

Ruth felt lightheaded. She stared at Elizabeth, gazed around the room, the tentacles of Zane's mastery overwhelming.

Oltipa rode behind Jessie, the weight of her head and her great tiredness forcing her dark hair split by her braids onto the girl's head. She jerked away, then allowed her eyes to close, the drone of the Randolph man coming back to her like a mosquito refusing to light. More words than she understood, sounds taken by the wind as he talked back over his shoulder. She recognized *beauties* and *learn* and *soft.* David Taylor used those words too, but with a different meaning.

She looked down at her legs. They were covered in the tiny blue flowers clustered on pink stripes of the dress David Taylor gave her. Beautiful," he had called her when she put it on and later when *Wita-ela*—Ben—first pushed up onto his knees and rocked back and forth as though to crawl to her, had reached at the "flounce." David Taylor had clapped and shouted as she saw other white men do. His eyes sparkled and he said, "Look what our boy is learning." His eyes showed tears. "Getting soft," he'd said.

She did not like those words used by this Randolph man, about what his "beauties needed to learn" about their being "soft" from doing nothing through the summer.

The skirt of the dress bunched up on her legs, pushed between her and the child. My Jessie, her name was. Young. Scared but with eyes hard as marbles. Oltipa wished she had her grass skirt on so when she killed this Randolph man, she could move quickly, wouldn't be stopped by calico catching at her ankles. And if he killed her in her effort and she died, she would already be dressed for her ending.

"I wish his mouth would be quiet," My Jessie whispered. Oltipa nodded, her chin bumping the girl's head.

"I wish him dead," Oltipa said. "For what he does to my boy."

"You think your baby's dead?" My Jessie whispered. Oltipa nodded, fought back the pounding in her chest. "He missed the dog he shot at. Least, I didn't see him when we got hauled out to your horse. Maybe he messed up with the baby and he's all right too."

The image of Ben smiling, crawling, arrived on wings of hope. She scolded herself then, for not paying attention to what she knew as real. The shaking and bruising of her baby while he screamed, that was real. The dropping of him, that was real. The silence when the light went out in the cabin, that too. He would have cried if he had lived, his eyes stayed searching for her through his tears. She would have heard his wails as they rode away. And they'd been gone now, two, three days. How could a small child live without someone to tend him, someone to hold him for safety and love? No, she would be honest with herself. Her family was gone, all gone. The thought made her as dried and wizened as the manzanita berries she saw clustered on the bushes.

"I'm hungry," My Jessie said.

"You girls having a chat, are you? Regular little sisters back there. Not tired out yet? Not as soft as I thought." He clucked his tongue. "Unfortunate," and he rode faster, jerking the rope that bound them. At night, he gave them hunks of food they ate like animals, gobbling. He was smart to bind them. Oltipa would have found a way to hurt him if he hadn't.

She wished he had chosen the trail along the McCloud River where the Pit Indians raided for horses and food. Few white men traveled there now. They might have been freed by the Pit River people. On this Trinity trail north, none would interfere with a white man bound to a woman and child.

The Randolph man looked back, again smiling, a silk scarf blowing out in the hot breeze from his throat. Then he turned and faced forward. They rode down a steep ravine, the horses' front legs sliding, back legs bending so that the animals nearly sat on the hillside as they slid down the slope. Oltipa lifted her legs in protection, the steepness pushing them forward toward the saddle horn, the rope wrapped around them loosened slightly in the shift. She noticed the man held his right foot out higher, then quickly back. His foot must hurt.

Oltipa's thighs ached. She had rarely ridden, always a walker, gathering acorns and roots. David Taylor had given her the horse they rode on, but she did not know the animal's ways. They rode beside a stream. A trickle of water splashed up as they crossed it, then back again. Her eyes followed him, studied the horse's ways. Her thoughts plotted.

"How should we do it?" My Jessie whispered.

"I do it," Oltipa said. "Silver spoon I carry will be sharp inside his eye. You run then."

The man turned, his hand holding the lead rope high, the rough hemp pinching their arms. "Pretty steep," he said as they climbed away from the little stream and headed up to a ridge where they could see mountaintops and timber, silver streams of water pressing out from rocks. They rode, one horse following the other, as though they were simply friends out riding. At the top, the ridge widened. Oltipa dropped her head again, rested her chin lightly on My Jessie's head. She must think how to get free.

"Look awake," the man said. "You, too, My Jessie." He yanked on the rope.

"Not your Jessie," the child whispered.

Oltipa looked up, scowling. Then her heart quickened. She recognized a rock! She'd seen it in the summer as she'd grown up. At the base of its gnarled gray and sunset yellow grew manzanita berries, ripened in the heat. Glossy dark green leaves could not hide their luscious fruit. She had picked them in season when they were dry and powdery inside. Here she'd mashed them on a rock, made them into a fine powder, a soup. And later, added seed-filled chaff to water and soothed her throat with the drink. Those dried old berries gave much!

Her digging stick had sunk into this dirt once, twice, many times. Beyond were lilies and wild onions found at another time of year—*oltipa*—spring. It was a distance from the river of her birth, but she knew this place. In late summer, her husband had climbed black oaks in the distance and had shaken the acorns like tiny pebbles covering the ground. Over there, she'd twined a basket, later served salmon in it in the fall. Her father had built a hut for them not far from here. She'd heard rain tap-tap into a steady rhythm on the cedar bark, and they'd moved toward their own river before the snows fell. A *pam-hal-lok!* A cave! Where she once looked out to see the rock formation. Her eyes scanned the shrubbery and trees.

She knew her people were gone, raided and taken, just as she had been. Yet something about recognizing where she was, seeing the familiar, lifted her spirits like a hawk's wings, just above the mourning of her loss.

She smiled at this gift given in a groaning time: that this *eltee-wintoo*—white man—who meant to take her far away and sell her to another was heading north, through a place Oltipa knew as home!

Suzanne and Lura's wagon rattled up the lane to Ruth's place. Suzanne beamed with her newfound sense of direction. She could hardly wait to tell Mazy, Seth, all the rest. As the wagon stopped she heard Mariah whoop.

"Well, I'll be," Lura said. "It's my Mattie."

Suzanne imagined hugs and hellos, heard expressions of joy. Made out Elizabeth's voice, children, and a baby. In a lull, Suzanne accepted Matt's hello, then asked "Isn't Mazy here?"

"She and Seth headed out a week or so ago," Ruth told her. There was something different in Ruth's voice. A quietness. Defeat? "I expect they'll be back next week. Matthew's milking for her."

"And me too," Jason reminded Ruth.

"Yes. And doing a fine job," Elizabeth said. "From what Ruth tells me." She turned to Suzanne. "We do have some things to talk about, Suzanne."

Ruth sighed. "And it isn't happy news."

"What?"

Elizabeth was the one who spoke of Jessie's disappearance, of Zane Randolph's involvement. Finally she said, "Your Wesley Marks is one and the same as Ruth's husband. Zane Randolph, and the snake grabbed Jessie and is gone."

Suzanne felt struck by a split rail.

"You saying that Suzanne's suitor was already taken?" Lura asked.

"That isn't what the worry is," Ruth said.

"I...don't know what to say. He took Jessie? His own kin?"

"Our sister's gone?" Ned said, his voice quivering.

"It's my fault," Ruth said. "He followed me. I should have stayed in Ohio and faced him." Her voice broke.

"Come on, Ruth," Matthew said. "Let's let Elizabeth fill in details. Tell it without us. We'll get the milk cows up. The fresh air'll do you some good."

Suzanne heard Matt and Ruth walk away.

"Oh, that young man you sent my way went after them. He don't know that Jessie's likely with them. Least we're making that guess. And the baby you hear? That's his boy. Said you sent him to me. Ruth's a wreck. You can see that."

"She can't see anything, remember?" Lura interjected.

"I can see the man trusted my advice about Elizabeth," Suzanne said. "Baby's pretty quiet."

"Good as gold 'til you try to set him down or take him out of his basket. Then he wails like a stuck pig. Something happened to him awful when Zane took his mama."

Suzanne swallowed. "Wesley…I mean Zane…wanted things to happen in a certain way. He came in once when I wasn't there. I felt him there, though. And I asked him not to do it again. I should have trusted myself more, that it didn't feel right."

"He came looking for you first. Maybe when he couldn't find you, he—"

Suzanne gasped, her fingers to her throat. "This is my fault," she said, her newfound focus blurred by the errors of her past. "I had to do things on my own, didn't let you all help me as I might have. We would have found out. We could have warned Ruth. Instead, for a man like…him, a blind woman alone was…an invitation to invade."

"Don't be blaming yourself, now," Elizabeth said.

"I just…I need to go away. To Sacramento, and take my children with me."

They'd ridden into the city, easily locating the boardinghouse where Sister Esther stayed on J Street. The woman bent over tomato plants growing up along a picket fence, newly painted, the green against white and the woman's dark skirt a contrast fit for a painting to even Mazy's unpracticed eye. Seeing her gave Mazy's heart a lift. They shared a love of words and a living faith, both things Mazy had neglected of late. Esther turned at the sound of their call, her little black cap still tied tightly beneath her chin. The woman smiled, revealing that missing tooth.

"Mazy. A fine sight, that's certain," Esther said as Mazy released her from an embrace. Esther brushed at her apron, clasped her hands before her in that way she had. A Mexican man led Seth's horse and Mazy's mule to the stable around in back. Esther lifted her long skirt with her gnarled fingers and guided them toward the porch.

"Come have cake and iced tea," she said stepping straight-backed up on the steps. "Margaret makes the best there is. She's got fresh eggs daily and cows." She turned, one hand on the porch post, her index finger pointed to Mazy now. "Milk costs two dollars a gallon in Sacramento, but she lets her guests have all they can drink for free."

"Bet they pay dearly for the food," Seth said. He removed his tall hat and held it in his hands, his blond hair matted by the heat against his head.

Esther nodded. "Yes, but they'd pay dearly at any hotel and still not have the satisfaction of milk foamed against their mustaches. Milk is essential. But I'll serve you tea."

Esther brought a tray out, and they sat on chairs of pine stumps cut out with tall backs. Small cushions softened the seats, and Mazy wondered if Esther had made them. She gazed out at a street busy with wagons and freighters and women walking in newly dyed dresses. She took off her own hat, a bonnet tied with wide strings at the throat, and fanned herself with it. "I thought the city would be cooler, so close to the river," she said.

"Tell us what you know about Naomi," Seth asked.

Sister Esther's eyes pooled, her chin lifted. "So little. Only that she's gone back to her husband. Again. I don't know what to do. Marriage is a scared trust, not to be broken, but no woman deserves poorer treatment than stock." She pulled a hanky from the sleeve of her dress, wiped at her eyes, then dabbed at her neck above the white collar.

Mazy reached across and patted the woman's hands. "My only prayer is that Naomi knows she always has a home with me," Esther said. "And that she knows she has not been forgotten. Perhaps he will change. People do," she said.

Mazy cast a quick glance at Seth, then said, "And the other contracts?"

"Are being repaid," Esther said. "My night work at the Jenny Lind Theater permits me to pay a little extra, and my day work at the academy allows me a way to live. Mei-Ling is happy. I am well blessed, despite the losses. And you?"

"At long last, I'm here to face whatever I'll discover about Jeremy. And myself. Sometimes I think I've been blinder than Suzanne, waiting so long."

"I'd hoped that one would come visit and bring those boys," Esther said. "I held this secret wish after Zilah died, that Suzanne would find a refuge with me. The dreaming of an old woman."

"Did you ask her? Say something to her?" Mazy asked Esther.

Esther shook her head. "I didn't want to intrude. And then, I didn't think I deserved such a gift, not after my poor showing with bringing the Celestials to safe harbor."

"It's funny how we deprive ourselves of things we might enjoy," Mazy said. She considered her own words as she stirred her tea. Maybe her avoidance of language and Scripture these months were just one more way she had of getting "busy" so that she had no time for the things that gave her nurture. Perhaps, like Esther, she believed she just didn't deserve them.

David's only hope was that someone might have seen them, a man and a woman and maybe another, he didn't know who. But they'd be resisting. None of the packers he met heading south held any hope for him. Instead, they warned him about riding out alone with the Pit River's restlessness. "I haven't much for them," he said. "A little grub's all, and I doubt they'd kill me for that." One packer had shaken his head, mumbled words about David being blind to the facts, then moved on down the trail.

David knew it was crazy to even think that the dog could follow their scent. Chance was probably just chasing a rabbit or squirrel. Still, he'd camped out beneath an oak, and in the morning the dog had acted as though he knew what he was being asked to do. David had no other plan, nothing else that looked like the next step.

But on the third day, Chance stopped, stood in the middle of the main trail, dozens of hoofprints in the dirt. David watched the dog whining and panting, stopping, looking up and back, scurrying back and forth across the wagon tracks, horse droppings, barefoot markings. David swallowed. He knew they'd lost the trail.

"You did better than I could've." He sat with his hands crossed over the saddle horn, staring ahead at the twist of dirt winding through the timber, rocks, and streams beyond a few orange poppies huddled in the shade. Should he just keep on, believing he could make Oltipa appear before his eyes? He turned the horse and looked back in the direction they'd come. He got off and picked up the dog, leading the horse over to an oak. He leaned against the tree, scratching his back on the bark. "We're at the end of the line, Chance," he said. "Only a fool would keep going on into Oregon Territory with no more evidence than a dog sniffing." He set Chance down.

David eased himself down the tree then, hung onto the reins and let his horse graze. He'd have to live with the emptiness either way—that he should have headed south first, had wasted time coming north. Or if he turned back and never found her, he'd live with the thought that he should have kept going, that she might have been just around the bend. No good answer, no sure thing waited at the other end. He guessed that was all of life, no sure thing.

"Your faith need not be large enough to finish," his mother always said. "Only adequate to embark." He guessed it was adequate back at the cabin. Just not now.

What to do next?

He closed his eyes. "Help-me, help-me, help-me," he said.

Back south, he had Ben waiting. That was the surest thing. That was where his embarking should head now instead of on this wild chase into Oregon. Accept defeat. Head home. That decided, he fell asleep.

20

adequate to embark

Mazy watched the buggy pull up in front of Margaret Frank's boarding-house, saw Seth speak with the driver, adjusting his tall silk hat as he did. The men looked toward the house, and she knew they were speaking of her, probably saying something about waiting after women and then moving on to the weather, both looking up now, to a cloudless blue sky.

She tied the ribbon of her bonnet, spreading it out at her throat as she watched, then turned to the oval mirror. She'd always liked green, a color her mother said brought the chestnut out in her hair. At least her hair had shine to it now, the spring water of California restoring what the alkali had once taken out. She turned sideways, noted the burgundy sash that circled the back of the poke, stepped back, then stood full face. She wore the best dress she'd been able to have shipped up to Shasta. Before their appointment, Seth suggested they go shopping in Sacramento, but she was content with what the packers delivered. The whale bones of the busk held her stomach flat, and as she swirled, the skirt kept moving over the five petticoats, even after she stopped. She covered the green taffeta with a paisley shawl, straightening the fringe with her lace-gloved fingers.

Last evening, Seth had shined her shoes—he'd asked if he might—and she accepted. They were the last thing he handed her before he leaned just slightly and kissed her more than good-night.

"It isn't a good time, Seth," she said when he stepped back. "If you press me…"

"I'm not," he said, both hands up in protest. "That was just a kiss that says 'I love you,' in friendship now; more if you allow. I thought you might like to hear it before you face whatever you will tomorrow."

"Thank you," she said. "It is nice to hear those words, especially with no intent to…bundle me." He smiled, tipped his fingers in salute, clicked his heels, and backed away to the door. After she latched the knob, she wondered whether he was headed out to the gambling halls.

That was last evening; this was the new day. Mazy inhaled. Head to toe, she was ready. She picked up her reticule and the thick envelope she'd made sure was never far from her sight. This was it, the day she'd anticipated and put off for over a year. This was the day she would find out what kind of man she'd married those three years ago, what kind of man could woo her, win her, fool her parents and herself, then lift her from the familiar and set her feet on a westward course. She'd discover his story and, in it, hope to find herself.

She couldn't concentrate on the sights the driver pointed out to them, the buildings going up after Sacramento's own fire the year before. This history of the West could have been written by its embers. She noticed brick buildings, a few iron doors, and several buildings with metal roofs and a foot and a half of dirt on top for extra fire protection. *Just like at home,* she thought and shook her head. *Home.* So Shasta was becoming home. Seth reached over to pat her hand.

"I'm sorry," she said, turning to him. "Did you say something?"

"No," he said. He removed his hand. "I saw you shake your head. Thought you might be biting at your lip that way you do. Just offering comfort, is all I'm doing."

"Oh," she said and turned away, watched the brick buildings fade into wood-framed ones, then to houses with a rose climbing here and there and pies setting in windows. More than one yard had a goat bleating from the back, chickens scratching in the gardens. The clop-clop of the horse along the hard earth formed a soothing rhythm.

Seth reached to hold her hand again and she allowed it. She wondered if she should have let him come along. Perhaps these requests provided him a level of intimacy and assumption she didn't intend. It was too late now, but she decided she'd have him remain in the waiting area when she went in to meet the solicitor and Jeremy's brother.

"Sometimes two people can hear better than one, when the words are hard to hear," he said when she told him.

"I know. But I don't want the lawyer or Jeremy's brother to make any assumptions as men can do, about whether I make my own decisions. He might easily start talking to you, not to me."

Seth nodded agreement. "Maybe he'll have more sympathy for you if I'm not there. Tell you more than he otherwise would, about the child and all."

"I'm not looking for sympathy," she said and wrinkled her forehead. Then the driver stopped.

"Here's the place," he said. "Josh McCracken, Attorney at Law." He twisted in his seat, said, "If you don't mind my saying so, you two seem pretty happy together to be coming to a land and divorce lawyer."

"Divorce?" Mazy said.

"One of the best in the state," the driver said. Then, considering another option he might have missed, added, " 'less of course you're getting one from others, so you two can be together."

Mazy opened her mouth to protest but told Seth instead, "Why don't you stay out here? Set the driver straight while I'm gone."

"About our not needing a divorce or that we intend to be together?"

Her set jaw was her only answer as he helped her from the buggy.

The waiting area in McCracken's home had black horsehair couches with wide walnut arms curved around the ends. Ferns draped from huge porcelain pots below photographs colored with pastels of mountains and valleys. A chandelier hung from the high ceiling—and that was only the outer office. Mazy turned slowly around, feeling smaller than she wished, and decided there must be wealth in the dissolution of marriages, another of the West's hidden treasures.

"You must be Mrs....Bacon," a man said from behind her. The voice was high pitched, from a small man.

"Yes. Jeremy Bacon's wife."

"Yes," he said, adjusting his glasses on his narrow nose. "Follow me, please. Mr. McCracken will see you now."

The man across the desk from her matched her in height. His hand felt warm as he took hers, gently pressed her fingers with both hands then directed her to a seat, thanking her for coming, asking after her comfort, ordering his secretary to return with tea. She sank into the cushion of a leather chair, sitting much lower than the lawyer now enthroned behind his desk. Her chair had appeared equal to his before she sat. Now her chest caved in on itself from the chair's softness. Light from the window behind him masked features that faded into a clean-shaven face. Dark hair curled at the ivory shirt collar. She looked around, noted the absence of any other people in the room.

She took in a deep breath, took control. "I understood my husband's brother and his wife were to be here," she said, forcing herself to sit up straight, hands at her purse on her lap.

"Your husband's brother asked that I press their case for them," McCracken said, taking control back. "It's quite usual, I assure you."

"I hoped to meet the relatives of my husband."

"In due time," he said. "I'm sure he'll want contact with you, but for now, things are somewhat...awkward, to say the least. They're feeling a little remorseful that they've not made a greater effort to stay in touch with your husband's offspring. And they were uncertain how you might receive all this news."

Mazy's hands felt damp, and she thought perhaps the room was too warm, though the window behind him stood partway open and the lace curtains moved easily in a light morning breeze. The secretary returned, bringing cool tea and sugar cookies, both of which Mazy now declined, her mind spinning without knowing why.

"Your letter informing us of your husband's death came as a shock to them," McCracken told her, "as you might imagine. They'd had no word from him since just before you started out."

"As my learning he had a wife and child came as a shock to me."

"Children," he corrected. "He had two. A daughter and a son."

A hawk in flight carried a snake in its talons. Oltipa raised her eyes at the bird's cry of triumph, doing what it needed to stay alive, risking all for food, perhaps to feed its young. She watched as it made its way to a tree and disappeared. Staying alive. That was what she must do, not get caught up with her outrage at this man. And save *this* child if she could not save her own. She must return, for even the slightest chance that her son lived, for even the chance that David Taylor might come searching, be confronted by this Randolph man and lose the challenge with his life.

In a whisper she said, "Think how to stay alive. Go back."

"You got a plan?" My Jessie whispered.

"This is familiar place, these rocks and trees."

She tried to remember where the *pam-hal-lok* was, the cave, the one her family took refuge in when an early snowfall caught them in these mountains. The *yola* melted the next day, but they had watched it come in flakes as large as acorns thickening the manzanita bushes in front of the cave opening with wet white. They watched from a place safe and warm.

In the morning, out of gratitude for this surprising home found where they did not expect it, her family left behind a cache of food—dried acorn flour, some deer meat—for someone else in need. Their feet made wide tracks in the melting snow, and Oltipa had looked back, remembered seeing two crooked trees like eyes growing out of the rocks above it, the cave opening like the slit of a frown in an old man's pocked gray face.

The food would not be there now. But if they could get free and find the cave, it would provide shelter, a place for them to hide until the Randolph man tired of searching.

"I have plan." Oltipa said. "Tonight, to sleep. When we are not held like twists around a basket next to the fire, you will make noises like you are ill. When he bends to see your pain, I will slip my silver spoon from inside this pocket and press it to his back, make him believe it is a gun or knife. Force him to cut your rope. Then we will bind him to a tree and be set free."

My Jessie shook her head. "He won't care if I'm sick. 'Less I throw up on his boot, and that'd just make him madder." She whimpered. "I wanna go home."

Could such a man find an ill child too much work? Maybe leave her behind...as he did her child? Yes, she decided, the Randolph man was held hostage by hatred, blinded by rage. Oltipa shivered in the August heat.

Dried leaves crackled as the horses moved through them. It would be a time of fire if storms came, the ground so dry. Perhaps she could start a blaze, stumble through the campfire and in the smoke and dust, they could disappear.

Before another thought could fill her mind, My Jessie said, "I hurt his big toe. He can't run fast. Maybe we could take his horse. He'd be stuck."

Oltipa thought, then said, "When horse goes down steep slopes, toward the creeks, rope around us gets loose. He holds it high. On right side of saddle. He does not notice."

My Jessie whined. "I don't know my rights and lefts."

"His bad foot side. We slide down when the way is steep," Oltipa said.

"Won't he see us when he looks back?"

Oltipa considered. "Horses hit water. Much splashing, clop, clop. We slide off. Scare my pony. Confuse that man. We run. Hope he is blind, with his seeing eyes on this pony running past him."

"Maybe I can hit his foot again. If he chases."

"Shh," Oltipa said as the Randolph man turned. He didn't bark this time about their whispering. Perhaps the leaves and crush of branches covered up their words. She had noticed when he held the rope that bound her and My Jessie, that the Randolph man sometimes looped their mare's lead twice around the saddle horn, to control one rope at a time. The hemp line leading their mare would be held hard and fast then, and any effort of the Randolph man to dismount would be tangled by the rope's tension. But now, he held both ropes in his right hand, his reins in his left.

"Heading down," he called out then, pointing with his head toward the stream below. "We'll camp close to water tonight. You beauties might have a bath." He laughed, turned back, started the horses down the steep side, moving around boulders, past windfallen trees, finally to a landslide area, steep and smooth, that ended at the water's edge, free of shrubs and trees. He kept his arm out to hold the lead horse clear.

As they reached the smoother slope, the mare they rode fairly sat on its haunches, dust from the other horse doing the same in front puffing up around them. The Randolph man lifted the rope that bound them, and Oltipa felt it loosen, felt it ease up her back with her own shoulders hunching down. She felt the help of My Jessie's hands pulling it over her, freeing her.

Oltipa watched, and when Zane Randolph's horse hit the water, he did what they hoped for—he stayed within the stream. The two horses clop-clopped through the water, splashing and kicking up rocks. He looked back, saw them still there, the rope around them held to look tight by Oltipa's hand. Then he turned back, and she watched him take the lead rope and double hitch it around the saddle horn. He was resting his arm of the pulling. This was their chance.

"Now," Oltipa whispered and she rolled the hemp rope up and over

My Jessie's shoulders, off over her head. "I slide off back. You follow. Now!"

Their legs wide, still bound hands pressed on the horse's rump, they dismounted. Oltipa first, her heart pounding. She felt the mare startle forward. She hit the water, stepped aside to avoid the hooves, did what she could to pull the child. My Jessie was sturdy and strong and pushed herself back from the horse and landed on her feet. "Run," Oltipa shouted. "Run!" She threw a rock at the mare, which jolted, causing the Randolph man to turn.

Seth waited with the driver, only half hearing as he talked about the flood damage of the year before, rebuilding going on. Seth thought of the game of chance he'd entered with this woman and his life.

Last evening, he had gone to the casinos. He played the game of a lifetime, taking his winnings up and gathering others until it was just two of them left and a pot of fifteen thousand spilling on the table before them. A single turn of the cards and he either walked away a wealthy man or sank into indebtedness he'd spend a lifetime digging out from. It was the rush of his life, that game. Maybe Mazy was right. Maybe there was no other passion for him except risk.

When he turned over a queen of hearts and the other man held only a jack, he'd stayed calm on the outside. His insides swirled with triumph. He'd wanted to wake Mazy, to tell her. Walked to her door but did not knock. He had suspected she wouldn't have shared his elation in his newfound wealth even though it meant they might have a more predictable life. Still, he hadn't given her that option, had simply gone to his room and turned in. He wondered what held him back.

Zane Randolph heard the shout and felt the rope yank around his back in the same second as he saw the mare bounding up beside him on the left. No! He grabbed for the lead rope bound hard and tight at the horn, tried to yank it loose, couldn't, turned his own horse to the right, wanting to straighten the rope being pulled against his back, his thigh, frightening his horse. His horse, pulled by the frightened mare, frenzied it more. It sidestepped and lurched, pulled even tighter by the rope attached to Zane's saddle. The mare's neck stretched out now, its eyes wide in terror. Zane's horse spun around it. Water splashing, rocks rolling, horses slipping. The rope gouged tighter against Zane, the noise of water and a shrieking horse, and rocks tumbling, and his own shouts, of "Whoa, now, whoa now!" throbbing like a hammer at his head.

The rope stretched tight across his thigh, and his own horse pulled and sidestepped, and then the mare reared and whinnied and shrieked, and Zane heard the crack and grind of its neck just before it went down, strangled. The rope raked Zane from his saddle.

He landed on rocks while his own horse stumbled, then smashed a hoof onto Zane's throbbing foot. Pain seared through him, worse than at the prison, worse than any whippings he'd taken. Zane yelped as the horse slowly slid his hoof off. Through the throbbing, burning pain, Zane saw that his treasures were gone.

He could barely move, the pain in his foot an outrage. He cut the rope to the dead horse and caught the reins of his own still wild-eyed animal. He tried to stand, couldn't. The horse half-dragged him, hopping on one leg, toward the bank. He dropped to the ground, his foot throbbing, then cut off his boot. Even before he saw the torn flesh, he knew his foot was crushed. He cursed them. Hawk for challenging him, for spooking the mare as they ran, for forcing him off, for his own horse stomping his foot. He cursed the girl Jessie for his rotten toe, Suzanne for resisting him and disappearing, David Taylor for interfering. And Ruth. Dear Ruth, for causing it all. She would pay. She would have to pay.

His body shook now, from the cold of the water and the pain. He still hung to the reins of his horse. He needed to put his foot back in the cold creek to stop the swelling. When he could, he would pull himself onto the horse and ride out. He would find a doctor. He heard his own breathing, that sucking sound through his teeth. He'd been damaged, all because of her!

"You led me here, Ruth!" he shouted to the rocks. "You led me to this place! You owe me!"

Even in the cold, he was sweating. Fever. Infection. Blood poisoning. His mind raced. He looked again at his foot, the slightest touch shooting pain up his leg. The arch where the horse stomped it, already bruised purple around an open wound with shattered bone showing through. And the toe, the one Jessie had struck with the rock—it oozed yellow and green. A red mark moved up to the throbbing arch already. See! There it was! Even if he did find a doctor, he knew: his foot would have to come off. Ruth. She'd stolen his foot.

"I see I've already upset you." McCracken sighed. "Mrs. Bacon. Let me begin at the beginning, shall I?" Mazy nodded. "Your husband," he said, "lived most of his life in England, coming to this continent in the early 1840s."

"He told me. He came to Wisconsin in the migration of '48."

"Well then he has told you in some error. He did not come to Wisconsin directly from England and he did not come in '48. It was the fall of '49 I believe when he arrived in Wisconsin." He checked papers on his desk. "Yes. '49. But he grew up in England and came with his wife to Missouri several years after his marriage in"—he looked again at the notes—"1833. He was twenty years old at the time and had—"

"Wait." Mazy held her hand up. "Let me figure this." She thought, then said, "That can't be correct. He would have been only seventeen in 1833. He was just sixteen years my senior, not nineteen."

Josh McCracken gazed at her then, a look that held sweet sympathy; patience pooled there too. He lowered his voice, a father now talking to a daughter, not a lawyer talking to a wounded wife. "This must be dreadful for you. Let me just tell you what I know from the brother's figures and the documentation he's provided. Perhaps then we can piece it all together with what you know. See how we can go from there."

Mazy nodded, clasped her hands, wished she'd brought her writing book with her for taking notes, or had asked Seth for his set. She asked the elderly lawyer for paper and a pencil which, when McCracken handed them to her, provided her something solid to hang on to. She gripped the pencil, but her eyes never left McCracken's face.

"He came to California not long after the claim at Sutter's mill." He looked up. "His brother, Sinclair, at the time worked with him in Fort Vancouver and learned of the great need for a dairy industry in central and northern California as the frenzy for gold brought more and more people west. They'd both worked in the dairy barns at the fort—they were quite extensive, so I'm told. The plan apparently was for your husband to travel first to California and see what he could confirm, and if all went well, to then head east, acquire good dairy stock, bring them west. His brother planned to follow here, to California. Sacramento.

"Now then. Your husband, whose name was not Jeremy Bacon when he left here, apparently had an eye—"

"That wasn't his name?" She knew her mouth was open, and she snapped it shut.

"In due time, Mrs. Bacon. As I was saying, your husband had an eye for fast money and for..." He looked up at her and said, "Ah, never mind." He turned back to his pages, his fingers lifting the long parchment pieces, flipping them until he appeared to find what he wanted. "Upon arriving in California, he was apparently hit upon by the gold craze—it happened to many a good man—and he staked a claim. He'd brought his boy with him, and after some small gain was made, he supposedly came to his senses as far as his commitment to his brother was concerned. He notified Sinclair that he was heading east and urged him to come south, bring his wife and child, gather up the boy still working the claim, and he would meet them in Sacramento by the fall of '51."

"He left his son?"

"The plan was for only a short time—we can assume. But the brother was delayed in Vancouver. A family matter, I believe, his wife's illness." He perused his notes. "No, an accident, leaving the girl as a ward of McLoughlin, the former Chief Factor at Vancouver, and his Indian wife."

Mazy was rubbing her temple, still gripping the pencil.

"He abandoned his son?"

"The boy was fifteen, Mrs. Bacon."

"Fifteen? But..."

"A number of lads younger than that have staked claims and done well on their own. I doubt your husband would be found neglectful for that, though unsympathetic, perhaps. One can assume he asked for someone to look in on the boy until the uncle was expected. Hopefully he advised his son of that fact. That would have been essential to have him remain. Still, if he didn't...that might explain the difficulty his uncle had in locating—"

"If he was fifteen in '49..."

"Yes?"

"I was only sixteen then," she whispered. "He had a son just a year younger than me? *Has* a son a year younger?"

"That I do not know, not being certain of your age. I do know that your husband became injured in Milwaukee, sometime in late '49 or early '50. I believe that was when you might have met him?"

She nodded. "My father was a doctor. We had a small surgery in our home. Patients sometimes remained until their recovery. Jeremy did. I married him in April of 1850."

"Aha."

"But why didn't he leave then to come back?"

"The advance originally given him to make the proper investments was depleted, apparently when he purchased a farm in…yes, here it is, in Grant County, Wisconsin."

"That was his uncle's farm. A gift to him."

"Apparently not." McCracken slid the paper onto a growing pile, read at the top from another. "He did however notify his brother of his…delay, and after rather heated correspondence, I should imagine, over the next two years, he sold the farm, bought the cows and bull and headed west to do what he'd originally agreed to. By then, California was desperately growing and in need of active dairies. Of course, now your husband had the complication of a wife to whom he'd given an assumed name."

"Why?"

"I'm sure he did not plan to die on the way here. I suspect he assumed you would never know of his first wife or the children. When did you say your anniversary was?"

"April second, 1850."

"That might explain it." He looked up from the page, down into her eyes. "Your husband may not have known he was a widower when he married you. Your marriage would have been illegal, obviously, a small matter if he intended never to come back. And of course, that does present problems for this…settlement as well."

"But then he did decide to go home. Maybe to see the two children he'd left?" Mazy blinked back tears she knew were spilling onto her cheeks, knowing she wasn't following everything McCracken said, but clinging to a quality of goodness she desperately wanted to see in the man she had chosen to marry. "Why didn't he tell me? After she was dead? He knew, yes?"

McCracken nodded. "We can assume, but we don't know."

"He lost a wife, never saw his son and daughter again, and I believed he had a good heart. What happened?"

"It takes a remarkable man to stay secure, or may I say 'true,' to what he's about when all around him people appear to be falling into riches, gambling big and coming out bigger. There is a sense that only a fool would keep to the tried and true, a steady course of making do day-to-day, providing for one's family, meeting commitments and obligations despite the sacrifice. The daily drudge of milking, or shoeing horses, or putting up hay, even the law, if seen as a distraction to easy wealth, has made many a man—and woman—do things they later regretted. No one can see ahead how it'll all come out, and keeping a clear eye has never been easy, Mrs. Bacon. Without a clear vision, dreams are easily converted into entrapments. And your husband had an eye for taking risks or he never would have come to America, and would likely not have gone into business with his brother as he did."

She sat, trying to find her own still place, breathing prayers to help her understand what she was hearing, to draw the best conclusions, not judge too quickly.

"He left a wife and two children. What would he have done with me when we arrived?" She felt the tears spilling over. "Was he even coming here at all or heading to Vancouver?"

McCracken reached into a side drawer of his heavy desk and from it pulled a clean and perfumed handkerchief. Mazy took it, thanked him, thinking as she did that lawyers must have need of tending to such office essentials.

"Please continue."

"Yes. Well then. So you see, the money from the sale of the farm you had near Cassville, the money that went into the purchase of the cows and the bull, that is money that is not, ah, rightfully yours."

"Not the cows. Nor the bull."

"Not completely so, no."

Something in his tone told her negotiation space existed. "But surely part of the stock and proceeds should be considered mine, as part of my husband's estate. And he also had funds from my father's house, placed in Jeremy's name—because my father thought my husband would be a better manager than my mother." She laughed with no joy. "My father intended for any proceeds to be used for her welfare."

"Not unusual for a husband to secure his estate in that way."

"Some of the money Jeremy left, after he died, has to be my mother's."

Josh McCracken leaned back, as though reassessing. His fingertips formed a tent below his nose. "But the cattle, they do not belong to you."

"Half does. I've read somewhere that here in California, a wife can keep half the profits from a business made with her husband, even while they're married, and sue him if he refuses to give it."

McCracken flattened his forearms on the desk, his palms on the table. "It has been known to happen," he said, "but there is the question of the legality of your marriage."

"I have the cows," she said.

"Possession is important," he said. "And the bull?"

"The bull I sent with stock belonging to other survivors of the cholera epidemic, more cows and horses, too. It has just recently arrived." She stood now, taking in a deep breath of air, sure of what she wanted. "I propose this, to get us past this place," she said. "Jeremy's brother, Sinclair, may take ownership of the cow brute as his half of the estate. If he comes to get him. And the cows I'll keep for my part in successfully bringing them west. Sinclair would have nothing if I hadn't done my part. And now he at least has the hope of a bull. I'll assume the remaining cash my husband carried belonged to my mother." She stood. "Here are the papers for the registration on the bull. A signed bill of sale." She opened the envelope that lay heavy in her lap. "If Sinclair accepts, I'll not press further for all of it, what I believe I could rightfully claim—Sinclair's word against mine the only evidence. Why, I might even charge that the Jeremy you speak of is not his brother at all. They didn't have the same names, as you said."

McCracken stood then. He was nodding, rubbing at his chin. He'd stepped away from the window, and Mazy could see he wasn't an old man. But those eyes had seen sorrow enough to give them depth. She marveled that she could have this conversation and sound so firm while her hands sweated, her heart pounded, and tears of Jeremy's betrayal pressed against her nose. She fumbled with the papers, found them, handed them to him. She felt stronger with his nodding, his agreeing that what she said was fair. Lighter, that was what she felt.

"One more thing." She pressed at her nose with the perfumed silk, picked up her purse, handed him back his paper and pad. "If you agree to tell me who and where the children are, I will give them half of their father's estate. They are, after all, his only heirs."

"You had no children?"

She shook her head. "Almost. But for my mother, those two children are my only family now."

Josh McCracken allowed a lifting of his lips, enough she thought it might be a smile. His eyes crinkled at the corners. "Sinclair will have to accept the bull, but it is the more expensive item, and it's true, your work and time to bring them west need compensation. I was asked to handle this matter to my best judgment. I'll confer with him, and any papers you need to sign I can send to you by mail. As for the children..." He looked back down on the paper. "The girl's name is Grace. She is in Oregon City. The boy, he'd be nineteen or so, we have not located. Perhaps he's deceased as well. Or taken his own gamble and followed a dream. It's possible he's still near the claim, though his uncle didn't find him. You might. Mad Mule Canyon is near your home in Shasta. His name," he said then, "is David Benjamin Taylor."

21

kin

Stars glittered above him, silver stones thrown to light the night. "No moon," David said, his eyes sticky with sleep. His horse would easily stumble, traveling without a moon. He wondered if the sky was clear wherever Oltipa was. He stretched, his neck sore from the way his head dropped while he slept beneath the tree. He heard the crunch of his horse chewing, the rustle of the dog at his feet. Had he dreamed? He couldn't remember. He stood, reached for his packsaddle, took out a bite of dried meat, liking the pull of it against his teeth. A shooting star caught his eye, a single flash of brilliance. "So small, we are," he told the dog as he squatted to share his food. "So small in the scheme of things."

He'd done what he could do and would have to live with the failure of his efforts. He thought of heading into Oregon anyway, futile as it might be to find Oltipa there. He could see his sister, walk where his father once walked, try to understand how he could have left his wife and daughter behind. Maybe to keep them safe. Maybe doing what he thought best for them, at least that was what he wanted to believe. He preferred that explanation to the one he'd come to first—that his father chose the dazzle of a fire over its warmth. Gold was no end in itself, despite what all around him were saying.

He might never know what his father thought, or what happened to him either. Just another unanswered question life handed him, asking him to ponder and trust.

"Heading back," David told the dog. "Don't want our Ben growing up without knowing there was someone there for him. Got to tell him about his kin and what she was about." He could keep her story alive, and if she did live, if she did escape the hands of Zane Randolph, then she'd return to where she last saw Ben. "She might not come back for me, old boy," he said. "But you can bet she will for Ben."

Riding a straight trail, without the side trips of following the dog seeking Oltipa's scent, he arrived at the cabin sooner than he expected. His eyes scanned the simple room, noted the things Oltipa did to make it her place, their place. *Bos,* she called it, home. Baskets woven and filled with flour and berries sat on the plank floor; salmon she'd caught and dried in the wind were stacked on a crate in the corner. She'd been working a deer hide. It lay rolled up, fur outside, and there were other skins—squirrel, rabbit—whose softness smelled of her as he picked them up, brushed the nap beneath his fingers. He couldn't find the small spoon he'd given her. That surprised him. Nor the dress. She must have been wearing it when he left. His eyes watered. He assumed she took it off as soon as he left, returned to her chosen clothing. But he found a woven grass dress folded and lying on the raised bed he'd built her. Once-yellow flowers spilled out of a pot, dried wisps scattered across the table. Little things unique to them made this a home. They'd always had enough—some to give away. "Generosity toward others," his mother had said, "is the true sign that you're grateful for all God has given." This cabin had become a home that way.

He hadn't thought of the walls and roof as a "home" when he lived here with his father. They'd thought of nothing but gold then, using the wooden walls and rafters as a space to keep them safe from the wind and snow, healthy enough to change streambeds and shorelines the next day. He looked around, wondering if there was a single thing left in this structure that was personal to his father. He found nothing. No wonder it was so easy for him to leave it once his father left. Like his father,

David had given nothing of himself to the place, kept all of what he was inside. Until Oltipa came.

Maybe that *was* what his father left behind: a son who took a gamble not for gold but for a woman's life, for the stillness of his own soul.

This cabin would stay a home again, for him and Ben. They'd keep it ready for her.

He checked to see what supplies he would need, deciding then he would work the claim not as an end, but as a way to one. He could be with the boy, to stay close. And when Ben was older, then he'd find another way to make his living, not wanting the boy to believe that gold was the goal in life. Others had struck it rich, but many invested in hotels, mercantile businesses. They gave others work. Yet they lived in homes not much bigger than this. There were other things to be done with money. David would make his mark for Ben.

Elizabeth greeted him at the hotel door, flour drifting like snow down her front. "Come in, come in! Oh, I know you're looking for your boy. He's in good hands. Got him out at a friend of mine's, Ruth Martin's. He was just too much boy, here. He needed entertaining every time I turned around. I liked the fun, but my strudels suffered. Sarah wanted to be back home with her auntie, what with Jessie missing… you don't need all that news, now do you? So," she said, looking closely at him, "I'm pondering your eyes there and I'd say you didn't find her. Them."

"Lost their trail north. At least I think it was their trail. Could be they went south or toward the coast. I don't know."

"Will you head south, then?"

David shook his head. "Maybe. But I'd just be chasing dust, I expect. He'll sell her, sure."

Elizabeth patted his shoulder. "I got news for you too. Not good either. That man? He's been making Ruth's life miserable for years. He was her husband. Is, I guess. And he took her little niece with 'em."

"That must have been the treasures he meant. More than one. This Ruth might know where he'd go, then?" David's eyes brightened. The dog barked and scratched at the door.

"Haven't seen your dog since you left," she said. "I was worrying over that. Let him in."

"I should have said I took him. I don't know if he really had their scent or not, but I followed it until he got confused. At least I had a step to take." He thumbed at his eyes. "Where's this Ruth live? Maybe she can think of something about Randolph, about where he'd go. Give me a next step." He lifted the dog. "Got to play the hand I'm dealt," he said. "Play it good as I can."

They sloshed through the shallow creek, running as fast the slippery rocks allowed, lifting knees high despite their hands being tied. Oltipa fell. My Jessie helped her up. Jessie cried as she ran, and Oltipa crooned encouragement. Oltipa had looked back only once. The Randolph man's horse stomped and skittered around him, pulling back as he shouted. Her pony looked dead in the water.

David Taylor had given her the horse they'd ridden, the one lying dead. *No time to mourn now,* she thought and turned away. She bunched her dress up in her tied hands, and showed My Jessie. The child picked up the edge of her flannel dress, what she'd been wearing for three days now. Oltipa always made sure the child was off to her side or ahead of her.

Once, early on, she thought she heard the Randolph man's words carry over the water, a shout, and they lay still, as still as a rabbit too far from its hole with a coyote fast on its trail. She stared into My Jessie's frightened eyes, thought of her son, prayed for their safety.

"That rock," Oltipa said, pointing. They sat wet, shivering in the heat and panting beside a boulder. Oltipa eased out around the boulder to see what she could of the Randolph man. They'd come a distance, around a bend, and she heard nothing but the rush of water, the screech of a bird overhead. "Come," she said and led the child up the rock-pocked and brushy bank, into the shrubs and up the steeper side.

The heat began to press against their skin, drying them. Then as though the God of David Taylor truly did watch over her, she found the *pam-hal-lok*—the cave! There was no food inside, but here came safety and the time she needed to pull the spoon from her pocket and begin the long process of using it to dig at the ropes that still bound her hands.

"Spoon," she told My Jessie. The girl helped her fumble with the skirt, reaching for the inside pocket. "Hold," Oltipa said, then rubbed the hemp strings that bound her hands against the spoon. She made little progress.

"Won't we ever get free?" My Jessie said, her lower lip trembling.

Oltipa looked around the darkened cave until she found a sharp rock.

She rubbed her wrists across the point until the rope loosened, then told My Jessie to pull the frays free. Rushing, she did the same for the little girl, fumbling once with her tired hands, then putting the rock and spoon back in her pocket.

"I'm hungry," My Jessie said.

Oltipa grunted and nodded. "We go home soon," she said. She reached for the girl, a child the size of Oltipa's younger sister, and held her in her arms until she slept.

Through the opening of the cave, Oltipa looked out at *thooyook. Stars,* David Taylor called them. She wondered if he saw them. She heard a twig snap and held her breath. Nothing happened. She exhaled. They were safe here. Safe from this Randolph man. She decided then that when she found David, she would try to tell him that no matter where she was, when she saw the stars, she would remember the thousand kindnesses her life was given because of him. She'd tell Ben too, if he lived. A sharp pain stabbed beneath her breast with the thought. She did then what David Taylor told her once to do: "Ask for all you need."

She was a strong woman, that Mazy Bacon, Seth thought. Strong, sure, and straight as an arrow. He supposed it was the set of her jaw line as she left McCracken's office that told him she was on a new trail, likely one that didn't have room for him. Noble's Cutoff had been a glitch, he decided, an interruption of this woman's single-headed steering of her world. He couldn't fault her for it. He admired it. He just wasn't sure he was up to the challenge of finding a way to make her care for him without risking her losing herself.

He guessed he knew it from the beginning, when she didn't lean on him as a woman might, when she said she was willing to wait for more. Knew it again with the chaste response to the kiss he'd given. Passion, she said she wanted. Well, so did he, and it was a gift if two people found it together, seeking similar things, making their way side by side. His old grandmother had told him once that God had a partner picked for everyone, but some took longer to be ready. "When you find the right one, you'll know it," she told him.

He'd thought Mazy was. But he was wrong. He could see that now. Mazy was gathering resources to stay put, build her a house, milking cows two times a day, put up hay, then commit to being there through the seasons, day in, day out, the same. That wasn't him and he knew it. Maybe she'd become like a sister to him, someone he could spar with, love true and true without the entanglements of anything more. That was what he'd hope for. To be thought of as kin.

They took a day to visit Mei-Ling, who bowed and smiled and looked as if she carried a watermelon under her tunic top. "Why, you're expecting," Mazy said, and A-He grinned back the answer.

"You come be married in Sacramento?" Mei-Ling said to Seth. "You and Missy Mazy?"

Seth thought Mazy blushed. "No, we're just friends, Mei-Ling, like you and I are." He thought Mazy tilted her head in question at him.

"You come be friend for baby too?"

"We'll always be that," Mazy said.

"Naomi have baby too. She tell me."

"Well," Sister Esther said. "How lovely. Perhaps they have put their differences to rest, then." Esther had ridden out with them, and they all walked through the peach orchard A-He had started two years back until they reached Mei-Ling's bees buzzing around their boxes on the far end.

"We should go by Naomi's, too," Esther asked.

Mei-Ling shook her head. "She say husband not like visitors. I come see her some. She say things be better when baby comes. She bring baby, show Missy Esther."

"At least life'll be easier for her with a child," Esther said.

"Kids never seemed to me to make life easier," Seth said as they rode back to the boardinghouse. "Problems just seem to get bigger."

"Still, they bring a change," Esther said. "And it is much harder to stay self-centered after a child arrives. They often do help their parents get raised up. Those of us without little tykes to teach us skip some lessons," she said, the word *lessons* zinging in that way she had. "And we only know we've missed them by the ache in our hearts."

In the morning, Mazy told Seth she was ready to go home. Like an older brother, he sparred before relenting. "Might be we should wait to travel home with a freighter, packing north," Seth said. "Might be safer."

"Did you pick that information up at the local amusement house?" Mazy asked.

Seth wondered if Sister Esther tracked this double team of conversation. He cast a quick glance at the older woman, couldn't decide, then turned his ear back to Mazy. "The driver reported it. Not many are leaving except by stage. Or in packs. Just want you to be safe. Me too, for that matter."

"I can take a stage if that would suit you more, or the steamer. Leave Ink here with your ol' Snoz, if that's all right with you, Esther."

"That's fine," the woman said. "But when will you get your mule?"

"Seth can pack her back. You'd do that, wouldn't you? To help me out?"

"I'll take you now," he said. "Wouldn't want you behind on your schedule."

Mazy nodded. "I'll get packed up then."

Seth's smile was wistful. He knew as he gave it to her they would always be friends, nothing more. And yet he didn't feel adrift as he'd thought he might. He had planned to tell her of his turn of fortune at what Mazy called the gambling "hell" last night. He could settle down now. But it wouldn't have made a difference with her. She wanted passion, and she didn't feel it with him. Maybe that he wasn't devastated by her rejection said he hadn't been all that ready for more with her, just as she'd said. He might not be ready for the wealth he had rolled into his pack, either. It should have made him elated. Instead, he felt weary.

They headed back, Mazy riding Ink, only not sidesaddle. She'd found a good saddle at a livery, so new the stirrups were still stiff.

"The tongues will wag," Esther told her as she mounted up.

"Let them," Mazy said. "The world looks much better staring through the ears of a mule straight rather than off to the side. Besides, no self-respecting California woman will waste her time worrying over wags. Come on, Ink," she said. "Let's go home."

"What did you work out about your cows?" Seth asked as the clouds lifted over the Sacramento River.

"The cows are mine. The bull is theirs."

"That'll cut into your herd-growing a bit," he said. "Not that being without one for a year hasn't."

"True. But I've got a plan," she said.

"I'm sure you do," he said. Mazy was a good woman, but he knew she would never be his. He had plenty else to keep his interest, he decided. And what Esther said, about the emptiness of missing some little tyke's lessons, maybe that was speaking to him.

Ruth felt like a chunk of winter hail, hard and cold and sharp with no hope of melting. She bumped into things in the house, picked up Jessie's clothing and brought it to her face to inhale the scent of her. She tried not to ignore the others, now that all of them were back. She told Ned he looked healthy, and he did, not as chubby as he'd been. He'd stretched up. Stood almost to her shoulder. She remembered to thank Jason for helping Matthew, for graining the horses, for bringing in venison, for working beside him like a man. Especially after the other drovers down from Oregon had scattered into the gold fields, except for Joe Pepin, always loyal to the Schmidtke family. It was nice to have Sarah around again too. Even Suzanne and her little ones gave them all a distraction while she waited for Mazy to return. Lura didn't bother as she had either; the woman calmed some with the presence of her capable son.

It was Jessie's absence she mourned. She'd never gotten to tell Jessie the story, the whole story. She'd told her nothing at all. And now, it might be too late.

Ruth hung Jessie's jumper on the wall hook, fingered the bar of soap Jessie had made. Her eyes watered. She needed to finish the drawing of the girl. Zane's she'd completed, had printed, and given to the postman. Jessie's face she found harder to draw. She had not sketched it enough, had not really seen the child. Her child. She hadn't gotten to know her. She felt weepy again. At times, she couldn't seem to stop sobbing. She was an ice crystal waiting to shatter against a child's grinding stone.

She looked around. She controlled nothing in the end: not her life, not her feelings, not her future. At least Zane Randolph no longer controlled her thoughts. They were only of Jessie and her prayer that the girl still lived.

Oltipa's dress dried into twists of wrinkles that looked as though she'd just wrung the water out. She brushed at her skirt, the flounce at the bottom half torn off. My Jessie's thin nightdress exposed cut knees The gown was smudged with dirt and ripped from a bad fall she'd taken. But they were heading back. Going home. Oltipa allowed her heart to sing with the flush of reunion.

She finished ripping off the bottom of her flounce, then undid My Jessie's hair, running her fingers through it to get some of the snarls and twigs out. She did the same with her own, then twisted it with the blue calico on top of her head. "Just like David Taylor show me," she told My Jessie.

"He your man?" My Jessie asked.

"My man," she said. She tied the remainder of the flounce into a scarf she held with a knot at the back of her neck. She would not look Wintu as she walked back, but like one of David Taylor's people. The child with her would protect her too. Hard to believe that a small child could lend a woman her dignity, but Oltipa welcomed it on this journey. Walking beside this white child she would not be whisked away as a slave. In her grass dress here on this trail she would have stood out. So it was good, though she did not know it then, to be dressed in David's gift when the Randolph man took her. And she was there for My Jessie, showing her berries and roots they washed down with spring water, provided to keep them alive. Who could know what was ahead? Who could see far down the trail?

When they heard a rider, Oltipa pulled My Jessie off to the side, peered to see if one was David Taylor, waited until the man passed, then kept on, steady, sure, heading home.

No dog barked as they approached the cabin a day later. No wind moved the dried leaves. The tin wash pan hanging on the log end had not been moved. An ax still creased the splitting log.

And then she heard it.

At first, Oltipa thought it was a bird, and then she thought the stream rippled, singing over rocks. But it rose higher, lifted like a hawk, and then she saw them and she knew a sound so deep, so filled with joy. A greater treasure than just arriving home—the laughter of her son riding high on David Taylor's shoulders.

She was a woman split by a sharp whip, cut down the middle. Two children she had failed to protect. Two children, gone because of what she'd done or failed to do. Ruth heard voices outside, children chattering. Pig barked. She cupped her hands in the basin, flushed the cool water onto her swollen eyes. Would she ever feel whole again? Would the tear in her heart ever heal? Now she could hear laughter. Would she ever take a full breath again? Squeals and shouts, then, "Auntie, Auntie, come quick!"

Ruth sighed and stepped to the doorway. She watched Matthew moving from the barn, his long strides taking him swiftly toward a wagon bringing visitors. As though dreaming, she gazed as Matthew pulled a child from the wagon, hair twisted in blue calico on top of her head. She wore a thin nightdress, like Jessie's. And then she knew. *Jessie! My Jessie!* Her heart felt whole enough she could run.

Mazy'd seen the plat of the claim bearing Jeremy Benjamin Taylor's name. One afternoon, she rode there, coming over the ridge on Ink, seeing the cabin that Jeremy had built. Her heart thudded like a butter churn, and she blinked back tears. Part of her felt as though she eavesdropped on another person's life. But this was part of her life, her coming to terms with the past. She wasn't sure how she'd tell him, almost wished the boy wasn't there, so she could wander about and sense her husband's other life, try to understand what drove him.

Smoke rose from the chimney. He'd built a good hearth, it looked like. Perhaps he had planned to stay, to bring his family here one day. Not a good place for milk cows, though, with the steep ridges and no place to raise hay.

Then she'd arrived, slipped off the mule and tied it to the corral. A small dog with black feathery feet stood at the door announcing her with a high-pitched bark.

"What is it, Chance?" the man said, and Mazy looked up to see what her husband must have looked like all those years before. Brown curls around a slender, handsome face, thin lips, softer though, more prone to smile. Blue eyes with warmth coming through the curious. "Can I help you?" he asked. He rolled his sleeves down as he talked and stepped off the porch. He was taller than Jeremy'd been, finer boned, but with wide hands. Now she saw a woman come around behind him. She looked native and carried a chubby baby on her hip.

Mazy blinked back tears, not wanting to make a fool of herself, wishing now she'd done this another way, maybe asked her mother to come with her. She had not told her mother yet. Didn't know why she waited.

"I'm sorry," she started, then stopped. "I didn't want to intrude, but I'm looking for David Taylor," she said.

"That's me," he said. His hands were on his hips now, his head canted to the side. "Do I know you?"

"No. My name is Mazy...Bacon, but we have family...in common."

They invited her in, and she eased into her story, told him of her farm in Wisconsin, the cows and how she'd brought them west with her husband who had died along the trail. Mazy watched his eyes for recognition, noticed how he protected the boy as he bounced the baby on his knee. David expressed sympathy for her loss, and she nodded, smiled at the child whose round face and dark eyes heavily favored his mother.

But then Mazy spoke of their arrival here, that she sold milk in Shasta, and that her mother ran the Popover. "I know your mother," he said, and Mazy smiled. "She was very helpful."

For a moment more he seemed to think that was why she'd come, to bring some bridge of commerce around a bakery or dairy, or to simply pass an afternoon with a new friend, not to lift a burden she had carried, not to set her own past free.

Finally she said, "David, I know some things about your father."

"My father?" he said. "How could you?"

"When he left here those years ago, he came to Wisconsin. He bought a farm and cows."

David stared at her, his face as still as winter snows covering cold ground. The boy stopped pulling at David's ear and looked at the man. David took Ben's tiny hand inside his own, his fingers gently rubbing the child's fist. "It's all right, fella," he said. The woman noticed something too and came forward, her hands on his shoulder, pressed her dark fingers at the red of David's shirt.

"My father lived in Wisconsin? When? He left here, said he'd be back. Never came."

"He went on east. He never mentioned his family here. And I married him."

David's mouth dropped. He ran his finger through his hair. They talked longer then, and Mazy found a comfort in the boy she'd never known with his father. Someone tender and authentic sat across from her, hands now wrapped around a tin cup, a man strong and kind whom she might be pleased to call her kin.

"I have a gift for you too," she said. She pulled a paper from her reticule. "The cow, one cow at least, is yours. As half the estate. And these glasses, they were your father's."

Mazy stood then, watching David's silence. "I'd like to bring my mother out, have her meet Oltipa, seeing how she hasn't yet."

"Yes," he said. "Bring everyone, your friends." He looked shyly at Oltipa. "We'll have a gathering. Never had one here, have we, Oltipa? That's what a home's for, isn't it? I met a few of the women, when we took Jessie back. Lura and her child, again, the blind woman and her dog."

"Pig," Mazy said. "He used to be mine."

"Yes, let's get your mother out to meet her...grandson. Sort of. I guess," he said and laughed. "Maybe even great-grandson, except I'm not Ben's father."

"You're more father than you know," Mazy said. She watched, surprised when he handed the boy to her. She held Ben and blinked back tears. The child reached up to touch her face, and it came to her then: She had come to put her past to rest and found instead the threads that wove her future.

Ruth wondered if she should tell the children with the others around. Suzanne hadn't left yet. She and Seth were sorting through her theater props, from what Ruth could tell. Esty had arrived that afternoon, too. And Lura and Mariah were talking decisions with Matthew, using Ruth's place as home base. With her luck, about the time she planned to tell the children, Adora and Charles would appear. She wondered if Tipton and her mother corresponded or if their relationship was forever severed by hurt feelings and betrayal.

She wouldn't let that happen in her family, not anymore. These women were almost like sisters. Not that she'd ever had one. But it was how she imagined sisters would be, people who shared, who disagreed, who encouraged, who loved despite how different from each other they might be. Blood tied sisters together, though, so no matter what was exposed, it would be understood if not accepted, believed if not honored. At least that was her image of sisters. She couldn't be sure if such allegiance lived within Lura and Suzanne, even Elizabeth and Mazy.

Ned sang after their supper of fresh corn on the cob and venison stewed with potatoes in the cast-iron pot. Suzanne strummed the harp, and Lura clapped her hands in time. Even Mariah looked refreshed, smiling between Jessie and Sarah, a big sister to those two. Jessie was still a pistol with her easy sass, but she stayed close to Ruth. And more than once, when Ruth turned around, there the girl stood, breathing fast, her face white as stone, her eyes as though she'd seen the devil. Ruth always bent to hold her then, whispered, "It's not happening now. You're safe, you're home," until she heard her daughter's heartbeat come to quiet, steady, and her breathing calm. She had to do something more, though. Tell them the truth.

If they were family, Ruth thought, if they were people she'd come to care for and was willing to accommodate for, stretch a bit from what she really wanted in their time of need, could secrets then be shared? This was risk, greater than driving a herd of horses across the plains, greater even than facing Zane. It was the risk of being herself, edging toward being someone different, someone a little more willing to expose and hope she could endure the result. She didn't want to curl up like a caterpillar every time someone chose to touch her.

They finished the song. Joe always stayed at the barn, but the rest were there in the cabin. Matthew sat rubbing oil into a bridle. The children played quack, as Matthew called it. She'd heard it as blindman's bluff and wondered that they didn't fall over each other trying to make their escapes. The laughter filled her. It was a perfect scene, Ruth decided. A fireplace flickering with low embers left over from cooking. She smelled the scent of herbs in soap, Jessie's cake now on the washstand. Brought in to comfort Clayton, the cat purred quietly at his stroke; Pig lay beside Suzanne, his ears alert, his eyes poised at the cat. A hearth. The focus of home. She wished she could paint it instead of talking of what she knew she would. Her heart pounded and her mouth felt dry. She cleared her throat when the game ended. "I have something I want to tell."

"You look so serious, Auntie Ruth," Ned said.

"Is it bad news?" Lura asked. She had her pipe out but just chewed on it with no tobacco lit. "I can't take any more bad news. Just let it ride until after we go to bed if that's what it is."

Ruth shook her head. "You'll have to be the judge of how bad it is or not. It's meant for good, even though…" she hesitated, took a deep breath. "Even though Zane Randolph would have it another way."

"Who is that Zane Randolph, anyway?" Mariah asked.

"That snake is my dad," Jessie said.

Ruth gasped. "You knew?" Her mouth dropped open. "You knew that Zane Randolph was your…father? Who told you?"

"He did. Kind of. He called me 'his Jessie.' I didn't like it, but I knew I was anyway. Before I mashed his toe."

"Guess I told first," Jason said quietly.

"How did you know?" Ruth said, turning on him.

"I asked Mama who that was when you wrote his name on that sign. Where people decide if they're going north or south," Jason said. "You said his family was heading to Oregon."

"And she told you," Ruth exhaled.

"Well, you told a lie there," Jason said, not looking at Ruth. "And I wondered who his family was, and Mama told. Said you were married to him. And one reason we were heading west was so you could be free of him. Start over the way other folks do." He looked up at her then. "She told me not to tell. But I told Ned and I guess Lura overheard it, and then pretty soon I was just saying it to Jessie. She had a right to know."

Ruth shook her head as though to clear it of…exclusion, she thought it was. Everyone else knew and didn't want to tell her.

Jason lowered his head. "I didn't mean any harm."

"You had no right," Ruth said then, a kind of hot betrayal pushing up against her throat. They had carried on without her. She felt her nose sting, her eyes itch. "None of you had the right," she whispered. "It was my story to tell."

"I didn't know," Suzanne told her, reaching out and patting her hand on Ruth's. Ruth allowed it, brushed at her eyes.

"It wasn't like we was talking behind your back," Jason said. "Just helped me know why you were so grum and edgy sometimes, why you kept going, going. Helped me not be so mad when you left us just before Mama died. Mama said it was you trying to keep your head clear about what mattered even when things swirled all around you."

"She said to keep you in our prayers," Sarah said.

"And that what mattered to you was keeping me safe," Jessie said. " 'Cause you hadn't been able to do that for my brother. Did he really do that? My dad?"

"Don't call him that, Jessie." Ruth softened her voice. "He is not a good man, and that is mine to carry, that I fell in love with him and allowed him to cower me and hurt others through it. Yes, he is the man who fathered you, but he is not nor will he ever be 'your dad.' Your dad—Jed—cared about you, encouraged you, guided you. That man did none of that, not an ounce. And I won't have you believing he contributed to who you are or who you might become. You'll make better choices."

She knew her words were racing, running together. She caught Matthew's eye. He looked up at her, a wash of care across his face. She couldn't stop. "My brother was your dad. My brother and Betha raised you best they knew how."

"Why didn't you take me and move away?" Jessie asked.

Here came the dreaded question.

"Why'd you leave me behind?"

"It was the best choice I could make for you. I knew Z—" she stopped herself, not wanting to hear herself use his name, pretend he was a normal man. "The court trial, it took so much. And I felt so...responsible for your brother's death. I had nothing to give you except to give you away to someone who could love you and take care of you. And Betha and my brother did."

Lura stood up and lit the lamps, and the light reflected on the pools in Jessie's eyes. Ruth rose, went to the girl sitting beside Mariah, her arms hunched forward, hands clasped between her knees. "And then later, I knew he would come after me, and I thought to keep you safe, away. It was always to keep you safe."

"That why you just kinda settled here but not really, like you was always waiting to go away?" Jason asked.

"I was frightened," Ruth whispered. "That I couldn't love you enough, that I couldn't keep you safe. And frightened that I still allowed myself to love that man despite what he had done."

Ruth wiped at the girl's cheeks with her fingertips. "And do you now?" Jessie asked.

Ruth shook her head. "Do I love *you* now? More than anything in the world. Do I think I can keep you safe? Yes. That's why I chose to tell you—though you already knew." Ruth shook her head. She reached for the girl then, and Jessie held her, the thin arms like spiders legs clinging to her neck.

"But do you love Da—that man?" Jessie whispered.

"No, not anymore. Not anymore. Your Aunt Mazy said once that when we women cared about ourselves enough we'd stop trying to fill the empty spaces with men who only know how to hurt us. She said we wouldn't bind ourselves to men for the wrong reasons then. I think I'm moving there." She caught Matthew's eye and he winked.

Ruth released her daughter, looked around the room. "All this time of keeping it a secret, and everyone already knew." She saw no judgment in their eyes, nothing but acceptance. "So here's the other news. We're leaving here. He'll be back—I know he will. So we're going north."

"Now wait," Matthew said. He stood up.

"Are we leaving your horses?" Jason asked.

"I decided once that I wouldn't run from what I had to face, that I wouldn't let that man decide my thinking, my life. That I wouldn't move away from him but toward the things I loved. But I did it anyway. Wasted all that time on worrying over how you'd take it, Jessie, over whether I could be a mama to all of you, raise you right. Blamed all of you for the awful things he did in this house. And you all already knew about him." She shook her head. "I'm not running away this time. I'm moving toward something."

"I think we get the chance to see if we've really learned a lesson. A second chance, so we can move on," Suzanne said. "It's the test at the end of the schooling."

"I'd sure like you to consider taking another look at that lesson, Ruth," Matthew said. He stood next to her now and the room felt warmer. Her face felt hot.

"Which lesson?" Ruth said.

"The part about not running from something. At least not running before...well, some conversations."

"I have a family to look after," she said, then saw what looked like sadness on his face. "But I don't have to do that alone."

"I remember Elizabeth telling you that a man holding a baby was as catching as a cold," Suzanne told Seth. "Remember that, back on the trail?"

"I do," Seth said. "Your Sason here has put on some pounds."

"Got an orange for you, Sason," Lura said walking up to them. "Packed right into our county. Isn't that chirk?" The scent of orange drifted to Suzanne.

"At Lower Springs, someone's planted two palm trees," Esty said. "If they survive, we could grow whatever we want in Northern California. Not have to ship in a thing."

"Mazy has a watermelon coming on ripe too, in that garden she's planted." Lura must have taken a bite as Suzanne heard a slurping. Then, "What'll you do in Sacramento, Suzanne? Decided to let yourself get married?"

Suzanne laughed, then smoothed the tucks in the sash at her waist. "Would you get Sason a drink of water, Lura? It's pretty warm."

"I'll take him to the house, if you'd like," Esty said.

Suzanne nodded.

"Could use a refreshing splash myself," Lura said as Suzanne heard them walk away.

"Lura found a suitor for you, has she?" Seth asked.

"Marriage is Lura's solution, not mine. I just want to find the right person for us, not a husband. Someone…to assist us all, not just the children. I need help with Clayton, especially. To discover why he doesn't talk more.

"I thought real freedom was being independent," she continued. "That I could do it all myself, not have to let a person live next to me as though they were a mother or father. Or husband. It's a different kind of intimacy, I guess, giving up privacy without giving up myself. I just wanted to control my life. But I lost focus. For a time. It's my boys who come first. Keeping them safe and getting them grown. I'm finding that real independence lies inside surrender. Isn't that ironic?" she said. "I don't need someone like a Wesley Marks 'tending' me like I'm a broken harp string. I want nothing to do with the likes of him, not ever. If and when I'm ready for marriage, I'll want someone who'll be just as strong beside me, but who recognizes we're two separate instruments who've agreed to play the tunes together."

"So you're off to Sacramento. Could be dangerous. I'll take you, if you'd like," Seth offered. "No harp strings attached."

Suzanne considered. "No," she said. "Esty's coming with me. She's going to give her love of millinery a try once she's there. And I've written to Sister Esther who's agreed to help me find a…keeper, if you will. For me and my boys."

"Going by stage?"

Suzanne nodded. "David Taylor's promised to take us on his last run south. Says he's taking Oltipa and her baby, too, and that they may get married there or come back here. So we'll fill the stage right up. It'll be fine. All we need will be provided. More, if we don't set limits."

"Look who's here," Suzanne heard Lura shout from a distance.

"Who is it?" she asked Seth.

"Mazy with David Taylor and the rest. Elizabeth, too."

While Elizabeth filled them all in on her latest visit with her expanding kin, Suzanne listened to the shifts and pitches of voices, sharing in joy and surprise. It was like a reunion, the telling of tales, and here she was, a part of it. Maybe she should just stay here, get Esty to live with her, here, in Shasta City. Begin anew. She felt Clayton and Pig beside her. "Mommy?" he said. Her prayers had been answered—her children were safe. That was her focus now. It must be.

"We're needing some singing for this celebration," Elizabeth said. "Will you sing for us, Suzanne?"

"I've no harp," Suzanne said, raising both palms to the air.

"I'll get it for you, Auntie," Jessie said.

"You don't need one with your voice," Lura said. The others agreed.

"All right then," Suzanne said, pleased to be asked. "One of my favorites, perfect for a time of new beginnings."

With a voice as clear as spring water and just as refreshing, she sang:

> "Be thou my vision, O Lord of my heart;
> All else be naught to me, save that thou art—
> thou my best thought, by day or by night,
> waking or sleeping, thy presence my light."

A silence followed. "Is something wrong?" Suzanne asked. "Seth, what's happening?"

"Everything's chirk," Elizabeth said. "I think we was all pondering your insight, helping the rest of us learn to see."

They pressed Ned into singing next, while Suzanne's mind wandered back to the words of her song. *Perfect for me, too.* She listened to the sounds of safety around her, the clapping and laughing, felt a fresh breeze of hope. She imagined the faces of the friends she'd never seen but knew as kin, and she smiled. Whatever the future might bring, she now had a vision, a focus. She might stumble some, but there'd be friends to pick her up. What mattered was, at last, she could see.

epilogue

"Oh, look, Nehemiah. At long last, Mazy's sent the quilt! It's a wonder she ever got it finished." Tipton hovered over her husband as he tapped at the cooper's seal and pulled the oak lid. He lifted the heavy, felt-stuffed material from the barrel while Tipton pulled the cream-colored paper from around the cloth. She inhaled a deep breath. "Oh, smell this!" She said. "It is morning sunshine in December if I ever knew it!"

"A little woodsmoke in there too," Nehemiah said.

"She must have hung it on the line before she put it in the barrel." She breathed again. "I miss the smells from Shasta," she said. "I never thought I would."

"We'll go visit next summer," he said. "You can breathe it back in then."

"Maybe," Tipton said. "Maybe." She didn't look at her husband, didn't want to think of old hurts. "She didn't stitch it all herself," Tipton said, making her voice light. She felt the soft cotton, the smooth pieces of silk stitched in swatches. "These look like Sarah or Jessie's work. Let's lay it out over the bed. This'll be cozy when those coast winds blow. Looks like she dyed the backing with tea to get that rosy color."

Somehow, Mazy had stitched the quilt into what looked almost like a book, with the outer borders dyed a darker brown as though they might be leather and then three, four, five tiny tucks of white material stitched all around to make the border look like pages. Inside were all the stories, separated with blocks of white on which Mazy had drawn with black ink—tiny letters. They were done in Spencerian Script, the slender loop on the tail of the *Y* rising to flow into Sarah's block, the line barely showing through her replica of a sampler, then becoming a firm *A* in the border, the long side of that letter taking her eye into Jason's block, a tin whistle and a hoop he'd rolled across Nebraska.

The letters strung the stories together.

Tipton kneeled on the quilt then, pointing and oohing, interpreting for Nehemiah, guessing which stories revealed the author of each block. Her face flushed with excitement. Here was Elizabeth's—a tree house with an antelope looking up at it; Ned's with a musical note. There was Ruth's with an open book and a Scripture reference. "John 8:32," Tipton said. "Let's look it up."

"No need," he said. "'Ye shall know the truth, and the truth shall make you free.'"

"Huh," Tipton said. "I wonder what that was about. Our truth-or-lie game? Oh, maybe she finally told Jessie the truth, or Jessie finally told her that she knew." She looked up at her husband. "I thought these quilt squares were supposed to be related to our journey across the plains. Ruth's is about what happened after she arrived."

"Hard to separate the past from the present if we're paying attention."

"Oh, well, my block is sort of about being here as well as there, too," she said. "See. I put your silver work with the blue stone on Tyrell's spurs. Is that all right? Do you like it?"

He looked closer. "Well done," he said. "Quite fine, indeed."

Tipton beamed. She turned the quilt over then. On the back, Mazy had made a signature block, she called it, listing all the names in the order of their "chapter" of the book. Three blocks were placed throughout and left blank: *for Cynthia, Betha, and Zilah,* Mazy had written. *And all the others we lost. The pages that didn't get fully written.*

"I never thought of it that way," Tipton said. "That Tyrell's life didn't get fully written."

"Only because we want more," he said. "Some shorter stories carry more meaning than long ones."

Tipton nodded. She reached for the letter Mazy'd packed in the barrel: *Something for you and Nehemiah to put under your Christmas tree.*

Nehemiah kissed the top of her head as she curled into the quilt to read, wrapped herself in the stories while deciphering Mazy's words.

"Wind is up," Nehemiah said. "I'll go latch the shutters."

"Oh, listen to this," Tipton said when he rose. She reached for him and he held her hand. "The shutters can wait," she said. "Please?" She released his hand and watched him sit back down, put his feet up on the leather-covered stool. She read again, glancing up occasionally from her catching up on the past, listening to the wind rattle the shutters. It was a good tight cabin. A good place to be. Nehemiah was a good man to share it with.

"Mazy's mother is spoiling a great grandson, sort of. Gosh. There's a story behind that. A long section. You'll have to read it." She read silently again, then, "Lura is staying in town, now, sharpening knives. Oh." She swallowed hard.

"What?"

"She's working at my mother and brother's store."

"Maybe your mama'll get some free time then. To come and visit."

Tipton raised her eyes to his, said nothing, returned to the letter. "Oh, listen to this: *I have finally set aside my fear that the husband I chose was none but bad. Perhaps I'll plunge again someday, remembering as he once told me, that 'things aren't always what they seem.' Sometimes they're even better.*

"Geese fly overhead, Tipton. I can hear them as I write. I confess, one will give its life for our Christmas dinner. I've heard the storms are fierce where you have set your roots, so let our stories warm you, hold you close. The stories of the past we captured here are like the cooper's ring around the barrel, not meant to bind or hold us hostage but to define us. Without that ring, the pieces of our lives would fall apart. I've come to see my faith in that light, too. Not to bind me, but define me."

Tipton let the letter drop onto the folds of the quilt. "Not to bind us but define us," she said. "I like that way of looking at the past. Oh, here's one more page: *Which brings to mind one last note of explanation for the quilt. Suzanne's block. She designed it, Ruth drew it out, and mother and I and all the rest here who took time stitched it, Mariah, too. But she wished this explanation written.*

"When we were at the choosing point of Noble's Cutoff, the morning Zilah became scattered in her thinking, Suzanne dreamed. She dreams little, she says, even before she lost her sight. But in this dream she could see, and she was crossing a stream to her husband. Her foot slipped and she thought she would drown. Her husband called to her and said to look up, not get caught up in the swirling water, the fears around her, but to keep her focus, to look always above the fray. She did not have the dream again, but she remembered it. And that the word for focus in Latin means hearth. So that is what she wanted drawn, a fire burning in it, all of us—her family—warm and content around it. We are all together there in Suzanne's block, Tipton. She says she can almost see us. And in the corner is a tiny 'Lover's Eye' drawn in ink. Suzanne says that it is God's eye on us all, and if we look up to him, that is all that we will ever need to see.

"Next year, send the quilt to Suzanne. She was second in the choosing.

"Blessings to you both,

"Love, Mazy"

Author's Notes and Acknowledgments

"Stories tell us who we are and who we might become," D. H. Lawrence wrote. This story, though fiction, grew from the realities of the 1850s, a time when stories of easy wealth drew people west with consequences far reaching. To help readers step into this place and time and story, I've relied on many resources, but what emerged is mine, for which I bear responsibility.

Special thanks go to the State of California for maintaining the Shasta State Historic Park, especially Ranger Jack Frost, who has not only taken the Noble's Cutoff, but who grew up in Shasta County, provides tours of Old Shasta, and carries in his heart the story of the city's once vibrant past as "the Queen City of the North." Tom Hunt of Eureka, California, provided maps, diaries, articles, and moral support about the Noble's portion of the trail. His enthusiasm is matched by the Oregon California Trail Association whose dedication to preservation of the Oregon-California story is commendable.

I am particularly indebted to author Dottie West whose four books proved invaluable to whatever success I had at recreating Shasta of 1852-53. *The Dictionary of Early Shasta County History, The History of the Indians of Shasta County, Registered Historic Places in Shasta County,* and *The History of the Chinese in Shasta County* are the works of a woman passionate for history and for truth-telling about the lives of all the people in early Shasta, including people of color. Her inclusion of the Protection Act provided a detail related to the auctions I had long heard about, but had never seen documented. The Protection Act was amended in 1860 and repealed in 1864, but the practices continued for some years after.

History records that the *Courier* operated in 1852 under Sam Dosh's editorial guidance; there was a St. Charles Hotel, a Hong Kong, a Kossuth House. There were two fires in Shasta City. That is fact. That Kossuth's name was Nehemiah, was a silversmith, a friend of jeweler and gunsmith Ernest Dobrowsky (who did exist), or that he married Tipton Wilson, is not. Poverty Flat, located close to the Sacramento River, was a major grazing area of packers. Mad Mule Canyon did give up gold along with its fascinating name. There were five bookstores in Shasta by 1855 along with more than three thousand people. True enthusiasts can visit Shasta Historical Park and see what remains of the brick buildings, mercantiles, and bookstores for themselves.

Peter M. Knudtson's work *The Wintu Indians of California* provided a glimpse into the lives of these mountain and river people. Few remain to tell their stories. To my Hupa/Wintu friend Kadoo Trimble and her brother Wesley Crawford, I express appreciation for allowing me to read material compiled by Jack and Jana Norton regarding the genocide perpetrated against native peoples in Northern California in the 1850s and for their insight based on stories of their own Wintu connections.

Fellow Women Writing the West member JoAnn Levy's books *They Saw the Elephant, Women in the California Gold Rush; Daughter of Joy;* and *For California's Gold* are treasures. Her research about the lives of the Chinese and the varied roles of women in the mining camps, theaters, boardinghouses, and mercantile shops and about laws related to divorce, business, and more that affected women on the western frontier and her personal encouragement were invaluable. Women did indeed perform many a new task in their new landscape.

Gary and Gloria Meier's *Knights of the Whip, Stagecoach Days in Oregon,* and numerous works by the Oregon Historical Society and Carlos Arnaldo Schwantes' book *Long Day's Journey* provided background information about stagecoach transportation and commerce. These authors provided an understanding of the connection between these two great western states.

Finally, some personal appreciation. To my brother, Craig, and sister-in-law, Barbara Rutschow, for making the meaning of family real in our lives; and for their introduction to the Ayrshire cows of their neighbors Joe and Kathy Tousignant of Red Wing, Minnesota. The list of friends to thank is long and often repeated, but special note does go to Blair Fredstrom, Kay Krall, Carol Tedder, Sandy Maynard, Millie Voll, Katy Larsen, Bob Welch, Harriet Rochlin, Michelle Hurtley, Wade Keller, Bobbi Updegraff, agents Joyce Hart of Pittsburgh and Terry Porter. Special thanks and admiration belong to editors Lisa Bergren and Traci DePree for encouragement and desperately needed focus. I thank all the fine staff at WaterBrook Press for their confidence in me and this story.

And not least, to my husband, Jerry, thank you: for sharing our own adventure along Noble's Cutoff and our life's journey through the wilderness of landscapes, relationship, and spirit. Your love and support are unending and without equal.

Finally, to you readers, I extend my deepest gratitude, for caring for these characters and so graciously for me. I hope you'll want to follow their stories into book three and find nurture in the journey. Thank you.

Fondly,
Jane Kirkpatrick

You may write to Jane at: 99997 Starvation Lane, Moro, OR 97039 or visit her Web site at www.jkbooks.com.

The following is an excerpt from Jane Kirkpatrick's
What Once We Loved
Book 3 in the Kinship and Courage series
Available in stores fall 2001

1854

It was as soft as a lamb's ear, as sweet as Mei-Ling's honey. Ruth Martin had never been kissed like that, not in all her twenty-five years. His lips were tentative at first, like a colt just learning to stand. His hands on either side of her face felt warm, his fingers mere butterflies at her ears. She smelled leather, and then his tentativeness moved to something firmer, something safe and as strong as the log corrals that bound her horses. She drifted like a leaf caught in the backwater of a stream. He moved closer, and she became aware of the distance between their bodies even as their faces touched. A sound of surrender gathered at her throat, stopped the air that flowed.

Ruth pulled back, opened her eyes and stared at the blue of his, surprised once again at the smoothness of his face. As she stepped back, his wide hands traced down her cotton-covered shoulders, lingered at the crook of her bare elbow, reached to clasp the palms at her side. She offered one. With the fingers of her free hand, she touched at the knot of hair caught beneath the brim of her wide hat. She felt rattled, uncertain. She rubbed at the back of her neck, swallowed, gathered her breath, her thoughts, her senses. "You're much too . . . This isn't . . ."

He put his finger to her lips, quieted her, and she looked at him again, perhaps for the first time. She saw goodness in that face, with more experience than she credited him. Wisdom. And strength. "My Irish grandmother, on my ma's side, used to say 'Better one good thing that is, than two good things that were, or three good things that might never come to pass.' This is a good thing, Ruth. Something rising from all the bad. We don't know what'll come of it or if it'll wipe out what's gone before." He kissed the back of her hand as he held it. "But we can accept this, just as it is."

A quail clucked in the manzanita bushes, and her eyes moved there to watch the mother hover her covey out of sight. The air smelled rich with pine scents, and behind him she could see a spring burbling out of the side of the Oregon hillside that marked this place as home now. He lifted her chin and moved to bring her eyes back to his. The leather and smell of his boiled shirt blended with the memory of this first kiss, and she felt herself blush.

"It's a gift, our having this moment," he said. "Along with finding a spring near a meadow. That promises good, God willing."

She nodded and smiled up at him, feeling young and inexperienced, not a mother and an auntie.

"Come on, let's go get us a drink," he said and pulled her along, a gentle bear leading her. "Nothing more refreshing than spring water."

Savor the moment, she told herself. Hang on to the promise of a spring. It was a gift she could have. She just had to learn to receive.

JANE KIRKPATRICK

JANE KIRKPATRICK is the author of eight books, including two non-fiction titles and six novels. *A Sweetness to the Soul,* her first novel, earned the Wrangler Award from the Western Heritage Center as the Outstanding Western Novel of 1995. *All Together in One Place* is the first book in her Kinship and Courage historical series.

A Wisconsin native, Jane holds advanced degrees from that state's universities and is a licensed clinical social worker and former mental health director. She continues to consult with Indian tribes in Oregon and non-Indian communities, encouraging families and children with special needs. She speaks often at retreats and conferences throughout the country about the power of faith and stories in our lives. Jane has two stepchildren, and she and her husband of twenty-four years live with their two dogs on a remote ranch they "homesteaded" on the John Day River in eastern Oregon.

Jane welcomes your comments about how her stories have touched your life. She can be reached at the address below or at her Web site, which she accesses via the seven mile phone line she and her husband and friends buried (twice!).

99997 Starvation Lane
Moro, OR 97039
http://www.jkbooks.com